ON CIMARRON

ON CIMARRON

PAUL JOSEPH LEDERER

FIVE STAR
A part of Gale, Cengage Learning

GALE
CENGAGE Learning

Farmington Hills, Mich • San Francisco • New York • Waterville, Maine
Meriden, Conn • Mason, Ohio • Chicago

GALE
CENGAGE Learning·

LIBRARY OF CONGRESS CATALOGING-IN-PUBLICATION DATA

Lederer, Paul Joseph.
    On Cimarron / by Paul Joseph Lederer. — First Edition.
       pages ; cm
    ISBN 978-1-4328-2988-9 (hardcover) — ISBN 1-4328-2988-2
    (hardcover) — ISBN 978-1-4328-2981-0 (ebook) — ISBN 1-4328-
    2981-5 (ebook)
       1. Frontier and pioneer life—Fiction. I. Title.
    PS3559.R6O5 2015
    813'.54—dc23   2014047831

First Edition. First Printing: May 2015
Find us on Facebook– https://www.facebook.com/FiveStarCengage
Visit our website– http://www.gale.cengage.com/fivestar/
Contact Five Star™ Publishing at FiveStar@cengage.com

Printed in the United States of America
1 2 3 4 5 6 7 19 18 17 16 15

ON CIMARRON

CHAPTER ONE

The woman, Ki-Ki-Tai, rested on the riverbank in the shade of the giant sycamore tree. The river was silver and lazy in its passing. The breeze was no more than a whispered hint through the leaves of the overhanging boughs. The day passed in a languid dream; only the happy shouts of the boys at play broke the stillness.

Ki-Ki-Tai lifted from the warm earth, propping herself up on one elbow, watching the boys splash, playing with their father. Now Ketah, naked and brown, would be lifted over his father's head and thrown back into the water; now his brother, Tema. They swam like fish, their bodies gleaming in the sunlit river.

And between them, laughing, turning from one to the other of his sons, was Nakai. Ki-Ki-Tai watched her husband with a warmly amused smile. Nakai, whom the Kiowa men now called Hungry Wolf, had changed not over these last ten years. Still, his body was lean and powerful. Still, his heart was large and filled with love for his family, with pride, and a fearsome hatred for his enemies. For those who would harm either his family or his people.

The river was beginning to color as the sunset splashed the high, flat clouds with crimson and gold. Nakai's powerful arms swept up from the water, and in one easy motion he grabbed the overhanging bough of the sycamore and swung himself up onto it, sitting there briefly before he walked, still naked, along the mottled sycamore limb to the riverbank where Ki-Ki-Tai waited.

He wrapped his loincloth around him and stood, hands on hips, watching the boys. Ki-Ki-Tai tied a thong around his hair, kissing his bronzed back once. He turned and wrapped her in his arms, kissing her deeply, his strong thighs hard against her.

Ki-Ki-Tai laughed and half-gasped. He was so strong, apparently unknowingly. It seemed that at times when he took her passionately in his arms, the breath rushed from her body.

Nakai stroked Ki-Ki-Tai's sleek dark hair and looked down at her with the wonder that had always been in his black eyes, the wonder of a male studying a female, yet much more deeply; the wonder that such love could occur between two living beings.

"My husband," she said, putting her head against his naked chest. He held her closer and she trembled. He was so strong, from his legs to the column of his neck. He had always been so.

As children they had played together, from their earliest remembrances. She had seen Nakai run in foot races. He was never the swiftest—Winter Owl, his cousin, was far swifter—but Nakai would never quit, and as the race wore on it would be Nakai who won. There was something indomitable about him.

She stepped away from Nakai, pushing his chest lightly with her palms, and they stood arms encircling each other, watching as the boys splashed in the river and the shadows began to settle and pool beneath the trees.

Nakai's silhouette was strong and proud against the orange and crimson of the sundown sky. She loved him so much still.

She remembered again when he and Winter Owl, Roto, and some others of the Kiowa had gone on a long hunt one year and all of them returned . . . except Nakai.

For weeks he had not returned and no one would tell her anything. In the evenings she would stand out and watch the long-running sky with its brilliant stars, watch the rising rabbit moon against the deepness of Manitou's heavens. Still Nakai did not return and she had cried herself to sleep in her father's lodge.

And one bright morning with the rising sun red above the yellow plains, Nakai had returned, and behind him was a string of six ponies, Pawnee ponies; newly washed and painted, Nakai had swung down from his horse's back and walked to Ki-Ki-Tai's father, giving him a beaded Cheyenne vest, a long-bladed steel knife with a bone handle, and the lead rope to the string of ponies.

Outside the lodge, Ki-Ki-Tai had waited while Nakai smoked a pipe with her father, and when the young man emerged, he had said, "Get your things then, woman. Now you will live in my lodge."

His gruffness was only a sham, she knew, only a pose for the warriors who had gathered to watch. There was a haughtiness in his eyes as he stood, hands on hips, watching the distances, but when he glanced at Ki-Ki-Tai, she saw the laughter behind his warrior's posturing—and even sheepishness.

He had done whatever it had taken to come by those marriage offerings. Out of love. The rest was just a man-thing. She tried to hold back her own smile as she bowed and went to gather her few belongings.

And later in the still of the cold, moonless night, in their wedding lodge, they had laughed together over it. They had laughed and then made long and exhausting love with Nakai kissing her throat and eyes, her arms and hands, his warrior's body lean and strong and proud against her . . .

"Tell your sons that they must come out of the water now," Ki-Ki-Tai said. It was getting dark, the sky fading to deep purple as it cooled from the sun's passing.

Nakai walked confidently back onto the overhanging sycamore bough and pulled the boys up by their outstretched hands, one by one, and swatted their rumps as they passed him, squealing with pleasure, and ran toward their mother who waited on the shore, her blanket wrapped tightly around her against the oncoming chill of night.

The camp was quite a distance from the river, perhaps a quarter of a mile. There was a reason for this: an enemy can glide noiselessly over water and attack a camp. Over land, however, even if they have no horses, there are small night sounds that reach the ear, or others that fade to silence to alert the village. The frogs will cease their croaking; the cicadas will fall silent. A startled fox will bark.

They were on the bank above the village, striding toward it, the boys running and wrestling as they went. The sky was deep umber and faded red above the far hills. The camp itself was two hundred tipis covering a space of ten to fifteen acres. In the center of the village was a square where the lodge of the civil chief, Winter Owl, stood. Leading into the square were regularly laid-out paths, the tipis in orderly lines. The men of rank had their tipis nearest the square, so the home of Ki-Ki-Tai and Nakai, the Kiowa war chief, was on the perimeter of the square.

From a distance they could tell that something unusual was happening. As they walked down the long-grassed hill through the scattered live-oak trees, they could see men and women scurrying about.

"What is it?" Ki-Ki-Tai asked her husband. "Can you see what is happening?"

"No," Nakai answered. His face was set as they walked on a little more quickly. There was an urgency in the air. They spoke to the first woman they passed.

"What is happening?" Ki-Ki-Tai asked her.

"A messenger has just arrived," the woman said, pointing toward the camp. "Osolo is coming with fifty warriors."

"Comanches? What for?" Ki-Ki-Tai asked her husband, but

10

Nakai did not answer. They hurried on until they met Koto, a squat, powerful warrior who was both good-natured and fierce in battle. He and his wife, Momo, had been married for ten years and produced eight children, the oldest a girl, the rest boys.

"Nakai!" he said. "Good. You have heard?"

"Only that Osolo is coming."

"Yes, well what do you think it is about?" Koto asked as he fell in beside them, taking nearly two steps to every single stride of Nakai.

"I don't know. He will ask a favor; that's certain. Osolo never visits without a reason."

Nakai did not like Osolo; still they were closely allied with the Comanches through blood and tradition, and the man would be made welcome.

"Where is Winter Owl?" Nakai asked.

"In his lodge, preparing himself," Koto told him. "I must do the same."

There were women building fires in the square and men applying fresh paint to their faces. Some of the women were taking the scalps, which usually hung in the tipis, and tying them onto their husband's deerskin shirts or to their belts.

Once inside their own tent, Ki-Ki-Tai and Nakai began to prepare themselves for the meeting with the Comanches. Ki-Ki-Tai fixed her long glossy hair into one braid and dressed herself in red buckskin leggings, a blue broadcloth skirt embroidered with beads, and over these a bright, striped calico short gown. She also wore a tin band around her head. Nakai wore a white elkskin shirt, fringed leggings, and permitted Ki-Ki-Tai to braid beads into his hair, an affectation the "Hungry Wolf" usually disdained. Then he carefully painted his face with the sign of the Sun Dog.

It was already dark. There was only a line of beaten gold following the horizon to mark the sun's passage; the drums had begun. The square was crowded with welcoming Kiowas, and as Ki-Ki-Tai and Hungry Wolf emerged from their tipi, a runner entered the camp from the south, shouting:

"Osolo is coming. A mile away!"

Nakai saw his cousin, Winter Owl, standing before the chieftain's lodge and, taking Ki-Ki-Tai's hand, he started that way.

"And what is this?" Nakai asked.

"I do not know, Cousin," Winter Owl answered a little nervously. Winter Owl was a brave man, but it took little to make him nervous. Perhaps he should never have been placed in high office. He, too, wore white elkskins on this evening, with an axe and a long-bladed knife on his belt. He held a feathered war lance. Silently they looked southward, and in another five minutes they could hear the approaching hoofbeats, then cries of greeting, and in another minute Osolo emerged from the oaks and entered the camp, riding toward the square.

Osolo rode at the head of his warriors, his face painted blood red on one side, black on the other.

War was on his mind.

"I greet you, Winter Owl," the Comanche leader said from horseback.

"And I you, Osolo."

"I greet you, Nakai," Osolo said then, his tone altering just enough so that it was noticeable.

"And I you," Hungry Wolf said unemotionally.

Osolo slid from his white horse's back and the animal was led away by a young brave to join the other Comanche horses grazing on the prairie. The horses had been ridden through camp only in display. The mules, however, remained behind, for they carried gifts from Osolo. As these were unpacked, Nakai became more certain that the man had come to ask a large favor. Osolo did not have a generous heart.

"Come into my lodge," Winter Owl said. "Let us smoke."

Ki-Ki-Tai took Nakai's arm and as he leaned down she whispered in his ear. "If you don't wish me to stay, I am going to visit White Moon."

"If you like," Nakai said. "The boys . . . ?"

"They will go to Momo's to eat. Will this take long?"

"I think so," Nakai replied. The Comanche leaders were ducking into Winter Owl's lodge. His mouth tightened. "There is Wotasha," he said, indicating a tall scarred man with a hatchet nose. Wotasha was the war leader of Osolo's band. Seeing him, Nakai became certain that it was war Osolo had in mind.

Ki-Ki-Tai looked up at her husband, squeezed his hand, and then walked away across the village where the bonfires were burning brightly and the din of drums and flutes mingled with the shouts of people and the constant snarling and snapping of truculent dogs.

Ki-Ki-Tai walked slowly northward, passing the tipis of friends and family, speaking to those she saw, until she was out of the camp proper, beyond the smoky glow of the fires, into the deep shadows of night along the river.

A lone tipi sat quite near the dark river on a high-rising bluff where a single wide-spreading pine tree stood, black against the starry sky. There was a tiny fire burning within the lodge as Ki-Ki-Tai approached.

Ki-Ki-Tai called out, and when she was bidden, she lifted the weighted corner of the buffalo skin entrance flap and ducked into White Moon's tipi.

The old man sat staring at the soft glow of the tiny fire in the center of his lodge; a wisp of smoke curled upward toward the vent hole. White Moon was very old, his face creased with the cares of nearly a century of living. His hair was snow white, worn loose over his shoulders. He wore a beaded buckskin shirt and a bear claw necklace. His eyes, younger than the rest of his body, sparkled with delight as Ki-Ki-Tai entered.

"Hello, Grandfather," she said, seating herself, her legs tucked under her.

"Ki-Ki," the old man said warmly, taking her hand in both of his.

White Moon was not her true grandfather, but he had been her own grandfather's friend when the prairies were still very young.

"There is a commotion," White Moon said.

"Osolo has ridden into our camp."

"I see," White Moon said wearily. "Who does he want us to fight now?"

"I don't know. Nakai will tell me later."

"Winter Owl will do as he is bidden," the old man said heavily. "Falcon will tell him what to do. Washai will tell him what to do, and so he will do it."

Washai was now the shaman, the spiritual leader of their band. Once, not so long ago, that had been White Moon's office, but he had lost the power of his spirit vision. Ki-Ki-Tai remembered when that had happened although she had been quite young, still living in her father's lodge.

White Moon had been gone for a long time, a year in fact, and had wandered far to the east, to the land of the whites, and he had returned with an unwelcome vision.

"There are a thousand lodges in their villages," he had told those assembled to hear him. "A thousand thousand. They will keep coming. From far across the sea in their wooden boats, a thousand and a thousand and a thousand more."

Washai had disparaged the concept. No one had believed it although White Moon claimed to have seen it with his own eyes during his travels.

"They will keep coming until we are pushed into the

14

mountains or broken on the prairies," White Moon had told them ominously.

At that, Washai had leaped up angrily and shouted, "This is not a true vision! Can you not even remember the promises Manitou has made to our people? The visions of the elders or the way of fire!"

What Washai referred to was one of the oldest of legends. The truth of it could be seen in a hidden canyon. There one could see the ruins of a large town, its walls of cut stone, two feet thick and in some places fifteen feet high, the inner surface of which were adorned with elaborate carvings. There was a broad street there leading to a massive stone platform that seemed to have been used as a stage or a pulpit.

Now the entire area was covered with broken pumice to a depth of twenty feet except for where the winds and rains of time had cleared the debris.

This, the legend said, was where innumerable moons ago a race of white men, more powerful and larger than any who lived today, inhabited all of the country neighboring the town of stone. They had built fortifications on the mountains to protect their city in the intervening years. They were brave and warlike and masters of all crafts.

They drove the Indians from their homes and put them to the sword, but at length, at the height of their pride and glory, Manitou had descended from above, sweeping them away with fire and a following flood, erasing them from the face of the earth.

Therefore Washai had challenged White Moon, demanding: "And so, is it not the vision of the true prophets that should the white man ever invade our lands again, he will again be swept aside?"

The two shamans debated the question for a long while, for years in fact, but finally as White Moon grew older and weary of argument, Washai assumed his mantle.

"No one is a true prophet who reveals what the people do not wish to hear," White Moon had said to Ki-Ki-Tai at the time.

Yet he was not bitter over the loss of his high office, only saddened because in the depths of his heart he knew not only through visions, but through what his own eyes had shown him in the eastern lands that the fate of the Kiowa was already sealed.

Ki-Ki-Tai talked with White Moon for a while of her children, and listened as he talked of the old days before anyone had ever seen a white man, how the first trappers and hunters had dwelt among them in harmony, taking Indian wives. How quickly time ran on, changing all in its way.

"Can I do anything for you, Grandfather?" Ki-Ki-Tai asked as the evening wore on and the old man appeared to be growing tired.

"I hate to ask this of you . . ." He handed her a very old pair of moccasins. The lacing had broken on them and needed to be replaced. Ki-Ki-Tai promised she would repair them for him.

Rising, she asked, "Is there anything else you need, Grandfather? Anything you would like?"

"No." He paused and smiled. "Well, perhaps a fat dog, Ki-Ki."

She smiled and promised him that as well. Then, kissing the top of his head, she bowed out of the tipi and started back toward the camp, which was quieter now, darker as the fires burned down.

Ketah and Tema were still outside Momo's tipi, playing sticks with Koto's sons. Their older sister, Kianceta, stood by, watching indulgently.

Seeing Ki-Ki-Tai, the girl rushed to her and hugged her.

Kianceta was nearly thirteen years old. Willowy and athletic, she was a lovely child with huge brown eyes and long slender legs. Already many among the tribe were thinking of her as

16

bride for Ketah when the two were older.

Kianceta was one of those who thought that.

Her eyes hardly left Ketah as Ki-Ki-Tai's older son, his shoulders now widening and filling with the muscle of a warrior, played or ran races or strutted in a boyish way through the village, well aware of his approaching manhood.

"Won't you come in and talk to me, Ki-Ki-Tai?"

"Not tonight, Kianceta," Ki-Ki-Tai told her. "I want to hear what Nakai has to say about the Comanche visit."

The girl looked disappointed; she was immensely fond of Ki-Ki-Tai. "But tomorrow? We will pick berries?"

"Yes," Ki-Ki-Tai said with a laugh. "And then we can talk as long as you like, about anything you wish."

Kianceta's mother, Momo, loved her daughter dearly, but with seven younger children, she didn't have much time to spare to sit listening to her daughter, and so it was important to Kianceta to have Ki-Ki-Tai, a grown woman, to talk to as the girl herself approached maturity.

"Come home then, boys," Ki-Ki-Tai told her sons. "It is too dark for sticks anyway."

"Another few minutes, Mother?" Tema begged. He was losing the game, but hoped his luck might change.

"All right. A few more minutes." She turned and kissed Kianceta lightly. "In the morning then? Goodnight."

Slowly then Ki-Ki-Tai returned home. Even from a distance she could tell that Nakai had not returned yet. Entering the tipi, she prodded the fire to life and sat to mend White Moon's moccasins. She should really make him a new pair, she thought . . .

And glancing around, her eyes lit on Nakai's warbag, and she knew she should begin to provision it, for she knew Osolo as well as Nakai did; she knew that soon Nakai would be riding to make war.

★ ★ ★ ★ ★

The warriors, Kiowa and Comanche, sat on blankets around a low fire in Winter Owl's lodge, passing the red sandstone pipe. Hungry Wolf took one puff and bowed, holding the feather-decorated long-stemmed pipe in both hands, and handed it on to the Comanche war leader, Wotasha.

Both men were expressionless. There was no lost love between the two war chiefs; perhaps each was too much a man of his own people.

Wotasha was very tall and thin with a high-arched nose. One of his ears was much higher than the other and bent like a dog's. His hands were large and scarred. Nakai knew that Wotasha still carried an Apache bullet in his chest.

The gifts had been distributed, the pipe smoked. They had dined on broiled mustang meat, and now it was Winter Owl's place to speak.

"My brothers," Nakai's cousin said, "the Comanches have traveled a long way to visit us. How can we repay our guests for the kindness of their gifts?"

Osolo was not one for mincing words; he was considered rude, in fact. Now the Comanche chief leaned forward and told the Kiowa leader: "We have been offended, my brother."

"Offended? How?" Winter Owl asked the round-faced Comanche civil chief.

"Four weeks ago we traded with some Mexican men. Two hundred prime buffalo robes, three times that number in beaver pelts we gave them. They promised us new rifles, knives, and silver ornaments. Instead, when morning came, we found that they had stolen away, taking twelve horses and three of our daughters."

"You did not pursue them?" Nakai asked. Osolo shot the Kiowa war chief a dark glance.

"There were many of them, all armed with new rifles. By the

18

time we found them, they had retreated into a walled pueblo."

Wotasha continued the story. "We waited. For many days we circled their town and called out challenges. I, myself, hurled down the lance at their gates, but they would not come out to do battle."

Nakai had little sympathy for the Comanches. For one thing, the growing trade with Mexico had increased the slaughter of buffaloes. Their winter hides, the best because of their full coats of hair, were not given to the women and children of the Comanches, but traded for rifles and mescal that made the Comanches crazy.

"What is it that you wish to do?" Winter Owl asked.

"Destroy their town," Osolo said passionately. "Destroy it as if it had never existed. I am offended. My people are offended!"

"And you ask us to make war with you?"

"If your goodwill toward my people continues," Osolo said. He was very careful about his phrasing. Much meaning was attached to the few words.

Nakai said to his cousin, "We should counsel alone, Winter Owl, before a decision is made." The Comanche leaders both gave him a hard look.

"I think so, too," Koto put in. The Comanche chiefs ignored the stocky Kiowa warrior.

"You, Falcon?" Winter Owl asked, speaking to the massive young warrior who had not been heard from. Nakai did not like Falcon or trust him, but he was Winter Owl's cousin as well, on his mother's side and not his father's as was Nakai. Falcon was bold in battle, but erratic, choosing his own tactics when it pleased him, rather than obeying Hungry Wolf.

Then, of course, there was the other reason . . .

"If our brothers, the Comanche, need us," Falcon said, "we must fight beside them. Will not these treacherous Mexicans also cheat us and steal away our women if we do not teach them that it will not be tolerated?"

Nakai smiled inwardly. That was well-said, except that the Kiowas seldom traded directly with the Mexicans, preferring to barter needed goods from the border tribes.

"Nakai?" Winter Owl asked, looking nervously into the war leader's eyes.

Nakai sighed. He did not wish to make war on behalf of the Comanches, but he could see already that he was going to be outvoted in this decision. He asked, "How many fighting men are in this band of Mexicans?"

"Only thirty or forty," Wotasha said immediately.

Nakai asked directly, "Winter Owl, what is your wish?"

Winter Owl hesitated, but it was clear what his wishes were— not because of any hatred he felt toward the Mexicans, but out of fear of offending Osolo whose implicit threat still hung in the air like smoke from the pipe.

Finally Nakai's cousin said, "It must be done, Hungry Wolf."

"Then so we shall," Nakai said grimly. "If that is your wish." Then to Osolo he said, "But who will be the overall war leader?"

"You, of course," Osolo said quickly, but Nakai thought disingenuously. Wotasha's lips had parted to object, but a look passed between the two Comanche leaders and Wotasha closed his mouth without speaking.

"So it shall be, then," Nakai said. Etiquette decreed that he should then have taken Wotasha aside to discuss plans for the raid, but instead he told all present what he meant to do.

"We will not storm the town no matter how many warriors we have. Not with men with rifles on top of adobe walls. It will be a long battle, because we must wait them out. First we shall demand the return of the women hostages. Then, that these criminals be cast out of the pueblo and handed over to us."

"And if they refuse to do that?" Wotasha asked sourly.

"Then," Nakai answered, "you will have your wish. We will burn the pueblo to the ground."

★ ★ ★ ★ ★

Sometimes the land grew too silent and the wind whispered broken promises. Meadowlarks sang across the prairie and the river flowed brightly, but the day was empty all the same. It was always so when Nakai was gone from home.

At times Ki-Ki-Tai wished they could live differently, but how? And who would protect the people—the young and the old, the weak, if it were not for bold men like her husband, Hungry Wolf? Sometimes there was a deep weariness in Nakai's eyes as he prepared for battle. This time had been like that, except he had thrown back his head to laugh, his even white teeth flashing, as, painted and adorned with beads and silver, he had mounted his war pony, bent and kissed Ki-Ki-Tai, and ridden from the camp, leading the war party. It was his way of re-assuring her, she knew. His promise to return alive.

Along the oxbow where Ki-Ki-Tai now walked, a sandy island formed when the flood time of the year had passed, and there raspberries grew in incredible profusion, their snarled thorny canes filled with ripe fruit. Picking them was work accompanied by numerous scratches, but still Ki-Ki-Tai normally enjoyed it. Kianceta, accompanying her, threw herself eagerly into the job at hand, filling her woven grass basket. To Kianceta it was a holiday from the necessary drudgery of scraping hides and carrying buffalo dung fuel for their fires.

"Why aren't you smiling, Ki-Ki-Tai?" the girl called to her. She had her skirt tucked into her belt and stood deep in the tangle of berry vines. "Is it Nakai? Do you miss him so much?"

"Yes," Ki-Ki-Tai answered, "I do."

"And you have been married so long! I hope when I am married I will love my husband so much. I think my mother is happy when Koto has gone hunting or raiding."

"I don't think so. It is just that Momo does not wear her sorrow on her face."

21

"I don't know." Kianceta shook her head and smiled widely. "Mother says that when he is gone it's the only time she gets any rest at night!" Then the girl laughed. "Well," she said, "there are eight of us children!"

Ki-Ki-Tai smiled in response. Then, shrugging off her mood, she returned to her work. A dozen crows perched on the limbs of an oak tree, scolding them as they went through the vines. Kianceta turned and threw a stone at them, laughing when the birds took to wing in a swarming dark cloud. Still a child, so nearly a woman, Ki-Ki-Tai thought . . .

Then her musings were broken off by approaching sounds. As she turned, she saw a line of horsemen, ten in all, filing slowly past along the western bank of the river. Winter Owl was at their head, dressed in his white elkskins, eagle feathers in his hair. He was followed by his brother, Eagle Heart, Falcon, and several of Falcon's own brothers. Wotasha was with them, his hawkish face stolidly set.

Kianceta had paused in her work to watch their passing. "Where can they be going?" she asked. Ki-Ki-Tai could only shake her head. Surely not to the Osage country, not in the direction they were traveling, but they were heading toward the ford to the west bank; and this was an official delegation, there was no doubt about that.

Disturbed, Ki-Ki-Tai handed her basket to Kianceta. "I must leave now. I am sorry."

"But, Ki-Ki-Tai . . . what is the matter?"

Ki-Ki-Tai ignored the girl's question. She ran back to the camp and in minutes was astride her pinto pony, riding in the tracks of the Kiowa leaders.

They were indeed at the ford, a place along the river where a spit of stones had collected sand and formed a bar reaching nearly halfway across the river.

They rode on, splashing across the silver river, disappearing into the dark oaks on the opposite bank, and Ki-Ki-Tai followed on her pony. Keeping her distance, she followed them across the undulating prairie beyond.

It was not until mid-morning that they were met by the white soldiers.

Watching, Ki-Ki-Tai's breath caught; her heart raced faster as the weary pony shuddered beneath her. Ahead and slightly below where she rested on the knoll, Winter Owl and his party of delegates rode forward toward a group of blue-coated Americans. And beyond them . . .

Beyond them were many other soldiers building a fort! Ki-Ki-Tai's mouth went dry as she watched Winter Owl and the leader of the white soldiers dismount and speak together briefly. Then some of the other whites brought presents from pack horses, and all of the men sat in a circle on the grass to talk.

Where had the soldiers come from and why were they here? How could Winter Owl have let them build a fort so near to the Kiowa summer camp with impunity?

And why had Nakai not been told of this before he went away to war with the Mexican bandits?

Ki-Ki-Tai watched as the silver-mustached soldier gave Winter Owl a blanket and a steel knife that gleamed in the sunlight.

"Now what can they be doing?" she wondered, and then she knew. Winter Owl and the counsel had given the soldiers permission to build their fort there. Ki-Ki-Tai found herself wondering if there was not more treachery involved in this. Was it only coincidence that Hungry Wolf had been sent away with the Comanche raiders to fight their enemies? The timing was much too coincidental. She knew Nakai would never agree to what she was observing from the grassy knoll.

"The whites may make war against us because they hate us," he had once told Ki-Ki-Tai, "but when they build a fort, it is for one reason—other whites are coming to live on the land. Our land. And they mean to hold it."

Ki-Ki-Tai watched the scene below incredulously. The faraway hammering sounds echoed across the prairie in constant, threatening rhythm as they built their fort. The white soldiers had come, and they had come prepared to stay.

And the Kiowa leadership had accepted their presence.

Secret councils must have taken place. Councils to which Hungry Wolf had not been invited, and the decision had been made without him. Nakai would be furious! More than furious. Yet what was there he could do now? The treaty, it seemed, was being made at this moment. What, she wondered, had Winter Owl and the leaders given away? What that was not theirs to give.

It seemed Eagle Heart had agreed with him. Even Falcon! All of this done as Hungry Wolf was away in the south fighting another tribe's battle at Winter Owl's instructions.

There was a bitter taste in Ki-Ki-Tai's mouth as she leaped aboard her little pony and turned it roughly homeward. She had a wild impulse to ride after Nakai, to find him and tell him what had happened, but she knew that was foolish.

Slowly she forded the river toward the western bank, her pony's hoofs sending up little silver fans of water. Kianceta was gone from the berry patch when Ki-Ki-Tai returned. Probably the girl had grown bored working by herself.

When she reached the outskirts of the village, Ki-Ki-Tai turned her pony loose to graze and started toward her tipi. She felt betrayed and hollow. She thought of going to talk to White Moon, but what could the old man say to soother her anger?

She stood before her lodge, her arms crossed beneath her breasts. Watching the long sky, she shivered, although the breeze off the river was not cold. She realized suddenly that she was frightened, frightened of an uncertain future that seemed to be rushing toward them all too rapidly.

"They have more men than we had expected," Nakai said to Wotasha.

The Comanche war leader lay beside Nakai on the dry grass hill two hundred yards from the pueblo called La Mesa. The town where the Mexican thieves had hidden was walled and well-fortified, with a good field of fire in all direction.

"Not all of them are fighting men, Nakai. Besides we have enough warriors to defeat them."

"Yes, if they would come out from behind their walls," Nakai agreed, "but they will not leave the protection of the pueblo unless they are forced to do so."

The wind was brisk, shifting the grass, their hair, and the horses' manes and tails. La Mesa, technically in the United States since the war fifteen years ago between the Americans and the Mexicans, was still a Mexican pueblo. Too far away from any American outpost for anyone there to care about it and so far from Mexico City that it might as well have been on the moon, it was an isolated, self-contained, well-fortified island on the prairie.

"What is your decision, Nakai?" Wotasha asked, lifting himself on one arm.

"At the hour before sunset we will show ourselves," Nakai answered. "All along the skyline. After they have seen us, I shall ride down partway and see if they will send out a messenger to speak to me. If they do, I shall tell them what they must do for us to leave them in peace. If not . . . we shall see."

"As you will have it," Wotasha said, although Nakai knew the Comanche war leader still favored an all-out attack on the walled pueblo. Such a tactic would produce unacceptable casualties for the joint Kiowa-Comanche force, Nakai believed.

"I will ride with you if you wish," Wotasha said.

"No. Then if there is treachery, who will lead the warriors? Have the warriors assemble. Let the drums begin and the war chants as well. Let the Mexican men know we are here. Let them consider their fate for a few hours. They will know why we have come. Let them counsel concerning what must be done."

In late afternoon in the pueblo of La Mesa, what had been an ordinary working day, with people going about their daily routines, was suddenly filled with fear, growing toward panic as the nerve-shattering hours passed by.

There was nothing at all to be seen, only the golden hills in the late light. There was no movement anyone saw, although men scanned the hills with spyglasses from the parapets of the pueblo walls. But, down the long canyon the constant blood-chilling sounds of war drums and chanted war songs continued. The unseen menace was a hovering, vibrating sound over the town.

Women rushed about, looking for children, dragging them back inside their houses. Men raced toward the adobe walls of the town carrying rifles, and a thousand excited conversations went on at once.

An hour before sunset the sounds ceased. The total silence was even more unnerving than the singing and thumping of the drums had been. Now the men along the pueblo's walls fell silent as well.

In a long, slow line, they appeared against the skyline, black figures on horseback against the crimson and deep orange of the sunset sky. A hundred, two hundred warriors with lances or rifles in hand. They sat motionless for long pregnant minutes, until with a wild whoop, one man, feathers tied into his hair, his face painted wildly, rode forward at a gallop on a tall gray horse. He rode down the hill and across the flats toward the pueblo,

26

and men shouldered their rifles, watching as the warrior reined up so harshly that his horse went nearly to its haunches. The rider raised a lance and hurled it into the earth.

Nakai sat waiting in the near-darkness, his horse tossing its head so that its white mane swirled around its neck.

Long minutes passed. Then half an hour. Then nearly an hour as the sun dropped behind the mountains far to the west and the shadows crept from their hiding places, merged and pooled.

The high wooden gates of the pueblo opened just enough to let a single man on horseback pass through and then quickly closed again. A single envoy, carrying a white flag tied to a Mexican lance, dressed in the tight trousers and short jacket of the vaquero, rode to meet Hungry Wolf.

Halting five feet away from Nakai, he lowered his lance's head and said, "I am Don Herredia, the *alcalde* of La Mesa. What is it you want?" he asked in Spanish.

There was no fear in the man's eyes, Hungry Wolf noted with approval. He was a short man, probably balding underneath his wide-brimmed black sombrero, with thick hands and the marks of pox on his face.

"There are men in your town who have stolen away Comanche women, stolen twelve horse and many buffalo hides and beaver pelts. These men must come forth."

"No," Herredia said flatly and Nakai's mouth twitched. "I cannot turn men over to be tortured."

"They will not be tortured."

"Killed?"

"Almost certainly," Nakai answered. "These men will be killed, or perhaps fifty of you. And fifty more. And fifty more until there are none, and your village is ash against the earth, nothing more."

"I can't agree to send them out. I cannot send people out to die."

"Then they shall die where they are along with many others," Nakai promised him.

"I can't . . ." the *alcalde* showed deep concern now. "I will need time to talk to the other officials of the pueblo. Perhaps the criminals will surrender themselves for the good of all of our people."

"I can give you until morning," Nakai said. "No longer."

"Thank you," the Mexican said with strained relief. He lifted his lance head as if he were ready to turn and go.

"The women, however, must be released now," Nakai said.

"Now!" Nakai said forcefully. "Release the three women unless you are ready for battle, ready to die before the sun has fully set."

Herredia was perspiring despite the cool of the evening. There was only one possible answer to the Kiowa leader's demand.

"I will find them and send them out," he promised Nakai.

The *alcalde* turned his horse and started slowly back toward the walled Mexican town.

Nakai did not move as the sky darkened and purple twilight spread over the land. It was perhaps half an hour before the gates to the town were opened and three small figures staggered through them. They stood, looking bedraggled and confused, before the pueblo for a minute. Then seeing Nakai and the silhouettes of the massed warriors on the hill behind him, they started to run toward him, holding their skirts high, their hair flying out behind them. On the hill Wotasha shouted out an order. And three warriors rode toward the flats, their horses at a dead run, the braves yipping as they came. They circled the young women and scooped them up, retreating to the hills with the girls swung up behind them on their horses' backs. Nakai sat his tall gray horse awhile longer, staring at the town where not a single fire burned. Then, with a satisfied nod, he swung his horse's head around and rode back to where the others waited.

They camped without fires that night. There was a chance that the Mexicans might become suddenly emboldened and slip out of the pueblo and fall upon them. They would light no campfires to show them their way.

The captured girls had exhausted themselves giving thanks earlier and then had fallen asleep; now as midnight approached they had awakened again and clustered together, singing softly, charmingly.

Nakai was still awake. He sat with his friend, Koto, in a hollow on the northern hillslope, speaking quietly.

"What will happen in the morning?" Koto asked. He had a stick in his hand and was drawing aimless patterns in the earth as the silver quarter-moon rose slowly in the east.

"I do not know. If they are men of good sense, they will turn the bandits out."

"I wonder what Wotasha is really thinking, Nakai. I feel that he would like to attack the pueblo, raze it, no matter what is done."

"Then Wotasha is a fool. Glory is one thing; attacking recklessly is only foolishness."

"I believe this Comanche thinks like Falcon. Of himself, not of the whole of the people." Koto looked up curiously. "And why is it that Falcon did not ride with us, Nakai?"

"Someone must remain with the camp. What if our camp itself were attacked by raiders while we were gone? The Pawnee cannot have forgotten that last battle so soon."

"True." Koto was silent for a time. Did Nakai know . . . ? Of course he must. Everyone knew that Falcon was beyond being polite to Ki-Ki-Tai; he wanted her and always had. Could that be why Falcon had remained behind, perhaps hoping that Nakai would be killed?

"One thing good," Koto said at length. "At least there are no Mexican soldiers in the pueblo. Wotasha says there used to be many camped around here."

"That was long ago. After the war with the Americans, they withdrew across the Rio Grande."

"Yes!" Koto laughed at some memory of those times. "That was a good war for us, was it not, Nakai?"

"Very good," Nakai answered. To the whites there didn't seem to be very much difference between the Mexicans and the Indians. To the Indians there was no difference between the Mexicans and the whites. It was only that the Spanish people had been on the land longer. Now they apparently assumed that it was theirs, forgetting who they themselves had taken it from. Now the Mexicans had been driven away, and, it seemed, it would be a long time before many Americans came into the lands of the Kiowas and the Comanches. North Texas, southern Kansas, New Mexico . . . all were still free lands, and must remain so.

That was one reason Nakai had agreed to aid the Comanches in this puny dispute. All intruders, Mexican or American, had to be reminded strongly whose land it was that they trespassed on.

"Change the lookouts," Nakai instructed his friend. "Every man must be as fresh as possible for tomorrow. We do not know what might happen. Then sleep yourself, Koto."

Without another word, Nakai rolled up in his thick red blanket, closed his eyes, and went immediately to sleep. There might be battle in the morning, a bloody battle, but this was Nakai's way of life. Battle, the thought of death, were nothing to be feared; worrying about these things accomplished nothing.

All things were done as the Great Spirit's will dictated. A man, no matter how brave, must die sometime.

The morning sun was a red ball behind an eastern mountain haze when Nakai rose and began painting his face freshly. Smearing his hand with crimson, he went to his tall gray horse and made a red handprint on its shoulder, the ancient warriors' sign for "I drink my enemies' blood."

Then he leaped onto his horse's back and rode slowly through the camp to where Wotasha waited, seated cross-legged on the ground. Two of the released captive women were still tying feathers into his beaded hair.

"This is the morning, Nakai," he said in ritualized greeting. In the same tone, Nakai answered the Comanche war leader.

"This is the morning, Wotasha."

Then, fully adorned and painted so that if they should die, they would not humiliate their ancestors by appearing unkempt on the Shining Path, the two men started on horseback from the camp.

Wotasha's voice rang out in a shrill, ululanting cry and was answered by the throats of the massed warriors. They walked their ponies forward. They crossed the separating hills and looked down upon the pueblo where not a man or woman was visible, where the gates stood firmly closed and all was as silent as if the town were now abandoned.

Side by side, the two war leaders rode forward onto the yellow grass plains, moving at an even pace. Nakai raised his feathered lance and called out his orders, and two parties of warriors broke off from the main band, one group flanking right, the other to the left. They approached to within a hundred yards of the Mexican town and halted, the sun warm against their backs, the morning breeze pushing gently against them from the west. Their war ponies blew through their nostrils and

31

shuffled their hoofs restlessly.

There were no other sounds except now and then, distantly, a dog barking and the cawing of a passing swarm of crows, black omens against the blue-white sky.

"How long will you give them, Nakai?" Wotasha asked, and Nakai glanced at the Comanche leader, his face painted with wavy black lines, two on each cheek. Wotasha shifted eagerly on his buffalo skin saddle, staring at the pueblo, still deep in shadow within.

"We shall see," Nakai answered. Wotasha was dissatisfied with the answer and only grunted a response.

Nakai, meanwhile, was forming a strategy, measuring their chances if they did have to mount a full assault on the pueblo. It would be a difficult fight, certainly. The adobe walls would not burn readily. Fire was a good offensive tactic always. The riding flames reduced a man's nerve, the smoke confused him, giving him two enemies to fear—the fire itself and the attacking enemy.

It was then that the front gates to the town swung open and Nakai tensed, becoming fully alert.

His pulse rate lifted; he could feel the blood pounding at his temples, and his hand tightened around his lance. Then the Mexicans, on foot, with the *alcalde* leading them, emerged holding a flag of truce.

"So!" Wotasha exclaimed in pleasured relief, "It is done!" He glanced at Nakai, his expression almost hungry, his eyes glittering strangely.

The Mexicans had capitulated.

A burdened oxcart rolled toward them first, and then six men, their hands bound, were prodded forward by a dozen Mexicans with rifles. The captives were disheveled, their heads bowed submissively. Two of them had badly marked faces. Nakai saw fresh bruises, scratches, dried blood on each thief. One of them was no more than a boy. He was trembling violently, sobbing as he was prodded forward.

Fifty feet from the front gate a command was given and all of the prisoners were thrown roughly to the ground where they remained as the *alcalde* spoke again to his escorts; the cart was unloaded, and dozens of buffalo hides and perhaps a hundred beaver pelts were tossed onto the ground beside the men who had taken them from the Comanches. The men who did not now have long to live.

"It is done," Wotasha said again. He started to knee his pony forward, but Nakai touched his elbow and he halted.

"I promised the thieves would not be tortured, Wotasha."

"How could you promise that!"

"To salve their consciences. But I did give my word."

"It was not your right."

"It is what I have said," Nakai answered levelly. The two men locked eyes for long seconds; then angrily. Wotasha nodded and started his horse forward toward the prisoners, signaling to some of the war party to assist in carrying away the prisoners and recovered goods. Nakai ignored all of their activity. He recalled his flanking warriors with a wave of his arm and then turned back toward the hidden valley. On the parapet, he saw the *alcalde*, all alone, staring after him.

Long upright poles had been raised in the camp by the few warriors who had remained behind to protect the women, and as the captives were brought into the camp and dumped from the horses that carried them, strong hands jerked them to their feet and took them to the posts where they were tied with rawhide thongs. The youngest of them kept crying until a black-bearded Mexican bandit yelled at him to shut up and be a man.

The girls who had been their captives moved around them taunting them, waving knives in their faces. The Mexican prisoners became stoic, even the boy, although tears still flowed down his cheeks.

Wotasha stood before the prisoners, his hatchet in his hand. He looked darkly at Nakai with an impenetrable scowling expression. Then he turned to the gathered Comanche warriors and spit out a command.

Instantly a dozen Indians leaped forward and the Mexicans were dispatched, hatchets biting into their skulls. In seconds all were slumped dead at the foot of the poles.

They were left to feed the vultures, a testament to the vengeance anyone cheating the Comanches would suffer.

At the little creek called Del Bosque, the two tribes parted company. Wotasha and Nakai shook hands and spoke the formal words of farewell—but that was all it was, a formality. If anything, Wotasha liked Nakai even less than before, despite the Kiowas' aid in his expedition to punish the Mexican thieves. He was a man who did not like to be frustrated in his desires or having his power usurped, and that was what Nakai had done in forbidding what he considered to be the well-deserved torture of the prisoners.

Nakai was glad to be rid of his company, and the Kiowas rode slowly across the Del Bosque and out onto the long prairie beyond. The youngest Kiowas were cheering themselves and mocking the Mexicans. Nakai was silent. It had not even really been a battle, but the young men needed to have something to have pride in. Let them reflect on it, and tell it larger than it had been. No matter.

Nakai's thoughts were already far from the incident, reaching out across the plains toward home and Ki-Ki-Tai, who would be there waiting for him at the end of the long trail.

★ ★ ★ ★ ★

The war party was welcomed warmly on its return to the Kiowa camp. The young braves rode through the camp at a run, swinging from side to side on their horses' backs. Nakai watched them with a wry smile, unable to even remember the time when he had been so young and exuberant. He wanted only to see Ki-Ki-Tai, to hold her, to hug the boys to him, but it was his duty to report to Winter Owl, and so with Koto at his side, he rode to the civil chief's lodge, and after calling out to the lodge and receiving an answering invitation to enter, the two warriors ducked inside the smoky tent.

Winter Owl was there alone except for one of his wives, the matronly Sho-Wata, who had been his first bride when all of them were so much younger. Winter Owl looked up in surprise, and Nakai thought, with some apprehension, but then Winter Owl's nervousness was well known.

"Welcome back, Nakai! Friend Koto! Please seat yourselves. Rest and tell me how the battle went."

"The Comanches obtained satisfaction," Nakai said. Then rapidly, simply, he told the story to Winter Owl, who nodded and smiled but still appeared nervous. "None of us was so much as injured," Nakai concluded, thinking that perhaps that was what was troubling Winter Owl.

"Good, good," Winter Owl said. His eyes kept going to the entranceway, and now as Nakai heard a small shuffling sound behind him, Winter Owl sagged with relief. Nakai turned his head to see Falcon appear at the entrance to the lodge.

"Welcome back," Falcon said, seating himself without an invitation. "Have you told them yet?" he asked Winter Owl.

"Not I . . . not yet."

"What is this?" Nakai asked. Something of importance had occurred. It was obvious in the two leaders' demeanor. Falcon appeared to be gloating. Winter Owl was more than nervous—he was fearful. What was it, then?

Nakai asked, "Winter Owl? Cousin? What do you have to tell me?"

"We have made a bargain that benefits the tribe greatly," Falcon said casually.

"A bargain?" Nakai asked, puzzled by the two men's secretiveness.

"A treaty, Nakai," Falcon told him. "We have signed a treaty with the whites. We are to be paid forty mules and a hundred blankets. In addition . . ."

"What treaty! What whites?" Nakai interrupted furiously.

"This demands explanation," the normally reticent Koto said.

It was Falcon who answered. Winter Owl looked down at the blanket he sat on, a new, finely made blanket. A white blanket.

"Soldiers, Nakai," Falcon explained. "They wanted a strip of land across the river. A small strip."

"What did they want with it?" Nakai demanded.

"They wished to build a fort," Falcon shrugged.

"And you agreed!" Nakai was incredulous. "While I was away?"

"It was the wise thing to do," Winter Owl said weakly. His eyes were watery, pleading for Nakai's patience. "What are we to do? Fight over a few miles of land? They are *soldiers*, Nakai. They would fight for that. It would be a stupid war over so little."

"Over our birthright," Nakai said coldly.

"Over so little! When do we hunt across the river? When do we travel to the east? This way we have settled matters without bloodshed, and we have enriched ourselves at the same time," Falcon argued.

"It is wrong," Koto said softly, shaking his head.

"I have given my word to the white leader," Winter Owl said, his voice growing firmer. "His name is Macklin, and I believe him to be a man of his word as well. The east side of the river is now given to the whites. They will remain on their side, we on ours."

"It is a good bargain we have made, Nakai," Falcon said.

"Be quiet!" Nakai was fuming. He began to realize now why he had been sent on a foolish pilgrimage with the Comanches and why Falcon had remained behind. He went on, subdued but still angry, "When the mules are dead," he said slowly, "when the blankets are filthy and filled with holes, the land will still be. Rich and sustaining. You are fools, traitors to your people."

Winter Owl became incensed. Perhaps Nakai's words were too close to what he knew the truth to be. Nevertheless, the Kiowa chief rose sharply to his feet.

"I remind you whose decision it was, Nakai. The council's. Myself. Eagle Heart. Washai . . ."

"Washai! The prophet gave his blessing?" Nakai asked in disbelief.

"Yes."

"Then he is no true prophet," Nakai said.

"It was our decision—all of the tribal leaders together," Winter Owl responded. "I cannot talk to you when you are in this mood, Cousin. Leave my lodge. When you are calmer, I will tell you what the treaty promises."

The words were barely out of Winter Owl's mouth before Nakai stormed from the lodge, Koto trailing him uncertainly.

"You let him order you out of his lodge?" the squat, sincere Koto said.

"It was that or grow even more angry. I would have said much more, too much, Koto. Maybe Winter Owl is right. I must calm down before I can think about all of this."

"Yes," Koto said. "But Nakai, when you are calm, you and I both know that you will feel the same. Winter Owl is wrong, and we know it. I do not know who among the council convinced him that this thing should be done, but it brings the whites to the fringes of our village. Only the river now stands between us. Nothing good can come of this," he said, shaking his head. "Nothing."

Nakai had found her and had taken her hand gently. Now as sunset began to color the western skies and send a flush across the long golden plains, he walked silently with her toward the knoll where the three oaks stood, their shadows long and deepening. The grass was sweet-smelling and long. The river flowed by, silent and touched by late sunlight, making its way toward its ocean dreams.

Nakai halted and turned Ki-Ki-Tai toward him. He kissed her roughly, taking her breath away. His hands were on her hips, pressing her against his body.

He did not speak. He undressed quickly, throwing his garments aside. Then he lowered Ki-Ki-Tai to the grass and lifted her skirt, his hands lingering on her thighs. She waited for him, seeing the terrible concentration on his face, and he came to her with a shuddering need.

He was quick, almost violently so. He mauled her body, needing it that much, kissing her throat, her eyes, her breasts. When he had finished, her rolled from her, staring up at the sky. His hand sought hers and held it for long minutes as the sky went slowly dark and the first stars appeared. He took her neck and rolled her to him and he clung to her as if she were his shelter against the battering tides of life.

They lay together, wide awake, without speaking for nearly an hour. Finally Nakai rose and dressed. Returning to his wife, he took her by her hands and helped her to her feet. Then he hugged her again, this time gently as if he were cradling a child in his arms, his fingers stroking her neck, tracing the whorl of her ear, following the line of her breast and abdomen.

His hands fell away and for a moment he only looked at her, his eyes unreadable, but quite soft. Then he took her hand again and they walked to the very top of the knoll where they could gaze out across the river.

Ki-Ki-Tai leaned her head against his shoulder as he stood watching the distances. Far away to the east, she could see them too—pinpricks of light, no brighter than fireflies, immensely distant, incredibly near. The campfires of the white soldiers who had come upon their land.

The following month found Nakai gone again. A band of Osage had raided the northern Kiowas. Apparently it had been only a band of a dozen or so youths meaning to prove their manhood, but a woman had been killed, and the Osage youths had killed an old man as he tried to protect her. A messenger had arrived the week before asking Winter Owl for help in punishing the Osage.

Falcon had remained behind again. Once, bathing in the river, Ki-Ki-Tai had seen him peering at her from the willow brush. She would not tell Nakai that. Hungry Wolf would certainly kill Falcon, leading to a serious rift in the tribe. Nor would she ever tell her sons! Still young, they were beginning to think of themselves as warriors, especially Ketah, the older of the two. They might believe it to be their responsibility to confront Falcon, and the older, much stronger man could hurt them seriously or even kill them with the same result—an irreparable rift among the Kiowas. Not a vast tribe, they needed to protect what strength they had by avoiding divisions.

Now Ki-Ki-Tai walked alone along the river. The frogs grew silent as she approached and then resumed their croaking after she had passed. Dragonflies skimmed low across the water, iridescent blue and orange. Killdeer sang in the long grass.

She thought of Nakai, of her love for him. She meant so much to her husband, and she knew it. She understood all of his moods, as she understood his rough, needful lovemaking on the night he had returned from the raid with the Comanches and found that Winter Owl had made the terrible treaty without consulting him.

He had been silent, concentrating on some secret quest, so intent on hiding himself away in her flesh, needing release and comfort, to be for a time forgetful of the world and all of its problems. And she could provide that for him.

Most often he was gentle with her, caring about her needs. He had been that way since the first night she had gone to his lodge, nervous, but not really frightened as some young girls on their wedding nights. He would never hurt her, she knew. Never. He was too much of a man. Nakai had never so much as raised a hand to his boys, this strongest of warriors.

Thinking these thoughts, Ki-Ki-Tai found that without conscious intent she had wandered back to the knoll where the three spreading oaks stood. Reminiscing, smiling to herself, she climbed the knoll to look out across the river, past the sacred island where the pine trees—the only ones around for miles—stood in deep profusion.

The breeze was gentle, the sky a pale blue with scattered lace-thin clouds.

Her heart stopped.

For they were coming! Across the river she saw them moving wearily westward.

White settlers had reached the banks of the river.

CHAPTER TWO

In the chill and misty twilight Elizabeth stood on the low grassy knoll and looked out across the flat expanse of crippled grass toward the long rambling river. The Cimarron was umber and deep purple in the late shadows, half-hidden in mist as it curved around the bend where withered willows crowded its banks. It was a sere and awful land, she thought, a land unpromising and dreadful, every bit as inhospitable-appearing as the miles of prairie they had crossed to arrive here.

Tom O'Day stepped up beside his wife and looped his arm around her waist, and they stood together in the sundown silence.

"There it is," Tom said, and there was pride in his weary voice.

The answering smile Elizabeth managed was weak and exhausted. She leaned her head against his shoulder, but her eyes were damp behind lowered eyelids. What was this madness, she was thinking? The boys, Kent and Oliver, jumped and tumbled and ran up and down the knoll with the exuberance of youth . . .

The land was no different than what they had traveled over for the last 47 days in that dismal cart drawn by their two mules who now stood, heads hanging, almost too tired to nibble at the withered buffalo grass.

The land was empty and raw, a God-neglected weary place. Elizabeth had tried to believe, wished to believe, that there was a golden land beyond the long plains. There was nothing, after all, left for them at home in Indiana. The drought had seen to that; the landowner had seen to that. And so they had come West. *West.*

Such a word. Thousands of men and women poured westward, all of their dreams pocketed into one slender hope. They struggled on toward an imagined place where there were wide spaces, freely flowing water, a dreamland beyond the Mississippi.

Tom had purchased the section of land, six hundred and forty acres, sight unseen for a dollar an acre, most of the money borrowed from family and friends. Elizabeth knew there had been no real choice. Twelve hours behind a mule and a wooden plow, working from sunup to sundown had profited them nothing in Indiana. They could afford no shoes for the children . . . but in the West, Tom had believed, as did many other thousands, there was nothing but rich land! More acres than men. Sweet water and freedom. An opportunity to improve their lot.

Elizabeth looked across the desolate, empty land. What had she expected? Tom's enthusiasm had carried her away as well. But now that the end of the long trail had been reached she just saw a lonesome land without a house, without a school. They had no store, no money, no food. They had nothing left but their dream.

Tom's big black-and white-patched horse, "Domino," pawed at the dry grass and whinnied once. Tom O'Day hugged his wife again.

"You see, I told you we would make it! This is our land, Elizabeth. From the skyline to that oak grove, and no one can take it from us."

Elizabeth tilted her head back and smiled. A wisp of blond hair drifted across her eyes and Tom wiped it away with his strong tanned hand.

"We'll have to camp beside the cart again tonight," Tom O'Day said, "but in the morning we shall begin."

Begin what? Elizabeth wondered. There were no forests here, nothing to construct a cabin of. Tom said he had learned to build a "soddy" from the old-timers. What would they use to heat it when winter came? Scraps of broken driftwood? Buffalo dung?

But tonight they would camp again beside the two-wheeled cart as they had since crossing the Missouri River. At St. Louis and St. Jo, the hopeful emigrants from the blighted East had discarded almost all of their goods as their Conestogas crawled up the western hills. Iron stoves, pianos, trunks, steel plowshares had all been cast aside by the side of the road as they traveled relentlessly on, the men grim-faced, the women wearing masks of hopeless endurance. But Tom had guided them alone further southward, far across the Arkansas hills onto the unvarying Texas plains. He was so sure, so intent, that even the Indian menace meant nothing to him.

In this year of 1860, he felt convinced that the Western lands had been secured.

It had been two years since the Texas Rangers under Captain Ford had crossed the Red River and defeated the Kotsoteka Comanches. Major Van Dorn had also defeated the Comanches at Cripple Creek the year before. Almost all of the hostile tribes had previously agreed to the Grand Treaty of 1851—Sioux, Cheyenne, Arapaho, Crow, Gros Ventre, Shoshone, and Pawnee. Only the recalcitrant Comanches and the Kiowas among the major tribes had refused to sign that treaty. But in general it was believed that there was no longer an Indian threat in the Southwest this side of Apache country.

Fort Supply, Fort Reno, and Fort Cobb stood nearby. Fort Defiance, it was true, had been captured by the Navajos, but that was farther west, and besides, there was little doubt that

43

Brooks would retake it.

The Comanches were running with their tails between their legs. As for the Kiowas—their bold leader, Hungry Wolf, as he was called, had not been seen for almost a year and was presumed to be dead.

"In the morning," Tom said, kissing the top of Elizabeth's head, "we begin our new life."

Her bonnet had slipped behind her neck. It was the same sun-faded bonnet she had worn since St. Louis. Her patterned blue calico dress was no newer. Her petticoats were in tatters after fording creeks, trudging through bramble country. When again would she have new cloth against her body? She sighed and smiled at once, for as she turned in the sunset light to watch Tom walk away to unhitch the mules and roughhouse with the boys along the way, the empty framework of the Kansas plains seemed promising again, the journey all worthwhile.

Tom was strong, well-meaning. The boys . . . watching them brought a gentle, sweet ache to her loins.

If this was to be her life, she would make what she could of it.

The last light of day passed away in crimson glory and the night set in rapidly, deeply. Beside the cart Elizabeth lay in Tom's arms. In his weariness he slept deeply, but she could not fall asleep. She watched the tapestry of the stars spread across the sky. Hours passed and still she could not sleep; she tried her best to pretend it was the abrupt chill of the prairie night and not fear that prevented it.

The night was still and yet there were many sounds, muffled and mysterious if one lay still and listened. Most she had heard before: the hoot of an owl, the distant desperate howl of a coyote, the occasional gust of wind ruffling the dry grass. Familiar sounds, yet different out here somehow. New sounds in a new land.

And there was the constant and vaguely disturbing sound of the Cimarron River in its slow progress toward the sea. It should have been a constant, lulling sound, but Elizabeth imagined in the cold night that she could hear each eddy and backwash as the water worked around exposed roots and sawyers, whispering over sandbars, gathering uncertain new momentum. It had its own mysterious vocabulary, and Elizabeth thought that she would always hate the sounds the long river made.

With the bright new sun, the riders came.

They rode directly out of the sun, dark silhouettes against its brilliance, and Elizabeth shaded her eyes to watch them coming.

"Tom!" she called.

He turned from his work, unloading their meager goods from the cart, and took his rifle from beside the wheel. Striding up beside her, he motioned the boys to stay back.

"Are they Indians?" she asked in a taut whisper.

"No," Tom answered after a long minute spent studying the incoming riders. "No, they're soldiers. I think."

After another few minutes it became clear that that was what they were. Five of them were at least. Altogether there were six riders, but one of them wore the buckskins of an old plainsman. Tom and Elizabeth watched silently as the riders approached.

The man in the lead was an officer. They could tell that even at a distance because he rode a dapple gray horse. Officers, they knew, were allowed to select their own mounts while ordinary troopers were required to ride uniformly colored bay horses.

As the men drew nearer, Elizabeth could see that the officer in charge wore a saber at his side. It seemed somehow incongruous to her out here. It glittered brightly in its sheath. Nothing else about the officer was crisp. His uniform was dusty, open at the collar. His hat was dented. He was young—Elizabeth

45

guessed he was not more than twenty-five—but he was grim-appearing.

The body of men slowed their horses to a walk and finally halted, and the officer swung down from his saddle. Coming forward, still appearing stern, he offered Tom a firm hand.

"Lieutenant Benjamin Ramsey," the officer said as the two men shook hands.

"Tom O'Day. This is my wife, Elizabeth," Tom replied.

"Hello." Ramsey touched the brim of his hat and nodded to Elizabeth, his eyes running briefly over her.

"I'm sorry we have nothing to offer you . . ." Tom began, but the lieutenant waved the offer aside.

"Nothing needed, thanks." He smiled, but it was a humorless smile. Ramsey removed his hat briefly and wiped back his dark hair. Already, Elizabeth noticed, there was silver showing in it.

The officer had handed the reins of his gray horse to a very young corporal with a pink face. He spoke sharply to the young enlisted man.

"Huggins, see to it that the horses are watered."

"Yes, sir!" came the automatic response and the soldiers along with the older man in buckskins started down toward the banks of the Cimarron. The plainsman, Elizabeth thought, seemed amused by the goings-on. The boys had emerged from their hiding places to stare at the cavalry officer.

"I hope there is no trouble nearby," Tom O'Day said earnestly.

"None that I'm aware of," Ramsey said. "We spotted your cart tracks some miles back and decided to follow along to see what your intentions were."

"Our intention," Tom answered very firmly, "is to take up residence on this land."

"Fine," the lieutenant said. Elizabeth did not like the man's smile at all. It was like a lesson he had learned by rote but never really understood. "So long as you weren't planning on crossing the Cimarron.

"You see," Ramsey went on, "we have no official treaty with the Kiowas, but we have an understanding with their young Chief, Winter Owl, that there will be no hostilities as long as the whites do not advance beyond the river. We can't allow any new settlers to cross the river. Not," he added, "until Fort Cimarron has been fully manned."

"We hadn't heard of that fort," Tom said.

"Small wonder," Ramsey answered. "May I trouble you for a drink of water from your water barrel, Mr. O'Day? Small wonder," he repeated as they walked to the barrel strapped to the side of the cart and Tom offered the cavalryman a dipper of water, "since construction has only begun in the last few months. At present we have only one company of men there, but by the end of the year we expect to have the fort fully manned."

The officer finished his drink, pouring what remained in the dipper across the back of his neck to cool himself. Elizabeth spoke up.

"This Winter Owl . . . the Kiowas, they have no objection to another fort being built along the river?"

"Madam," Ramsey said, "the Kiowas have nothing at all to say about it. Since they refuse steadfastly to sign a formal treaty, there are no terms to be dictated by them. White settlers must be protected, and that is what we intend to do. There will come a time, I assure you, when whites will cross the Cimarron, and when that time comes the Kiowas will have to simply move westward or be pushed."

Tom glanced at Elizabeth. She knew he thought no more of Benjamin Ramsey's manner than she did.

"What of this Hungry Wolf we've been hearing about?" Tom asked.

The officer made a disparaging gesture. "That one? I don't

47

know frankly. Except that he was a self-proclaimed war chief and seems to have fallen out of favor with the Kiowa leadership. We have information that he was killed along the Smoky Hills by a contingent of cavalry and their Arapaho allies."

"For now . . . ?" Tom looked at his two boys who had run barefoot down to the river to watch the soldiers water their horses.

"For now, O'Day, you are perfectly safe, I assure you." Ramsey hesitated, looking at the covered cart. "You are prepared to build here?"

"I am prepared to do my best, sir," Tom replied. "Frankly, when I acquired this land, I was led to believe there was some timber along the Cimarron."

Lieutenant Ramsey laughed. "No, I'm afraid not. The wood we're using for our palisade is being freighted all the way from Independence. No, I'm afraid you'll just have to make do."

And that was that. With a half-hearted invitation to visit the new fort and a brief handshake, Ramsey started toward the river where his men waited.

"It must be hard to swagger like that down a slope," Tom muttered as they watched the officer, and both of them laughed.

"I don't like that man, Tom."

"No, I don't either—but the fact that they're constructing a new fort nearby makes me feel a little more secure."

"Someone's coming," Elizabeth said.

From the river, riding very slowly on an old buckskin horse with black ears, came the plainsman they had seen, carrying his rifle across the saddlebow.

Reaching them, he halted his horse and without swinging down, asked. "Do you know what you're about?"

"What do you mean?"

"I mean, have you got a steel-blade plow?"

"Yes," Tom answered.

48

"Have you ever built a soddy before?"

"No, sir . . ."

"My name's Donovan Hart," the plainsman said, "not 'sir.' I'll be back in a day or so with some off-duty soldiers from Fort Cimarron. I reckon we'll be able to help you slap a soddy up in a day. It won't be pretty, but it'll keep the weather off you and the kids."

"Mr. Hart . . ."

"No 'Mr. Hart' either, thank you. I'll be back and we'll see what we can do to help you out. Right now it looks like the lieutenant is eager to be riding on. I'll be seeing you folks."

Then Donovan Hart nodded, turned his horse, and slowly rode back down the knoll to where Lieutenant Ramsey, his impatience visible even at that distance, sat waiting.

Donovan was true to his word. On the second day following that visit, a small group of soldiers, loose and laughing and singing as they rode, approached. There was no officer in charge of them and they were obviously enjoying their day of freedom. Elizabeth was at the cart, Tom O'Day at the river with the boys, drawing water.

"Mornin', Mrs. O'Day," Donovan Hart said as the small contingent arrived.

"Good morning, Mr. Hart."

"This is Sergeant Callahan, another good Irishman," he said, introducing a dumpy, merry-looking man missing a few front teeth. "And this is Corporal Huggins who you might remember. Caffiter, Swift, and Yount are those three lazy looking privates."

Elizabeth smiled and nodded to all of them.

Tom had arrived, and to him Hart said, "Yount is especially good with a plow. The rest of us are good for nothing, but these young bucks have strong backs."

"Welcome, all of you," Tom said sincerely.

49

"It's nothin', Mr. O'Day," the plainsman said. "We've brought a few trinkets along from the sutler's at the fort. Huggins?"

"We knowed you folks couldn't have much," the soldier, his cap in his hands, said shyly, "so we brung . . . well." Caffiter, the baby-faced blond trooper, untied a sack from the pommel of his saddle.

"Just nothin'," the trooper said, inexplicably blushing. "An iron pot, fairly good-sized. Ten pounds of beans, a few small things."

"Horehound drops for the kids," Sergeant Callahan reminded him, and the soldier produced a paper sack with the candy in it.

Kent and Oliver, who had seen no sweets for three months, gathered eagerly and the trooper passed the sack to them.

"Thank you so much," Elizabeth said feelingly, and Caffiter blushed still more deeply.

"Now, then, men," Sergeant Callahan said, "let's help these people get started here."

Elizabeth said to Donovan Hart, "I can't tell you how much this means to us . . . we need so much help."

"Ma'am," the plainsman replied quietly, "you don't know what it means to these men. Most of them haven't so much as seen a woman or a child in almost a year. I could've gotten fifty volunteers if Lieutenant Ramsey would have allowed it."

All day long then, with Elizabeth and the boys hauling water to the hardworking soldiers, with the mule in front of Tom O'Day and then Yount, cutting long squares of sod eight to ten inches thick from the prairie carpet, they worked to build their house on the plains.

The work went more quickly than Elizabeth would have believed possible. Donovan Hart and Sergeant Callahan laid out a ground plan, and row upon row of sod squares were stacked one on top of the other. There were two rooms only to the soddy, which was thirty feet long by twenty deep. The walls were thirty inches thick—"Enough to keep the cool in come summer, enough to keep the heat in through winter," Hart had told her. "Don't worry about the door or window frame," he had said with a wink. "We'll pinch some lumber from the fort and bring it along tomorrow."

And so the squat, quite unremarkable but functional sod house went up over the next three days.

"It'll do for now," Tom said firmly, studying the house. "Until I can plant the crops and bring our own timber from Missouri."

He was so determined, so hopeful, that it caused Elizabeth's eyes to mist over briefly. He wanted to do so much for her and the boys.

She remained unsure. It was a strange, wild land, a lonely land, but she allowed herself to feed off Tom's certainty, and in the evening when the orange sun sank low across the Cimarron behind the scattered sycamores and twisted oaks, coloring the lazing river, there were times when she could almost share his dream; for although the land was wild, broad, and empty, still there was a haunting beauty to it. They now had a roof over their heads, new friends, and day after day, from sunrise to sunset, Tom plowed his land as she tried her best to start a small garden. Each day the land seemed a little more tameable. Each day the boys, who had seemed wan and weakened after the long trek across the plains, seemed to grow in strength and thrive on the wilderness living.

They swam in the river, helped where they could, and seemed at times to be poised already on the threshold of manhood.

And at night in their bed, she and Tom talked of what he wished for, what he wanted to provide for them, and sometimes she almost believed it would all come true. His dreams were beautiful and strong. But still Elizabeth feared this land on Cimarron. It was too vast, too empty.

One day when the bright green leaves of the new corn were

shimmering in the sunlight above the dark, rich loam of the earth and there seemed to be some hope for her kitchen garden after the broiling days of summer, Tom arrived on Domino in great excitement.

"I've found what we need, Elizabeth," he said, beginning to speak even before he had swung down from his horse.

"What do you mean, Tom?"

"Why, the one thing we've really lacked, dear. Timber! There's an island not a mile upstream with a fine stand of yellow pine. Enough to begin a decent house and start a barn. This soddy will have to do over the winter, I'm afraid, but I can begin a wooden house soon. Some of the men from the fort will help us. I'm sure of it."

"But, Tom . . . the Cimarron is the boundary of our property, isn't it?"

"Which bank of the Cimarron?" he asked with a careless laugh. "It's a midstream island, Elizabeth; no one can claim to that stand of timber."

She hesitated, taking both of his hands in hers. "Not even the Indians, Tom?"

"Indians have no use for timber. Besides, they've all cleared out. You heard Lieutenant Ramsey saying that."

"I heard him. But I don't think Donovan Hart agrees with him on that point. Tom . . . maybe you shouldn't do it."

Surprised by her caution, Tom answered. "We need that timber, Elizabeth, to build our home. There's not a man around for a hundred miles with any claim to it but me."

Still Elizabeth shook her head worriedly. They were in a new land they knew so little about.

"Darling," Tom said, gently touching her cheek with the back of his hand. "This is important. So important. This is our home, and we have to seize every opportunity to make it a fine place. For us, for the boys."

"Yes, Tom. I know. I suppose you're right, but . . ."

"We have to, I tell you," Tom said, and now there was just a hint of anger in his voice. It was an unusual emotion for Tom O'Day. It meant only that he was determined to do what he had promised her on the long western trek and would not be frustrated in his attempt. There was little Elizabeth could say against the project. She knew they needed lumber badly, and her objections seemed without foundation.

Still, she was uncomfortable when the timber began to arrive from the island upriver, most of it hauled by their two mules on the old cart, although on several occasions, Sergeant Callahan and Huggins brought out a four-horse team and wagon from the fort to help out.

There was one other thing that bothered Elizabeth deeply. She said nothing to Tom about it.

The boys were now being taught to shoot. Knowing that they would need those skills to hunt or to defend themselves in this wild country, she bit her tongue and remained silent. However, the sounds of gunshots as the boys took target practice still disturbed her.

And then there was the day she saw the other woman.

It was so sudden and unexpected that it startled Elizabeth violently.

The boys were working with their father in the fields, so Elizabeth had taken the opportunity to walk down to the river to bathe. The day was warm and the river slipped past silently. Cicadas sang along the bank, and quail spoke somewhere in the underbrush as the sun glittered down through the branches of the overhanging sycamore trees.

Wading nude into the river, Elizabeth felt suddenly that someone was watching her, and she immediately covered her breasts with crossed forearms, looking around. Far across the silver-blue river then, she saw a shadow against the trees.

It was another woman, simply standing on the opposite bank of the river, staring at her. Indistinct and unmoving for a long time, the other woman eventually turned and moved silently away.

"Don't you see, Tom," she said that night as they sat before a low-burning fire in the soddy, "she had to be an Indian!"

"Yes," Tom answered slowly, "of course she had to be."

"Well then, Lieutenant Ramsey was wrong, wasn't he! All of them are wrong. There *are* still Indians around here."

"Only a few wandering bands, one imagines," Tom answered quietly, but she could see the uncertainty in his eyes. "So long as they stay on their side of the river and we stay on ours," he said with a shrug, "there won't be any trouble. That was the agreement we made. Still . . ."

"Still what, Tom?" she asked.

"Well, maybe I should report it to the soldiers. We'll go over to the fort tomorrow, all of us. We haven't seen the post yet and we could all use a little break from the work."

The fort, when they reached it the following sun-bright morning, was bleak and primitive-looking. Set on a humped knoll that rose only slightly from the surrounding dry grass plains, the outpost had a low, square palisade of unpeeled timbers with catwalks along the inner walls. The flag flew on a pole in the center of the parade ground. To one side as they entered through the high gates, a squad of men stood at attention, being lectured to by a sergeant they did not recognize.

The buildings were laid out in an L shape, the officers' quarters and the barracks adjoining on the north side, the armory, mess hall, and supply rooms along the longer side. At the juncture of the two sides rested the sutler's store, which was the best constructed of all the buildings, it seemed.

All around them men were working in shirtsleeves. Hammers

rang out, saws hummed, orders were shouted as timbers were lifted into position.

"That should be the headquarters," Tom guessed as he reined in the mules pulling their cart. There was a door between the officers' quarters and the enlisted barracks, as yet unmarked, but in front of it Ramsey's horse stood at the hitch rail and a young corporal stood guard beside the door.

Ground-hitching the mule team with a heavy lead weight carried for that purpose, Tom removed his hat and wiped back his hair. Helping Elizabeth down from the cart, Tom said, "The boys will be all right out here. They can watch the soldiers work." Eagerly the boys leapt from the cart.

"But don't get in their way!" Elizabeth admonished.

"Mr. O'Day!" a familiar voice called from across the parade ground, and they turned to see Donovan Hart striding toward them. He asked, "Here to see the lieutenant?"

"Yes, we are."

Then to the boys, Hart said, "Hello, Kent. Oliver. You know the sutler's got some new peppermint sticks in his store. Maybe we could go over and get you each one . . . if it's all right with you, ma'am."

"That's kind of you, Mr. Hart."

"It's nothin' at all, Mrs. O'Day. Be more than happy to do it."

With the boys under Hart's escorting arms, walking off toward the store, Tom and Elizabeth stepped up onto the unfinished boardwalk in front of the headquarters building. The corporal on guard there merely nodded at them, giving Elizabeth a second glance, and they entered the office where a big sergeant sat behind a puncheon desk, scowling down at the papers spread out before him.

"May I help you, sir?" the sergeant said, looking up.

"Is Lieutenant Ramsey in?"

"Yes, sir." The soldier rose. "May I give him your name?"

Tom told him and he and Elizabeth stood waiting for a moment, staring at the big map on the office wall and the Indian blanket someone had tacked up there. The sergeant re-emerged from the inner office.

"You're welcome to go right in, folks," he said, holding the rough door open for them.

Lieutenant Benjamin Ramsey, looking slightly harassed, but impeccably groomed as they had not seen him on the prairie, rose and extended his hand to Tom O'Day, bowing his head to Elizabeth.

"I'm happy to see you both again," Ramsey said, offering them each a chair beside his desk. Then he seated himself again, leaning back slightly, hands folded together on his lap. "What can I do for you folks?" His manner was affable, but there was the beginning of a frown on his wide mouth.

Briefly Elizabeth told him about seeing the Indian woman. Now that she was repeating the tale, it seemed such a trivial occurrence that she became slightly embarrassed. Ramsey's frown, however, continued to deepen.

"I'm sorry," Elizabeth apologized, "it seems like nothing now."

"It is nothing. Now," Ramsey said, "but I have been told by our scouts that the Kiowas have moved north with the coming of summer. I would like to know if a band of them has remained behind, and for what purpose. We'll increase our patrols in that area, I promise you."

"Thank you," Tom said. He, too, seemed a little embarrassed now. It seemed such a minor episode to bother the officer about. He explained, "We just thought you should know. And naturally, since this Kiowa was seen directly across the river from our farm . . ."

"Yes, yes, I understand," Ramsey said. "Your concern is quite natural."

Ramsey rose and went to the window, which was nothing more than a space created by sawing away sections of two logs. He stood there for a long while, the slanting rays of the sun illuminating his finely hewn face.

"I was hoping all of this trouble with the Kiowas had been sorted out." He turned with a feigned smile. "I'm sure it has been." Sighing, he returned to his chair and sagged into it. "It's just that with all of this mess in the East, it's worrisome."

"I don't understand what you mean," Elizabeth said, but Ramsey waved a hand as if such matters shouldn't concern a woman.

"He means," Tom told her, "that they are still talking secession in the South. Isn't that correct, Lieutenant?"

"Yes." Ramsey admitted. "The last St. Louis newspaper I received is filled with nothing but rhetoric and speculation concerning that. And, of course, no one knows which way Missouri or Kansas would tilt if it ever came to that."

"Surely there won't be a war," Elizabeth said, deeply concerned.

"I'm afraid no one can say just now," Ramsey answered. "But let us talk of other matters. I do have a bottle of brandy if you care to . . ."

"I do not drink," Tom O'Day said sternly. The son of a Presbyterian minister, Tom had been taught early on that liquor was the devil's tool.

"If *you* wish to," Elizabeth said quickly. Ramsey looked as if he would like nothing more, but he made a dismissive gesture.

"It was only a courtesy."

"And we do thank you for that," Elizabeth said pleasantly. Ramsey was on his feet again, smiling.

"While you are here," the officer said, "you must, of course, visit our sutler's store. He has a surprisingly large stock of goods, and I'm sure you need many small items you weren't able to bring across the plains."

"Yes, we do, thank you," Elizabeth said gratefully. She had hoped they would offer the use of the army store to them. She had carried her small purse all the way from the farm, clutching it tightly. In it, she knew, was exactly four dollars and twenty cents in silver. All of the cash money they had remaining in the world. This was a major concern to her, of course. Although she believed they could survive with the farm, there would be nothing at all for the boys but garden crops and the occasional deer.

Since the day they had learned about the construction of Fort Cimarron, Tom had been excited about having discovered a potential market for his corn. That had been another reason for coming to the fort—to discuss the possibility of selling his crops to the army. Now, the two men hung back as Elizabeth walked with them to the sutler's store past the respectful soldiers, and she felt certain that was what Tom and Ramsey were discussing.

Her sons, with well-licked peppermint sticks in their hands, were sitting in the narrow band of shade cast by the awning in front of the store. Donovan Hart, who they always had liked, sat with them. Donovan rose at Elizabeth's approach and removed his hat.

"Is everything all right, Mrs. O'Day?" he inquired.

"I think so, yes." Briefly she recounted the Indian woman's appearance as Hart listened intently.

"What did the lieutenant say?" the scout asked.

"That he would increase the patrols near the river."

Hart shook his head worriedly. "I see."

"You don't think that's a good idea?" Elizabeth asked in surprise.

"Truthfully," Hart answered, looking toward the headquarters building, "no, I do not."

"But *why*?"

"Ma'am . . ." Hart struggled to find the right words. "I say, let the Kiowas alone. The lieutenant—I could tell you a few stories—he's just too eager to engage them, ma'am. And making them angry is much more dangerous for you and the children than leaving them be."

"I see," Elizabeth said. "Well, at least I think I do. But, Mr. Hart, wasn't there a more senior officer commanding this post? The one who made peace with the Kiowas?"

"Yes, ma'am. That was Captain Macklin, a fine soldier. He's the one who did the negotiating with Winter Owl."

"But, then?" Elizabeth asked in puzzlement. "Where is he now?"

"He went home, ma'am," Hart said solemnly.

"Home?"

"Yes, ma'am. Captain Macklin, he's a Southerner."

The subject of impending war came up only seldom after that. The O'Days were too busy on the farm, concerned with the corn crop and the fast-approaching fall and following winter. It was impossible for Tom to do all he had planned although he worked from sunrise to sunset, worked until he had no sooner eaten his supper than he fell into bed to sleep, often too tired to even undress.

But the corn crop, tall and waving, did come in, a good plentiful crop, and most of it was sold to Lieutenant Ramsey at Fort Cimarron where the horses had little but wild grass to nourish them and the corn was welcome. Elizabeth was able to buy a few things for the boys and herself. She was frequently disappointed, of course; she still wore her old blue gingham dress. The sutler, his customers all men, had no reason to stock such items, although he promised her that in the spring he would order some bolts of cloth and buttons and such from St. Louis.

Most important to Tom, with the corn in and the time to work on a house, the wooden structure began to go up quickly. It had already snowed, but not heavily, and he worked steadily at the framing. The boys collected stones along the river for the chimney, and it was nearing completion as well.

Elizabeth hated to see Tom working so hard—in all weather he was out with his tools, building their new house. But when it rained, Elizabeth prayed he would manage to finish it quickly. The rain streamed through the sod roof, and muddy water stained everything, pooling on the earthen floor, making everything cold, damp, and messy.

In the second week of October, it snowed all night, leaving twelve inches of new-fall behind.

Rising, Elizabeth went outside into the cold morning. The sunlight was so bright off the new snow that she had to squint into the distances. Her shawl, wrapped around her shoulders, did little to protect her against the chill. It would be a long, cold, desolate winter.

The boys were untroubled by the weather. They romped across the hills, sometimes with permission to take a rifle along to hunt for rabbits. These were the only times the boys really quarreled. Both wanted to carry the rifle. Kent, being the older, usually won the argument, and Oliver, on the verge of tears, would pout at length.

"I *am* the oldest," Kent would tell his younger brother. They looked so very much alike with their flyaway flaxen hair and blue eyes, Elizabeth thought, but their temperaments were different. Kent was bolder, more outspoken, perhaps he took after his father. Oliver was reserved, given to keeping his own thoughts. At night by candlelight, he would read the Bible or Jonathan Swift while Kent cleaned the rifle or sharpened his pocket knife on a stone.

"Still, I should have a turn, shouldn't I, Mother?" Oliver pleaded.

"Of course, you should. For today, let Kent carry the rifle. Then next time it will be your turn, won't it, Kent?"

Kent opened his mouth to object, but he saw the look in his mother's eyes. "Yes'm," he said unhappily.

Oliver brightened a little. "We'll bring two rabbits home today for sure," he promised.

"All right," Elizabeth said, "Just remember everything your father has taught you. Walk abreast. See your target clearly . . ."

"Mother!" Kent moaned.

"I want you to remember always that guns are not toys," Elizabeth said.

"Mother!"

"All right, then," she said, "get along now." She watched them with a smile as they ran out into the yard, pausing to wave to their father who was on the roof of the new house, before they headed out through the new snow, confident that they would be able to track rabbits easily under these conditions.

When they were gone over the knoll she still stood watching. Watching the cold river run. Now the banks of the Cimarron were fringed with icicles and in places there were ice floes on the river itself. The willows stood bleak and leafless against the bright background of the new snow. The birds were still and quiet, most having moved on, with only the black crows cawing, winging across the crystal-blue sky. Still, Elizabeth watched the river, and the silent land beyond. Not long ago she thought she had seen a wisp of smoke to the west, but Tom had laughed and assured her that any Indians who might have been there through the summer had surely moved on to the south when the snows began.

The soldiers seldom rode by their farm any longer. Perhaps it was the weather, but a passing stranger, a ragged-looking mountain man with a beard that flared out to his shoulders, had told them that Lieutenant Ramsey had led a force north, searching for Hungry Wolf.

"Though they got as much chance of findin' him as you'd have findin' a penny under this snow," the mountain man had said around spoonfuls of Elizabeth's venison stew.

"Why do they want him?" Elizabeth had asked. "I thought we had a pact with the Kiowas."

"That pact was done with Winter Owl, ma'am." The mountain man shook his head. "But Hungry Wolf, well, he is a different kind of animal altogether."

"We could set snares like Donovan Hart showed us," Oliver suggested. He was breathing hard as he labored to keep up with his older brother. Kent sneered at the idea.

"And suppose we snared one, Oliver? What then? Suppose it snowed tomorrow again? Or for three days running and we couldn't get back to the snare? Why, you'd have an old frozen rabbit good for nothing. No, sir, we'll shoot us some and get them back home while their blood's still warm."

"I was just thinking . . ." Oliver said rather weakly. "What do we have to go on so fast for?"

"Don't have to," his older brother said, looking over his shoulder at Oliver who was struggling through the snow. "I just naturally walk fast. If you're tired, go on back home."

"I ain't tired," Oliver responded, and he trudged on doggedly through the snow.

"Hey, now, here goes one," Kent said, halting suddenly, and he pointed out the tracks of a rabbit in the snow. "Quiet now."

"He's long gone."

"Maybe so. Just wait, and keep your eyes open for a place where the wind's cleared the snow off the grass. That's where they'll be headed."

"Or back to their burrow," Oliver thought, but did not say. No matter what he said these days, Kent mocked him.

They walked on more slowly now. There were scattered oaks here, twisted and stark against the sky. Beneath the trees the snow was thinner, and they did come upon places where the grass showed through.

Abruptly a rabbit started in front of them, running in a zigzag pattern across the snowy ground, and Kent shouldered the rifle. It was a difficult shot, but Kent was skilled with the rifle and he had made kills on running rabbits before. He was sighting down the long barrel, his finger slowly easing back on the trigger when his brother, at his elbow, shouted.

"Look here, Kent!"

Kent fired the rifle and missed wildly, the rabbit bounding away into the underbrush. Kent spun to face his brother, his face, red with the cold, growing redder.

"What did you have to yell for?"

"Look, Kent," Oliver said. He was pointing at an old white oak tree and there, three feet above the ground, its obsidian head embedded in the bark of the tree, was an arrow.

"Well, what . . . ?" Forgetting the rabbit and his anger, Kent went with his brother to examine the arrow. Handing the rifle to Oliver, he yanked the arrow from the tree. Not firmly embedded, it came free easily.

"So, it's true; there are still Indians around," Oliver said in a taut whisper, his blue eyes growing fearful.

"Ah, this thing could've been there forever," Kent said. Yet, he found himself surveying the snowbound landscape carefully.

"What if we see 'em?" Oliver asked in a near-whisper.

"It's nothin' to me," Kent replied with false bravado. He took the rifle back from Oliver. "I'd just shoot 'em, I reckon. See if I wouldn't."

"Kent . . . let's head on home."

"What are you, a sissie?" Kent sneered, but he had already forgotten about rabbit hunting himself. "I guess I'd better take you home, though, if you're scared."

They began trudging wordlessly back across the new snow, which crunched underfoot. After a long while, Oliver asked, "What do we tell Mother?"

"What do you mean?"

"You know she's afeared of Indians. More afeared than she lets on."

"Then we won't tell her," Kent said after a moment's indecision. "We'll show Dad the arrow in private. But he'll tell you what I just said. That arrow could've been there forever. If there was any Indians around, I'd have seen 'em."

When the boys got home, Tom was inside the new house, nailing down the flooring. Wordlessly he listened to them as he looked at the arrow. He told them essentially what Kent had said.

"They lived on this land for a long time, boys. This could have been lost in a hunt long years ago."

Nevertheless, it bothered Tom, and he agreed with his sons that Elizabeth shouldn't be told and worried needlessly. The three of them made a pact to say nothing to her.

Winter inevitably began to encroach on their time and freedom of movement. The days grew short and when it did not snow, the rain fell in heavy sheets with a thrusting wind behind it, prodding massive black clouds across the plains. Tom had completed the roof of the new house and so they were able to work in most weather, the four of them a unit, a family, although Tom naturally outlasted them all with his seemingly boundless energy. Elizabeth went to bed no less weary, for after working on the new house she had to return to the soddy and cook dinner in an iron pot suspended over the fire on chains.

Still the soddy leaked and dripped mud constantly. Tom

cursed himself for not having done a better job of building it, but with the materials at hand, there was no way he could have done more.

And yet, Elizabeth counted herself lucky. They would have a new home. She and Tom were still in love. The boys were healthy and strong. On one rare day after the skies had been clear for three mornings in a row, Tom judged the trail dry enough to travel to Fort Cimarron and purchase the last of their winter supplies.

The mules moved the cart along the road with surprising enthusiasm. Perhaps they, too, were tired of the inactivity of the past few weeks. The fort was nearly completed and as they passed through the open gates, a few troopers waved to them in recognition.

Inside the stockade they found a new family of westward migrants. They seemed quite dazed by it all; Elizabeth understood fully. Their name was Kittinger. Nesbitt Kittinger, called Ned, and his wife and daughter. The woman, Isadora, was dressed in black, her dark hair pulled back severely in the style of a matron although she appeared to be in her early thirties. She was very attractive except that her mouth was always tightly compressed. The daughter, Bettina, was dark complexioned like her mother, her hair raven-black. She might have been mistaken for an Indian herself except for her astonishingly blue eyes. She was, Elizabeth guessed, 14 or 15 years old, already developing into a woman. Kent made friends with the girl immediately, although Oliver said enigmatically:

"She isn't our sort, Mother."

The reason for Isadora Kittinger's displeased, nearly hostile mood, was readily apparent to everyone. Crossing the plains this late in the year without a waiting shelter was foolhardy at the least. "The man's a fool," was Tom's opinion. They had arrived too late to have a hope of even building the poorest of soddies with the snow falling unpredictably. The earth was frozen and defied the plow. Therefore, the Kittingers were living in an army tent pitched on the bare, cold earth of the fort's parade ground.

"Like common blanket Indians!" Isadora had complained to Elizabeth.

There were a few Indians now living just beyond the walls of the fort as well, which was astonishing to Elizabeth.

"They're Osage Indians," Donovan Hart told her. "Looking for safety. It seems they're pretty scared of Hungry Wolf and his band."

"I had always thought that Indians didn't make their wars in winter," Tom O'Day remarked. The plainsman shook his head.

"Most don't. But don't you remember, Tom? I told you once that Hungry Wolf is not your average warrior. Somehow the Osage got on the wrong side of him and he's still looking for blood."

"Weren't we told that he was dead?" Elizabeth asked.

"Rumors, speculation. If it's not Hungry Wolf, it's his ghost that has frightened these people so much they'd shelter outside a white man's fort rather than risk confronting him."

"I'm surprised Ramsey allows them here, knowing how he feels about Indians," Tom said.

The scout shrugged. "Whatever Ramsey is, he's not stupid, Tom, it never hurts to have allies. The Osage can give him a lot of information he did not have before. For example, through these people, we have learned that the Kiowas and the Comanches have kissed cheeks and made up."

"Does that mean trouble?" Elizabeth asked with concern.

"Not necessarily. Not for now. It seems they have some kind of grudge war still going on with the Mexicans. Nobody seems to know what started it, but neither Hungry Wolf nor the Comanches have attacked a single American camp these last two years. For the time being matters are remaining calm. Maybe Winter Owl is insisting that they stick to the treaty, I dunno."

"But there will be trouble?" Tom asked.

"One day," Donovan Hart said. "One day when there are just too many settlers comin' into this country so that the Indian feels threatened by us."

"Let's hope that day's a long way off," Tom said. He himself not only wished for peace, but he had no need of many neighbors, towns, and all their problems.

"I feel so sorry for the Kittinger family," Elizabeth said, changing the subject.

"Yeah, well, so do I," Donovan Hart responded, "but like your husband says, the man was a fool to start West this time of year. It makes no sense."

Across the parade ground they could see Bettina and Kent talking, playfully shoving each other. There was mock indignation on Bettina's pretty face and Kent was grinning from ear to ear. Oliver hung back near the sutler's store, picking up stones and tossing them.

Elizabeth said, "For a woman and a young girl to have to sleep in a tent in this weather! No one around but rough soldiers . . ."

Hart nodded his agreement. Then he glanced toward the headquarters building where Ned Kittinger, a tall spare man with ridiculous muttonchop whiskers, was emerging from Lieutenant Ramsey's office.

"There's the one I save my pity for," Donovan Hart said. "Lord, the way that woman rails at him! You can hear it all over camp. The soldiers stand out on the boardwalk in front of the sutler's of an evening and listen to her for entertainment."

"That's sad," Elizabeth said. They all nodded to the narrow, stooped man as Kittinger shuffled past, returning to his army-tent home.

"It is," Hart agreed after he had passed them. "The truth is, though, a man like that just don't belong out here. Worse, it seems his wife comes from a wealthy family. Her father is a Boston banker or some such."

Actually Isadora's father was a Baltimore financier as she later told Elizabeth in private.

"Father despised Nesbitt," Isadora confided. "He thought he was worse than a poor match for me. But," she went on with a heavy sigh, "I was young and thought I was in love. After Bettina was conceived, of course, there was no going back. And Father refused to let us in his door or help us with expenses. Nesbitt had a dry goods store in Maryland, but he's never been much good at anything, and it folded. And so," she said with a harsh laugh, "here we are."

She complained about Ned Kittinger until Elizabeth could take no more of it. They parted promising to be friends. "After all we are the only two women around." But Elizabeth doubted they could ever really be friends. Perhaps Oliver had been right after all—they just weren't their "sort" of people. In any event, Elizabeth was less than fond of the woman's manner.

Nor did she like the way Isadora looked at the muscular, laughing Tom O'Day when she thought no one was watching her eyes.

"Well," Tom, oblivious to all of her thoughts said on the way home, "at least there's another woman now for you to talk to from time to time."

"Yes," Elizabeth said in a flat, low voice. Shrugging mentally, Tom drove the cart homeward. Watching him, Elizabeth was glad her man was no fool like Nesbitt Kittinger. He was hard-working, caring, filled with good humor. A good husband and a good father. She leaned her head against his shoulder unexpectedly, and Tom smiled in surprise, touching her head briefly, thumbing back an errant strand of hair from her eyes.

On the first of December, Tom announced that the new house was complete enough for them to begin moving in. On that clear morning with the snow deep and the sky a magnificent blue, the wind slight from the north, they moved their few possessions into the log house. The boys were thrilled. They had their own bedroom with a door and a window. Elizabeth and Tom had their own at the opposite end of the house. In between was the large main room that served as kitchen, living room, parlor, and hall. Tom had built a fire in the stone fireplace as a welcoming, and smoke twisted skyward from the chimney.

"Maybe," Tom said thoughtfully as they worked on arranging their house, "we should offer the soddy to the Kittingers. They'll be condemned to spending the rest of the winter in that miserable tent."

"No," Elizabeth said, too hastily. Quickly she added, "They would just be too close, Tom. Besides, Isadora would probably prefer to be close to the sutler's, safely sheltered in the fort."

"Maybe." Tom stood, hands on hips, looking out the window at the empty soddy. She knew that Tom had no idea what she meant, but he acquiesced. "I'm sure you know best, Liz."

They returned for one last look inside the muddy soddy to make sure they had left nothing behind. After Elizabeth had made one final survey, during which she was touched by a curious sense of sentimentality at the raw emptiness of the place, they went out and Tom closed the door with finality. "Come now," he said, "let's go *home*." He grinned. "Shall I carry you over the threshold?"

Before Elizabeth could answer, he swept her up and she let out an involuntary, girlish squeal. The boys began to hoot and laugh as Tom walked through the snow to the front door of the new cabin and entered with a flourish, Elizabeth cradled like a new bride in his arms.

He didn't immediately put her down. He looked into her eyes, bent his head, and kissed her deeply. The boys stopped their jeering and went outside silently, embarrassed now.

"Now we are home, Liz," Tom said.

"Yes," she said breathlessly, "now we are home, Tom."

And that night in the bed Tom had made for them was more of a honeymoon night than their first had been, when inexperienced and clumsy they had fumbled their way to completion. Now they were comfortable together, Tom's hands familiar and comforting on her breasts and on her thighs. On her back, Elizabeth could see the white half-moon through the high window and Tom's eyes sparkling, his face pleasured and strong above hers. The boys slept in their own room, warm under quilts, and the long, silent snowbound land around them insulated them from any evils of the world.

They were finally home!

Winter was long and bleak, but not nearly so brutal as Elizabeth had been told to expect. It was scarcely colder or harsher than winters back home in Indiana. Occasionally the wind swept savagely, unhindered, across the plains and the snow banked itself against the northern wall of the cabin, but overall it was not a dreadful winter. The new house was tight and dry and warm. Once Elizabeth had wandered through the old soddy, looking for a misplaced frying pan, and had found the floor a muddy muck. She pitied all the women across the prairie who were wintering in such houses and blessed Tom for his zeal.

Once, surprisingly, the Kittingers drove out from Fort Cimarron in their covered wagon. For a moment Elizabeth panicked, thinking that they wanted to occupy the soddy as Tom had suggested, but Isadora not only sneered at the soddy, but disparaged the new house as well.

"I suppose it's all very comfortable," the sleek, dark-haired woman had said, "it's very . . . cozy. I intend to have my house built of finished lumber, not logs, and of course my kitchen shall be a separate room."

"How about the servants' quarters?" Tom muttered, but only Elizabeth heard him.

"When do you expect to start building?" she asked Isadora quickly.

"Very early in the spring. Father has relented; he has wired money—a substantial sum—to St. Louis, and when the weather clears, Ned and I will go over and order our lumber and household items, hire some workingmen to come on Cimarron."

"So you are determined to stay out here, Ned?" Tom asked as the two men sat at the table, sipping at chicory coffee.

"Yes . . ." He looked to his wife as if for confirmation. "There's no point in returning East. And I do have four sections along the river, as you know."

"Yes."

"I wanted to talk to you about last year's corn crop and ask you what you thought about trying wheat out here," Ned went on, his eyes suddenly showing interest, almost passion. Isadora turned away and looked out the window as if all of it were of no importance whatever to her.

Outside the children were playing, throwing snowballs at one another. Rather—Kent and Bettina were—Oliver, silent and solitary, was beginning to build a snowman.

Tom slipped up beside Elizabeth as she watched the play and told her, "Ned is going to bring some chickens out from St. Louis and maybe some ducks. Some hogs. I've agreed to buy a few from him."

That would be a great help, Elizabeth thought. Fresh eggs and some meat besides game! It was something to look forward to.

"If you can find any vegetable seeds, Mr. Kittinger . . ."

"I'll be sure to do that, Mrs. O'Day," Ned answered. He was more animated than Elizabeth had ever seen the muttonchop-whiskered man. He did have grand plans for his farm. It was too bad he had no one to share them with.

"There's one other thing we could use, Ned," Tom said. "If you can manage it."

"Sure, Tom, anything. Make a list and I'll . . ."

"This doesn't require a list. I believe it will be quite simple."

"What is it you are wanting then?"

"A dog," Tom said. "I'd feel better if we had a dog around the place."

And that was how "Regret" came to the O'Day farm. In late February the Kittingers returned from St. Louis with their wag-onloads of lumber, hogs, and chickens, an iron stove and factory-made furniture.

And "Regret."

He was five months old, black as sin with only a few white hairs on his left ear and at the tip of his tail. His coat was long, as thick as a bear's. There was no telling what his parents had been, but they had been very big dogs, certainly. Regret had huge paws, a sure sign that he was going to be massive, and in fact, when he was full-grown, his paws were nearly the size of a man's hands. He was affable, but far too energetic.

In his first week on the farm he got into the chicken coop and tore a hanging deer haunch from its hook in the new smoke-house. He would charge through the house with muddy feet, tongue dangling, mouth set in what seemed to be a grin. Hence his name.

It was Elizabeth who said, "You'll regret the day you brought that monster home, Tom O'Day." And, "I regret the day I agreed to you adopting a bear." The name stuck.

In time his puppy ways fell away and he became nothing

more than a huge ball of black fur sleeping by the fireplace except when the boys wanted to go out to play or to hunt. Then Regret was up in a flash, bounding along beside them across the land.

It was late March when Lieutenant Benjamin Ramsey rode out to the O'Day farm and changed their entire way of life in that one visit.

Ben Ramsey rode slowly over the muddy plains toward the O'Day house. Here and there patches of snow remained in the sheltered areas under trees or in the coulees. The day was brisk, cloudless. An aimless white moon drifted across the daybright silver sky. The big gray horse Ramsey rode moved easily under him. The cavalry officer's thoughts were dark and jumbled.

He was only twenty-seven years old, but he felt that his career was slipping away from him. He should, at the least, have been promoted to captain after that traitor, Macklin, returned to his home in Virginia to prepare for the approaching war, but he had been denied even that. Promotions were slow in coming on the plains. Only in warfare did they come to even the most deserving of officers. He had anticipated a few skirmishes with the Kiowas and Comanches, but even those warlike tribes had kept their distance, and Fort Cimarron was nothing more than a useless stockade sitting alone on the prairie.

Ramsey could see Tom O'Day in the distance, shovel in hand, a huge black pup romping around him. A sodbuster. It was a new term and one Ramsey had adopted quickly and used disparagingly.

What sort of *man* could live like that? Grubbing in the earth, planting seeds? Where was the challenge in his life, where did the glory lie? It required no valor and one received no recognition whatever.

Well, he reflected as Elizabeth O'Day appeared on the porch, shading her eyes as she looked toward Ramsey, at least the man had a woman's comfort. Ramsey was fond of women, quite fond of them, in fact, although he did not think he could ever love one of their treacherous sex. He and Isadora Kittinger had been playing a flirtatious game. Ned Kittinger, the boob, smiled indulgently at their teasing remarks. The man was too stupid to see the underlying passion in his wife's eyes. Ramsey was only too well aware of it, and frustrated by it.

"Good morning, Tom!" Ramsey called from across the yard. He rode his horse slowly forward. The bear cub–sized pup had come up to harass the gray's hocks and the boys were chasing the dog, trying to snatch him away before he took a hoof in the face.

"Good morning, Ramsey! Step down."

The lieutenant nodded and swung down from his saddle. "I need to talk to you, Tom," Ramsey said in a grim voice.

Surprised at his tone, Tom said, "Certainly. What's the problem?"

"Can we go inside?"

"Of course. Follow me."

The two men walked to the porch, scraped the mud from their boots, and proceeded into the house where Tom gestured for the army officer to take a seat at the table.

"Coffee?" Tom offered.

"No."

"All right then." Tom seated himself across from Ramsey and remarked, "This seems serious. Mind telling me what's on your mind?"

"It's very serious, Tom. Can we speak privately?"

Tom shrugged and glanced at Elizabeth, who shrugged in return and went out into her garden.

"Now then," Tom O'Day said after the door had closed behind his wife, "what is this about?"

"It's happened, Tom," the cavalryman said, and he took the folded newspaper from his pocket and spread it on the table so that Tom could read the banner headlines.

FT. SUMTER ATTACKED!
STATE OF EMERGENCY DECLARED
WAR IMMINENT

The entire front page of the newspaper carried stories of the rebellion: Emergency session of Congress; Lincoln's terse comments; Jefferson Davis elected president of the seven breakaway Southern states. Tom refolded the paper and looked glumly up at Ramsey.

"Well, you said it was coming," Tom O'Day said.

"Yes." There seemed to be a flush of satisfaction on Ramsey's face, an expression Tom could not understand. "Now, the question is, Tom—which side are you on?"

"Which side?" Tom said in some confusion. Why, I stand with the Union, of course!"

"I thought so. And so the next question has to be: what are you going to do about it, do for the Union? For your country?"

Tom asked carefully, "What do you mean, Ramsey? I'm not sure I follow you."

Intently, Ramsey leaned forward and said, "I mean, Tom, will you fight for your country, or will you not?"

"Ramsey . . ." Tom gestured helplessly around him. "I have a family, my home."

"So do all of the thousands of men who will be going to war, Tom. Are you any different than an Ohio farmer?"

"It is different . . . out here."

"Is it! Why, Tom? Listen, you've got your corn down already, most of it anyway." Ramsey leaned back in his chair. "This war will be over in three months, Tom. Six at the most. You'll be back by harvest time. Meanwhile, there is the fort nearby if your wife and sons need anything at all.

"Tom, we're going to need some good men to head up the Kansas volunteers, and you are the kind of man we need. I will recommend you and see that you have an immediate commission."

Elizabeth had returned from her garden. Closing the door silently behind her, she looked questioningly at Tom, seeing the concern on his face.

"I don't know, Ramsey," Tom said in a lowered voice, "you see how it is."

"Yes," Ramsey replied with a hint of contempt in his voice, "I see how it is. It's your country, but you don't care to sacrifice for it." The officer rose abruptly.

Tom also rose. "I'll think about it, Lieutenant. I'll promise you that."

"Promises aren't going to save the Union, Tom," Ramsey said stiffly. Then he picked his hat up from the table, nodded curtly to Elizabeth, and spun on his heel to walk out the door, Regret snapping at his bootheels.

"What is it Tom?" Elizabeth asked. "What did he want?"

Tom unfolded the newspaper again and showed it to Elizabeth, and she sank into a chair opposite as she slowly read the headlines.

"He wants you to . . ."

"Yes."

"What did you tell him, Tom?"

"You heard me. I said I'd think about it."

He did think about it as he had promised. Deeply, at length, almost obsessively, so that he could not sleep. Men were dying at that moment to preserve the Union. Their country. Tom had always hated the institution of slavery. His father, a Presbyterian minister, had driven the wrongness of that into his head, saying, "Tom, if it's right to enslave a black man, why, may not these men one day decide that it right to enslave us? Anyone who may be weaker, be different, or simply hold different opinions."

Elizabeth said nothing to Tom about this decision; she could see his mind at work, watch him as he looked out over his land, the land he had improved and struggled to tame through hard labor as he fondly watched his growing sons. *What if he did go?* At times panic rose in her breast at that thought. True, everyone said the war would be over in a few months; the South could not stand; but what would she do without him?

And what if he did not return? So many could be killed, would be killed. One day she did raise the courage to ask him directly. They were sitting alone at the table late in the evening with the fire burning low, Regret sleeping by the warm hearth, the boys safely tucked into their beds.

"Tom," she asked as her fingers worked uncertainly across his strong, work-hardened hands, "what will you do? What will *we* do?"

He looked up with bleary eyes and shook his head. He took her hand in his, and they sat in silence for a long while before they rose silently and went into their bedroom where the warmth from the fire still lingered faintly, but the gathering chill of night drew them closely together.

Elizabeth knew he had made up his mind. In the morning the indecision was gone from his eyes. Tom's mouth was set firmly. There was a sadness about him, but it was a determined sadness, and already she knew; she knew her Tom that well.

She said: "You'll need plenty of warm socks, Tom; I'll see to it."

"It won't be for long, Elizabeth."

"No, I know it. How will you tell the boys?"

"They're nearly men. I'll tell them straight out what has happened and what must be done. They'll take good care of you, Elizabeth."

"I know they will," she said, fabricating a smile. What she wanted to say, but did not, was, *They are still only boys, Tom.*

Then one chill and cheerless morning as they stood watching in the yard, Tom swung aboard Domino, waved, and rode the black-and-white horse eastward toward the fort, toward the conflagration beyond. Regret chased after the horse and rider for a long mile until he was too tired to run any more, and he returned to the three small figures standing in the yard of the farmhouse, looking still across the plains, which suddenly seemed so much larger, so much more empty and threatening.

CHAPTER THREE

Ki-Ki-Tai had a red-and black-striped blanket wrapped around her shoulders as she stood watching. Now, as the rains began, she lifted it over her head, crossing her arms to grip it tightly to her. The river was iron-gray; the leaves on the oak trees were thinning. Already the willows along the river were barren. The pines on the sacred island, of course, were thick and so green as to almost appear blue in the dull light.

For months now, she had come up onto this knoll to look out across the river toward the white fort after first checking on White Moon's well-being. The old man seldom left his lodge. It seemed he had banished himself from a faithless tribe after the ascent of Washai to the position of shaman.

Concerned about the incursion of the white soldiers, Ki-Ki-Tai had kept a watchful eye on their fort from a distance. Now she felt foolish. The soldiers, far from increasing, were diminishing in number. Three separate times she had seen small bands of the blue-men ride away to the east, never to return. Why, she did not know and could not guess. Perhaps White Moon's vision of their coming like locusts onto the plains had been wrong. Ki-Ki-Tai could only hope so. She did not want to see Hungry Wolf war against these blue soldiers, and—if he felt his people threatened—she knew he would do so.

The white woman remained.

Ki-Ki-Tai could see her at that moment, riding slowly back toward her lodge of logs through the rain, a bundle of goods tied behind her on the horse's back. Ki-Ki-Tai had not seen her husband for a long time. Perhaps he had died, but she thought he had ridden away to the east with the others. Eagle Heart had told her there was a war between two white tribes somewhere far away. A mountain man named Kyle, with whom he had once hunted as a young man, had told him that. Ki-Ki-Tai did not know if she believed this tale or not.

Now, she watched as the white woman rode into her yard and a huge black dog came bounding toward her followed by her two white sons.

The woman's corn had not all been picked. Now it was too late. She would have a hard winter with no man to hunt for them.

The rain increased and the wind gusted strongly.

Ki-Ki-Tai turned and started back toward her own lodge. Many of the tribe were preparing to travel northward already. The winter was approaching quickly: the time for a good buffalo hunt as their coats grew thick and woolly. Osolo's success trading with the Mexicans and Winter Owl's recent success trading with the Americans had convinced them all that the hide trade could lead to riches.

Of course, they had again waited until Hungry Wolf was gone from the village before reaching this decision.

Ki-Ki-Tai, Momo, and some of the others who had men away from camp in the war party had decided to stay behind and wait for the warriors' return. At least Falcon would not be around to bother her. The warrior had grown bolder in his attention to Ki-Ki-Tai. She did not know how to put a stop to it without making serious trouble. Rani-Ta, unfortunately, had also decided to remain behind.

Rani-Ta was only a nuisance, really, but Ki-Ki-Tai did not like having her around. She was Eagle Heart's niece. Her own father had been killed in a skirmish with the Pawnee when she was a child. Now Eagle Heart constantly touted his niece to Nakai.

"It is not right that a man of your rank should have only one wife, Hungry Wolf," Eagle Heart had said earnestly as Nakai sat eating and Ki-Ki-Tai mended White Moon's moccasins. "Look at Rani-Ta. She is strong! Loyal. She could help Ki-Ki-Tai with her work. She has no father. Yes, it would be better for all three of you if you would take Rani-Ta for your wife."

Nakai had continued to eat, never answering Eagle Heart. When he had finished, he rose, handed his bowl, and walked away, leaving his guest.

Outside of the tipi Rani-Ta was standing, waiting hopefully, her hair glittering with glass beads, wearing her best elkskin dress. Nakai passed by without glancing at her.

How strong Rani-Ta was, Ki-Ki-Tai did not know, but she was a lovely-looking girl. She had high, full breasts and slim hips, long legs, and slender arms. She had a way of walking with her pelvis thrust forward suggestively that Ki-Ki-Tai found annoying, but which caused many warriors to turn their heads. She could have had her choice of the young men, but she and Eagle Heart had determined that she must be wed to Hungry Wolf.

On this evening, when Ki-Ki-Tai had returned from the knoll, the boys were still not back. They had gone hunting with three of Momo and Koto's sons, and undoubtedly had sought shelter somewhere when the rains began.

Ki-Ki-Tai was shivering with the damp and cold, but starting a fire for herself alone seemed too much trouble. Instead she cast aside the wet blanket and crawled into her bed. The hard rain beat down on the sides of the tipi, the wind rumpling the buffalo hides as it gusted by on its way to the secret land. She lay with her eyes open for a long while, thinking of Nakai, worried for him, missing him so deeply that she ached.

Elizabeth O'Day saw only the end of the argument. Frank Skoglund, big and red-faced, stormed out of the headquarters building, turning to shake his fist in that direction before he mounted his black mule and rode angrily from Fort Cimarron. His interview had been with Sergeant Callahan, temporarily holding the rank of lieutenant with the departure of Benjamin Ramsey for the Eastern War, as they had begun calling it on the plains.

For the last half hour, first supplicating, then angered and finally incensed, Skoglund had tried to make Callahan see his position—the need for more patrols near his farm, which was two good bottomland sections near the Arkansas River.

"Indians, of course!" the big farmer said when he was asked what his business at the fort was.

Callahan had leaned back in his chair, brushing at his long sandy mustache. He looked and felt uncomfortable in his new officer's uniform. Callahan knew what was coming; he had had this conversation with so many men over the past few months.

"They were practically in my fields!" Skoglund shouted. Refusing a chair, he stood kneading his hat with his big, raw hands. "Kiowas and Osage. They've been feuding all summer out our way, Callahan."

"I know that, Frank. As you've seen, we have some Osage camped outside the fort here—though I'm going to have to send them on their way; we haven't got the troopers to watch them."

"Well, it seems you have enough troops to watch them and not enough to patrol my area."

"I haven't got enough troops to do anything, Frank. Damnit, you know that. I can't tell you how long Fort Cimarron is going to be manned at all just now, with everyone needed in the East."

"These damned Indians . . ."

Callahan interrupted him sharply. "I don't care about *their* feuds right now, Frank! If you've forgotten we white Americans have our own little feud going on."

Skoglund bit his tongue. He cared only distantly about the war in Virginia. He lived *here*. With his wife and six sons. Ben Ramsey had tried to enlist the two oldest boys and Frank Skoglund had run him off his farm. He was damned if he would send his boys off to fight over the rights of Virginia to secede from the Union or the right of some damned Mississippian to keep slaves.

"You'll do nothing?" he asked Callahan.

"Have they attacked you, Frank? Or any of your neighbors?"

"No . . . but, Callahan! How would you like to be afraid to let your wife and sons leave the house for fear some wild Indian might take a notion to lift their scalps? *And,*" he said as if he had been saving this topper, "they tell me that this Hungry Wolf is violating the treaty by crossing the Cimarron in the first place."

"He's not fighting the whites, Frank! God bless them all if they want to kill each other off."

"Then you'll do nothing?" Skoglund said, his face stony.

"I can't! We're stretched too thin. For now, it's all I can do to patrol this little stretch of Cimarron. Next month . . . who knows? Maybe we won't even be able to do that. Maybe we'll all be in Virginia by then."

"Then what the hell good are you!" Skoglund shouted, bringing the corporal of the guard, Huggins, in to see what the trouble was.

It was a minute after that exchange that Elizabeth O'Day saw Skoglund storm out of the headquarters building.

She had ridden to the fort alone. Earlier in the week, Isadora and Ned Kittinger had driven to her farm in a buggy from their new house, a mile and a half upriver, and told her, "If you want anything at all from the sutler's store in the fort, you'd best get it now. Wiggins is pulling out."

"Closing the store?"

"Yes. There just aren't enough soldiers left there to make it profitable, he says."

Even now there was a wagon in front of Wiggins' store being loaded with crates of merchandise. There was really no point in having ridden all that way, Elizabeth thought. She had scarcely two dollars in her purse. But if she was to find anything at all they needed, it had to be now. The corn was late; the boys were at home, picking through the remaining stand. But with the soldiers and horses being transferred East, the market for their cash crop was sorely depleted, and winter was going to be difficult.

"Oh, please, let this war end soon!" she thought. "Let Tom come home to us."

They had all believed the war would last six months at the most. Now it had dragged on into fall, and there seemed to be no end in sight. Tom had written to her from someplace called Manassas in July, and the word from there was not heartening. Lieutenant Ramsey's unit and Tom with his volunteer regiment had been attached to General McDowell's army. Tom had not come out and said it, but from the tone of the letter and the little they could glean from the censored war reports in the newspapers, it seemed that the Southerners under some Confederate general named Stonewall Jackson had driven them from the field with many casualties incurred.

The shelves of the sutler's store were nearly empty.

"Right now," Wiggins told Elizabeth, "I can't even get beer and tobacco, which, as I'm sure you know, ma'am, were my most profitable items with the troopers."

"I do understand," Elizabeth said, "but must you really close down your store, Mr. Wiggins?"

Wiggins only shrugged. "A man has to make a living, Mrs. O'Day." He managed a small smile and his eyes brightened a little. "Recollect that calico I got for you from St. Louis? You may as well take the rest of the bolt if you like. I've no use for it."

She thanked him; and taking the cloth, and purchasing a bag of salt and twenty-five pounds of flour from the sutler, Elizabeth started back toward the farm. The skies were heavily clouded, the wind strong from the northwest. It would rain again; if what was left of the corn crop wasn't brought in quickly, half of it would rot. It would be a long, cold, lonely winter . . . so lonely.

"Come home, Tom," she whispered. It began to rain then, a steady, cold rain that soaked through her long before she reached the house on Cimarron.

Morning was incredibly bright; the clouds had drifted away except for a few cottony stragglers, and the rising sun glittered against the dew-fresh grass, scattering tiny jewels. Rain trickled from the eaves of the house; the river ran fast and wide, swashed with white water.

"Hello the house!" a feminine voice called from outside as the O'Days were finishing their breakfast. "Anyone up, lazy boys?"

"It's Bettina!" Kent said excitedly. He got his feet tangled in the legs of the chair as he tried to rise, and nearly fell as he rushed toward the door. Elizabeth laughed. Oliver hooted derisively.

"Don't hurt yourself, Kent! She'll still be there in half a minute."

Kent didn't even hear him. Something inside him had changed nearly overnight. He had always liked Bettina Kittinger. He enjoyed playing games with her. She was easy to talk to; she seemed interested in things he had to say.

He had always recognized the fact that she was a good-looking girl, known vaguely that she was nearly a woman, but now that knowledge had a different effect on him. There was nearly chemical excitement that surged through his body when he saw her or even *thought* about her. No one else mattered when she was around.

He flung open the door and emerged onto the porch. Bettina sat her little roan horse there, mounted sidesaddle on its back.

"Well, mister," she said teasingly, "aren't you going to help me down?"

Kent blushed—this was a new phenomenon, he couldn't remember blushing in his entire life until these last few months—he went to her and took the roan pony's reins, leading it beside the porch so that he could reach up and swing her down onto it. He smiled at her, his hands on her hips. Then glancing toward the open door, he kissed her lips lightly.

It was not the first time he had done so, but that was their secret.

The first time had been on the banks of the river at sunset as the sky, garish with crimson and orange pennants of cloud, faded slowly to a deep purple and to a final lingering web of golden lace. Had she offered her lips to him or had he searched for hers with his own? He couldn't remember ever afterward, but it had been his first kiss, sweet and warm, and the moment would never be forgotten. Never.

"Well, Bettina," Elizabeth said in greeting, taking both of the girl's hands in her own, "what a surprise."

"Not much of one," Oliver said, but no one heard him.

"Mother wants to know if you'll come to dinner. All of you," Bettina said.

"I don't know. There's so much that has to be done around the farm."

"Mother . . ." Kent's eyes were pleading. He had never yet seen the new Kittinger house, though he had heard about it from Bettina. And, he wanted to be with this girl for as long and as often as possible.

"We got corn to bring in, Kent," his brother said. "The animals haven't even been fed yet."

"We don't have to leave this minute, do we?" Kent responded. "Not for dinner. We've got plenty of time to take care of the chores, don't we, Mother?"

Regret had ambled into the room. The big black dog sniffed around Bettina's legs, identifying her, and then satisfied, went to lie on the braided rug by the hearth, plopping down heavily.

"I hate to say no," Elizabeth said hesitantly. She was thinking of the corn in the field too. But she had inspected it only yesterday, and so much of it had fallen to frost and corn borers that there was actually little left of any use except for fodder for their horses and the mules. Finally, with a faint sigh, she answered.

"We'll be glad to come," she said to Kent's vast relief. Bettina clapped her hands together in girlish glee. She was like that, Elizabeth had noted on many occasions. One moment a woman of the world, the next still a child. Just now she certainly *looked* more the woman. Her hair was pinned up, decorated with a mother-of-pearl comb. There seemed to be a touch of rouge on her cheeks as well. Beneath her fur-appointed cloak, she wore a deep-blue silk dress with ruffle of white lace at the cuffs.

"Well, I don't care to go!" Oliver blurted out unexpectedly.

"Oliver! It will be fun," his mother said.

Oliver doubted it. "I don't care to go. I'll see to the chores and try to find a bushel or two of good corn. Don't concern yourself. Me and Regret will be all right alone."

"Well . . ." Elizabeth was hesitant.

"Let him do what he wants, Mother," Kent said. He was standing as near to Bettina as was possible without actually touching her. "We'll all be happier without sourpuss along anyway."

Oliver nodded his determination, and without speaking, he went out the front door, leaving it open. He clicked his tongue and Regret rose eagerly to bound after him.

"I don't know why he's gotten like this," Elizabeth said. She thought a part of it was his missing his father so much. Oliver had always been quiet; now he was nearly reclusive. And she did recall Oliver's comments when he had first met the Kittingers. He had never liked them very much.

"It's natural to be a little shy at his age," Bettina said.

"I suppose so. Well, let me make you some tea, Bettina. I think there's some left. Then you can tell me everything about your new house. It must be exciting to have it all finally finished."

They talked for a while then, sipping at their tea. Kent changed his clothes, and then sat around waiting impatiently. He was obviously relieved when his mother finally rose and went to her bedroom to wash and change her dress.

"Will we have any time alone?" he asked Bettina immediately, scooting over beside her on the striped divan.

"I don't know," she answered with a barely suppressed smile, "why?"

"Why! Because I want to be alone with you, why do you think?"

"It would be a little impolite of us to sneak off, don't you think?" Bettina asked.

"Why? They don't care to talk to us anyway, not really. When they do, it's as if we are only children."

"Well, we'll just have to see, Kent. Perhaps. Perhaps." Then lifting her eyes toward Elizabeth's closed bedroom door, she stretched out a hand toward his and squeezed it tightly.

Oliver fed the chicken and the hogs, forked hay for the horses and the mules, and then sat down on the lip of the hayloft, legs dangling down into the dank coolness of the barn. He waited while Kent saddled the horses and led them out—never noticing Oliver perched above him—and he and Mother rode off toward the Kittinger house through the brilliant light of the startlingly clear afternoon.

Then, with a sigh, he clambered down the wooden ladder and went out into the yard where red tulips and yellow daffodils were blooming. The rest of the world seemed drab and silent. Overhead two red-tailed hawks glided on a wind current, their wings not even moving. Regret sat in the mud of the yard, pink tongue dangling, watching Oliver for some sign indicating play to come.

"All right, then," Oliver said to the huge black dog. "Let's do something!"

He decided to try fishing upriver where the recent rains had caused a pond to form in the oxbow. He and Kent had discovered that catfish had been trapped there, one of them a twenty-pounder at the least. The day they had seen it they had had no fishing gear with them and could only throw stones at the fish, annoying it only a little.

Getting his pole and a burlap sack to carry any fish he caught, Oliver dug into the earth near the depleted vegetable garden and turned up a dozen earthworms that he placed in an empty tomato tin. Then he walked slowly toward the river through the cornfields, startling two cottontail rabbits that Regret pursued eagerly but futilely.

Following the river northward, he whistled a tune without a beginning, without an end.

Reaching the pond, which was very muddy again after the previous night's rain, he spread the burlap sack he carried on the ground under a broken cottonwood tree for a seat, hooked a worm, and cast his line into the pond.

He leaned his back against the tree and fell into aimless thought. What his mother suspected was true. He did miss his father. Horribly. Tom O'Day was a giant in Oliver's eyes. He had strong, kind hands. He did not curse at them or hit them ever, but was a tolerant older friend. Whatever job he put his hand to was done rapidly and well. Oliver loved his mother dearly, of course, but that was different. Sitting in the kitchen, watching her bake, listening to her hum old religious songs, was pleasant, comforting in a deep way, but it wasn't the same as going with Dad to saw, hammer, to plow, to pull tree stumps, to *do* things, to build and change the raw unformed world into something structured and strong and new . . .

The catfish was there. Oliver could see its dark form now and then in the murky water. Regret saw it once and followed it along the bank, barking at it. But the "cat" had no interest in Oliver's bait. He decided to try the river proper, although the quick current after the new rain was at odds with good fishing there on this day.

He walked moodily through the trees along the river. The ground underfoot was muddy; the boulders beside the trail patinad with moss. The willows shuddered more than swayed in the wind. Oliver walked up a steep hill, Regret lagging behind, distracted by a gray squirrel.

Cresting the hill, Oliver came face to face with the girl.

"Bettina!" he said in surprise. The black-haired girl's sudden appearance astonished him. He knew instantly that he had been wrong in thinking it was Bettina. It was not her at all—Bettina's eyes were a deep blue; this girl's eyes were as black as obsidian. She wore a buckskin skirt and a red calico short gown. There were calf-high moccasins on her feet.

An Indian! Oliver didn't move. His mouth was agape. The girl put her curled hand beside her head as if undecided whether to hide her face or form a fist to strike out at him.

"I'm sorry . . ." Oliver mumbled. He could think of nothing else to say, and some remark seemed called for.

The girl stood frozen as well for perhaps fifteen seconds as they stared at one another; then she turned, hoisted her skirt, and ran away, leaping a fallen tree, scampering through the oaks like a startled fawn.

Regret rushed up to Oliver's side and the giant dog barked twice from deep in its throat.

"Quiet, Regret!" Oliver said sharply, and the dog eyed him, its head cocked, and then sat down, silent.

Oliver stood there for a long minute, but the Indian girl, whoever she had been, had vanished. He reached out and scratched Regret's head. Then, shouldering his fishing pole, he turned and started thoughtfully toward home.

When Kianceta arrived in the village, her heart was still racing, her spotted pony weary. She had ridden it at a run all the way from the river. Now she leaped from the pony's back and rushed to Ki-Ki-Tai's tipi to tell her what she had seen.

Bursting in through the tent flap, she found Ki-Ki-Tai gathering up a few blankets she meant to shake out outside.

"Kianceta! What has happened?" Ki-Ki-Tai asked, seeing the wild expression on the girl's face.

"I can't . . . may I sit down, Ki-Ki-Tai? What a fright!" She put a trembling hand to her forehead.

"What is it? Tell me, Kianceta."

Kianceta related the encounter, her voice high-pitched with excitement, her hands still shaking.

"And . . . what did he *do*?" Ki-Ki-Tai asked with concern.

"Do? Nothing," Kianceta admitted. "But can you imagine what a scare he gave me! A white man appearing right in front of me! He had *yellow* hair, Ki-Ki-Tai. And blue eyes!"

"Was he armed?"

"No," she said, shaking her head, "he was fishing, that's all." Her encounter sounded less dramatic now as she retold it, but it had been frightening enough at the time.

"Was he a big man? A soldier?"

"No . . ." A strange smile touched Kianceta's lips and was quickly banished. "He was only a boy, Ki-Ki-Tai. No older than Tema."

Who was still just barely fifteen, Ki-Ki-Tai reflected. Kianceta had frightened herself, it seemed, from her recounting of the event.

"You should not have gone to their side of the river," Ki-Ki-Tai said gently.

"No, but Ki-Ki-Tai! Isn't it you who always says that the land there is ours as well? That the council had no right to give it away?"

"Yes," Ki-Ki-Tai was forced to admit. "Still, we have to live by the council's decree."

"I know that *I* will not cross over the river again," Kianceta said solemnly. But as she began to calm, she could see that she had been only a little foolish. Nothing had happened. It was a harmless encounter. She could have simply turned and walked away from the fisherman instead of running all the way home and lathering her spotted pony.

Later, when she found Eagle Heart's wife, who had also known the white trapper, Kyle, and therefore knew some English, Kianceta asked her what the words the young fisherman had spoken meant.

"What did he say?" the woman asked and Kianceta repeated the words as well as she could recall phonetically.

"I'm sorry."

"That is all, Kianceta?"

"That is all," she answered.

"I wonder, then, what he meant." And she explained what the words signified.

Kianceta wondered afterwards what the boy could have meant as well. For a long time thereafter, she practiced the words to herself: "I'm sorry."

The Kittinger home was the only house for many miles around made of finished lumber. It was long, painted white; there was a portico supported by Doric columns. The house had green shutters flanking glassed windows. Fifteen carpenters from St. Louis had spent three months building it.

Isadora greeted Elizabeth, Kent, and Bettina at the door as they arrived. She gave Elizabeth a tour of the house.

The dining room contained a richly polished oak table and chairs for eight, a sideboard, and two small, flat, elegant chandeliers with dazzling arrays of crystal reflecting the candlelight.

"They made the ceiling so low," Isadora complained, "so that they couldn't hang the chandelier I wanted. It's in the storage room."

The kitchen was separate. It held two iron stoves. Brass pans hung on the walls. A small black woman in an apron looked up, apprehensively, and then returned to her work, chopping vegetables for dinner.

"She's so slow," Isadora said while they were still in the cook's presence. "I have to tell her to start an hour earlier than I should have to for every meal."

The parlor was luxurious with a blue satin settee and matching chairs with high backs and carved mahogany legs. The fireplace in the room was white-painted brick. On the mantel was a row of crystal animals.

"The view is not what I would have really wanted," Isadora said.

In fact, Elizabeth thought, there was nothing about the house which would not have done a St. Louis family proud. Incredibly costly to have built out on the prairie with all of the materials hauled overland from Missouri, Isadora nevertheless found the house lacking. Elizabeth thought of her own log house and of the newest family on Cimarron, the struggling Rademachers, who were having to make do with a soddy and likely would for years to come on their poor land.

"This is my father's house in Baltimore," Isadora said, handing Elizabeth a daguerreotype of a huge two-story neoclassical mansion. "Those elms have been removed now," Isadora said, "and there is a new carriage house beyond the east wing." She looked wistfully at the picture for a while, and then put it back on the round mahogany table beside the settee.

"This house is lovely, Isadora, just lovely," Elizabeth said. "There can't be a finer house for a hundred miles."

Isadora's upper lip curled over her teeth, and she replied, "That's not saying very much, is it?"

There was no answer to that, so Elizabeth just followed Isadora to the back doors.

They were double Dutch doors, though in recognition of their circumstances, there was a heavy bar fitted into an iron bracket, which could be dropped across them in case of an attack. Swinging open the top halves of the doors, Isadora leaned out. Beyond, they could see Ned Kittinger plodding behind a black mule, plowing up the stubble field for planting. He was laboring mightily. It was obvious that the work was too hard for him. Elizabeth couldn't help comparing him to Tom, who walked along behind his mule ten hours a day, his powerful muscles sure and capable.

"Ned has no idea what he's doing," Isadora said to Elizabeth's discomfort. "He asks everyone's advice and then follows half of it. He'll never make a farmer. We're only trying to hold on until Father dies and I inherit."

Elizabeth was astonished. What sort of daughter was Isadora? What sort of wife?

If she could have seen Isadora's inner thoughts, she would have wondered more.

For Isadora had fallen into a brief waking dream, remembering another day when she had stood watching Ned Kittinger laboring in the field.

On that day, Lieutenant Ben Ramsey had ridden out from the fort. He must have knocked, but Isadora hadn't heard him. Her maid had not yet arrived from Independence, and she was forced to do some of the housework herself. Something had been spilled on the polished oak floor in the parlor—what, she could not recall, and still wearing her dressing gown, she had bent over to wipe it up. Incredibly flexible, Isadora could do that comfortably without bending her knees.

How long Ramsey had stood there in the doorway, watching her as she worked, she did not know, but glancing up, she saw him there with an enigmatic smile on his lips, his eyes softly glowing.

"Lieutenant Ramsey!" Isadora said, blushing. She had nothing on beneath her silk robe. She turned, clasping the top of the gown together.

"It's all right," Ramsey said, "go ahead with what you were doing. I was just taking in the view."

He sailed his hat onto the settee and folded his arms, looking out the open Dutch doors to where Ned was plowing.

"I'll only be minute," Isadora said. Her cheeks were flushed, and she was breathing shallowly, rapidly. She knew exactly what

Ramsey had been looking at, knew exactly what he was thinking.

It disturbed her in a way she could not deny. *Stop it!* she commanded herself, but she couldn't stop herself. Her thighs trembled slightly and her mouth was suddenly dry. She deliberately turned away from him and bent to her work again. *Don't be a fool,* she told herself. But all of the while she kept wiping at a stain that was long gone, and when he moved up behind her, she wanted him as much as Ramsey wanted her.

He flipped up her nightdress from behind and gripped her thighs so roughly that she had bruises from his fingers on the front of her legs for a week afterward. She braced her palms against the floor to keep from being pitched onto her face. Her robe fell open. She looked back at his intense face, then glanced toward the open door where, beyond, she could see her husband laboring clumsily with the plow, struggling to keep it balanced and cut a straight furrow. His face was red and streaked with sweat and dirt. Watching Ned somehow inflamed her, built her passionate response to Ramsey. It thrilled her to think that Ned might look across the field and see her. She wished they could do it right in front of his eyes, that he would be forced to watch Ramsey.

Ned had never *made love* to her. He was incapable of it; too puritanical or ashamed of his own body, he had never mastered the art of catering to his wife's needs any more than he had mastered anything else. As with his work, he was clumsy, inefficient, tiring quickly.

Their lovemaking was a quick interlude in the middle of a dark night, his hands pawing at her, entering, shoving a few times, exiting, falling to sleep to snore, his mouth hanging open. Unwashed, repellant, he was a failure at that as well.

Ramsey shuddered, tightened his grip on Isadora's thighs, and then went slack. She drew away and straightened up, grasping the belt of her robe to retie it; but she was mistaken in thinking he was finished.

Now Ramsey tore her robe from her and carried her to the blue settee, putting her down on her back. He lay on top of her, kissing her wildly, and she answered with wild, clawing, biting abandon . . .

"Dinner is ready, Madam," the tiny black servant said, and Isadora turned form the window and her remembrances to escort Elizabeth to the dining room, calling to Bettina and Kent who were talking in the garden.

But then the bastard . . . Isadora thought as they seated themselves at the table. Ramsey had come to her house unannounced several times after that. Once they had gone to a nearby hillock where he had stripped her naked without saying a word and placed her down on a blanket spread against the long grass to stand looking at her nude body for long minutes before slowly undressing to make love to her.

Then the bastard . . . had ridden over one day with fourteen men including Tom O'Day and told her he was riding off to the Eastern war. Isadora had cried all night long, telling Ned that it was because her stomach ached.

He would be back soon; everyone said that the war would end quickly. Maybe in the meantime Ned would cut his leg off with his axe as he chopped wood. Maybe Indians would kill him. Maybe he would just wither up and die from his constant laboring.

One thing was certain. Ben Ramsey would return one day and then he would take charge. She would tell him to get rid of Nesbitt Kittinger, and then they would share a life in the new house, making love day and night.

He had never actually said that was his plan, but Isadora *knew* it. She was beautiful and he loved making love to her; besides her father was extremely wealthy. He wouldn't have to remain in the army any longer. He could do whatever he wished—find a position in government, perhaps.

They had entered the dining room, and Isadora assigned them their seats. Once settled, Isadora spread her linen napkin on her lap and waited as the servant served the food. Then, before they had begun to eat, she made her announcement.

"I have something to tell you," she said, looking at Elizabeth, briefly toward Kent, and then steadily at Bettina, "there will be a new Kittinger in the world early next year."

"Mother!"

"Isadora!"

"Do you mean it, Mother?" Bettina asked. She was too stunned to feel either happy or unhappy. She appeared bewildered, her expression fluctuating between a smile and a concerned frown. "It's been so long, I thought . . ."

"I am with child," Isadora said.

And of course, it was not Ned Kittinger's child. That was why she was sure Ben Ramsey would return to her once she told him. When she had missed her period the first time she had not been concerned, but the second month brought the realization that she was indeed pregnant, and that the child could not possibly be Ned's. That very evening she had forced herself to make love to Ned—if it could be called that. In the middle of the night she had prodded and stroked his weary body until finally he had rolled heavily on top of her and made an effort that at least resulted in a feeble ejaculation. A month later she had informed him that he was to be a father again.

Ned had celebrated by plowing from sunrise to sunset, working until he was exhausted and trembling with weariness. "I've got twice the reason to make a go of this farm now," was what he said.

At the table, Elizabeth said "Congratulations" to Isadora, meaning it. There was a hint of wistfulness behind her words.

She had always thought she would like a daughter, but it had never happened. Now, with Tom gone . . . she feared she was getting too old for conceiving.

They ate for a while in silence. Then Bettina began wondering aloud if it would be a boy or if she'd have a baby sister. Elizabeth began to reminisce about her own babies, to Kent's occasional embarrassment, and by the time Ned came in to wash for dinner and seat himself still in his work clothes at the head of the table, they all offered heartfelt congratulations. Isadora dabbed at her lips with her napkin, rose from her chair, rested her hand on Ned's shoulder, and kissed his cheek, and Bettina thought that her mother must indeed be happy, that this was just what she had needed all along. She had never seen her mother kiss her father before. Now Ned's face glowed; Isadora's eyes had a deep mysterious glow in them. All thing happen for the best, Bettina thought, although God did sometimes work in mysterious ways, as the preacher had always said.

Returning home, Elizabeth and Kent found Oliver sitting on the plank porch, although the sun was nearly gone and the evening was growing cold.

"How are you?" his mother asked as Oliver's brother led the horses to the barn. She rested a hand on his head. He did not look up.

"I'm all right."

"Did you catch that big catfish?"

"No."

"What is troubling him?" Elizabeth asked Kent later. Kent, who had little time for anything but his thoughts of Bettina, shrugged.

"You know how Oliver is. It'll pass."

"Dearest Elizabeth,
    I can't tell you what everything is like here. Lying in

99

frozen mud with little to eat.

It would only worry you, dear, if I told you everything. Do not be afraid for me, Liz. I am strong, as you know. Some who were not so strong have died—well, I won't discuss that either. I cannot tell you, my love, how much I miss you and all that is good and stout about you. Nor can I tell you how much that little piece of land we have labored so long and hard on means to me!

Memories of my home and family are all that I have to keep me going on some dreadful days . . . and dreadful nights!

The boys—I cannot tell you how much I miss them (I even miss dumb old Regret).

I pray you found some kind of help with the crop. I have apparently made a vast mistake in following Ben Ramsey. I wanted to tell you some of what has happened to us in Virginia, but you would have trouble visualizing it. Truthfully I can't recall it all well enough to visualize it myself! All I see, when I reflect, is cannon smoke, trees scorched to black, burning farmhouses.

I will try to give you a little picture of things. During the first week we met the enemy at some town called Manassas, on July 21, having been temporarily attached to Gnl. McDowell and we encountered a Rebel army under Johnston and Beauregard (as I understand their names to be.) At a small place called Blackburn's Ford we were involved in a minor skirmish. I would think that five hundred of us perished that day (such is what they call a minor skirmish.) We marched through the smoke and confusion. I have no idea who won this battle. I'll leave that to future historians. I only know who lost. I suppose you wonder why I, a cavalry officer, was on foot. Poor old Domino was killed by cannon fire and later eaten, our supply train having been cut off. After that first thrust, we attempted to attack a Rebel position called 'Henry House,' but we ran into a brigade commanded by this Confederate officer they now call 'Stonewall' Jackson, and we could do nought but retreat . . . shamefully.

And so I think of home, Dear, your loving arms, more than you'll ever know. And my small patch of land, such as it is, on Cimarron . . . God only knows when this war will end. I have been thinking about my grandfather leaving Ireland when the Irish were not even allowed to own their own land. Maybe this is what has instilled a certain sort of fierceness in my wish to have my own property.

I am not sure of Ramsey's state of mind. He has fallen under the sway of this young brevet colonel named George Armstrong Custer, a very reckless young officer. Ramsey scoffs at him, but I believe he is jealous of Custer's success to the point where Ramsey is even wearing a red kerchief around his neck as he rushes into battle. (That is the insignia of Custer's brigade.)

Let us hope that in this last month of 1861 this collision between North and South is nearly at an end.

I love you so dearly.
1st Lieutenant Tom O'Day
Fourth Kansas Volunteers."

Then, having read the faded letter for the fortieth time, still failing to find any comfort in it, Elizabeth rolled over and slept with it crumpled in her hand.

Hungry Wolf sat alone on the grassless knoll. There was nothing there to comfort the soul: yellow-lichened boulders, scattered laurel-leaf sumac, the tips of their leaves red in the late light, a few yucca trees, and purple sage. Below his vantage point, he could see weary warriors resting.

It seemed no one had the heart for this battle, but a man went on; that was what a man did when it was necessary. A band of the Osage tribe called the Yatha, led by a Ghost Dancer, had decided to wage war. The Yatha leaders had come to believe that all the whites were withdrawing from the prairie and that now was the time to strike. Hungry Wolf did not believe this. He did not believe the shaman, Washai, or Winter Owl's hopeful predictions. The gathered tribes had forced the so-called Fort Defiance to close only the year before. But there had been swift retaliation—the "Baylor Massacre," in which the whites struck back with a force of Texas Rangers and militia surged onto the plains, resulting in the slaughter of hundreds of Comanches in Texas and New Mexico. The Kiowas, being their allies, had also paid a blood price.

And so as a lazy sundown settled, Hungry Wolf only wondered if there would ever again be peace for Ki-Ki-Tai and their sons.

It seemed unlikely now. The white soldiers would return from their Eastern war, he believed. No matter which side won, nothing would change for the Kiowas. And almost every adult male they now would see would be a warrior, a veteran of the war. They would be hardened and angry men.

There was a rumor that the Southern people in the East had recruited the Cherokees, the Choctaw, and the Seminoles onto their side. Hungry Wolf did not know of these people except secondhand. Promising the Indians that he would protect their land rights forever, this man called Jefferson Davis had summoned the forces of these tribes to fight for the Southern cause.

Nakai did not really understand this all. He only knew this— the whites would one day return from the East, and being more numerous and carrying better arms, no valor would stem the tide of their infringements.

Some of his people had run away for safety. Hungry Wolf

wished he could take Ki-Ki-Tai and his sons far to the north and west and live peacefully; but a man does what he must—and his people needed his war leadership.

Nakai, Hungry Wolf, rose stiffly and slowly walked down the knoll toward the camp below, trying to elevate his confidence as he prepared for a two-sided war against both the Osage and the American whites.

The young men rested on the ground beneath the wide-spreading oak tree in the camp of the Kiowas. Among them were Ki-Ki-Tai's sons, Ketah and Tema, and two of Momo's boys, Lakad and Opaga, sometimes called One-Feather, the emotional one of their group.

"And what shall we do?" Lakad asked. He sat cross-legged, tearing a dry oak leaf into thin, ragged strips.

All of the young braves knew what he meant. They were tired of being left out of the warriors' adventures. They did not feel too young or inexperienced to make war on the enemies of the Kiowas. They wanted to ride with their brothers and fathers and count coup, but the leadership of the tribe refused to let them accompany the older braves on their excursions, reminding the boys that someone must remain behind to guard the camp.

"We should strike across the river," Opaga believed.

"My father has said that is not to be done," Ketah said. "And so has Winter Owl."

"The white fort is nearly empty now. There is no one left to protect the farms along the river."

"No," Ketah repeated, shaking his head heavily. He would do nothing to contradict his father's wishes.

It was just then that Rani-Ta strolled past, her head held high, her strides fluid and haughty. She only glanced at the young warriors, but their eyes couldn't help following her swaying progress.

"I envy Hungry Wolf," Lakad said. That remark angered Nakai's older son.

"What do you mean!" Ketah demanded, half-rising.

"Oh, don't be angry. Everyone knows Eagle Heart's niece wants to be Hungry Wolf's second wife, Ketah."

Ketah's muscles had bunched and his hands had clenched, but he forced himself to relax, knowing that his friend was only speaking the truth.

"Ketah is the only one who doesn't notice Rani-Ta," his brother, Tema, said with a laugh. "He doesn't even see any other girl than Kianceta." Everyone smiled. It was a foregone conclusion that Ketah would marry the beautiful young woman one day. The boys returned to their discussion. Manhood was approaching and they were growing restless with inactivity.

Kianceta, feeling slightly traitorous, stood on the west bank of the Cimarron, looking across its slowly flowing waters. The stars were high and sharp against a silky blue sky; the moon had not yet risen, but the river was silvered by the starlight. It was a mysterious, meandering dark band as it made its way southward.

Kianceta could not understand her own feelings just then.

The white boy's image remained in her mind. Fair-haired and mysterious. Who was he? He had seemed so shy and kind. She did not even know his name, and yet she thought of him sometimes when she tried to sleep.

Knowing that her man was Ketah and that she would marry him and that her great friend, Ki-Ki-Tai, would be her new mother. *Knowing* all of this, she still wondered about Oliver O'Day.

I am sorry.

Sometime later when Ketah had gone to look for Kianceta, and his brother, Tema, had returned to the lodge of Ki-Ki-Tai and Hungry Wolf to sleep, the young warriors remained gathered around Opaga, Momo's oldest son, as he prodded a low campfire.

"We have to wait for Falcon before anything is done," Opaga said carefully. His eyes searched the quiet camp.

"If Nakai discovers it . . ." Lakad objected.

"Nakai is not here! Washai has said this is the time to remove the whites from the plains. Do you doubt the shaman?"

"No," Lakad said, "but Ketah . . ."

"Ketah repeats whatever his father says," Opaga interrupted again. "Both of them have nothing but women on their minds! And so they think like women and treat us as if we were children."

"What is it you want of us, Opaga?"

"If we crossed the river . . ."

"Winter Owl forbids that!"

"What is he? Only another old man." Opaga waved a derisive hand. "If we cross the river," he said, leaning forward conspiratorially, "there are not enough white soldiers to defend that fort of theirs. Burn it! Drive the invaders out."

"It can't be done," One-Feather said hesitantly, but he knew it could quite easily be done. But such a raid went against the wishes of the council against the decree of Winter Owl and against the promise of Hungry Wolf. He could see the determination on his brother's firelit face, however, and he ceased his objections.

Slowly and silently, the young warriors walked away from the camp to where they could not be overheard. Crossing on their ponies to the sacred island where the pines grew tall, to where their ancestors were buried, they pledged a blood oath, forming a secret society that came to be called Ta-Hai-Kai.

The Ghost Warriors.

By the time the eerie white moon, pocked and mysterious, rose over Cimarron their oaths had been taken. It was done.

Still there was a candle burning in Elizabeth O'Day's window far across the moon-shadowed land. She read again, with waning optimism, Tom's second letter of that difficult too-long year.

"My Darling," she read on that night, "one never believed that this horrible war could go on so long. Daily men are blown to bits. Only fodder for the stern ranks of cannon.

We have no morphine; the surgeons are sorely pressed. Nothing can be done to help the men's suffering, nothing whatsoever.

I can only pray that everything is calm and safe on Cimarron, that you are not suffering much and that the boys are now strong enough to help you get through this year! And that it will be the last year I am away from you. I do not even know if this letter can find its way to you— there was a brilliant burst of flares just then, I do not know what it signifies—I do not.

I do not even know if the two opposing forces know who they are firing at. All is confusion. Vast and general.

I want only peace for the rest of my days, Liz! And pray for it. There are men who seem to glory in this conflict. That Armstrong Custer I have mentioned, for one, and Ramsey who is now *Major* Benjamin Ramsey. (They have decided that I deserve to be a 1st Lieutenant now for something called 'conspicuous gallantry.' I don't even know what this is supposed to mean—so many men die around me each day; it seems you are promoted simply for surviving. It doesn't matter—our uniforms are in such rags that one can't tell a general from a rank private were it not for the officers' horses and sabers.)

Most of my men are simple farm boys, afraid and alone. I have to send them against the muzzles of cannon and withering musket barrages. Most of them believed (as I) that they knew what this dreadful war was about; now I wonder if any of us does.

Then, when these simple boys get scared or defeated at heart, Liz, and they desert singly or in pairs, in whole platoons, it is my job as an officer to punish them. I won't tell you how swiftly and in what way that is done on the battlefield. Dear God! There is so much blood on my hands now. I remember when you did not want me to allow Oliver and Kent to pick up weapons, and wonder now if you were not right.

I know you cannot write me. No missive could find its way to me in the midst of this turmoil. The battles are so confused and seemingly disjointed. Perhaps the generals understand our seemingly random thrusts and retreats. I can't explain all of it, nor would it mean much to you, I'm afraid. Through Ramsey's efforts we have found ourselves more or less attached to Custer's command. We are east of a place called Chickahominy where, as far as I could perceive, we were beaten again, but Custer led a brilliant cavalry charge and from what I understand has been promoted again to brevet general.

I do not mean to worry you, but I did take a musket ball in the hip. The surgeons have given me something, laudanum, for the pain, though I have developed a limp!

The medication does make me sleepy at odd moments, Elizabeth, so now while there seems to be a lull in the fighting, I am going to try to sleep and dream of the times to come when I can one again lie peacefully in your loving arms on our little farm."

Elizabeth tried to sleep herself, watching the ghostly white moon rise and gloss the land, recalling the nights when she and Tom had made love with it peering through their high window; but sleep was impossible. Pulling her blue cotton robe around her, she walked out onto the porch in the chill of night and gazed across the silkily running Cimarron. All was still except for one distant bark of a lone coyote. She stood silently for a long while, really looking at nothing at all until she bowed her head and began to weep.

CHAPTER FOUR

Winter began to arrive early and very hard with a flurry of snowstorms followed by days of gray skies and torrential rains. The soddy on the O'Day farm began to resemble a mudpile with patches of straw and fallen logs imbedded in it. Elizabeth, seeing it, wondered how the new neighbors, the Rademachers, would survive a winter on the prairie at all.

There were occasional days, crisp and bright and clear as October stretched into November, that made it a pleasure to rise from one's bed, to be alive. They never saw Kent on those days; when travel was possible, he rode to the Kittinger house to spend time with Bettina. Now and then Kent talked of building his own house, and of course Elizabeth knew what he had in mind, and she supposed it was the natural course of events, although it made her feel prematurely old.

Where was Tom!

Oliver spent his days as before. Still in boyhood, his deepening chest and lowering voice proclaimed change. He hunted, fished, walked long with Regret who had now gotten his full growth—a fearsome-looking dog if one didn't know him, with a huge black head like a grizzly's.

In his winter coat he looked even more massive.

Together one early winter day, the two roamers came upon a troublesome sight.

"Look, Regret," Oliver said, frowning. In his hand was the

old rifle and his grip tightened on it as he crouched. "Moccasin tracks."

Regret watched Oliver, trying to understand his master, but if this was a hunt, the prey didn't smell right. Not rabbits or deer or squirrels . . . something entirely different. A human? It didn't smell of salt or sugar or coffee—none of the familiar human smells.

But Regret could sense that his master was agitated and he shook his huge head, looking up to see what his leader wanted him to do.

What Oliver saw, sensed, thought, made no immediate sense to him. The tracks were those of a large child or a small woman. On this side of the river! He felt suddenly very protective of the farm, his mother . . . what would his father do if he were here?

Oliver trudged on. The ground underfoot was ice-melt, reddish mud with here and there patches of snow.

He entered the coolness of the oak grove. The sun flashed brilliantly through the trees at intervals. He was faintly disturbed, uneasy. Yet he knew there was some other sensation hovering around him; he knew he should not be afraid, not of a single Indian girl when he had not only the rifle, but Regret at his side—what then was that hotness across his cheeks? That sudden knowledge . . .

He walked around the huge broken oak tree and came face to face with Kianceta.

He recognized her instantly. Although he automatically began to raise his rifle, he never shouldered it. How long they stood and stared at each other neither one of them could afterward remember, but it was quite a long time. The wind shifted Kianceta's raven hair and Oliver saw her shiver. The wind was very cold, moving the piles of loose snow where they were still banked in the shade of the big trees.

Kianceta did not know what prompted her to say her

practiced words. Perhaps, as Oliver, she knew nothing else to say.

"I am sorry."

"Why are you here?" Oliver lowered his rife, holding it loosely at his side. "Who are you? What is your name?"

Kianceta looked at the damp earth and then lifted her black eyes to his. She answered with a small shrug. Even had she understood his words, she could have given him no answer that was sensible.

Regret had walked cautiously near to her; then, recognizing her scent from an earlier day, he wagged his heavy tail. His memory told him that she was a friend, not seen for a long while.

And in some distant way, Oliver felt that way himself—she was a friend not seen for far too long.

They walked for a little way and then sat on a massive flat rock heavy with moss as the wind gusted over them and a redheaded woodpecker rocked his head against a scraggly pine tree. Regret sat looking up at them, hoping to be enlightened. Now and then Kianceta would scratch him behind the ears or beneath his great shaggy ruff.

They spoke.

Again, for a long time afterward neither of them could recall what was said. Now and then, embarrassed, they would point at a tree or to the dog and try to exchange words to describe them, but the language they communicated with was neither Kiowa nor English. It was an ancient and well-known language spoken only with the eyes.

Within an hour the rain began again in earnest, and Kianceta rose, looking toward the violent darkening above the oaks. The Cimarron, beyond the grove, was rain-pocked and growing suddenly swift.

"I have to go," Kianceta said in her own tongue. "I do not

111

know why I came."

Oliver understood that she was going. It had grown very cold; soon it would snow. Regret's deep coat was soaked through already. Oliver had no idea what to say.

"I want to see you again," he said, keeping his gaze cast down. Looking up he saw no comprehension in her obsidian eyes.

Feeling both awkward and ignorant as the down-pouring rain streamed through the upper reaches of the oaks, Kianceta said again the only words she understood, "I am sorry."

She started away then, toward the river crossing, and Oliver followed her briefly.

"My name is Oliver!" he yelled above the silver slash of the downpour. He touched his chest.

"Oliver!"

Kianceta paused, her head turned toward him. She understood him. But the smile on her generous mouth indicated well enough that that seemed the funniest name she had ever heard.

"Oliver! Don't forget."

Just for a moment she paused again, and as the rain washed down, she touched her own breast and said, "Kianceta."

Then she was gone, vanishing through the woods. Regret bounded after her briefly, understanding none of this, but Oliver whistled him back and started slowly, thoughtfully back toward home through the increasing rain.

That was the start of it; not nearly the end.

They met secretly many times after that. If Oliver had had his way it would have been daily, but of course that was impossible. In time they became able to speak a few words in each other's language, frustratingly few at first. Their meetings were witnessed and understood only by old Regret. Oliver did not dare say a word to anyone about the Indian girl. And, of course, Kianceta, who was promised in marriage to Nakai's son, Ketah, would say nothing. Not even to Ki-Ki-Tai.

But there inevitably came a day when the young people were found out. In mid-November with the snow deep and pristine on the ground Ki-Ki-Tai had followed a lost pony across the river and stumbled upon the tracks of a woman's moccasins beside those of a white man's boots. She knew whose sign it was; only Kianceta had left the camp on this sharply cold morning. Ki-Ki-Tai was deeply disturbed, but what could she say to the girl? What could she say to her son! Nothing without serious consequences for one or all of them. *Nothing.* Ki-Ki-Tai bit her lip and vowed she would say nothing to Ketah at all.

Besides, she had not even seen her son for a month or more. Nor, for that matter, had Nakai returned from the north. There was something quite ominous in the air, and Ki-Ki-Tai knew she did not like it. Something very bad was bound to erupt on Cimarron.

"Hello in the house!" the familiar voice called out one frosty morning, and Elizabeth, shawl around her shoulders, opened the door to see Donovan Hart, wearing a buffalo coat, sitting his horse in the yard. The scout smiled.

"Got a cup of coffee, Mrs. O'Day?"

"Certainly. Come in where it's warm, Mr. Hart."

Hart slid from the back of his buckskin horse and said, "I'll never break you of calling me 'Mister,' will I?"

Stamping the mud and ice from his boots, the army scout followed Elizabeth into the warm interior of the log house. Seating himself at the table while Regret sniffed inquisitively at his legs, Hart watched Elizabeth bustle around the fireplace. In the back room he heard Kent say something and Oliver mutter a reply. Then they both laughed.

"The boys sound fine."

"They are." Elizabeth approached the table and lowered her voice. "If only I could keep Kent from wanting to spend all of his time around Bettina Kittinger."

Hart laughed. "It's nature's way, Mrs. O'Day. You know that. If you can figure out a way to put a stop to it, I guess you'd be the first one in history."

Elizabeth laughed as well. Of course Hart was right. She poured coffee from the big blue enamel pot, its handle wrapped in her apron. The frontiersman nodded his thanks and leaned back in his chair.

"I wonder why you're here, of course," Elizabeth said, seating herself opposite Hart.

Hart, reading the hopeful gleam in her eyes, shook his head. "I'm sorry, I'm not here with a letter from Tom this time. Lines of communication are either destroyed or in vast confusion just now. No, Mrs. O'Day, I just drifted by to say goodbye."

"You're leaving?" Elizabeth asked in surprise.

"Yes, ma'am. This new world and I don't agree any longer."

"What do you mean?"

"Well, what's an army that intends to go nowhere need with my services?" the scout asked. "The fort has only a skeleton force. Callahan—well, he's doing the best he can with what he has, I guess, but sitting by the stove is making my old bones feel even older. I think I'm going to drift down to Mexico. The Comanches know me, the Apaches too; they won't bother me. Did I ever tell you—I've been scalped twice already—it seems to give me some kind of immunity with them."

"Scalped!"

Hart grinned at her shock. "Yes, ma'am. Lots of folks don't know that the Indians generally just take a piece of scalp about as big as a silver dollar. It don't feel real good, but there's many a man walking around who's survived a scalping."

"Dreadful!" Elizabeth said.

"Yes, ma'am, but it beat having them kill me."

The boys, having heard conversation, wandered out from

their room followed by Regret, who scurried around for attention until he seated himself beside Hart, who scratched the dog's massive head absently.

"Mornin', boys," Hart said.

"Did I hear you say you were moving on?" Kent asked.

"That's right. There's no point in me stayin' around. The army's goin' nowhere. Things are at a standstill. The Kiowas have all gone north anyway."

No one noticed Oliver's expression at that statement.

"North?" Elizabeth asked, surprised that a nomadic people would be traveling that way at this time of the year.

"Yes, ma'am," the scout answered. "Buffalo hunting."

"In winter?"

"That's when their hides are full and woolly, good for trading," Hart told her.

"I see. I didn't know that. One would think that it would be the reverse, that they'd be traveling south to avoid the winter cold."

"Like us old-timers? Well," Hart said after a sip of coffee, "it used to be that way, but the traders have kinda changed all of that. It's the same with beaver trapping; it's better for pelts in the winter. Economics, as a man told me, changes things a lot. Firearms have changed things for the Indians."

"Speaking of which . . ." Kent said with an air of excitement, and he reached into a closet and brought out something Elizabeth hadn't seen before. A Springfield rifle. He handed it eagerly to Hart for the scout to examine.

"Nice piece," Hart said. His eyes lowered, "That's no squirrel gun, is it?"

"No, sir!" Kent said proudly.

"Where'd you come by it?" the frontiersman asked. It was an army-issue .45-70, and as Hart had remarked, far from a squirrel gun. It was man-killer, pure and simple.

"I got it from Mr. Kittinger who got it from one of those soldiers deserting South. He figured that since I was riding back and forth to visit Bettina I should have a good rifle. And, of course, when I was with Bettina . . . should anything happen."

"Kent!" Elizabeth hadn't seen the rifle before either.

"Mother. It's a rifle, that's all. I heard Mr. Hart talking about buffalo hunting. Maybe I could do some of that myself. I hear there's money in it, good money."

"What do you need with money?" Elizabeth asked, feeling foolish before the words emerged from her lips. Kent wanted a rich girl for his wife. Bettina was accustomed to money. Hart took over.

"It's a thought, of course," the plainsman said, handing the Springfield rifle back to Kent, "but it's tough, dirty work, son. The Indians now, they kill a buff and the women skin 'em out. They live on the plains while they're at it. You, you'd need a wagon, a crew of buffalo skinners, and supplies for them.

"It might sound like a good way to make some easy money, but they're easier ways than shivering though the cold and bloody nights surrounded by carcasses. You'd have to cart the hides to market. In daydreams I guess it seems like just popping a hundred of the useless beasts, but it don't work that way," said Hart with the tired smile of one who knew. "Try skinning a frozen buff once, and you'll soon see what I mean. Yeah, the Indians have done it for a long, long time, but for those who ain't used to it . . . well."

From Kent's expression it was obvious that he didn't want to hear the hard facts about buffalo hunting. All of this had come as a surprise to Elizabeth; she had no idea that he had been building up this plan. Perhaps she had been thinking of Bettina and Kent as children rather than as young adults looking for a way to make their beginning.

"I'm sorry," Kent said tightly, and he walked to the closet, replaced the rifle, and banged the closet door shut, stamping his way out to the front porch.

"Ma'am," Hart said after a minute. "I do thank you for your hospitality. I suppose I should be on my way now while the weather is clear. I don't wish to get caught in the next blizzard."

Oliver asked, "Where are you headed, Mr. Hart?"

"Texas first. Mexico? I won't know until I get there, Oliver. There are some crazy people in Texas who have been shipping cattle to the Confederate forces in Alabama, who are already thinking of war's end and a transcontinental railroad! Some screwball named Goodnight who's thinking of driving longhorn cattle north from Texas all the way to Kansas! I dunno," Hart said, shaking his head. "But if they try it, they'll need an old trail hand like me who knows the plains.

"I just know I have to go now. Nothing good is going to come now on Cimarron . . ."

He realized what he had said and stuttered an apology to Elizabeth O'Day.

"I know what you meant, Mr. Hart," Elizabeth said with more cheer than she felt. "May I pack you a sandwich or two for your ride?"

She bustled around in the kitchen for a time, pressing the scant meal on Hart. Oliver then followed Hart out onto the porch, and together with Elizabeth, waved goodbye to one of their first and few friends on Cimarron. When Elizabeth went back inside as Donovan Hart became only a memory on the horizon, Oliver remained behind, the cold wind lifting his fine blond hair. Not long afterward, Kent emerged from the barn, leading the black gelding, which was not his horse but Bettina's. He swung into the saddle and rode slowly across the muddy yard. Kent had recovered the .45-70, Oliver noticed, and Kent rode with the rifle across the saddlebow. He watched his brother's departure with a strange sense of loss. He had never been really close to his brother, but now he felt there was a growing and somehow irreparable schism between them. Some secret scar they could no longer bridge. Oliver felt like shouting out to his brother, "Come back!"

As if Kent would understand what he meant by those words.

As if Kent would not shout the same thing to him if he had any idea how he felt about Kianceta.

And Mother—he looked toward the log house—God love her, was really aware of none of it. She lived in her daydream world, waiting only for Father to come home.

Who knew if he ever would! Oliver slammed the side of his fist against one of the pole uprights of the porch.

Who knew if his father would ever come home!

Damn this endless war. Damn all wars!

Oliver whistled up Regret and they started northward along the river.

Elizabeth watched Donovan Hart until his dark figure merged with the far horizon. Minutes after that she saw Kent riding away on the black horse. She knew where he was going, of course.

Not that the young man was shirking his work. There was little to be done at this time of year. The boys had dragged in all of the dead wood they could find and chopped it into manageable lengths, and they had collected buffalo chips until the new snow covered them up. The house would be warm . . .

She heard Oliver whistle and saw Regret bound after him. She watched them go with a sort of indistinct sadness. Even had they stayed with her on this clear, cold morning, she wondered what the three of them could have talked about. They were men, nearly, and she knew nothing of that side of them. It was no longer as if they were babies when she could bounce them on her knee or play on the floor with them, making silly faces, tickling them. Peekaboo, I see you . . . she could almost envy the haughty Isadora Kittinger. Not for her fine house, but for the new life ripening in her womb. Elizabeth touched her own belly and then shook off the passing mood. She picked up the bucket by the stove. There was wash to be done, floors to be scrubbed. Tom would be home soon enough. Soon.

She paused in her motion. A sudden fury swept over her. She took the oaken bucket and hurled it across the room, slamming it against the wall.

"Damn you, Tom!" she said once out loud. "I don't know what to do without you." Then, fighting back the convulsion of tears and the guilt about having said a thing like that to the man who had always wished only to do what was right for his family, she crossed the room, scooped up the bucket, and walked out to fetch water from the coldly frothing gray Cimarron.

The river swept past, a cold torrent going nowhere, nowhere, and Elizabeth, as she had a hundred times before, walked to it.

As a hundred times before, down the familiar muddy path, she picked her footholds. But as she rested her shoe on a black upcoiled willow root, it gave way, rotted through by time and the damp, and Elizabeth plunged headlong into the river, her skirts and petticoats becoming instantly waterlogged, dragging her down into the river's swirling depth. Her hand thrust skyward, finding no purchase. She strangled and coughed and felt the current, heavy cold and deadly, tearing at her body.

"Ta!" Ki-Ki-Tai had been fishing on the river from her canoe, and had seen the white woman's footing give way, had seen her plunge into the icy waters. Deliberately, Ki-Ki-Tai had turned her back. What did she care for this person, this invader? She said nothing more after her first startled expletive. She made no move to assist the white woman.

Slowly, she turned her head and watched Elizabeth's fingers clawing brokenly at the red-mud earth of the riverbank, the swift gray eddy tearing at her long skirts.

Then, almost angrily, Ki-Ki-Tai threw down the oar to her canoe, swam to the near bank, and raced toward Elizabeth. Ki-Ki-Tai clutched the white woman's hand and she dragged her, panting and freezing, onto the shore, where she lay inert and shivering.

What now!

Still angry with herself, Ki-Ki-Tai, knowing that the foolish white woman would not survive out in the cold, picked Elizabeth up. Ki-Ki-Tai was small, but very strong. Her life on the plains had left no room for weakness; now she shouldered Elizabeth in her sopping garments and slogged heavily back toward the white woman's lodge, clicking her tongue in disgust with herself.

A huge, woolly black dog, as large as a bear cub, came running to meet her.

"Go away, dog!" Ki-Ki-Tai said, and Regret, quivering with uncertainty, worried beyond barking, followed Ki-Ki-Tai toward the house.

How did they open these wooden doors? Ki-Ki-Tai wondered, fumbling with the latch string.

The door swung in and she marched forward, dripping water across the floor. She threw more than lay Elizabeth down on the striped couch.

"Now. There," Ki-Ki-Tai panted, staggering back a bit as she unburdened herself. "Now you may live or die, white woman. I have done my best."

Elizabeth lay in her sodden clothing, still shivering, but otherwise motionless.

"Ta!" Ki-Ki-Tai muttered again. She had started toward the door, wanting to leave the white lodge, but could not bring herself to leave. She started on again, halted again.

She looked at the stupid white woman again and then, pushing back her black hair, took a deep breath and began undressing Elizabeth, stripping off her wet clothing. She found a blanket in a hidden room. There were so many odd things around, but Ki-Ki-Tai had little time to catalogue them all.

She wanted only to be away. Dry the woman's pale body, cover her up with a blanket, go away quickly!

Ki-Ki-Tai had nearly finished, tucking the blue blanket she had found around Elizabeth, when two things happened at once. Elizabeth's eyes flickered open; and behind Ki-Ki-Tai, the front door banged open.

Oliver stood there, stunned, rifle in hand. Elizabeth, dazed, recognized neither of them immediately. Regret suddenly began to bound around the room, barking.

"What has happened here!" Oliver shouted, seeing the Indian woman standing over his mother. Elizabeth sat halfway up so that the blanket nearly fell away from her breasts; she clutched it to her. It was a full minute before both women realized that Oliver had shouted his demanding question in the Kiowa language.

"I see . . ." Ki-Ki-Tai said very carefully, watching the blond boy. Those few words had opened her eyes. So this was the boy Kianceta cared for.

"What did you say, Oliver?" Elizabeth asked from out of the haze of her semi-consciousness.

"Nothing," he replied. Oliver crossed the room and got to his knees beside his mother. "What happened to you?"

"I don't really remember . . . the river. I believe I was drowning." She shook her head exhaustedly. "Then this lady . . ." It was only then that Elizabeth realized that the woman who had saved her was an Indian. Her voice broke off. "I don't know what to say . . ."

"Do you want me to thank her?" Oliver asked.

"Of course! But how . . . ?"

Oliver rose and turned. He was a head taller than Ki-Ki-Tai, but he bowed slightly and said in perfect Kiowa: "My mother wishes me to thank you. You have saved her life."

Listening to her son, Elizabeth now also understood some of Oliver's mysterious comings and goings. She recalled once having seen a young Kiowa maiden not far from the farm, and oddly, Regret had not barked at the girl.

"It is nothing," Ki-Ki-Tai responded with an impatient gesture. She felt suddenly closed in in this strange wooden house. Oliver took another step forward and said in a lower voice:

"You must be Ki-Ki-Tai. I thank you again."

"How could you know . . . ?"

"She speaks of you often," Oliver said. His mother watched them uncomprehendingly.

"So . . ." Ki-Ki-Tai nodded her understanding. "I would tell you to stay away from her, but it would do no good, would it?"

"No."

"Then . . ." Ki-Ki-Tai shrugged her slight shoulders beneath her wet buckskin shirt. "Then be careful."

"Do you know this lady, Oliver? What is her name?"

"I have not met her before. But her name is Ki-Ki-Tai," her son answered. Elizabeth just nodded. There was a sudden residual weariness in her. Everything seemed dreamlike. Oliver speaking to this unknown Indian woman in her own tongue!

The Indian woman's eyes met hers for only a fragment of time, then returned to Oliver. "She may simply call me Ki-Ki," Ki-Ki-Tai said, and then she spun away, waving a hand in the air. "Some day I may visit."

Regret leaped up again as Ki-Ki-Tai left, leaving damp moccasin tracks across the floor. The dog followed her for a little way as she went through the door, leaving it open, and trudged homeward across the slushy yard.

Elizabeth said: "Oliver, I can see that we are going to have a serious talk."

Then she yawned massively, stretched her arms, and rolled over on the settee, falling asleep in minutes.

Oliver stoked the fire, putting water on the stove for tea in case his mother should wake up still chilled from her ordeal. Then he went thoughtfully to the door and closed it, the remainder of the day passing in blessed peacefulness.

No one could have known it, but there had been another witness to the events of the day. In the chill grayness, Rani-Ta had seen. Seen Ki-Ki-Tai go into the white enemies' lodge; it was something to be saved away and casually mentioned to Nakai one day. The beautiful maiden smiled inwardly and glided away through the cottonwoods along the riverbank. Hungry Wolf would yet take Rani-Ta for his second wife. She would see to that.

"A cold night," Koto said. Nakai nodded. Hungry Wolf had been sitting alone on top of the rocky hill, watching the new snow begin to drift down. Around him the old snow, which had begun to melt, was freezing again. Below, huddled around several small campfires, his war party was motionless, bracing themselves for a fresh onslaught of winter.

"This is a bad time for warring," Koto said, settling himself beside Nakai. The two men faced each other silently for long minutes as the feathery flakes of the new storm settled on their blanketed shoulders.

"It is nearly done," Nakai said from the darkness.

"The Osage . . . what does it matter, Nakai? They have learned their lesson."

"It could be so," Hungry Wolf answered. And if Falcon and the other warriors had followed Nakai into battle instead of going to the north to hunt for buffalo hides to trade to the Mexicans, it would have all ended long ago. "But the Osage

must learn—never. *Never* to attack a Kiowa camp again, Koto."
He paused, looking into the distances. One star gleamed
through the dark clouds. He watched it until it was smothered
by the falling snow. "What would you have me do?" he asked.

Koto shrugged. A loyal friend, he followed Nakai's lead, only
Nakai's.

"Perhaps I only miss Momo's comfort on this cold night, Nakai."

Nakai smiled distantly. As he missed his Ki-Ki, but both of
their women understood a warrior's way, the life that had to be
led to protect their people. It always had been so.

"What is that, Nakai?" Koto asked. The stubby, broad warrior pointed eastward. Dimly, seemingly as far away as the star
Nakai had been following, they could see what appeared to be a
campfire on the plains.

"It is across the river," Nakai answered, "I pay it no mind.
Maybe the white war has come nearer."

Koto nodded. He knew that Nakai would not cross the river.
The council had given its word and that was Nakai's bond.
Still, sometimes his friend wondered if that time must not one
day come.

He said, "Sometimes our warriors wonder why we do not go
over the river and chase all the whites away, Nakai."

Anger flared in Hungry Wolf's eyes, although Koto could not
see it in the night.

"Winter Owl's word has been given," he said slowly.

"I understand, of course, but . . ."

"Then you understand," Nakai said evenly. "His word is
mine. That is the law. You know what I personally think of the
treaty, but the word of the Kiowas was given. The blue soldiers
are weak anyway. They cower inside of their fort. They have not
bothered us yet; why make trouble?"

"One day, Nakai . . ."

"Then, on that day, it shall be settled," Hungry Wolf said. He rose, drawing his blanket more tightly around his shoulders. "Go to sleep now."

Ketah had not slept for two nights running.

A light, gentle snow had begun to fall. Wildly painted now, he lay against the frozen earth in a shallow coulee. A trickle of cold water sluiced past. Ketah was sick at heart.

In the end, he had agreed to join the Ta-Hai-Kai, the Ghost Warriors. Washai. The Prophet had encouraged all of the young men. Ketah, Shansa, and Opaga.

"Who is listening to the old shaman?" Washai had demanded at a secret meeting. He referred to White Moon and his prophecy of destruction at the hands of the white soldiers.

"We are led by old men and *cowards*!" Washai shouted.

Ketah had come to his feet in a swift fluid movement and taken two steps forward. Washai, his face painted all in yellow except for the white circles around his eyes, stepped back.

"Are you speaking of Hungry Wolf when you use that word?" Ketah demanded. He could feel his limbs trembling.

Washai was pacifying. "You know I do not speak against your father, Ketah! He is our war leader, and a strong leader. It is," Washai went on, "that the old men have tied his hands. The old blood. Winter Owl, White Moon. They have assented to treaties that you know as well as anyone Hungry Wolf does not agree with."

That much was true. Ketah had heard his father rain scorn on the Cimarron treaty many times.

"Our blood is young," Opaga said, putting his hand to his heart. Koto's son's face was set. "Our people's fate depends on us. Who is the enemy now? Do we fear the Osage, the Arapaho! Bah! It is the whites who wish to push us to the farthest sea. Now, I say! Now is the time to strike while they are weak with their own tribal wars."

"Spoken truly," Washai said in a low voice. The firelight flickered across his weirdly painted face. Smoke rose in a slow curl and was banished by the breeze. The young men spoke among themselves on the sacred island, surrounded by the graves of their ancestors. The campfires of their own village were distant and small in the night.

Ketah, a reluctant convert to their cause, could find no argument against their words. "Then it is what must be done," he said softly. "In such secrecy that not even my father does not know of it."

"And so we all agree," Washai said.

"But no harm must come to the woman across the river!" Ketah insisted.

"They are the . . ." Yatha objected.

"No!" Ketah raised a palm toward Opaga. "My mother will not have it done, One-Feather. Besides," he reminded them grimly, "there would be no doubt as to who had done it, and we would all face Hungry Wolf's wrath."

"He speaks the truth," Opaga agreed firmly. One day Koto's son would be their new war leader. Ketah saw this ambition in the young brave's eyes.

"We strike!" Washai said violently, slamming a fist against his thigh. "It is decided. But we must circle far and wide across the river, moving in silence as the Ghost Warriors we must become."

That had been three nights earlier. Now Ketah lay in the coulee, looking toward the fort of the whites, remembering all that had transpired in the last few days . . .

The farmhouse had been a small one on the Arkansas River. It was dark and still. No dogs patrolled the yard. No one watched.

Nodding to the others, Opaga had started forward from the willow breaks, and stealthily Yatha, Ketah, and the new converts to their cause had followed in his footsteps. Ketah's pulse hammered in his veins. The war axe weighed heavy in his hands. Silver moonlight shone through the distances, catching the sharp blade of the weapon as they moved through the shadows on moccasined feet. Washai, their leader, had no weapon of his own, but Ketah could feel the savage energy of the shaman urging them on.

What am I doing! Ketah thought. What would his father think . . . but it had gone too far to stop now.

Accompanied by Opaga, Ketah neared the front door of the small farmhouse while other members of the Ghost Warriors circled the house toward the rear windows. Ketah crouched beside the door, panting with nervousness. Washai gave the sign to them, and with Opaga they sprang up and burst into the house, their shouts filling the air.

Frank Skoglund, in his nightshirt, rose from his bed as the war cry sounded. He hadn't managed to reach his rifle standing in the corner of the bedroom before Opaga clubbed him down with his war axe. Jane Skoglund screamed and tried to flee, but Yatha pulled her down by her hair and stabbed her a dozen times with his hunting knife.

Stunned by the violent suddenness of it all, Ketah turned at the rush of approaching feet. Skoglund's sons, none of them older than Ketah himself, appeared and two of them threw themselves at the Kiowas. The white boys were unarmed. It was madness, but still it was battle.

Ketah raised his axe and buried it in one boy's head. The other four, some very young, fled the house in terror, but they were caught in the yard and quickly killed.

Ketah stood watching the butchery and then turned back toward the inner room. He had killed.

He had killed, but it had not even been a true battle.

Opaga had retrieved the rifle from the house and he danced

with it overhead in the moonlit yard. The Skoglund boys lay scattered across the dark earth.

Ketah heard Washai at his elbow say, "It is necessary, Ketah. They are our enemies."

"Yes," Ketah replied weakly. But *what* would Hungry Wolf say if he heard of this? This was not the way Ketah's father fought his battles; he knew that.

"Let us go quickly before we are discovered," Ketah said in a trembling voice.

"Don't worry, Ketah," Opaga said. "No one will ever know. We are Ghosts—silent and swift."

Ketah didn't answer. He stared at Opaga's face, realizing that his young friend had *enjoyed* the slaughter, that he wanted to kill. Ketah knew that he wanted no more to do with the Ghost Warriors. And he knew that by the oath he had taken, they would kill him if he left the Society or broke their vow of silence.

Flushed with victory and elated with their "prowess" at killing unarmed boys and a sleeping woman, they had traveled back toward the fort on the Cimarron where they now studied the ill-manned outpost from the cold coulee.

They saw no soldiers on the ramparts. The blue soldiers seemed confident in the false treaty and expected no attack. Still, there were dozens of armed men within the walls, and a frontal attack against the palisades was illogical and foolish. They had discussed the problem on the way back from the Skoglund farm, dismounting from their weary ponies, crouching against the dewy grass.

After several strategies had been proposed, Washai had said, "Fire is a fearful enemy. We won't fight them, but burn their fort from under them."

And so it was decided. Ketah, himself, and Yatha had been elected to start the fire. The others would circle the outpost and watch for interference, although they expected no reinforcements to arrive from off the dark plains.

Slipping up beside Ketah, Yatha placed his hand on Ketah's arm and whispered, "Now."

Ketah nodded. Picking up his pitch-soaked torch as yet unlit, he crept toward the fort with Yatha.

The ground around the fort had once been cleared, but as time went on, it had grown back—sage, sumac, and chia covered the ground. It offered little concealment, but the two young warriors wove their way from shadow to shadow as the pale moon shone; and still the fort remained silent.

It seemed still and deserted, but the young warriors knew that soldiers with rifles were stationed within.

Ketah drew up beside the fort, pressing himself against the unbarked stockade walls. His breath whistled in his lungs. His hands trembled. He gave no sign of his nervousness to Yatha as he and Koto's son stacked loose brush and bark against the wall of the fort and arranged their tinder in the darkness, their eyes going constantly to the palisade walk above them, knowing that at any moment a sentry might appear.

Yatha scooted nearer to Ketah and nodded. Crouched in the darkness, Ketah watched as Yatha drew flint and steel from his pouch and struck sparks, huge and red-bright in the darkness.

The brush pile caught almost immediately, and despite being damp, it flared up rapidly in the night. Nothing moved except the golden flames and fire shadows. The fire licked at the stockade walls and then, as they had hoped but not really expected, the dry pine pilings of the stockade caught fire, and Ketah and Yatha turned and ran recklessly at full speed back toward the coulee. Ketah fell once over an unseen tangle of chaparral roots, rose again, and rushed on.

It was a full minute after they had dived headlong back into the shallow coulee before they heard a cry raised and saw shirtless soldiers appear on the parapet.

A bucket brigade quickly formed, but by then it was already too late to stop the fire's advance.

The fort's source of water was the Cimarron itself, and beyond a few barrels of water kept for drinking, they had nothing to fight the blaze with.

The wood itself, despite the damp weather, was old and dry beneath the bark and once started, it burned with great intensity, spraying golden sparks and violent crimson flames against the solemn night sky.

That fire was the one that Nakai and Koto had seen on that night as they prepared to make their last punitive raid against the southern Osage.

The Ghost Society warriors halted again that night to take a new oath of silence on the sacred island, but it was unnecessary. What could any of them say to Winter Owl? What could Yatha or Opaga have said to Koto—they had broken the treaty.

What could Ketah have said to his father, Hungry Wolf?

Ketah washed in the river, and when he returned to the still, dark village he slunk into his mother's lodge, hoping that Ki-Ki-Tai was sleeping so soundly that she would not hear him come in.

His younger brother, Tema, had been awake however. Tema's eyes were open to the night, catching starlight through the vent hole of the tipi. He said nothing, whispered not a word as Ketah rolled into his blankets, but his eyes were questioning. Angrily Ketah threw himself onto his other shoulder, turning his back on his brother, drawing his blankets high around his head.

Only one other member of their band was aware of what had happened that night, but she said nothing as she silently walked back to her own tipi. Rani-Ta was very pleased with herself. She now had many things to tell Nakai upon his return—and what she had to relate would one day draw him into her arms.

Elizabeth could not say what had awakened her on that night. The scent of distant smoke, the faint glow of fire against the sky, dreams of Tom? She sat up in bed, realizing that Kent had not returned from the Kittinger farm either. She only knew she was unsettled in her mind.

Walking out onto the porch, her hair loose around her shoulders, shawl pulled tightly against the chill, Regret rubbing questioningly against her leg, she saw that there was indeed a fire on the plains.

The fort?

That seemed incredible, but perhaps someone had grown careless with a lantern. At least it was not, as she had feared, a prairie fire—although the weather made that unthreatening at this time of year. Not as in summer when the flames and devastation could sweep across the plains uncontrolled, incredibly destructive, uncaring of life.

Elizabeth watched the fireglow, her hand resting on Regret's huge bearish head. The night seemed to drift by in confusion. Where was Kent? Fireflash flooded the sky. She was a strong woman, she told herself—or that was how she was perceived.

No! She *was* strong. But how long could anyone, man or woman, remain strong in this world of uncertainty and danger? She knew it was wrong, but she clung to her single fantasy— that when Tom came home from the war everything would be all right. *He* would know how to say things to the boys that she did not. To Tom, fighting in the East, Cimarron was a refuge away from war in his thoughts. A distant dream, helping him to hang on to his reason to struggle on. To Elizabeth it was only growing vastly more confusing, vastly more difficult and sad and lonely.

The boys . . . she continued to watch the fire burning against the sky for a while. There would one day be trouble between those two young men. She knew that. They had drifted too far apart.

Regret nuzzled her leg and she smiled at him. "No. It's too early for your breakfast. Let's go back inside."

Elizabeth wandered back into her cold bedroom, turned up the wick on the lamp, and pulled the down comforter up nearly to her ears, reading again that last letter from Tom. The letter seemed somehow mysterious, and despite his tender words, it did not sound like Tom O'Day at all! Was the war changing him so much? It leant her one more fear to deal with on this cold and empty night.

"Dear Heart," Tom's letter began.

"For the moment I have respite to write you. I am in a tiny makeshift hospital in a town called Winchester in the Shenandoah Valley of Virginia. (I am not seriously hurt! Do not trouble yourself with worry!) I have been plagued with 'blackouts' as they call them. Lapses in consciousness, that is—hardly a benefit when one is trying to fight! I believe that is caused by this morphine they continue to give me when it is available. I am not a physician, and half of those we have working in this capacity do not seem to be knowledgeable physicians themselves. It is this damnable musket ball I now carry in my hip that is at the root of it. None of these 'doctors' seems willing or able to remove it.

The months, the years roll by in this hellish war.

How are things on Cimarron?

Three nights ago, Liz, I was alone in a fire-scourged blackened forest and came across a young Confederate soldier no older than Kent. A musket ball had pawed his mouth open grotesquely. He lay there sprawled and I saw he had no shoes. I don't know if someone took them from his dead feet or if they in the South are now sending their boys into this Virginia winter shoeless and coatless. I wanted to bury him! But there was no way to do it in the frozen earth. And it seemed, anyway, quite futile.

As time goes by, it *all* seems quite futile. So different from when we first rode in proudly behind our guidons. I wonder if any among us now can remember why we are fighting!

As you may or may not know, Jefferson Davis has already forbidden the importation of slaves. On their side, too, they now have many Indian regiments—Cherokee, Choctaw, Seminole, and Shawnee among others. Davis has promised them their lands in perpetuity if the Confederates win. We have engaged a few of these hard-fighting men.

I wonder what our own side will do to these people when the Union does win—which almost everyone now agrees is inevitable. I fear the people in Washington will deal with them harshly. Rumor has it that they will all be sent away to the West.

It seems, anyway, that everyone is fighting everyone in vast confusion. None of us here on the lines can make any sense of the major patterns of the battles. One assumes men like Grant and Lee have some grand overview. The rest of us are merely weary. And our hands are so bloody, dear Elizabeth.

Oh, yes—Ramsey! He still finds some glory in all of this. I've told you several times about this Custer fellow (a major-general now!). Ramsey has patterned himself after the man. I wonder what happens to their type when finally the war's end comes.

We fought a fearsome battle at a place called Newmarket. A blunder by General Sigel cast us into an ill-advised offensive. General Lee cut us off with Hampton's cavalry. None of this could be seen from my perspective through the smoke and confusion, you understand. It is all gossip gathered later as we lay in these cots in the hospital. All I saw was a gray horde swarming through our ranks slashing with sabers. Yet now it seems we have finally been re-inforced, because yesterday when they let me stand and go to the window, I saw Sheridan himself riding past at the head of a column all in fresh uniforms, riding east by south.

I wish to return to my company, Liz, but truthfully, I do not know if I am capable of fighting on now. A man doesn't wish to be considered weak, but this war has taken its toll. *And* I have gotten to where the 'jitters' have taken me over. (This may be a result of the morphine as well.) I am as apt to shoot at a tree-shadow or one of my own men as a Rebel soldier!

I won't bore you with more of this. We will have many years for me to tell my stories around our hearth. (Though I don't think I shall ever wish to tell some of them!)

I have been told that a courier is departing in an hour or so for Knoxville with some military dispatches. The lines of travel from there on to the west are said to be clear. I shall try to post this. I have no idea of how many of my let-ters—if any!—you have received over these past few years.

I love you with all of my heart, Elizabeth. Give the boys my love as well. I wonder how much they have grown! Forgive my scrawl–I must hurry if I hope to catch the courier.

1st Lt. Tom O'Day
4th Kansas Volunteers

(We are required to sign letters in that way, Liz. I promise to see you again soon. This damnable war can't last forever.)"

134

★ ★ ★ ★ ★

The Kittinger farm looked like a fortress these days, Kent O'Day thought grimly as he approached it riding Satan, the black gelding Bettina had given him. They had begun building a miniature stockade around the big house. Five mounted Mexican vaqueros patrolled the perimeter of the Kittinger property. Hard-faced men, they took their duties seriously. Recognizing Kent, they let him pass without a challenge.

How much was this costing Ned and Isadora, Kent wondered. Not that it mattered to Bettina's mother. Her father, as age had set in, had come to forgive and forget the past. Well, Kent speculated, maybe it was the war, which still raged on not far from Baltimore. Or the new baby that had softened the old man's heart.

For Ned and Isadora now had a young son, more doted on by Ned than Isadora, it seemed. But Kent didn't concern himself with trying to fathom their relationship. All he cared about was Bettina.

He rode the black horse, which moved lightly and so smoothly that one would think it had oiled bearings for joints, to the front door of the big house, and almost before he had swung down and tied the animal to the hitching rail, Bettina was in his arms.

"Not here!" Kent said, looking toward the house. He didn't mean it, really. Let the world know about their love. Her warm young body pressed against his, destroying all of his inhibitions.

"They're in a state!" Bettina warned him as they walked across the canopied porch to the front door. Kent carried his Springfield rifle; it had become habitual with him.

"Oh? Is it something I've done?" he asked lightly.

"You haven't heard then." She paused and turned her troubled face up to his.

"What?" he asked searching her deep blue eyes.

135

"The Skoglund family . . . they were massacred by Indians."

"How could . . . ?"

Bettina went on breathlessly. "And they burned down Fort Cimarron! There's an Indian uprising, Kent. Mother is terrified. All she keeps saying is that if Lieutenant Ramsey were here none of this would have happened. The soldiers are living in tents near the ashes of the fort."

"Jesus!"

"You shouldn't talk like that, Kent," she admonished. "Mother says Sergeant Callahan is a nice enough man, but he has no idea what to do about these raiders. As he was only waiting to serve out enough time to earn his pension."

"I don't know what he *could* do," Kent commented. "There can't be more than twenty or so men remaining at the fort. Does anyone know who is responsible for it?"

"Well, it has to be Hungry Wolf, doesn't it?"

"I don't know." Kent shook his head. "From what I understood of the treaty . . ."

The door beside them opened. "Good morning, Kent!" Isadora Kittinger had appeared in a salmon-colored dressing gown, filmy and ruffled. Kent blushed faintly as he usually did. Bettina's mother never seemed to be fully dressed these days.

"Hello, Mrs. Kittinger," he mumbled. "How is the baby?"

"Oh," she said offhandedly, "Charles is fine. Missie is bathing him." Missie being the Negro do-all of the household.

They all advanced to the coolness of the parlor. Isadora asked, "Have you heard from your father? Is the war any closer to an end?"

"Mother's gotten a letter," Kent said. "She hasn't shared it yet. Usually she digests them for a day or so and then gives up a synopsis. I imagine there are personal things in them she doesn't wish to share."

136

"But what does he have to say about the war? Will it end soon?"

Kent glanced at Bettina, whose eyes were blank blue mirrors. It was difficult for the young man to penetrate Isadora's mind. She had asked about his father in a way that seemed to be only polite conversation, yet her attention as to when there might be an ending to the war was deeply intent.

It was natural enough, he supposed; everyone wanted it to end, this national tragedy. Maybe, too, he conjectured, Isadora was growing more and more fearful of the Indians after recent events and wanted the soldiers to return to the plains from the East.

Yet it seemed like there was some other reason behind her concern.

"How is Mr. Kittinger?" Kent asked, relieving the conversational hiatus.

"He's fine, quite fine," Isadora answered, waving her hand carelessly. "I don't know what he does with himself these days."

Neither did Kent. He had seen Nesbitt Kittinger walking his fallow, snow-crusted fields, doing nothing. Simply looking at the frozen soil. Then one day as Kent and Bettina had looked for a place for stolen kisses, he had seen her father standing on a low knoll where a broken oak tree stood like a truncated giant. Ned Kittinger stood in its winter shadow staring westward, as still and silent and forlorn as the oak.

"Have you met Ernesto?" Isadora asked apropos of nothing that had gone before.

"I'm not sure, ma'am," Kent answered. "I don't know any of the Mexicans' names."

"He is the tall one . . ." Isadora's eyes grew briefly dreamy. She rose abruptly. "We must have some coffee. Missie! Where are you?"

Kent shifted uncomfortably in his seat. At times he understood why his brother, Oliver, felt uneasy around this family.

"Well," Isadora said, "you'll know all of the hands soon enough. When you two are married."

Kent started. Of course he and Bettina had discussed marriage, but this was the first time her mother had mentioned the possibility. Isadora turned toward him, a fleeting smile on her lips.

"I want Bettina to have a man she can love. A strong man. You are strong, Kent."

Kent lowered his eyes and remained mute. What was there to say to that? Why did Isadora's eyes go to the window and remain fixed there as if she could see a silent, lonely figure wandering his frozen fields?

Bettina tried to lighten the moment. "Let's go see what's keeping Missie, Kent. Or I'll make the coffee myself, Mother. There's no sense in bothering the poor woman."

"That's what she's paid for," Isadora said with sudden savagery. "Missie!"

The two younger people exchanged a glance and rose. "Let's see if we can find carrots or some other treat for Satan," Bettina said, meaning the black horse she had given to Kent.

Isadora was not finished yet. "Bettina is not a poor girl, Kent. And when my father dies she will have quite a bit more."

Kent, who had seen little money in his life, thought about it only in terms of *making* it so that he could provide for his mother and Bettina. He was dumbfounded by Isadora's words.

"I'm sure that . . ." he began.

"Tell your mother to come over here, Kent. The two of us will see to the wedding. There is still a chaplain at the fort . . . or what's left of it," she said. Then Isadora left the parlor, shouting again for Missie.

Embarrassed, the young couple wandered out into the garden

where lifeless, pruned-back rose bushes stood in dark, thorny rows.

"I guess . . ." Kent began, his head lowered.

"Sh!" Bettina said, putting a finger to his lips. "I know mother has an abrupt way about her, but weren't you going to ask me one day, Kent?"

"Well, it's the strangest proposal I've heard of!" he laughed.

"I know how brash mother is," Bettina said, "but it's all out in the open now, isn't it?" She lowered her eyes. "You always said we had to wait until we had some money. Mother has just offered that to us. Unless . . ." she hesitated, "unless you really don't want to marry me, Kent."

"Bett . . ." Words failed him and he drew her into his arms and held her tightly, astonished to feel a hot tear rivuleting down his cheek.

"I love you, Bett," he said kissing her soft hair. "That's all there is to it."

"Yes," she said, touching the tear on his face, her sparkling eyes locking with his, "that's all there is to it. Shall we find Father and tell him?"

Ki-Ki-Tai walked slowly across the frozen earth toward the O'Day farmhouse. It was all so strange, but with time's inexorable and unpredictable passing, she felt more welcome and less a stranger here than she did in her own village. Hungry Wolf was still gone; the boys were absent, and their young friends now seemed so distant, holding secrets, falling to silence at her approach.

Walking to the porch of the lodge of the O'Days, she knocked.

Elizabeth had been scrubbing the floor with a stiff brush and strong lye soap. It was hard labor, but no one could know what that floor meant to her after living on a muddy earthen floor in the soddy. The knock at the door brought her head up. She

139

rose, pushing her hair back out of her eyes, and went to meet Ki-Ki-Tai.

Their relationship, any outsider would have said, was odd. Speaking so little of each other's language, they spoke more with eyes and gestures, yet somehow they understood each other at a deeper level. They were friends and did not need to speak that much to enjoy each other's company.

"Tea?" Elizabeth asked. The water was already boiling on the fire iron above low coals, the pot whistling gently. Ki-Ki-Tai nodded. Still uncomfortable with white furniture, she sat on the striped couch and waited. Elizabeth made them both tea, making sure to brew Ki-Ki's light. After the sycamore and other light teas she was used to, she found pekoe and any English tea too strong. Nor did she use sugar, ever.

Elizabeth returned with the teacups. Ki-Ki nodded, accepting the tea. Elizabeth, weary from her work, sagged gratefully beside her guest.

Ki-Ki-Tai looked around. The bear-dog was gone. That meant the boys were gone. Good . . . it was hard to be comfortable in this house when she and Elizabeth were not alone.

"I apologize for the mess . . ." Elizabeth began, but then the two young people accompanied by Regret appeared, framed in the open doorway.

Oliver and Kianceta.

Oliver's mouth was set firmly. His arm was around the Kiowa girl. He appeared uneasy but determined. They came slowly into the room; Kianceta's eyes dropped briefly as Ki-Ki-Tai looked at her.

"Yes, Oliver?" Elizabeth asked, putting her cup and saucer down on the table. Her heart had begun to flutter; she knew her son, and this was not his usual manner.

"We've come to tell you—Kianceta and I are going to be married." He spoke first in English to his mother, and then in

Kiowa to Ki-Ki-Tai. "It doesn't matter what anyone else says. We are in love and that is that!"

There was a bleak silence for a moment. A hundred thoughts flitted across the room. Both of the older women seemed slightly stunned. What would Hungry Wolf do? What would Tom say! What about Ketah, to whom Kianceta was promised? How would they marry? In an Indian ceremony? Would a white preacher agree to a mixed marriage . . . ?

"That is how it will be, *Mother*," Kianceta said to Ki-Ki-Tai. "I do not know what else can be said. This is what we have determined to do, the two of us."

Elizabeth was still stunned. She should have guessed, she supposed, but there was a dreamlike quality to this all. The young people began talking in a strange mélange of Kiowa and English, each trying to explain it in a torrent of words.

"Mother," Oliver said pleadingly. "Try to understand, please."

One wanted to warn them what lay ahead, but looking at their young flushed faces—determined and filled with love— there was nothing to say.

Without thinking about it, Elizabeth turned toward Ki-Ki-Tai and held her, and the two of them began to cry, embarrassing the young people.

"Well, this is quite a charming scene!" said the voice from the doorway, and they looked up to see Kent O'Day standing there, face rigid, rifle in his hands.

"Kent . . ." Elizabeth began.

"I came back to tell you something important, Mother. Bettina and I are going to be married. I thought it would be something we could be joyful about . . ."

Oliver stepped toward his older brother, hand outstretched. "Good Lord, Kent! This is a remarkable coincidence."

"Is it?" Kent ignored his brother's hand and stared at Ki-Ki-Tai and Kianceta. "Don't you people even know that Hungry

141

Wolf has burned the fort and slaughtered the Skoglund family?"

Ki-Ki-Tai came sharply to her feet. "It is not true."

"Oh, yes it is, squaw-woman. Ask the corpses of the children."

"Kent!" Oliver objected.

"Shut up, Oliver. Take your own squaw and be gone!"

Oliver launched himself at his brother and they hit the floor, winging blows at each other.

Ki-Ki-Tai had only understood half of the words spoken, but she understood well enough what the brothers' fight was about.

Elizabeth stood and demanded: "This is my home. Stop this now!"

Kent struggled to his feet and drew back, panting.

"All right, Mother. It's over now. Oliver," he said turning slashing eyes on his brother, who was still seated on the soapy floor, "you go your way and be damned. Traitor!" Kent snatched up his fallen hat and rifle and stomped out of the door.

Oliver rose slowly then, staggering briefly back against the wall. He glanced at Kianceta, who was concerned and uncertain, and then said, "Mother—I think we shall have to go away. Kianceta and I. We have discussed it. North or west, to the south perhaps. We know there can be no peace for us on Cimarron. As you see, there will be too many to condemn or simply shun us. I want you both to try to understand this decision . . ."

Then with hardly a backward glance he and Kianceta went hand in hand out into the yard and slid onto the backs of two Indian ponies. Regret ran in circles, barking, as they rode from the yard, understanding none of it at all except that there was trouble among the humans.

Elizabeth began to rise and then sagged back onto the striped couch again, and Ki-Ki-Tai joined her. Shoulder to shoulder, they sipped their cold tea, and there were still tears flowing from both of their eyes.

★ ★ ★ ★ ★

"I'll be damned! I will be damned! I will be goddamned," Corporal Huggins muttered to himself as he walked through the ashes of the fort toward where Sergeant Callahan sat on his camp chair in his still-uncomfortable, smoke-smudged lieutenant's uniform.

"What in blazes are you muttering about, Art?" Callahan asked sourly. His temporary command had been burned down around him and he was in a black mood.

"Sergeant . . . that is, *sir,* a dispatch just up from 14th Headquarters." Huggins dropped to his haunches and handed the message to brevet-lieutenant Callahan, who read it in slow disbelief.

War over. Repeat. Over
Lee has surrendered this
Day, Apr. 9, 1865 at
Appomattox Ct. House, Vgna.
Hostilities ended.

Callahan read the dispatch three times before he put it on his lap and smoothed it. "I'll be damned," he said, looking around at the charred and ruined fort. "I'll be damned!"

CHAPTER FIVE

"One wonders, Tom," Benjamin Ramsey said as the two men let their horses rest and graze in the shade of the twin oaks on some nameless rivulet.

Tom O'Day barely glanced up as Ramsey spoke. His concerns and Ramsey's were no longer the same. They had fought together, survived the war, in part, because of each other. Now, for Tom O'Day, all of that was over.

"One wonders about these damned Kiowas," Ramsey, undeterred by Tom's silence, said.

The two men wore beards and trail grime as part of their costumes. Four years of battle and two months on the homeward trail had hardly improved their appearance. Tom wore his faded and torn blue issue uniform. Ramsey, following the lead of his hero, Custer, wore fringed buckskin jacket over black jeans. He wore his major's oak leaves on his shoulders, though that brevet rank had probably been revoked, leaving Ramsey a permanent captain. The paperwork involved was so clogged up in Washington after the recent chaos that no orders reducing rank had come through. Tom knew that many battlefield commissions, promotions for gallantry or for currying some commander's favor, would soon be worthless as the army returned to peacetime.

"I don't know," Tom said wearily. He was tired of Ramsey's company. He had been alone with him on the trail for two long months; the officer had spoken about little but the old war, the new wars. Word had reached them of a massacre on Cimarron by Hungry Wolf and his Kiowas. Ramsey was invigorated by the prospect of battles to come. Tom wanted peace. Only peace.

Tom reached into his saddlebags, removed his steel flask, and drank deeply of the laudanum it contained . . . the very last of the opiate the doctors had given him. Ramsey eyed him darkly.

"You ought to get off that stuff, Tom."

Again Tom O'Day ignored the remark. After four years of flame and war, he had learned to ignore any advice or counsel from those "in charge." He had learned, in fact, to despise all authority.

"I think the horses are rested enough," Tom said, rising. Fortified by his morphine, he felt intensely alert mentally. The lowering sundown sky was an exhilarating display of colors and seemed to be charged with mingled thoughts.

Despite the new alertness he felt, Tom's limbs were unsteady as he swung aboard the bay horse he rode. He patted its neck and once absently called it "Domino," forgetting that his favorite black-and-white horse was long ago lost in the channels of the dark war.

"If those damned redskins think they have seen the last of us . . ." Ramsey rambled on. Tom heard him only in disconnected fragments. The sundown sky was flooded with pale color and deep purple clouds. "With impunity . . . our weaponry . . . the restructured regiment . . ."

Tom had learned to let all these jingoisms fly over his head. He only wanted to part company with the army, with Ramsey, and go home to Elizabeth and the boys.

"Well, Tom," Ramsey said sharply as they rode on, "if it comes down to your family's safety, you'll think differently! If they were harmed, what would you do then?"

Tom's head was hanging now. They continued their weary trek, silhouetted against the sundown sky. Tom lifted tired eyes to his companion and said:

"Well, Ben, I guess I would just kill every Indian I could find."

What, anyway, was one more dead man, red or white, on his conscience after four years of bloodshed? He would not be drawn out into conversation, however, and so they rode silently on, comrades-in-arms, but never friends. Silent, uncompanionable tribesmen bonded only by shed blood.

"Unless and *until* they take these maple leaves from my shoulders . . ." There was no shutting Ramsey up! Could he actually be missing the terrible excitement of war? ". . . Custer for God's sake! They've busted him back to colonel, Tom! Can you imagine? What an indignity!"

Tom lifted his weary head again. Fuzzily he reached toward the epaulet on his shoulder and removed his lieutenant's bar. Without a word he bent the sign of rank between his thumb and forefinger and hurled it away to glitter dully in the prairie grass.

He reached automatically for his flask. It was empty, only a few bitter drops of the laudanum in it. He told Ben Ramsey: "The first lamp you see, Ben . . . first little town. I need some whisky, badly."

Then the son of a Presbyterian minister lifted himself erect in the saddle. Breathed in deeply and stared ahead into the purple dusk. His hands trembled on the reins. Ben Ramsey watched Tom with surreptitious disgust.

Well, Ramsey thought, *it doesn't matter, then.* Tom O'Day had seen his day. The war had broken him. He would be of no use in battles to come.

Ramsey had seen gallantry, heroism, and reward through courage. O'Day, it seemed, had seen only the dark side of the conflict. Not everyone was cut out to be a soldier. Let O'Day go back and plow his miserable fields on Cimarron. Ramsey knew where the glory lay.

There was the smallest shadow of regret across Ramsey's thoughts. He, too, recognized that there was a bond between them. Once, according to all accounts, Tom had saved Ramsey's life.

An exploding rocket nearby had stunned Ramsey and knocked him to the ground so that he had no personal memory of it. He recalled only fire and smoke and snow. But they told him that Tom O'Day had shouldered him and taken him from the field as Jackson mounted one of his savage cavalry charges. It was the very day that Stonewall Jackson was killed by one of his own sentries at Chancellorsville.

It was a shame to look at O'Day and see what the war had done to him. Ben Ramsey had been invigorated by it, reconstituted after years of rotting on the plains. He knew very well what O'Day thought of him—that he hated Indians and wanted to wipe them out. He did not! Ramsey didn't care a whit about the Indians one way or the other.

But they held the key to his path to glory.

"I see lights to the south, Tom. I think it's Graves' Crossing. They'll have whisky."

They rode slowly through the settling night. Ramsey was silent, his thoughts drifting in a new direction now.

Isadora.

She had sent him a hastily composed letter that had taken six months to reach him in Virginia.

They had a son!

Now that was another matter that had to be attended to. Was that fool Nesbitt Kittinger still alive and living with her? One assumed he must be.

That was one more item to be taken care of. Back on the Cimarron there was no complicated chain of command. Ben Ramsey would be his own law on the plains this time.

It was an arrogant thought, he knew. But for a nation weary of war, the goings-on in the far West involving a few savages was of little importance. Ramsey shifted in his saddle and reached out a hand to nudge Tom, who had managed to fall asleep on horseback.

"Wake up, Tom," Ben Ramsey said with sudden enthusiasm. "I'll find you some whisky. Maybe a doctor with some morphine. Tomorrow sees us home on Cimarron!"

It was cold outside the hastily built lean-to, but incredibly warm and tender inside.

Oliver had never known such a night. He and Kianceta lay naked and at peace with the world beneath two blankets and a buffalo robe, the cedar scent of the newly cut boughs overhead flavoring the air with a natural perfume. There was no world outside of the lean-to, and if there was, it did not matter. Not on this night. Oliver lay awake in wonder; Kianceta was awake too; he could see the starlight in her eyes. Oliver ran his hand over her flat abdomen, across her breasts, still amazed by her body so gently strong. He rose slightly and leaned over to kiss her throat and her lips. Her arms stretched out to him and he rolled to her.

Earlier they had stopped to let the horses drink at a quick-running rill where pine trees crowded the banks of the stream, casting shifting shadows onto the water as a breeze flitted through the treetops.

They were riding south and west with no firm destination in mind. Oliver had lifted Kianceta from her pony, and he held her close for a long minute as the river ran and squirrels chattered in the pines. Drawing away, he had asked her, "Are you afraid, Kianceta? Are we making a mistake?"

"I am afraid . . . a little," the Kiowa girl said. "But we are not making a mistake, Oliver. There was no place for us to belong back there. No one who would dare take us in."

"Where then . . . ?" he began, but she silenced him with a warm kiss.

"We can survive on our own for a while," Kianceta said confidently. "I know the wilderness. It can be a friendly place. Sometime, somewhere," she said with a small shrug, "we will find people to live among. If not, we shall build our own home."

Oliver shook his head, marveling at her sureness. His own boldness and hasty decisiveness had faded to uncertainty. The two of them had virtually no supplies with them and the weather was still far from good.

"Come," Kianceta had said. Taking his hand, she had led him a little away from where the horses drank. There was a shelf of granite lying ten feet above the river, and rising behind it a series of dark, brooding cliffs.

"We must bathe while we can," Kianceta had said, and without another word, she slipped from her short gown and broadcloth skirt to stand naked before him. The breeze, moderated by the rising bluffs, was cool but gentle. Oliver could only stare at her. He had never before seen a naked woman, and her lithe body, with its long legs, high breasts, and slender hips, took his breath away and started the blood surging through his body. He reached for her, but she laughed and dove neatly from the low granite shelf, knifing into the shallow rill. She emerged, shaking her hair back, beckoning to Oliver.

He turned his back modestly; then realizing there was no point in modesty, he stripped off his trousers and shirt and dove in as well.

He rose next to Kianceta in the quick-running, cool water, and their damp bodies met in close embrace. Her lips were parted, her eyes half closed; Oliver's heart was hammering wildly. She reached down and touched him uncertainly.

"Here?" he asked, and she had kissed him roughly, pushing

her body against his. And so for the very first time they made love, there in that shallow creek. It was hasty, unskilled, but necessary and bonding. They needed no other ceremony to declare that they were now man and wife.

Afterward they had clambered up onto the ledge where the rocks were sun-warmed beneath them and the gentle breeze still flowed. They made a bed of their discarded clothes and lay in each other's arms while the horses dozed lazily in the sun and crows cawed in the tall, staggered pine trees along the deserted wilderness rill.

Later that afternoon they had built their lean-to of branches, which they cut and slanted up against the lowest limb of a huge old cedar tree. They had made love again, still experimentally, but more comfortably.

There was so much to worry about. Food, shelter, the threatening weather. Would the Kiowas pursue them? Also they were nearing Comanche country. How would they be treated if they were discovered there? Wotasha, a fierce and widely known warrior, was said to be in the area.

"Are you sure," Oliver asked Kianceta once more when it was nearly midnight, "that we have made the right decision? That we haven't . . ."

Again she put her supple lips to his and quieted him with her kiss and they loved the night away. She was sure! Oliver marveled at this woman—his woman. In ways she was stronger than he, and she was proving that again at this troubled moment as his own thoughts whirled and snaked into uncertainty. He cast away his own fears as her arms slipped around him and he drifted into some deep land where there were no worries in her embrace.

"I ought to have beat the life out of him!"

"Where did they go?" Bettina asked. Kent spun away from

the window, his fists still tightly clenched.

"They were still at Mother's house when I left. For all I know, they're still there. How could he do such a thing?" For a moment Kent's throat was so tight with rage that speech was impossible.

"Bringing those squaws into my mother's house! My father's house—while the Kiowa men are out massacring settlers, burning the fort!"

"Don't get yourself so furious, Kent," Bettina said, taking his hands. "I hate to see you this way."

"It makes me sick!" Kent looked away briefly and then back into Bettina Kittinger's blue eyes.

"And on the day I went to tell Mother that you and were to be wed. I tell you, if he weren't my brother, I think I would have killed him."

"Kent!"

"I mean it. I loathe the thought of going back to that house. What am I going to do if I find those . . . people there still?"

The voice from the parlor doorway was smooth and quiet.

"You don't have to go back at all, you know, Kent." Isadora entered the room in a swirl of frilly white dressing gown.

"What do you mean?" he asked, his eyebrows drawing together.

Isadora was briefly silent as she seated herself on the blue settee, sweeping her long gown between her knees.

"You can stay with us, Kent," she said.

"Here, but . . . !"

"Of course," she said easily. "We have plenty of room, Kent. I don't want to see you go home in your present mood and get into trouble. Of course you can stay here! For as long as you like." She glanced at Bettina and smiled. "And of course we can make other arrangements for you two when the time comes that you two wish to be married."

"I don't care to wait at all," Kent said impulsively.

Bettina was momentarily astonished, but she stepped beside Kent and took his hand. "Neither do I," she told her mother.

"Good," Isadora said, unruffled by the young couple's decision, "then it's settled. I'll send one of the vaqueros for the army chaplain in the morning." With a single movement she rose to her feet, her smile quite enigmatic. She kissed Bettina lightly on the cheek, turned the smile again toward Kent, patted his hand, and flowed, rather than walked, from the room in a flourish of white satin and lace.

"Leave it to your mother!" Kent said in amazement. "She gets us engaged one day, and the next she's planned our wedding. I wonder which of your parents proposed to the other—her or your father?"

"I wonder too," Bettina said, laughing. Then she grew serious. "I know my mother's wildly impulsive, Kent. But you'll find her instincts are generally right."

Then she kissed his lips very gently and her eyes searched his. "You will be happy here, Kent. I'll see to that, believe me."

"Wildly happy," Kent murmured into her hair as he drew her tightly to him. "I know it too."

Evening was settling on the Cimarron. Elizabeth O'Day stood on the front porch of the empty house. A fire burned within, but there was no cheer to its warmth. The river slipped past silkily, touched only here and there by the dull flames of the sundown sky. To the east the skies were already starry. The wind lifted Elizabeth's loose hair and drifted it across her eyes. She didn't even lift a hand to brush it aside. How could the night be so empty, so lonely?

Regret bounded across the yard toward the barn and then ambled back, sniffing the air inquisitively. He clomped up onto the porch, circled Elizabeth's legs, and seated himself, leaning his massive head against her thigh.

"They're gone, Regret," she said in a whisper. Where, for how long, she did not know. They were just gone—all of her men.

She tried to keep from blaming herself. After all, what had she done? But still there was a stony, guilty feeling in her heart. If she had *not* made mistakes, and grave ones, then why had they all gone?

The prairie had never seemed so vast and empty. She looked at her bare rose bushes, the sterile winter garden. Nothing flourished. It was a dead land and the house was empty and sterile as well.

There was no color left in the sky when she finally turned and went back into the house. The fire had burned down to softly glowing embers, but she made no effort to prod it to flames or bank the fire for morning. She walked into her bedroom and, still fully dressed, curled up onto the bed, drawing her comforter over her, listening for footsteps that never came.

"Hello the house!" a voice boomed out. Elizabeth opened her sleep-clogged eyes. It was very early. There was the faintest hint of dawn flush in the iron-gray sky beyond her window, no more.

"Hello!" the voice roared again and Elizabeth came suddenly alert.

It couldn't be!

The voice was too familiar to be mistaken. *Maybe I'm still dreaming,* she thought, but her heart was racing wildly. Regret began to bark excitedly. Elizabeth rushed from the bedroom to the front door and threw it open, her hair unbrushed, her dress folded with night wrinkles. She threw the front door open to the chill of the morning.

"Is it all right to step down from my horse?" Tom O'Day

asked with a grin.

It *was* Tom! He had a beard, wore a dirty uniform. His face was lined and travel-grimed, but it was her Tom.

Elizabeth rushed down the steps, nearly tripping on her skirts. Tom swung from the saddle stiffly, grinning widely. Regret ran to him, sniffed his leg, and then began to run in circles, barking joyously.

Elizabeth clung to her husband, tears welling up uncontrollably. Tom stroked her back silently. She looked up into his eyes, laughed at the brush of his beard, kissed him deeply, and hugged him again, so tightly that the joints of her shoulders cracked. Tom was home. Now everything would be all right. He would know what to do.

Together they walked back into the house. Tom stumbled against her as they mounted the steps and Elizabeth glanced at him worriedly.

"You must be so tired, Tom!"

"Weary to my bones, Liz. None of that matters now. I'm home."

There was, she had noticed immediately, something different about Tom. His eyes were overbright yet weary looking. However, after all that he had been through, some change had to be expected. What he needed was rest and good food.

He listened as they crossed the threshold and asked, "Where are the boys, Liz?"

"They're off . . ." Elizabeth said hesitantly. It was too soon to tell Tom all about it. Let him rest first, catch his breath. "They went off."

"Awful early, isn't it?" Tom asked.

He let go of her waist and walked to the chair by the fireplace. Again Elizabeth saw him stagger. Oh, no! The musket ball in his hip, the wound he had written to her about, she thought.

She sat on the arm of his chair, her arms around his neck.

Looking into his eyes, she said, "Tom," again and again. It had been a long, terrible four years, but he had come back alive to her.

"What am I thinking of!" she said, rising, brushing at her skirt. "I'll get the fire going and make some coffee."

"Sounds fine, Liz," he said, but his voice was only a murmur. His eyes were nearly closed. No doubt he would fall asleep in the chair before the coffee was even boiled.

Cheerfully now, kissing him again, she put on her apron and turned her attention to the fire, jabbing at the dormant fuel with the poker, grateful for the few hot embers that remained in the fine gray ash: enough to catch fresh kindling quickly into flame. She added a little dry wood and watched with satisfaction as the fire caught. Then she rose, wiping her hands on her apron.

"I'll get the coffee on, Tom," Elizabeth said, as nervous as a girl with her first beau calling.

"I'd better see to my horse," Tom said, rising heavily. "He's had a long ride as well."

"All right, Tom."

She watched as he walked toward the door in his dirty uniform. The hard years seemed to weigh him down. He opened the door and left it standing open to the cool morning. Elizabeth watched as he walked to where the bay horse, its head hanging miserably, stood. Tom patted its neck and then went to his saddlebags.

He reached into the near one and took out a silver flask. As she watched, he drank deeply from it. When he lowered it, she saw his shoulders shudder. He shoved the flask back into the saddlebag and took the reins of the bay, leading it toward the barn.

Elizabeth turned back toward the pantry.

After coffee, Tom seemed much brighter. It seemed to have

revived him tremendously. Now he sat with his boots off, feet propped up on the table by the sofa.

"I have got to wash up, Liz. God knows there has been little enough opportunity on the trail."

"Tom," she asked, "did Ben Ramsey come home with you?"

"Yes, he did. Of course he went directly to the fort."

What's left of it, Elizabeth thought. That would be a nice homecoming surprise for Ben Ramsey. As they spoke, Elizabeth began heating water for Tom to wash with. She found his favorite red-checked shirt and jeans and laid them out for him to change into.

Leaving him to bathe and dress, she went out to feed Regret, the chickens, the white ducks, and the two hogs they had left. She sang softly as she worked. The sun was rising, bright and yellow into a cloudless sky. Doves winged past overhead, on their way to water, and quail sang along the river.

"You see, Regret," she said to the curious black dog, "you can't let things get you down. Just when things seem to be at their lowest, something comes along and make everything all right again."

Returning to the house, Elizabeth started to speak. "Tom . . ." but he was not in the room. He called to her instead from the bedroom.

"Liz, come in here, will you?"

Glancing at the sofa, she saw his clean clothes right where she had left them, and with a smile, she began untying her apron.

She found Tom propped up in bed, his chest bare. He reached out to her.

"It's been such a long time, Liz. Come here."

She was out of her dress in moments and in bed beside him. Tom rolled suddenly, roughly on top of her, his bearded face pressed roughly against her. He held her so tightly that she knew she would be bruised by his passion. He mauled her, taking her violently, and she tried to roll her head free, to laugh lightly, but there was no restraining him. He was through in minutes. And, with the act completed, he rolled away from her and fell immediately asleep. Elizabeth lay there through the silent, following minutes feeling deprived, cheated. It was not the homecoming she had dreamed of. It was only the war that had caused it, she thought charitably. The gentleness seemed to have gone from Tom.

It was only the war that had caused that.

Tom would be himself again one day. With rest and normalcy back in his life . . . Elizabeth lay with her hands across her belly, staring at the ceiling.

He would be himself again, gentle and kind. Sadly she touched his shoulder, leaned over and kissed his cheek, and then rose, surprised to find that there were tears in her eyes and the powerful odor of raw whisky in her nostrils.

When he awoke three hours later he dressed, stamped into his boots, and started toward the door, his shirt untucked.

"Forgot my saddlebags," he muttered as he passed her, rumpling his hair absently.

"Don't you want to shave, Tom?" she asked. "I can boil some more water."

He didn't answer her. Elizabeth saw him step off the porch, lurch forward, and march on silently toward the barn. Regret romped beside him, playing for attention, but Tom turned on the dog and kicked it savagely. Regret yelped once and then hobbled away into the fields. Tom went into the barn and closed the door behind him.

Elizabeth turned back toward the bedroom, her own words returning hollowly. "Just when you things are at their lowest, something comes along and makes everything right again."

Tom spent the rest of the day sitting in his chair before the blazing fire, occasionally rising to wander out to the barn to see to his horse or his gear, or to look at the hogs, or so he said. To Elizabeth he seemed profoundly unhappy. He was also unresponsive with words or simple gestures when she addressed him.

Tom had never asked her about the boys again, and finally she realized that it would be up to her to approach the subject.

He listened silently to her halting explanations of the events, staring at his cracked hands or at the wooden floor as she tried to sort out the incidents.

When she was finished, he finally raised brooding eyes and said in a dull, low voice, "That was stupid of you, Elizabeth. Extremely stupid."

"But you see, Tom . . ."

"To let Indians into this house! My God, what were you thinking, woman?"

What she had been thinking of, she wished to reply, was companionship. All that long and lonely time if she could not have her husband home, she at least wanted a *friend*, and Ki-Ki was her friend.

"All right," Tom said brusquely, "we'll solve all of this. Do you think Kent followed Oliver?"

"No. Kent left first."

"Then it will take some tracking to bring the boy home," Tom said. He rose, his mouth set, his eyes fixed on the flickering firelight.

"Tom, if he wants to go . . ."

"With a Kiowa squaw!" He turned sharply toward her. "What sort of life do you imagine lies ahead for the boy if we allow this to happen?" Anger shone in his eyes. "Oliver is only a boy. I can understand him letting himself get mesmerized by the first girl he sees. You, Elizabeth, are not a child! You must see what sort of mess he's gotten himself into. Where is Kent?"

"I don't know, Tom." She hesitated. "At the Kittingers, I suppose."

"I see. Then he won't be coming back here, no. I can see why he wouldn't wish to."

"Perhaps, Tom," Elizabeth said, touching his arm, "they're better left alone."

He didn't bother to answer her. He stood rocking on his heels before the fire. "I'll go over to the fort. I have to track Oliver down. Maybe Ramsey will let me have Donovan Hart and a few men. We'll find him and the squaw."

"Mr. Hart has gone away," Elizabeth said, but again he gave no indication that he had even heard her. He was tucking his checkered shirt in, strapping on his revolver.

"I'll find the boy and bring him home, and then I'll take some hide off him. I'm going to talk to Ramsey and then find Kent. We're going to drag his brother home no matter what it takes."

"Tom!" Elizabeth said. "Oliver is a grown man now. You've never so much as put a hand on the boys before."

"No, but Oliver has never pulled anything like this before. I couldn't very well have been here to tan his hide earlier, could I?" he asked sarcastically. "But *someone* around here should have."

He started for the door then and Elizabeth grabbed her shawl. "Tom . . . wait, I'm going with you."

"No you aren't. You are not going on the trail with me, Liz," he said sternly.

"Tom! I want to talk to Kent. I want to be there when you talk to him."

"I don't know what you could say to the boy, Elizabeth," Tom said coldly, "but very well, come along. Just hurry up."

★　★　★　★　★

The fort, when they reached it, was chaos. Dozens of men were hauling off burned timbers, sifting through the ashes for anything of value. Behind and above the old one, a new fort was being built. Hammers rang; men shouted and cursed. Two wagonloads of new finished lumber sat to one side of the building site. In the midst of the confusion a wild-eyed, red-faced Benjamin Ramsey strode, shouting angry orders to his men.

There was something that had changed in the man's demeanor. Ramsey had always been fairly arrogant, but now he strutted and swaggered among his perspiring men, browbeating them. *The War.* Elizabeth suspected that none of them who had returned from it would ever be the same again. Dressed in a fringed buckskin shirt, Ramsey halted in mid-stride, put his hands on his hips, and half-smiled as the buckboard carrying Tom and Elizabeth braked to a halt.

Tom leaped down without so much as a glance back at Elizabeth. In days gone past he would have come around to her, helping her down. Elizabeth, encumbered by her skirts, eased down to join the men. She looked around at the busy confusion in the fort. She still knew many of the men—Callahan, who seemed to have his temporary lieutenant's bars taken away, grinned and waved to her. Corporal Huggins was still there as well.

"Hello, Mrs. O'Day," a voice called, and she turned to see Eric Donahue, the post chaplain approaching, hat in hand. "We surely missed you," the short, white-haired man said. "Terrible that you couldn't make it."

"I don't understand," Elizabeth replied.

"I mean the wedding, of course!" Donahue said. He seemed to waver between cheerfulness and abashment. His eyes were uncertain. "Your son's wedding at the Kittingers' . . ." Then he realized that she had known nothing about the ceremony.

Murmuring regrets, he walked away.

Stunned, Elizabeth watched his back and then closed her eyes tightly. Kent—married—and she had not even been informed of the wedding. He had not cared that much about his mother's feelings. "Oh, God!" she thought. How can the world turn around so quickly? Oliver gone and now . . . A murmur went through the ranks of laboring soldiers. Heads lifted and Elizabeth turned to look westward, toward the Cimarron.

What she saw was Kent arriving at the fort at the head of a dozen Mexican vaqueros. Rough-looking men. Far back in their ranks rode Nesbitt Kittinger, looking forlorn, his absurd muttonchop whiskers full and gray.

Kent did not so much as glance at his mother. He rode past silently on the black gelding and approached Tom and Major Ramsey. Elizabeth could not overhear their conversation. One name did escape to drift to her on the breeze. "Hungry Wolf."

She did not know what the men spoke of. Their gestures were animated. Their voices loud and then secretive. She believed she knew what it meant, however. There was going to be more war.

And there was nothing anyone could do to prevent it. Elizabeth walked slowly toward the river, wondering if she felt more sorry for herself or Oliver, Tom or Ki-Ki-Tai. Because war was in the air, coming rapidly toward Cimarron now that the soldiers had returned.

The Mexicans in their wide sombreros and tight jackets, proud-looking and cocky, stood by their horses, smoking. Ramsey, Tom, and Kent stood in close conversation. The breeze drifted gently across the land. Elizabeth lifted her eyes briefly toward the river and then lowered them again, wishing she knew how to curse like a man. "What about my son, Oliver?" Tom O'Day demanded. "Can I have a few men to cross the Cimarron with me and track him down?"

"No one's crossing the river yet," Ramsey responded. "I'm sorry, Tom. Soon, though, we'll have the fort rebuilt, and we'll be up to regimental strength again. A lot of the men who fought with us in the East are coming back."

"That doesn't do me any good right now, does it?" Tom asked bitterly.

"It doesn't matter, Dad," Kent O'Day said, "let my brother go if that's what he wants."

Ben Ramsey seemed to be paying no attention to either one of them. "You ought to see what's going on up around the Rademacher place," the officer said. "A few people are trying to throw a town together. More than that, there's hundreds of immigrants coming in. Most of them Southerners displaced by the war. Men who went home to find their homes gone, burned down. They can't find enough prime land here, Tom. Between you, Rademacher, and the Kittingers, you own most of the good sections on this side of the river."

"Let 'em go someplace else then," Tom said brutally. He wanted to talk about Oliver. He noticed Elizabeth, hands behind her back, strolling farther toward the river, but his attention was not on her. "About Oliver . . ."

"Don't you see, Tom," Ramsey said. "We all know we'll have to cross Cimarron one of these days when the time is right. I can't hold back these new settlers forever; but we can't afford to cause an incident just yet. Not until we're at full strength, I cannot let my men cross over to search for your runaway boy.

"One day," Ben Ramsey said, looking westward, "we will cross, but not just yet."

"What's the government going to say about that when you do decide to cross Cimarron?" Ned Kittinger asked. Tom glanced at the ineffectual little man with the muttonchop whiskers. He and Kent exchanged a look of pity. "You're talking about starting a war, Ramsey!"

"I'm talking about natural expansion, Ned," Ramsey said softly. In fact he was talking about where his future glory lay— across Cimarron. "Do you want these newcomers squatting on . . . your land?" Perhaps only Kent caught the officer's slight hesitation and gained a sudden insight into the relationship between Ramsey and the Kittinger family.

"Kent?" Tom O'Day said single-mindedly. "Will you ride with me after Oliver?"

"I don't care how far he goes with his squaw," Kent answered, his eyes flashing. Kent saw his father's expression begin to change from disappointment to anger.

Ned Kittinger put in hastily, "For God's sake, Tom, your boy's just married. To my daughter. You wouldn't want him risking his skin in what's probably a futile search. Besides, I need Kent now."

"For what?" Tom asked.

"We're . . . well, it's all Kent's idea, really," he said with a sideways glance at the young blond man. "We're changing the farm around. Everyone knows I haven't done real well with the land . . . I guess I'm not cut out for it."

"We're bringing cattle up, Dad," Kent said. "That's why I have these vaqueros riding with me." He nodded toward the hard-looking Mexicans he had ridden in with.

"Cattle!"

"We've been talking about it for some time, Tom," Kittinger said. "Bringing up a Texas herd. This is the right time for it."

He continued: "You just heard Major Ramsey say that the regiment is going to be back at full strength before long. And everyone knows there's a host of new settlers up to the north of Rademacher's place. People have to eat, Tom. They tell me that down in Texas, with all of their boys being off to war for four years, there's thousands of wild new-bred longhorns practically for the taking. Those people in Texas are hard up for cash money. Their Confederate bills aren't worth a penny. And Tom, the rest of the country is hungry for beef."

"I think it's a lot of foolishness," Tom O'Day said.

"It's not, Dad!" Kent argued. "There's money in it, a lot of money."

Ramsey said, "The Western army would buy almost all the cattle anyone could manage to drive up from Texas, Tom. I'm sure of that."

Tom believed it was too much of a risk. "What happens if it doesn't work, Ned? Are you just going to let your crops go to hell while you're gone?"

"Tom," Kittinger answered, "frankly it doesn't matter." Embarrassment turned his eyes downward. "I . . . Isadora has enough money from her father's estate to carry us through for any conceivable period of time."

"I still say it's crazy. And so is trying to build a town out here! Who is going to supply it?"

"The railroad, Tom. Yes! Don't look so surprised. Times are changing rapidly in the West, too fast maybe, but the railroad crossed the Mississippi way back in '55."

"But that was up in Illinois," Tom said.

"Yes, that's true—but this will happen, Tom," Ned told him. "Believe me. A man's got to grasp at opportunity."

"Or grasp at straws. It will be *years* before a project like that could be completed, assuming the Indians let them do it."

Kent said, "It might take years, Dad, but when the time comes, we will be ready to take advantage of it, I guarantee you. Kansas beef will be riding the rails to the East Coast."

"You could come in on this with us, Tom," Ned Kittinger said.

"I haven't the money. Besides, I'm no cattleman. No, Ned, with me, it's back to business as usual on my farm . . . as soon as I find Oliver and bring him home."

"Let that go, Tom!"

"No, sir," Tom said deliberately. "I'll not let it go. Now I have to be getting home."

He had begun to grow increasingly nervous; his hands had begun to tremble a little. He had to get back home to where he had his laudanum. Only Ramsey noticed the signs, but he said nothing.

Walking with Ramsey back toward the buckboard, Tom signaled Elizabeth to return. He said to Ramsey, "Ben . . . I need you to get something for me."

"All right," Ramsey answered, knowing what Tom meant. He watched Elizabeth approaching them and lowered his voice. "We've plenty in the hospital. I'll be by tomorrow or the next day."

"Make it tomorrow, Ben. I'm running very low."

"All right," Ramsey agreed.

The two men grew silent as Elizabeth drew nearer, the breeze shuffling her skirts. Kent, Ned Kittinger, and the vaqueros had mounted their horses and were riding slowly southward, toward Texas. Once Elizabeth thought Kent was looking back to her and she waved a hand, but the wave wasn't returned.

Ramsey, too, watched them ride from the bang and confusion of the new fort. Then, after helping Elizabeth O'Day onto the buckboard seat, he turned his attention northward, toward the Kittinger farm. Isadora would be alone for quite some time now, too long for a healthy woman like her. He watched the O'Days start the wagon and team southward toward their home, Tom silent and brooding, Elizabeth silent and broken-hearted beside him. Then, whistling an odd little tune, Ramsey turned and started back toward his nearly completed quarters, calling for his houseman.

★　★　★　★　★

A morning mist lay across the land, gray and distorting. Trees appeared magically, black and twisted, and then disappeared again into the damp, low-lying clouds. The land was red bluffs and broken canyons, red earth and deep arroyos. Pinyon pine trees grew here, yucca and huge fields of nopal cactus.

Oliver plodded on, carrying the young mule deer buck across his shoulders. He had risked a shot at the buck although he and Kianceta were deep into Comanche country. They had not seen a single person for four days, but from time to time they had spotted a distant campfire glowing across the plains. They kept to the high country, moving steadily southward and westward. They still had no plan for their future. They were sharing the first glow of love and nothing else mattered. In time they would need people around them, companions for each of them, but not now, not just yet. The land grew rougher as they traveled on, but the weather was warming, the nights almost mild. Oliver had brought his Bible and his Bunyan with him. And on some evenings he would sit reading to Kianceta. She didn't understand all of the words, and when he explained some of the stories, they amused her with their foreignness.

And of course there was the lovemaking, the long silent nights in their lean-tos or simply on the open ground beneath their blankets and buffalo robe, long, sweet nights when they murmured lovers' eternal promises . . .

"And so! A fine young buck," Kianceta said as Oliver reached their campsite. A tiny tendril of smoke twisted upward from their small fire and merged easily with the ground mist. Oliver unshouldered the deer and hugged her. His wife. Weary, he sat for a moment and she joined him. Their camp on this day sat on the rise of a convoluted ravine, which spun out to nowhere they knew of, leading only away from all they had left behind. Kianceta leaned her head against his shoulder and they held hands, content to say nothing on that morning.

Oliver had left his fears behind long miles ago. He had made the right decision; there was no longer a bit of doubt in his mind.

"Kianceta," he said, stroking her dark hair. She smiled up at him. "I think I shall never be so happy again."

"I shall make you happier," she promised.

"I don't see how!" Oliver laughed. "I don't wish for anything else. One day, though . . ."

"Sh!" She suddenly put a finger to his lips, drew away from him and half-rose, crouching like a wary young animal.

Then Oliver heard it too. There were horsemen approaching slowly through the morning mist. Three or four horses at least, he thought.

Oliver rose, snatching up his rifle, but it was already too late to run or to hide.

There were four of them and they emerged like specters from the fog. Oliver braced himself.

Comanches!

He started to raise the rifle, but Kianceta put a hand on his arm and he lowered it again, and they stood silently, side by side, watching the warriors approach.

Abruptly they were seen and the Indians reined their ponies in, grabbing for their own weapons. Obviously they were surprised themselves; the Comanches made no move for a long minute. They simply sat their ponies, watching with narrowed eyes.

"Now what?" Oliver asked in a hoarse whisper.

"I don't know. Let me speak to them." She studied the men one by one and then recognition flashed in her eyes. "The one on the left is Wotasha," she told him. He was recognizable by his thin nose, his ear that was folded—as children, they had said he had a dog's ear.

"Do you know him?" Oliver asked.

"He knows my father."

"Perhaps, then . . ."

"But," she added, "I do not think he likes my father because he rides with Hungry Wolf." She took in a deep breath. "Do nothing. I shall talk to them."

Walking forward through the mist, her hair damp and loose, she approached the Comanche warriors.

"Who are you, Kiowa girl?" Wotasha asked. "I seem to know you."

"I am called Kianceta. My father is Koto."

"Ah, now I recall you. What are you doing on Comanche land? With a white boy!"

"He is my husband, Wotasha," Kianceta said, careful to keep her head bowed down respectfully. "We had to run away because my father would have killed him. We only want to pass through your land and find a place to hunt and have babies."

"Does Koto know this?"

"I do not know. I think not yet."

"Does Hungry Wolf know?"

"I think he cannot yet."

Wotasha rubbed his mouth thoughtfully and then suddenly threw back his head and began to laugh. One of the braves with him understood and laughed as well.

"It is a great joke on Koto. And on Nakai, I think," the Comanche overlord said. "They will be furious."

"Very furious," Kianceta agreed.

"Bah! Go your way. Wotasha has said you may. You are too young to be made a widow. What do I care for Koto or Nakai?"

Then the Comanche warriors continued on their way, vanishing into the fog again, and Oliver came up beside Kianceta, still feeling the trembling in his legs.

"He is allowing us here. He would rather leave us alone, Oliver. Otherwise he'd have to kill you and take me back to my father. He's happier to be able to spread the story that Koto's daughter has run away with a white man rather than marry Hungry Wolf's son."

The Comanche's joke was a grim one, Oliver thought. He said, "I hope he doesn't tell Ketah which way we have gone." They did not need Kianceta's jilted suitor following after them.

"I do not think he will."

"Would Ketah come if he knew?"

She answered seriously, "Yes."

"Does he love you so much?" Oliver asked, turning her by her shoulders to face him.

"You have taken his property, Oliver."

"I see," he said quietly. All they could do was to ride on, to put hundreds of miles between themselves and the Kiowas. Thinking that, he began kicking out the campfire. He tossed the gutted deer over his horse's withers. There was time for butchering and skinning the buck farther along.

"You are worried, Oliver?" she asked as he tightened the cinch on his saddle. Her arms slipped around his waist.

"Plenty worried," he said. "I have only just gotten you, Kianceta. My only regret about having to fight Ketah and dying would be that I would lose you."

"You cannot lose me, Oliver," she said, putting her forehead against his chest. "I would follow you."

"Don't talk like that. I wouldn't want that. No, we simply have to ride on and cover our trail better from here on, I think. Maybe ride north for a while and then double back from time to time. We won't make it easy for anyone to find us!"

Oddly enough it was on the day following that the most unexpected person did find them in the most unexpected of places.

As the morning had worn on, the mist burned off and the

169

day grew warm despite the fact that here and there in sheltered places they still saw patches of snow. They had been sticking to high ground where only sage and stunted, wind-deformed pinyon pines grew. Water, naturally, was scarce on the high ground, and in mid-afternoon, they decided to drop down to where the snow melt would have collected into ponds so that the horses could be watered.

They wound down along the side of the red canyon where the land was already in shadow and saw from a distance a stand of cottonwood trees, their leaves turning silver in the sun. Riding that way, the horses picking their way carefully across the steep slope, they eventually emerged again into bright sunlight. Kianceta pointed ahead and Oliver nodded. Like a brilliant mirror reflecting through the trees, a large pond lay among the trees. Far from any known habitation, hostile or friendly, they approached the water cautiously.

The trees overhead painted them with shifting shadows. The horses, smelling water, lifted their heads eagerly. An annoyed red-tailed hawk rose from a cottonwood tree and circled overhead at their approach. Dismounting at the pond, they looked around. And saw a man in buckskins emerge from the trees.

"That can't be who I think it is!" a familiar voice said.

"No. It can't be," Oliver said. "Donovan Hart!"

" 'Fraid so," the old frontiersman said, approaching. He looked at Kianceta curiously, took Oliver's hand warmly, and added, "There's got to be a story behind *this*." The scout had grown a beard over the months since Oliver had last seen him, but he looked basically the same—wiry, alert, and merry-eyed.

Sitting around Hart's tiny fire where a coffee pot boiled, Oliver told the scout what had happened. Donovan sipped his coffee and listened thoughtfully, never interrupting.

"I feel sorry for your mother," Hart said finally. "But, Oliver, you two did make the right decision to my way of thinking. They'd never have let you have any peace back on Cimarron. Prejudices run too deep."

Kianceta took a taste of the strong coffee Hart had brewed, made a face, and gave the tin cup to Oliver. Hart smiled, "Sorry, ma'am," he said and then continued.

"But you two will have to find a place to settle one of these days. And you'll be needing flour, salt, ammunition—traps and such if you mean to live off the land. No woman, not even an Indian, wants to just wander about forever, Oliver."

"I know that, Donovan," Oliver said worriedly, "but there was no time for us to plan for all of this. We figured we'd just have to trust to luck."

"Maybe you've found some," Donovan Hart said. He tugged at his beard meditatively and then came to a decision.

"I can help you. Or maybe I can. I'd like to, Oliver. Lookin' at me you wouldn't believe it, but I was young once too, and in love with a woman . . ." Temporarily Donovan's thoughts drifted back into the distant past. Then, catching himself, he drew out of his reverie and went on.

"I've a little cabin, Oliver. A man named Considine and I built it when we were trapping up La Junta way. That's in Colorado. It's pretty high up, near five-thousand feet, and it gets cold in the winters, but it's a pretty land. There's a few Ute Indians around, but they don't bother much if you get off on the right foot with them . . ."

"But, Donovan, we couldn't!"

" 'Course you could. If you want to. I don't know what the cabin looks like now. I'm sure the critters have gotten into it but it'll shelter you."

"I don't know what to say," Oliver said gratefully.

"Don't say a thing. Just talk it over with your woman here. She should have her say. Then, if you decided to do it, I'll draw

171

you a map of how to find it."

Donovan lifted the coffee pot, shook it, and found it empty. He frowned and put it back down. "Now then, Oliver, I reckon you two don't have any cash money."

Oliver laughed. "No, sir, not a nickel."

"That brings us to the second part of what I'm trying to say. You'll need some supplies to start you out. It so happens I have my mustering-out money from the army . . ."

"We could never do that! No, sir."

"Oliver, listen to me. I just plain don't need much money. I've lived off the land most of my life. It would give me pleasure to help you two start out. More than you'd know," he said, again growing reflective. "There's a little pueblo called La Paloma not far from here. We can ride over there and at least get you and your bride a few months' provisions."

"I don't know what to say. I have to accept your offer, Donovan. I'll never forget this. Someday I swear I'll pay you back."

"All right," Hart said, rising. "We'll leave that for someday, then. For today, let's use what daylight we have left to start toward La Paloma. We might be able to reach it by nightfall. The woman, of course, will have to wait out of the town somewhere."

"She goes where I go," Oliver objected.

"No!" For the first time Donovan grew stern. "It's no good stirring up trouble by bringing an Indian into their town. Talk to her now, Oliver. Explain everything I've said that she mightn't have understood. Me, I've got to pack my kit and saddle my pony."

The western sky was awash with crimson flames as Donovan Hart and Oliver trailed into the dusty pueblo of La Paloma, a tiny village of no more than fifty structures, a dozen of them of adobe, the others of barked wood and brush. What kept the town alive was anyone's guess. The residents looked up with startled dark eyes as the two men rode up the rutted, dusty street toward the general store. Children followed them excitedly, bare feet flying. Dogs yapped at their heels.

Kianceta, who had understood better than Oliver had why Hart had not wanted her to ride into the pueblo, waited for them at the base of the foothills in a secluded copse of sumac and scrub oak.

The sky was growing rapidly dark. Here and there across the pueblo, candles or kerosene lamps were being lit already. The two men rode past a small cantina, its doors open. They saw several men in huge sombreros standing at a bar, drinking. The store, when they found it, was already closed, but there was a light upstairs where the proprietor lived, and Donovan Hart rapped loudly on the door until the man came down, a tortilla filled with frijoles and rich red salsa in his hand. He was a burly man with a sour expression. He nevertheless opened the door immediately, sensing a profit, which on most days in this poor pueblo must have been small change indeed.

Hart led Oliver along the rickety shelves of goods, doing most of the selecting himself. Pointing out items which the store owner eagerly carried to the counter across the dim store. Hart ordered fifty pounds of flour, fifty of cornmeal, twenty-five pounds of beans, a case of tinned tomatoes, and another of peaches.

"Donovan," Oliver whispered at one point, "you're doing too much."

Hart replied. "Now what's the sense in doing his halfway, Oliver? Leave me be. Listen . . ." He opened a chamois sack he carried and shook three ten-dollar gold pieces into his palm. "You go find a mule to carry the provisions. And don't keep arguing with me. You'll pay me back, you said. You might as well borrow enough to do you some real good."

Hesitantly Oliver took the money. Starting toward the door

his attention was captured by a small display of Mexican-made jewelry. He picked up a silver and turquoise necklace, a beautifully crafted piece of work. Hart was at his shoulder.

"One day I'll be able to buy Kianceta things like this," Oliver said wistfully.

"I could . . ." Hart began.

"Absolutely not!" Oliver said firmly. "The necessities are one thing, and I thank you from my heart. But we did not come shopping for trinkets and such." He placed the necklace back carefully. "I'll go find a mule."

"Carlo here has told me that there's a man at the end of the street, on the west side, who might have one."

The store owner said something in Spanish that Oliver didn't understand.

"He says," Hart translated, "that you should offer him ten dollars for the mule and a packsaddle and dicker from there."

Oliver went out into the purple dusk of the evening and started toward the house he had been directed to, wondering how he would ever be able to repay the plainsman for his generosity. He wondered suddenly if he would ever see the scout again. And Hart *knew* that was unlikely to happen. Vowing he would find Donovan and pay him back no matter how long it took until the day came when he did have the money, Oliver walked on toward the end of the street, his step light, his thoughts positive. *Now* he and Kianceta would have some sort of a start for their new life. He knew things would be far from easy, but they would make it! He knew that to the depths of his heart.

Kianceta's heart froze. She did not move, scarcely drew breath. Hidden as she was in the thicket where the scrub oak grew head-high, she had been discovered. She could hear rustling movements in the brush as they, *it*, drew nearer.

She had no weapon but her skinning knife, and she drew it with infinite slowness from her belt and waited, her eyes darting this way and that, seeing nothing in the settling gloom of the silent copse. The sun had faded to darkness and the moon had not yet risen. She was lost on some dark island, surrounded by unknown predators.

She waited.

Suddenly the dark form emerged from the underbrush and rushed toward her and she raised her knife to strike out.

The *thing* hobbled toward her, its jaws slavering, and still Kianceta sat frozen against the earth, knife in hand, but now she lowered it as Regret came to her and lay his massive head on her lap.

"Dog!" she said in wonder, stroking his matted black fur, which was thick with stickers and clinging globules of mud. She felt his paws and found that they were raw and torn. One ear was split and there was a large patch of fur missing from his left flank. He was very thin beneath his wooly coat and exhausted, but he looked up at her with adoring eyes, his tongue lolling from his dry mouth.

"Where could you have come from? All these days!"

Regret wagged his heavy tail, flapping it against the earth three times. He had followed them! Followed their scent for four days across rugged country. Something had attacked him along the way, that was obvious, but he had fought and won and continued on. Kianceta felt a tear in her eye. She knuckled it away, bent her head, and kissed Regret's head.

"Rest, dog. When the men return you will have water and food. Rest," she said as she continued to stroke Regret's head, and the bear-dog fell asleep on her lap, his long trek to catch up to them completed at last.

★ ★ ★ ★ ★

It wasn't until the second morning afterward with Regret rejuvenated, although still limping a little, that Kianceta and Oliver started northward toward the La Junta country and the abandoned cabin, leading the black mule carrying their provisions. They had barely had time to say goodbye to Donovan Hart.

"I ain't much for long farewells," the scout had said after he and Oliver had returned to where Kianceta waited. Never even stepping down from his stocky buckskin horse, he had turned it again and swung onto a southerly course, riding away toward Mexico in the darkness.

One reason for Hart's hurried departure might have been the article Oliver found the next morning pinned to one of their mule packs. Gleaming brightly in the new sunlight was the silver and turquoise necklace Oliver had admired in the pueblo store.

He fastened it around Kianceta's neck and kissed her. The necklace, he supposed, was a sort of wedding gift from the old plainsman.

"We will be lucky to ever find such a friend again," Kianceta said.

The land they now rode across was less broken, though rising steeply, and they saw more pine and juniper, occasional big white oaks along the river bottoms, sycamore and cottonwoods.

The grass was greener, better for the horses. Donovan's map was amazingly accurate and detailed, and they had no fear of missing their landmarks.

They began to ride through hills where cedar and aspen grew and over meadows where purple lupine and black-eyed Susans flourished. There were many small silver rills winding across the grasslands. The air was sweet and fresh. Each day grew warmer despite the higher altitude.

On the sixth day they had a distant view of the town of La Junta itself, but they gave it wide berth, needing nothing that they hadn't already. And on the seventh day, still ascending the flank of the mountain, they came upon the cabin, exactly where Hart had described it to be.

They sat their ponies silently for a long minute, surprised by their own success.

"It still looks sound," Oliver remarked finally.

"It is a beautiful valley."

It was that. Cedar and fir crowded the mountain slopes above. A trickle of a stream—enough for their purposes—flowed across the valley where buffalo grass grew, dotted with wildflowers.

"Home," Oliver said in wonder. Well, maybe it wasn't much of a home now, but it would be, he swore it.

They rode slowly forward toward the cabin, following an overgrown trail that wound through the big cedars and then emerged onto the park where the tiny cabin rested. The log walls of the cabin had been carefully laid and there was a stone chimney. The front door, Oliver noticed, was no longer hanging properly, canted to one side. Undoubtedly they had used leather hinges and they had rotted away. There would be a mess inside, probably. Wood rats, owl nests, snakes, but the young couple was willing to work, eager to work, to make their way into a new and brighter world than the one they had left far behind on Cimarron.

CHAPTER SIX

He had ridden in with the dawn, weary and hungry and dirty. The fresh wound in his shoulder troubled Nakai. The Arapaho arrow had done no serious damage, but he had lost much blood from the wound. Now he wanted only to wash, to eat, to sleep with many hours with Ki-Ki-Tai and see his sons.

Koto, Eagle Heart, and the other Kiowa men had ridden directly into the camp, a long line of bedraggled warriors. Nakai wanted to wash himself first, to present himself. Hungry Wolf had his pride to protect.

Therefore as the sun shone through the black line of the trees along the river, he stripped the blanket and hackamore from his war horse and set it free to graze, and seated himself on the low hanging bough of the old sycamore, which overhung the river, and slowly, painfully undressed.

Walking out onto the low-bending branch of the tree, he dove into the river. His muscles were numbed by its cold, but it invigorated his mind, and he swam a distance upriver against the current with powerful strokes, returning the circulation to his weary muscles. Then Nakai floated on his back, letting it carry him lazily back downstream.

She was nude. Poised tall and elegant in the golden glow of the morning sun as she watched Nakai drifting toward her.

"Ki-Ki-Tai!"

But it was not Ki-Ki who stood on the grassy bank above him, but Rani-Ta, her smile enigmatic, her eyes deep and hopeful, expressing admiration for Nakai's warrior's body.

Rani-Ta had been waiting a long time for Nakai's return. Now she was prepared; she would do what she must do.

"Go home, foolish girl!" Nakai shouted. He was directly below her next to the bank, treading water.

"I have come to swim with you, Nakai. Don't you need a woman to wash your back? To make you a warm meal?"

"My wife will do that if I wish it," Nakai said angrily.

"Perhaps Ki-Ki-Tai is not in the camp. Perhaps that is why you should take a second wife, Nakai."

"I need no one," he responded. "What do you mean that perhaps Ki-Ki-Tai is not in the camp?"

"Perhaps she is across the river with her white friends. Again." Exultance built in the young woman's breast as she saw Nakai's expression darken toward savagery. When Nakai spoke his lips were tight.

"What are you talking about, foolish one?"

"Come out of the river now, Nakai. Let me dry you off. The sun is fading and you will grow cold."

"I asked you what you meant!" Hungry Wolf demanded.

"Nothing," Rani-Ta said, lowering her eyes. "I should have said nothing."

Nakai grunted with disgust. There was no hope of getting Rani-Ta to be reasonable about anything. He reached up, caught the sycamore bough, drew himself up, and walked along the shore, the naked maiden following him.

"I have a dry blanket for you, Nakai," Rani-Ta said, picking up a carefully folded red-and-blue blanket. She spread it open and lifted her arms to rub him with it. Nakai yanked it angrily from her hands and wrapped the blanket around his shoulders.

Glaring down at Rani-Ta, he commanded, "Dress yourself, woman, and then tell me what it is you have come to say."

Rani-Ta smiled and turned away, walking—gliding—to where

179

her clothes lay. She stepped very slowly into her skirt and even more slowly slipped on her short gown—obviously all that she had been wearing—and then put her moccasins on.

Nakai had hastily dressed himself and tied back his hair with a bit of rawhide thong.

Increasingly angry with the girl, he walked to her and grabbed her wrist, yanking her toward him.

"What is this you are saying about Ki-Ki-Tai?"

Innocence crept into Rani-Ta's wide eyes. Perhaps Nakai believed he was threatening her by gripping her wrist so ferociously, but it made her heart race with a strange joy. She wanted to be this near to him, to feel the power of Hungry Wolf.

"I mean no harm." She lowered her eyes demurely. "But everyone knows this. It is no secret—Ki-Ki-Tai visits with the whites across the river all the time. The white woman is her friend . . ."

Without warning, Nakai slapped her across the face. Blood trickled hotly down from the corner of her mouth. Rani-Ta tasted it with her tongue.

"I only wish that were the worst," she said, lowering her eyes again. "I will say no more. You will hit me again."

Nakai had regained control of himself. In a tight voice he asked, "What worse lies could you tell me?"

"I do not lie, Nakai," Rani-Ta said, pretending franticness while inside she was excited her drama was playing out. "I am a faithful bitch! A good wife." She clutched at his forearms and let her eyes rove his.

"You are not my wife! Tell me whatever it is that you know."

"All right." Rani-Ta hesitated for effect. "Ki-Ki-Tai was there. She was at the white woman's house when Kianceta, Koto's daughter, was given in marriage to a white boy."

Nakai dropped her hand. He shook his head many times. The

girl had to be lying! But what a preposterous lie! As soon as he returned to the village she would be found out. Either Rani-Ta had lost her mind or Ki-Ki, beloved Ki-Ki-Tai, had betrayed him while he was away on the war trail.

"I am a good wife," Rani-Ta said in a pitiful, tiny voice as she stared at the ground.

"I do not understand you, Rani-Ta! How can you make up such stories?" Nakai laughed, waving a negligent hand.

"There is more yet . . ." Rani-Ta said as if growing fearful to speak further although she had been carefully planning all of this for a long while, lying awake nights, relishing the moment now at hand.

"How could there be more!"

"It is about your sons, Nakai," Rani-Ta said, her voice barely above a whisper so that Nakai leaned toward her to hear. "Ki-Ki-Tai has allowed them to go to war on their own. To cross over the river. They are among the Ta-Hai-Kai. *They* are the Ghost Warriors who burned the soldiers' fort and killed whites across the river."

Nakai spoke carefully, trying to control his trembling voice. "And Ki-Ki-Tai knew of this?"

"Yes, Nakai. She did not care—so long as they did not harm her friends."

Nakai was incapable of speech. He would discover what had happened, of course, but for now it was too much to digest at once. Far too much. Was there treachery all around him? Only this girl had spoken a word to him about any of this . . . if it proved to be true. Perhaps he had judged Rani-Ta too harshly. Perhaps she was not as shallow-headed as he had always believed her to be.

And then, perhaps Ki-Ki-Tai was not the woman he had always thought she was. He could speak no longer just then. There was too much thinking to be done.

"Go on your way, girl," he said, not unkindly. "Leave me alone for now."

"Yes, Nakai," she said quite meekly, and then with her head still down, her heart exuberant, she walked slowly away, barely able to contain the smile that wanted badly to flood her lips. She tasted the blood in her mouth again and found that it tasted sweet to her. What a small price to pay for the victory she had just won!

Cookfires burned across the camp as Nakai walked heavily homeward. A few small boys saw him and waved excitedly, welcoming Hungry Wolf. The women were busy building fires, cooking, scraping hides. Dogs snapped at each other and raced across the camp. Children at their games screamed. There was morning activity everywhere. Reaching his own lodge, Nakai entered.

It was cold within. No fire burned there. Empty and desolate, it seemed as if it had never been inhabited, or as if there had been a recent death in the family.

Clenching his teeth together, he went back out and walked to Koto's tipi. Inside he found Koto eating heartily. His wife, Momo, sat to one side dressing her hair.

"Nakai! Welcome," Koto said, his broad face expressing genuine pleasure. Momo seemed to shrink away a little under Nakai's gaze. Nakai seated himself cross-legged across the blanket from Koto.

"Where is your daughter, Koto? Where is Kianceta?"

Koto's eyes were puzzled. He shrugged slightly and looked to his wife. "Where is she, Momo?"

"I do not know, husband," Momo said, but she kept her eyes turned down. Her fingers toyed aimlessly with a strand of beads she had meant to weave into her hair.

"She's probably out gathering wood or collecting berries," Koto said with another shrug. "Why do you ask, Nakai?"

"Where is Kianceta?" Nakai asked deliberately, and this time his voice was not that of a friend, but that of a tribal leader. Koto put down his bowl, stared at Nakai for a moment, and then turned to Momo again.

"Nakai wishes to know where the girl is."

"I don't know," Momo said, but her voice faltered badly. It was obvious that she was lying. Koto was to his feet instantly, standing over her.

"Where is she!"

Momo buried her face in her hands. "She has run away, husband. I am sorry! I could not say it."

Now Koto's face grew grim. He glanced at Nakai, realizing that something important involving his family had happened.

"Where has she gone?" Koto asked his wife.

"No one knows."

"Did she go alone?" Nakai asked severely.

Momo hesitated. "No, Nakai. She ran away with a . . ."

"With a white man!"

Momo began to cry. Koto gaped at her and looked uncomprehendingly at Nakai. Momo nodded.

"Yes," she said, "Kianceta ran away with a white man."

Nakai was stone-faced. "And Ki-Ki-Tai knew this? She was there?"

Momo seemed to be struck dumb. She braced her hands against the floor as if to scoot away as Nakai advanced.

"Tell me this, Momo," he demanded, "Where are your sons? Where are mine? Where are Ketah and Tema. Yatha? Where is Opaga?"

"I do not know," she said miserably. She hung her head and let it sway from side to side.

"Hunting?" Nakai asked. "Have they gone hunting?"

Momo leapt eagerly to that possibility. "Yes, that must be it, Nakai! They must have gone hunting."

"Must it? Or have they crossed the river despite my orders, despite those of Winter Owl and the council and gone to make a secret war on the whites, a war which could mean our destruction!"

Momo's lips trembled. Her mouth began to form words several times, but failed. She buried her face in her hands again. Nakai turned in a fury and ducked from the tipi. Outside, he stood looking across the village. He heard the harsh slap of a hand against flesh within the lodge. Then it sounded again, and a third time. Then Koto emerged, and the warrior stood there trembling. For a while the two men stood silently side by side.

"What can this mean, Nakai?" Koto asked finally. "When our women and our daughters and sons become treacherous? What does that augur?"

Nakai just shook his head, and after resting a hand briefly on his friend's broad shoulder, he walked away.

What *did* it mean? he wondered. What had become of order and justice, of truth and honor?

Nakai walked slowly through the camp. He was aware of Rani-Ta's eyes following him. She had dressed in her white elk-skin dress and put beads in her hair and around her slender neck. He did not wish to speak to her just now. But she alone had told him the truth. Harsh truths. He felt bad about slapping her for speaking the truth to him. He would make it up to her.

What was to be done now! Taboos had been violated. The treaty had been violated. The young men had spit on the council's promises; the women had allowed an unlawful marriage; his own wife was somehow involved with the white people . . . he walked on toward the river, alone and muddled in his desperate thoughts.

★ ★ ★ ★ ★

"He has returned, White Moon," Ki-Ki-Tai told the old shaman.

"Hungry Wolf? Have you seen him?"

Ki-Ki-Tai shook her head. "Not yet. He will be furious with me."

"It is not your fault, Ki-Ki, that a young woman chose to run away," the old man said, his eyes studying her face.

"No, but I did nothing to stop it."

"What should you have done? Fight the two white men and drag Kianceta across the river? There was nothing to be done," White Moon said sadly. His hand trembled a little as he reached for the buffalo-horn cup Ki-Ki-Tai offered him. He spilled a little of the pink sycamore tea as he tried to drink it.

"I think, Ki-Ki-Tai, that I shall prepare myself to die," White Moon said, lifting his clouded eyes to hers.

"Father! Don't speak like that."

"No. I believe I must," he said shaking his head. "I think my time has come. I am useless to my people. All of my friends are gone."

"You have me!"

"Yes, yes, Ki-Ki-Tai," he said with a smile. "You are my joy. But my time has passed. Washai has the ears of the young warriors. I live, but it seems I exist only as a memory of a distant time. No, it is time for me to prepare for my death. Please go now, Ki-Ki," the shaman said, "I have much to do."

Ki-Ki walked slowly away from White Moon's lodge toward the river, her hands behind her back, her moccasined feet moving in small arcs. The sun was above the willow trees along the river, brilliant and yellow-white. The birds stirred. Two herons swooped low over the sparkling river. Ki-Ki walked on. Without consciously having determined her destination, she went ahead, knowing that he would be there.

And there she found Hungry Wolf, sitting on the low-growing curved sycamore branch, legs dangling. He lifted expressionless eyes at her approach, rose, and walked along the wide bough to the grassy shore.

"You are well, husband?" Ki-Ki asked as he came toward her.

"Well enough," Nakai said expressionlessly. "Shall we walk or do you want to tell me here?"

"We can walk," Ki-Ki-Tai said, feeling a cold touch of shame that reason told her she did not deserve. Side by side then, they walked the river's edge over the warming grass where still jewels of dew sparkled.

"What have you done to me, Ki-Ki-Tai?" Nakai asked bluntly. "What have you done to us and our family?"

She halted. "Nothing, Nakai."

He studied her eyes for a long minute, perhaps searching for the truth, then they started on their way again, walking in silence until Nakai found his next words.

"You let Kianceta run away with a white man."

"She chose to go. I could not stop her."

"And you think that was right!"

Ki-Ki shook her head. "I think that she made a bad decision. No one asked me what I thought."

"It is an insult to me. An insult to Koto! Kianceta was to be our daughter-in-law. It is an insult to our son, Ketah!"

"Kianceta is not my daughter. I could not stop her."

Nakai halted again and sat down on the grass, watching the river flow. He plucked a clump of grass from the earth and threw it. Distantly he could see pale smoke lazily rising. Was it coming from the fort? He could not be sure.

"Why did you go across the river at all, Ki-Ki-Tai? How did you come to meet this white woman? Why did you feel that you needed her company?"

"It all just happened," Ki-Ki said, sitting beside her husband. "I meant to harm no one, especially you. I said nothing because you might have gotten angry with me. She fell into the river and could not swim in all the skirts she must wear. I helped her get to the shore, that is all. That is how I met her."

Nakai was silent again. She knew what he was thinking: why not just let her drown? Looking back, Ki-Ki could remember having the same thought herself at the time. But Elizabeth was a good woman; they were friends now. Ki-Ki-Tai had never regretted saving her from drowning.

"You have concealed so much from me," Nakai said. "Too much. No wife should keep these confidences."

She could feel his anger simmering beneath the surface of his calm, see it far back in his intense brown eyes. She rose and walked three steps closer to the river. Nakai leapt to his feet and followed. Suddenly he grabbed her roughly and turned her to face him.

"You have betrayed me," he said in a voice as cold and hard as winter-stone.

"No!"

"You allowed my sons to go off to war on their own, let them cross over the river and raid the whites! Burn their fort! Break our treaty. What will happen because of that bit of treachery, Ki-Ki-Tai? We shall have to run or fight to the death to protect our women and children. And who do you think will be blamed for what has happened? Hungry Wolf, who was far away in the Arapaho country!" His finger dug into her shoulders. She did not try to shake him off. Mentally she grappled with his accusations. Only a portion of it made sense to her. She shook her head.

"I don't understand you, Nakai. How could our sons have anything to do with this? That would mean they are . . ."

"They are Ta-Hai-Kai! Or have you not even heard rumors of

their existence? They are the secret warriors. Our sons and Koto's. Against our commands! While we are away fighting a just
and honorable battle, they sneak across the treaty river and
raid, beginning what will be terrible war! And you allowed it,
Ki-Ki-Tai!"

"I knew nothing of it. I know nothing now! Are you sure, Nakai? Who has told you this?"

"Someone who feels no need to lie to me," he said, shoving
her angrily away. His hand raised for a moment. He had the
powerful urge to slap her as Koto had slapped Momo, but his
hand lowered again. He could not strike her. Not the Ki-Ki of
his childhood, the comfort of his winters, the mother of his
sons. But was she even that Ki-Ki any longer? Or nothing but a
cunning liar.

He turned his back. Ki-Ki could see the tension across his
shoulders and up the column of his neck. She stepped forward,
reaching to him.

"My Nakai," she said, touching his arm, "you must believe
me."

"I believe nothing anymore," he said, brushing her hand away.
"I have said what I have to say. Now I must think of how I
mean to deal with my sons and the Ta-Hai-Kai."

"Nakai . . ."

"We have nothing more to say." He took three strides before
he turned back and said very coldly, "I have decided to take a
second wife. Rani-Ta shall be my woman too."

He walked on swiftly, his loose, powerful stride taking him
away from her. His words, however, had already taken him ir-
retrievably away from her. All that they had shared was suddenly in the shadows of the past. Ki-Ki-Tai turned back toward
the river, holding her breast as if a knife had been driven into it.

★ ★ ★ ★ ★

The village was bustling, but as Nakai looked around, he noticed that there were no young men to be seen in the camp. None but Ta-Ah-Omo, who was not right in the head and sat drawing in the dirt with a stick. Other than him there were no young men between the ages of sixteen and twenty anywhere to be seen. Nakai saw Winter Owl and he walked on more swiftly to catch up with the civil chief of the Kiowas.

"Winter Owl!"

"Nakai! Welcome, my cousin. It is good to see you."

"We must counsel."

Winter Owl frowned. "You are troubled."

"Very troubled."

Winter Owl took his cousin by the arm and turned him away from the camp. "We shall counsel if that is what you wish. Walk with me a way first and tell me what is troubling your heart."

The two men walked through the long grass to the north. Their passing startled three pheasants, a male and two females, and they took to wing.

"What is it, Nakai?" Winter Owl asked, watching the birds circle and return to the grass.

"These Ghost Warriors, what have you said to them, Winter Owl?"

"No one knows who they are," Winter Owl said, but he was obviously lying.

"They have defied the council, broken your treaty, Cousin."

"Yes," Winter Owl said, "I know this." He spread his hands. "What can be done, Nakai? You must talk to them."

"It is not my place to do so, Winter Owl," Nakai said with some heat, "it is yours."

They walked on slowly; the sun was warm on their backs, the scent of the grass sweet. A single puffy cloud drifted slowly past, shadowing the land briefly. Winter Owl asked, "Who is with us,

189

Nakai? Who can we truly count on?"

"Me, of course. Koto, certainly. And Eagle Heart. Falcon
. . ."

"Falcon is with the Ta-Hai-Kai," Winter Owl said sadly. "He
is a sort of tribal elder, an advisor."

"Who is their real leader?" Nakai asked.

"Opaga, I think."

"Koto will be furious with his son. With both of them."

"It is rumored that your sons ride with the Ghost Warriors as
well," Winter Owl said without looking at his cousin.

"Yes, I know. These young men have broken the council's
decree. They are risking all of our lives."

Winter Owl nodded slowly. As always, he was unwilling to
take the initiative, to make a decision. "Perhaps," he said finally,
his eyes brightening, "we could blame it all on the Comanches.
We could tell the white soldiers that . . ."

"No!" Nakai was incensed. "Are we to blame what our sons
have done on others? Is that honorable?"

"You have no love for the Comanches. Think of Osolo. Of
Wotasha," Winter Owl said.

"Speak no more of this," Nakai said with barely suppressed
anger. At times his cousin infuriated him.

"The white men have nearly completed their new fort, Nakai. Many more soldiers arrive daily. I think that one day they
will cross the river to exact revenge if we do nothing. Perhaps
we should move away."

"I will move when we always move, with the seasons, for the
winter buffalo hunt, when the corn is in and the green corn
festival has been celebrated."

Winter Owl shook his head worriedly. He did not like
confrontation. "Then what can we do, Cousin Nakai?"

"I don't know yet," Nakai said honestly, "I only know that
something must be done. That is why I believe we should sum-

mon the full council to discuss this."

"What will you suggest to them?" Winter Owl asked.

"I will suggest," Nakai said solemnly, "that we offer to counsel with the white leaders as well to explain matters and try to maintain the peace. *After* we have resolved to expel every member of this so-called Ta-Hai-Kai from the tribe."

"Your sons, Nakai . . . !"

"Each young brave who has broken the laws of our tribe and disobeyed the council must be banished forevermore. They have defied us and written their own code. Very well, let them live apart from us if they cannot obey our laws. Otherwise, we have no law."

Winter Owl was speechless, Nakai turned abruptly and walked away from his cousin, leaving the civil chief of the Kiowas gaping.

Did Nakai know what he was proposing? To anger the parents of every young warrior who followed the shaman, Washai, and the Ta-Hai-Kai way? It would destroy the tribe. And Washai himself! Could the true prophet be banished as well?

To banish all of those young men! It was the future fighting core of the Kiowa nation that Hungry Wolf meant to exile. The tribe would not have the strength to resist the white soldiers if the day came when there was open warfare.

Winter Owl walked on. Traveling through the oaks on the knoll above the old shaman White Moon's lodge, he looked across the river, the wind bending the feathers in his hair.

Yes, the whites had nearly finished their new fort, and he could see bare earth far to the north where more whites were carving at the soil, breaking ground for their settlement. Even more distantly, he could see structures of wood rising. They were building a permanent village for their people.

It was only a matter of time, he knew, before they crossed the river. When their numbers had grown sufficiently, they would

191

come. It gave even Winter Owl, the most timid of men, to wonder if Washai and his Ghost Warriors were not right— perhaps now was the time to strike, to drive them back before they gained still more strength. Later, visiting Nakai in his empty lodge, Winter Owl broached the subject again. Perhaps, Winter Owl had said, the whites should be driven out now while there was time.

Nakai had listened in silence and then said, "No, it must not be done. Our word has been given: that we would stay on our side of the river, they on theirs. I did not like that treaty then; I do not like it now."

"Then, Nakai, why . . ."

"Because our *word* has been given, Winter Owl! *You,* yourself, made the treaty with the white leader, did you not? They have not broken the treaty yet. If anyone has done so, it is us. We are an honorable people. Honor does not shelter lies."

Ki-Ki-Tai had no emotions left to spend. She had passed from fury to tears to quiet sullenness.

Now as she watched Nakai undress in the night of their lodge she found she had nothing left to stir her heart in any direction whatever.

The council had met and the decision had been made—Nakai had seen to it that her sons could never return again. Never. They had been banished from the tribe, irrevocably separated from their mother.

"It is right and honorable, Ki-Ki-Tai," Nakai had told her. How could it be right, she wondered, to separate her from her children? But it was done. The old men had banished the young—funny, she realized, when they all wanted the same thing: to expel the whites and hold their lands.

"Are you finished with your tears now?" Nakai asked, crawling into their bed. His voice was one she did not know. He was no longer Nakai, but only Hungry Wolf. She fed him; they spoke of things that did not matter. His eyes no longer followed her as she moved around the lodge. His thoughts were no longer really with her.

"I am finished, Nakai."

"Good. It was the only way. We shall speak of it no more."

Then he rolled against her, his strong length pressing against her body. She responded woodenly. It was her duty still. He clenched her without caress, his body tense and dominant.

Then abruptly he stopped, feeling no real response, only her deliberately summoned reactions.

She wanted to tell him why she could not respond, that he was clubbing their love and tenderness to insensitivity, but that would only anger him more.

"Not even that will you give me," he said, withdrawing furiously. She reached out to him. *I will try,* she wanted to say, but could not. Where was the gentleness, the bond between their hearts stirred through the joining of their bodies?

"Nakai . . ."

It was already too late. He had thrown a blanket over his shoulders and risen. Now he stood over her, only a dark silhouette in the night.

"You are a traitor in so many ways," he said brutally. "I am going to my wife's lodge."

He swept out through the tent flap. In the night she could imagine him stalking toward Rani-Ta, who would be lying there waiting, smiling at her victory . . .

Ki-Ki-Tai closed her eyes very tightly. A few small tears escaped. Her heart continued to pound.

She wondered if, after all, it was not Kianceta who had been the more clever. She and her Oliver leaving all of this rancor, frustration, and hatred behind. For Ki-Ki there was no place to go. None at all. She rolled over and tried to smother her emotions with elusive sleep.

He was naked, angular, and proud, very proud. Isadora Kittinger rose from her quilt-covered bed to find Ben Ramsey standing over the child's crib, staring silently down at him. Charles slept peacefully, his dark hair across his brow, his finely lashed eyes closed, his unformed nose snoring so softly that it was like a distant breeze in the willows. Isadora slipped up beside Ramsey and put her arms around his naked waist, resting her head against his strong shoulder.

"He really is mine," Ramsey said.

"Only yours."

"My son. Yes, I can see that," Ramsey said, still fondly watching the sleeping boy. "He should be living with me then," he said, turning sharply toward her. He held Isadora tightly. The moon was a silver half-globe beyond the nursery window. Ramsey continued quietly. "He should have his father to raise him. Not . . ."

"He should have a man for a father," Isadora agreed. "He should have his real father." Her voice lowered to a whisper. "I should have a real man, my real husband."

"Yes." Ramsey bent his head and kissed Isadora's lush mouth. How long could this continue? Ned Kittinger was bound to return from Texas soon. What if he arrived in the middle of the night, unexpectedly?

"I can't stand the thought of him in your bed," he said.

"I would never let him . . ."

"How do I know that!" Ramsey said so sharply that the baby stirred. "How do *you* know it, Isadora?"

"Because I swear it."

Ramsey looked into her eyes by moonlight and then took her hand for a moment, squeezing it. He walked from the nursery then, and because Bettina and Missie were in the house, he walked back to the bedroom and began to dress. Isadora watched him with a sense of loss. She wanted to make love to him again.

"What can we do?" she asked. She had gone to the French doors and drawn one of the curtains back to look out at the moon dangling above the dark land.

"About what?" Ben Ramsey asked, as he rose from the bed to button his trousers, although he knew full well what she was talking about.

"We can't go on like this!" Isadora said too loudly. "It's too painful, Ben. Pretending. Wanting you all the time."

"Does Bettina know about us?"

"I don't think so. She's so involved with her pregnancy, knitting, decorating the other room, planning for Kent's return from Texas . . . I envy her happiness."

"Don't I make you happy?" Ramsey asked, tucking in his shirt. She let the curtain fall and put her arms around him.

"Of course you do, darling. That is the point. I have to have all of you. All!"

"Then we'll find something to do about it," Ben Ramsey said in an almost offhanded way.

There was something chilling in his tone. He had said nothing, really, but she was suddenly afraid. After all, he had killed so many men in the war . . . but perhaps that was not what he had meant at all. She looked into his eyes, but she could read nothing in them.

"I'll be back to claim what's mine," he said. "My child, my woman."

"Everything is yours, Ben," she said, her breathing rapid and excited. "I have money, you know. Lots of money. You wouldn't need to stay in the army. You could resign your commission and run the ranch."

He smiled a different sort of smile now, enigmatic and distant. "Never, my dear. Never. I *am* a soldier. It wasn't chance that put me into uniform. The part of me that is a man needs conflict to thrive, to exist."

"I don't understand that."

"Nevertheless," he said flatly as if his lecture had ended, "that is the way I am. I crave it. Can you understand?"

"Yes, of course!" she cried out a little desperately. "Yes, Ben. I can accept anything that you need to do. It is what makes you Ben Ramsey."

"Yes," he said, kissing her forehead, "it is."

"Our other trouble . . . ?"

"I will take care of that. One way or the other. I won't be able to see you for a little while, Isadora. You know that, don't you?"

"I know that," she said, her cheek against his chest, her arms around him.

"But it won't be for long," he promised. "Do you believe me?"

"I believe everything you tell me, Ben."

"Good." He lifted her chin. "Take care of my little son. There are solutions. Leave it all to me."

"I just want to get home to my wife," Nesbitt Kittinger was saying. "That's all I am waiting for."

"You and me both," Kent O'Day agreed. The two of them sat around a low-burning campfire with two Texans, Pritchard and Amos Starr, the firelight glow highlighting and shadowing their faces. It would be sunup in an hour. Beyond the light of the small fires the cattle lowed and milled, having risen early, ready to move on despite the weariness they must be feeling after the long drive north.

"I envy you, men," Pritchard said. He was young, pale, and

freckled, an amiable and adventurous wanderer Kent had hired to help drive the herd of cattle back from Texas. "Havin' womenfolk and a home to go back to. Us," he nudged Amos Starr, "we're riding away from any home we ever had, it seems."

"One place is as good as another. They're all the same," Starr said, drinking his strong coffee from an enameled steel cup. He was also young, younger than Kent O'Day, perhaps, but he gave the impression of wide experience. Dark, perpetually unwashed, there was a strange cast in his eyes. It was difficult to read any expression in them. Unfortunately, he was overly fond of the twin pistols he carried. More than once Kent had had to admonish Starr about firing at rabbits from horseback with his .44s, heedless of the chance of stampeding the herd of long-horns.

"Come morning," Ned Kittinger said, stretching his arms overhead. He was grinning with satisfaction. He had secretly doubted that he had the strength for this trip, but he had made it and not disgraced himself, although the work was something that did not come easily to him. "When morning comes, we'll be home on Cimarron, Kent!"

"You know, Ned," Kent O'Day said. "It'd be all right with me if you wanted to ride ahead. Surprise Isadora."

"No. No, Kent," Kittinger said seriously. "We started this drive together. We'll end it together." He tossed the dregs of his coffee into the low-burning fire and rose, stretching his back. The first glint of golden dawn was touching the eastern horizon. "Let's get those steers ready to move down the trail, men. Tomorrow night, Kent, we sleep in our own beds."

"My God! Elizabeth, come here!"

Elizabeth O'Day turned from her cooking and looked toward the yard where Tom stood, hands on hips, staring southward. Wiping her hands on a towel, she went onto the front porch.

She shielded her eyes and looked southward as well. Then she, too, saw them. A huge reddish dust cloud rose into the air above the dry grass plains, and there was a rumble as of distant thunder beneath her feet.

"They made it!" Tom said, turning red eyes toward her. "I'm damned if Kent didn't make it!"

Elizabeth slowly lowered her hand. She could now see more clearly, and the anonymous dark mass on the horizon took on form and substance; she could see the herd of longhorn steers and the outriders pushing them forward, hear the whistles and yells, the complaining lowing of the cattle.

Tom had forgotten his usual etiquette in his excitement and drank openly from the jug of whisky he was carrying, all pretense momentarily lost.

Elizabeth braced herself against the porch upright. Her heart raced a little. True, the herd had made it, but was Kent all right?

"Look at all that money on the hoof!" Tom said exultantly. He drank again from his jug, celebrating the arriving wealth although he had no stake in it.

The herd grew larger in their eyes, more vibrant as it approached, each animal taking on an individual shape. Their long horns clacked together. They were being driven directly toward the farm!

"They'll trample everything!" Elizabeth said anxiously.

"He'll turn 'em. Kent'll turn 'em. He just wanted us to see 'em."

It didn't seem possible for anyone to turn that mass of onrushing animals. They seemed to be moving much more quickly now.

"Not that it really matters," Elizabeth thought bitterly. There was nothing to trample, really. Tom had not worked a day in the fields since he had returned from the war. Perhaps he thought this year's corn would raise itself. She thought that he did not even know how many days were passing unheeded, lost in the endless repetition of his pattern of drinking and sleeping, rising and drinking again.

Tom was very excited about the herd. It was as if he had encouraged Kent in this project, supported him in his efforts, and now Kent was returning to show his father what *they* had accomplished. Elizabeth knew it had been nothing of the sort. Tom had spent many evenings complaining about Kent's absence when it was time to begin turning earth for the new crops.

About Oliver, Tom never said a word.

"Look at 'em come, Liz! There must be a thousand head, easy."

Elizabeth said nothing; she stood watching the wall of heated steers approaching their farm. She glanced around looking for Regret, wanting to get him out of the way, forgetting that the dog had run off a long time ago. On the day Tom had kicked it so savagely. But then, with dogs, one never knew. They sometimes came home after the longest time . . .

"There he is!" Tom shouted, pointing.

Elizabeth peered into the sunlight and then she, too, saw Kent riding point for the trail herd. He wore a Texas-style hat and chaps. His face was sunburned and whiskered. He looked years older, much tougher. He rode up to the house ahead of the herd, bringing with him a dirt-smeared, weary Ned Kittinger. As Elizabeth watched, smiling now, the vaqueros did manage to turn the herd slightly, just enough so that they missed her yard. Kent turned his head and yelled back to the vaqueros.

"Let 'em run, men! They smell that water now."

The cattle streamed past in an endless dark rush, racing uncontained toward the Cimarron. The cowboys let them go.

Kent rode toward the porch, swinging down while his horse

was still moving. He walked to his father and the two men shook hands. Elizabeth stepped down from the porch. Kent looked at her and then turned his eyes away. It was as if an arrow had pierced Elizabeth's heart. Still! Would he hold his anger forever? She wanted to scream, "I am your mother!" but she held her tongue.

Nesbitt Kittinger, seemingly embarrassed, dismounted, and with a nod to Tom O'Day, walked stiffly to the porch, leading his weary horse.

"Good morning, Mrs. O'Day," he said, lifting his hat. "Have you a drink of cool water for a thirsty man?"

"Certainly," she answered with a wavering smile. "Come into the house, Ned." She glanced again at Tom and Kent, deep in celebratory conversation, and led the way inside.

"I expect a lot of people didn't think they'd ever see us again," Ned said, nodding his thanks as Elizabeth poured a glass of water from the pitcher in the coolness of the kitchen.

"I don't know, Ned. I suppose everyone only wished you success."

"Well," Ned said, drinking his water in three gulps, "they don't have to wish any longer."

He was flushed with the pride of his success. Proud beyond words. Had the excursion to Texas been a sort of odyssey, searching for his manhood?

"Was there much trouble on the trail, Ned?"

"A lot of different kinds of trouble, Mrs. O'Day, but we didn't lose a man. I can't say I'd want to do it again anytime soon," he said with a laugh, "but I wouldn't have missed it for the world!"

"Your cattle are really scattered now," Elizabeth said, looking out the window to where the steers were lined up in what seemed to be a miles-long line along the Cimarron, drinking from the quiet river. "Won't it be terribly hard to gather them together again?"

"No, ma'am," Ned said with careless pride. "We have a good crew. They'll bunch them again in no time. They won't fight it after their bellies are full of water. Then, there's nothing left to it. We just push them up to my land.

"You know, Mrs. O'Day, I sure owe your son a debt of thanks. I wasn't much for the idea at first. He and Isadora—they're the ones who were sure it could be done."

"Will it be hard for you, Ned, to switch from farming to ranching?" she asked.

"Well, once I would have thought so, but I've gotten used to these beasts along the trail. Then, you know," he admitted, "I wasn't really much of a farmer to begin with. Maybe I've found my calling. Finally."

"I hope so, Ned. I know you worked hard for this."

"Yes, I really did . . . sorry! Kent's back in the saddle, ready to go. Thank you for the water, Mrs. O'Day. It was fine to see you again. Come over for supper some night, you and Tom, won't you?"

"We'd be happy to, Ned," she said with a manufactured smile. He put on his hat and walked toward the door, the unique sound of his Texas boots with their spurs ringing against the wooden floor as he went out into the bright sunlight where still fine dust from the passing herd filtered down toward the dry earth.

Elizabeth followed him back out onto the porch, watching as Ned Kittinger swung aboard his horse and rode to where Kent waited, bent forward in his saddle, still talking to his father.

Then, laughing at some remark, Kent straightened up, lifted a hand to Tom, and he and Ned rode slowly from the yard. Tom was beaming with pride as he watched them go. He took one more drink from his jug and then walked slowly toward the barn, smiling, talking to himself.

Elizabeth returned to the house, shutting the door against the dust and the emptiness outside.

Ki-Ki-Tai stood looking at the fresh grave. Nothing moved on the sacred island but the breeze from the river. There was no sound except that of the cicadas and the frogs. The ranks of pine trees swayed in silent unison.

The old shaman, White Moon, was dead.

Only the women had come to bury him, to cut and raise the burial stakes around his grave and make a roof of bark. Ki-Ki-Tai and Momo had done this along with White Moon's nearly blind sister, Oh-Ka-Shay. Momo had taken the old woman home hours ago in her canoe, leaving Ki-Ki-Tai alone on the island.

If White Moon had had horses or mules, they would have been slaughtered at the gravesite to travel the Bright Trail with him, but White Moon had nothing left. He had burned his lodge with all of his goods in it the night before he had died. They had found him in the cold of morning, arms crossed, sleeping the long sleep beside the gray ashes of his life. Now there was nothing left of the shaman on this earth.

Ki-Ki had visited her own father's grave earlier, sitting against the cold earth, trying to speak to him, to tell him how she felt. Her mother had been buried on the far plains at a place unmarked and unremembered.

Now White Moon was gone as well. Everyone was gone, and there were no good things, new things, to replace them. It seemed as if the world had quit growing, flowering, renewing itself. The only season was the season of death.

Nothing. There was nothing left but the breeze across White Moon's grave and the long river, flowing away never to return.

★ ★ ★ ★ ★

"There! You see, Ketah?"

"I am sorry, Opaga. I barely believed you when you told me."

The two young warriors lay in the long grass looking across the river to where hundreds, perhaps thousands, of cattle drank.

"And why do they need so many, Ketah? I will tell you," Opaga said. "To feed all of the whites who are coming. Washai was right, he is always right. We should have struck earlier and with more force. If only your father had listened to the true prophet. But Hungry Wolf has already grown old in his prime. His eyes are blind with age. His heart has grown too old."

Ketah was briefly angry. He didn't like anyone speaking ill of his father, the pride of his youth. Hungry Wolf, respected by all, admired by all. Strong and sure and brave. But perhaps Opaga was right. Perhaps his father's eyes had grown blind.

"It may be so," Ketah was forced to admit. "He has said he will not come forth to do battle with them."

"And those of us who would fight? Us! He has seen to it that we are banished from the tribe, Ketah." Opaga's eyes searched Ketah's deeply. "We are now our own band. The true shaman is on our side. He has spoken the truth to us. When has Washai told us lies?"

The two young warriors eased back from the river's edge and sat in the sun, talking.

"We have to counsel with Falcon," Opaga said. "He is an experienced warrior. He could devise a good war plan. It must be done, Ketah! The enemy is a stride away from us."

"I know it, Opaga," Ketah said, rubbing his eyes. Even after all that had happened he did not wish to go against his father, but everything One-Feather was saying was true. If the Kiowas did not make their fight now, then when? Were they to wait until there were thousands upon thousands of whites across the river and the People had no chance at all of survival?

Opaga stood and Ketah, dusting his hands, did the same.

"You are with us are you not, my brother?" Opaga asked.

"There is no other way. If my father cannot see what is happening, I can. We must do what we must."

"Yes." Opaga placed his hands on Ketah's shoulders, gripping tightly. Their eyes locked.

"Ta-Hai-Kai," the Ghost Warrior vowed.

"Ta-Hai-Kai, Opaga. As it must be."

CHAPTER SEVEN

It was a morning like few others. The sun was bright, splendoring on the Cimarron River, and the air was crisp and invigorating; the willows moved in synchronization with the light western breeze. Ned Kittinger rode across the short grass plains toward the fort. The buckskin horse he had purchased in Texas moved with fluid agility. It had a black mane and tail and one black ear. A quick cutter, long-winded and fast, it was a pleasure to ride. Word had reached Kittinger that morning that Ben Ramsey was ready to arrange for a purchase of a hundred steers.

Nothing could mar the morning's exhilaration.

Well, he reflected, Isadora had not slept with him the night before, but he had been gone so long, it would take her some time. And then, she had never been very interested in that sort of thing anyway. Still, Ned reflected, there were few luckier men than he. A successful cattle drive, an army contract for beef, a beautiful wife, two healthy children, a good horse . . . Ned began to whistle as he rode.

A mile from the fort he was surprised to see Ben Ramsey riding toward him. Reining in, he waited for the army officer to reach him. As Ramsey approached, Ned noticed that Ramsey was wearing captain's bars, his permanent rank, instead of a major's oak leaves. Ned vowed to say nothing about the reduction in rank.

"Good morning, Ramsey," he said as the officer halted his horse beside him. "Did I get crossed up? I thought you wanted

205

to meet me in your office."

"No, no," Ramsey said with a smile. He removed his hat and wiped out the sweatband. "There's so much noise over there with all of that construction that I thought I'd ride out to meet you." He replaced his hat and lifted his chin. "How about going down to the river, finding some shade?" He patted his tunic. "I've got the contract right here."

"Suits me," Ned agreed, turning his horse.

"That's a nice animal you've got there, Ned."

"Rode him all the way from Texas. I bought him from a cowboy who was down on his luck. He told me it could work steers with the best of them, and he wasn't lying."

They rode slowly toward the river, watching its sun-glitter through the trunks of the willows.

"Have you been over to see the new town yet, Ned?" Ramsey asked.

"Not yet. I figured Isadora and I would take the buggy over there one of these days and see how they're coming along."

"That's going to be good for you, isn't it? I mean those people will be wanting beef to eat too."

"It's great for me, Ramsey. I'll tell you, I don't see how things could be going much better!"

Entering a willow grove, they swung down in the shady cool of morning, leaving their horses to graze on the lush grass. Kittinger dipped his hat into the river and splashed water over his face and neck.

"A hundred head is what you were thinking of?" Kittinger asked. "That's what Isadora told me."

"A hundred, yes. In increments of twenty steers." Ramsey withdrew the contract from his tunic and handed it to Ned Kittinger to study.

It was a standard procurement form with Kittinger's name filled in in the right place. Ramsey had already signed it.

"I can't see anything wrong with this," Kittinger said.

"There isn't. It's a good deal all around, Ned. The men'll be damned happy to have a steady supply of beef again."

"Yes, I imagine so."

"If you just want to sign it . . ."

"Sure."

Ramsey offered a pen and a tiny traveling inkwell to Nesbitt Kittinger, who knelt down so that he could write on one knee.

He thought nothing about it when Ramsey came to stand behind him, watching.

Ramsey reached out and grabbed a handful of Kittinger's hair, yanking his head back, and in the same movement he slashed across the rancher's throat with a razor-edged bowie knife. Blood drenched Kittinger's shirtfront instantly. His nearly severed head lolled to one side as Ramsey let him fall forward to pitch against the earth. He rolled to his back and then twitched several times, staring up at the blank sky, and then Ramsey watched his eyes cloud over and all movement cease.

Panting, Ramsey stepped away, wiping the knife blade on his pant leg. He smeared his own face and hands with Kittinger's blood and then reached down to grab a handful of dirt, rubbing that on his face and uniform.

Standing over his victim, Ramsey did not move for a moment. His chest rose and fell with a strange, nearly sexual exultance. In a way, he supposed, that was exactly what it was.

Kneeling then, Ramsey grabbed a handful of Kittinger's hair, lifting his head. Deliberately he sawed a patch of scalp free and rose again. He walked to the river and threw the scalp in, watching as the current carried it away. Returning to the body he stood thinking. Ramsey grabbed the front of his own tunic and ripped it, popping three buttons so that it hung open.

Not good enough.

Deliberately Ramsey walked to a nearby moss-covered granite

boulder and took a deep breath. Then he slammed his fist against the rock, hard. Bones broke and pain shot through his hand and up his arm.

Gritting his teeth, he stepped back, holding the broken hand with the other. He drew his knife from its sheath again, staring at the bright polished steel of the bowie's blade before he raised the knife to his face and in one swift movement, slashed his own forehead. Warm blood trickled into his eyes, stinging them. He wiped it away with his sleeve. Removing his yellow scarf, he tied it around his head. Satisfied now, he took one last look back at Nesbitt Kittinger, walked to his horse, mounted, and rode slowly away, leading Kittinger's buckskin pony.

He had been five minutes gone from the grove before the man emerged from the willows where he had been napping, still exhausted from the long drive up from Texas.

"Well, well," Amos Starr said to himself, looking at the distant form of the army officer and then to Ned Kittinger's body. "It just goes to show you never can tell, doesn't it? No, sir, you just never can tell."

He stored the scene away in the compartment of his mind reserved for information that might prove useful in the future, and returned to the willows to saddle his own horse for the ride back to the Kittinger ranch.

The three men rambled on in disconnected discussion.

"Well, what can we do now?"

"It was Hungry Wolf—it had to be."

"Does it hurt much, Captain Ramsey?"

"Twelve hundred steers. What if they hit the herd?"

"We've got enough men . . ."

"No one's speaking of poor Ned."

"In the war we'd have known what to do."

"Got your head pretty good, didn't they?"

"How many were there, did you say?"

Elizabeth rested her elbow on the table, her head on the heel of her hand. It had been entirely the wrong night for a social dinner at the Kittingers'. Far from wishing to postpone the gathering after the death of her husband, Isadora had become even more insistent that they come, sending one of the Mexican riders over with a written invitation. Elizabeth and Bettina exchanged a glance as the men rattled on. The girl was no more comfortable than Elizabeth was. Her eyes were red from crying.

It would have been an uncomfortable situation in any event. Tom was growing very drunk at the table. Kent was ignoring his wife. Isadora was excited, frantically so at times. Then, as if remembering, she would let a tear or two trickle down her cheek. The men were going on and on about the need for retaliation; the women were silent except for Isadora, who constantly asked Ramsey about his injuries—a deep slash across his forehead that was bound with a fresh bandage but still showed a faint crimson stain through the gauze, and a broken hand, splinted and taped.

"When you rode in . . ." Isadora was saying.

"I apologize," Ramsey said, "I wasn't sure I could make it back to the fort."

". . . Torn and dirty and bloody!"

Did you even think about Father? Bettina thought. She was young, but not as ignorant as her mother seemed to believe. Isadora's concern for Ramsey was much more than neighborly consideration. It was obvious to Bettina, had been obvious for a long while, that there was something between her mother and Ramsey. Whether they had done anything about it or not, she didn't care to know, but she knew her mother.

"In the war we'd've known what to do," Tom O'Day repeated in a slurred voice. They had all been drinking a light white wine with dinner, but Tom had had no need for it. He had nearly fallen off the buckboard on the trip over to the ranch.

Kent sat scowling, running a finger around the rim of his wine glass. His homecoming had turned to ashes. And it had been such a glorious arrival on the morning he had returned in triumph to find Bettina, her belly rounded with his child, waiting at the gate, tears of joy in her eyes. The damned Indians! But then, it had been building on Cimarron for a long time. He glanced once at his mother, briefly met her gaze, and then returned to studying his untouched wine.

"What is the army's plan?" Kent asked.

"We've still got a treaty," Ramsey said with a doubtful shake of his head.

"Obviously abrogated," Kent said.

"That's up to Regiment," Ramsey replied. "One incident . . . well, I don't know what General Cox will come back with."

"Maybe the Kiowas could be convinced to turn the guilty parties over to us."

"I don't remember an occasion when they've agreed to anything like that."

"Don't any of you remember that it was *Father* who was killed, who is lying dead out in the barn!" Bettina exploded. Tears streamed down her cheeks. "All you seem to be able to think about is revenge!"

"There's no better way to honor him," Tom O'Day said, shocking Bettina and Elizabeth both.

"We do remember Father, Bettina," Isadora said, reaching to take her daughter's hand. Consolingly, she added, "Perhaps we are all trying to avoid thinking about his death too much."

It seemed obvious to Bettina that Isadora had other things she would rather be thinking of.

Ramsey.

"I think I'm getting a headache, Kent," Bettina said. "And I'm exhausted. I need to rest."

"Of course," he said with concern, rising. "You can't let this upset you so much that it ruins your health. We have a baby to think of."

He held her chair as she rose with a few perfunctory apologies, and offered his arm, escorting her down the hallway toward their bedroom. Halfway along the dark corridor Bettina stopped, turned, and put her arms around Kent's waist.

"Kent, don't forget what you just said."

"I don't understand."

"We *do* have a baby to think of, Kent. Do not let them talk you into doing anything that would cause our baby to risk losing his father."

"If it's decided . . ."

"No! I will not have you going off to any sort of battle. They have soldiers to do that sort of thing if it becomes necessary. I want you to promise me that you won't get involved."

Kent stood silently looking into her blue eyes by the faint lantern light. There was a light rain falling outside, playing through the trees.

"I can't make any such promise, Bettina. This is our land. If it has to be defended I will not shirk my duty."

Bettina's arms fell away. Slowly she turned and started toward the bedroom. Kent stretched out an ineffective hand after her.

"Bett . . ." But she kept walking, silent but for the sound of her rustling skirts. The bedroom door closed quietly, definitely behind her.

The dinner party was breaking up when Kent returned. His father stood unsteadily near the door, hat in hand. His mother was slipping a shawl across her shoulders. Isadora was helping Captain Ramsey with his cape, fastening it for him as he held his wounded hand high.

Isadora could not keep from looking into Ramsey's eyes. Their conversation was silent and deep. The others, if they had not already suspected, would read the admiration and the secret messages there and soon know.

Isadora did not *know*. Ramsey had told her the same story he had told the others. Four Kiowa warriors had attacked them as they stood near the river, discussing the contract for the army beef purchase. In a brief, furious struggle, Ned Kittinger had been killed. Ramsey had been able to fight his attackers off, but by the time he could assist Ned, it had already been too late.

Was the story true? Isadora did not know and did not wish to know *ever* with certainty. This was so much easier; to believe the story was to banish any guilt she might have felt about causing the situation. Her suspicions, she considered, should have made her slightly afraid of Ramsey, but they caused no such apprehension. She felt bonded to him—even subjugated, in a way: an emotion totally new to her experiences with men. She only knew that when she and Ramsey were finally together she would never have to fear other men.

Isadora felt only a vague unease about Ned's death, the way one feels uneasy in the presence of any death, a fear for her own mortality, perhaps. It was, she had to admit, much as if someone had taken an old dog she had not the nerve to put down, and taken care of the chore for her.

"Let me know, Ben," Tom O'Day was saying, "how the situation develops."

"I'll see that you're kept up to date, Tom," Ramsey promised. "For now all we can do is keep everyone on increased alert at the fort. Our patrols will be doubled and more frequent. If there's any word from General Cox, I'll be sure to notify you. He may want to come down here himself to assess the situation." Ramsey winced as he put on his hat. He could feel the wound on his forehead open a little. "We'll just have to wait and see what happens, Tom."

"Wait until more people are killed!"

"Yes, well, there's nothing else to be done, Tom. Things are different out here. We don't have a declared war. I'm a soldier. I can't ride without orders, you understand that better than anyone."

"Well if what they've done isn't an act of war . . ." Tom seemed to lose his train of thought. He mumbled a few more indistinct words, his face suffused with anger. Elizabeth wanted only to get away from this house, this belligerent talk.

She never thought the day would come, but it had. She was deeply and completely humiliated to be in her husband's company.

Kent opened the door, shaking his father's hand with both of his, and the O'Days went out onto the porch. A Mexican had brought their buckboard around and they clambered up onto the seat with a light, cool drizzle still falling from the dark, reckless sky.

Tom took the reins and they drove slowly away with no one watching after them.

"Goodnight, Ramsey," Kent said, shaking the officer's left hand.

"You're going to bed, Kent?" Isadora asked in surprise. "It's early still."

"There are some things I have to talk to Bettina about. If you see Miguel before I do in the morning, tell him I haven't forgotten the bonus I promised every vaquero who made the drive north with us, but he has to make his men understand the Kiowa situation—I can't have them celebrating with gallons of tequila."

"All right, Kent," she promised. "I'll tell him. Goodnight."

Ramsey and Isadora waited until Kent's bootheels quit echoing down the hallway before they said goodnight.

"How long do we have to wait?" Isadora asked, clinging to the lapels of his tunic, drawing herself closer to him. Ramsey smiled and kissed her very lightly on the cheek.

"Not long. People understand out here. They know a woman cannot be alone in this part of the country, not even a rich woman."

"Ben, was it . . . ?" She started to ask the question, then closed her mouth and shook her head. "Will I see you tomorrow?"

"No. There's too much to do. The threat of war with the Kiowas is very real."

"Don't say that. It frightens me."

"All right," Ramsey agreed. "I won't say it."

But the threat of war was very real indeed. Acquiring Isadora, her fortune, and the ranch was not the only benefit of Nesbitt's death. There would be military action on Cimarron. Regiment be damned! Ramsey would cross the river on his own if he had to invent yet another pretext. Now was the time to claw his way up in the ranks past these desk officers and cowards.

Captain Ramsey. It rankled. They believed he was only worthy of higher rank in time of war when his skills were needed? Very well, then there would be a war. With any luck, he would come out of the Kiowa war with silver oak leaves at the least. Yes, he decided, looking around the chandelier-lighted house—*his house*—and then down into the eyes of the adoring, dark-haired woman he held, things could be managed very well indeed by a man with a vision. The door to the future was open now and he had but to march through it.

Outside the wind had increased, making the rain seem harder than it was. Ramsey's horse had been brought around. He stood on the porch for a while, deep in thought.

He wasn't aware of the figure moving toward him from the deeper shadows until the man was nearly beside him. Startled, Ramsey controlled himself and turned cold eyes on the stranger. The man was a cowhand with odd eyes that seemed to look in no direction, in all directions.

"Yes?" Ramsey said imperiously. "What is it?"

"Nothing. I just wanted to have a closer look at you," the ragged cowhand said.

"Well, you've had your look," Ramsey said to the man in the shadows. "What is it you're looking for?"

"Nothing. My name's Amos Starr." When Ramsey didn't reply, he went on. "I work on the ranch here, you see."

"Is there a point to any of this, Amos Starr?" Ramsey asked, growing irritated. "I don't have the time to listen to your babbling. Why don't you go somewhere and sober up?"

"Oh, I'm quite sober, sir," Starr said, laying a slightly insolent emphasis on the last word. "I just kinda wanted to introduce myself to you. You won't forget my name?"

"Why," an exasperated Ramsey asked, "should I bother to remember it?"

"No reason," Starr said. "Just a funny coincidence. I know you're a soldier, sir. But you see, I know something about Indians, too. As a matter of fact, I saw a Kiowa attack not far from here. Down along the river." Starr smiled, showing broken teeth. "It wasn't a pretty sight, sir. Not pretty at all."

"Listen here . . . !"

"Goodnight, Captain Ramsey. That was all I had to say. Now I know who you are and you know who I am. Don't forget the name—it's Amos Starr. One day we'll have a longer talk."

Then Starr withdrew into the shadows. Ramsey watched him go, his eyes narrowed. The mist swirled around him. His horse stamped impatiently. Then, dismissing Starr as a maniac, he mounted and started back toward the fort, leaving Isadora to watch him from behind the draperies of the lighted house.

★　★　★　★　★

"Eagle Heart?"

"I will go, Nakai."

Hungry Wolf nodded. There was nothing more to be discussed. The council had decided that the only course of action left open to them was to talk to the white leaders to try to prevent war. They must be made to understand that the raiders had been branded as traitors and banished from the tribe.

As the men rose and parted, Winter Owl and Nakai stood outside for a moment. It was a damp night with mist falling off and on. A cool breeze flagged the smoke rising from their tipis. Even the dogs, those allowed to, stayed inside the lodges.

"This plan must work, Nakai," Winter Owl said anxiously.

"It is you who made the treaty with the whites. Do you not trust them now?" Nakai asked, deliberately looking away from his cousin.

Winter Owl expelled his breath harshly. "I no longer know. Things seem to have changed so rapidly. I still believe we should move on to our winter campsite."

"That would only bring us into conflict with the Arapaho again. We have an agreement with them as well, Cousin. We are to stay south of the prickly pines."

"I know it." Winter Owl rubbed his forehead. "Nakai— shouldn't we send a messenger to the Comanche camp? Talk to Osolo and Wotasha to see where they would stand in case of war?"

"They will refuse to join us," Nakai said positively.

"How can they! After all the times in the past we have aided them against the Mexicans? Against the Apaches."

"Send a man then, if you will," Nakai said. "For myself, I have no faith in Osolo." He was looking across the camp with narrowed eyes. He asked Winter Owl, "Is that not Falcon's wife and children I see?"

"Yes, I think so, Nakai. Why do you ask?"

"They must go," Nakai answered. "No wife of any Ta-Hai-Kai warrior may remain in our camp."

"But she has done nothing!" Winter Owl protested.

"No," Nakai answered firmly. "But if Falcon wishes to see his wife, he will try to return. That would mean more trouble for all of us. Then I would have to kill Falcon, Winter Owl. See that the woman leaves."

Nakai walked away then. He knew that his cousin thought his heart had hardened, but there could only be one *right* decision. Not one decision in favor of Falcon's wife and another for someone else. Falcon was the biggest of traitors in Nakai's mind. He was an older warrior, not a young man misled by the ranting of Washai. No, no one who had broken the rules of the tribe could expect to be granted the benefits of tribal membership.

Nakai was weary these days. He did not like what had happened between him and Ki-Ki-Tai. He did not like the fact that he had banished his own sons, his pride! He had fewer and fewer allies left in the camp; he knew that and it troubled him. But he would not be deterred. There was a right course and a wrong one. His cause was just and honorable. So it would be; so it must be. He turned and walked slowly through the cold mist of the night toward Rani-Ta's lodge and her comfort.

"Captain Ramsey, sir?"

Sergeant Callahan stood at the entrance to Ramsey's office, his broad face showing concern. Ramsey put down the telegram he had been re-reading. It had arrived from Regiment the day before and read in part:

"Your assessment of situation on Cimarron received. Pending command decision, advise you to pursue all possible peaceful solutions to Kiowa problem.

> Brig General Harlan Cox,
>
> Commander, Ft. Riley"

"Peaceful solution to the Kiowa problem," Ramsey thought bitterly. That was a contradiction in terms. They had tried peaceful solutions going back to before the war, and they had lost the old fort and a dozen lives to the Indians. Cox, the old fool, must not have gotten his pablum for breakfast.

"What is it, Callahan?" Ramsey asked, throwing the telegram into his desk drawer.

"There's an Indian messenger at the main gate, sir. He looks like a high mucky-muck of some kind. He's got a lot of feathers on his lance."

"All right," Ramsey said with feigned unconcern. *This* was interesting, he thought. What in the world was going on now?

Walking across the parade ground with Sergeant Callahan in his wake, Ramsey went out through the high gates to where Eagle Heart sat his paint pony.

"What is it you want?" Ramsey demanded.

"Where is the other man, the older chief?" Eagle Heart asked, looking past Ramsey. He referred, apparently, to Captain Macklin, who had engineered the original treaty with the Kiowas.

"He's gone. I am the commander here now," Ramsey told him. "What is it you want?"

"To counsel," Eagle Heart said, still sitting erect on his war pony's back. The night's rain had broken and thick white cumulus clouds drifted past, casting deep shadows against the plains.

"Who is it who speaks?" Ramsey asked carefully.

"I am Eagle Heart. I speak, but the man who wishes to counsel with you is called Hungry Wolf."

Ramsey maintained his mask of indifference, but his heart rate accelerated and his mouth went slightly dry. *Hungry Wolf!*

The possibilities were enormous.

"Does he wish to speak of peace?" Ramsey asked cautiously.

"Yes. Of peace. The Kiowas do not want war. We have not made war. It is a few . . ." Eagle Heart groped for the word he wanted, "a few outlaws. This is what Hungry Wolf wishes to explain."

"I see," Ramsey said. He glanced at Callahan, who wore a bewildered smile, half-hopeful, half-wary. "All right, then. I will meet with Hungry Wolf. At the river. When the sun rises tomorrow."

"I will tell Hungry Wolf," Eagle Heart said with a nod. His eyes lifted to the palisades of the fort where a dozen soldiers with rifles watched his every move. Then carefully, he turned his horse and rode it away at a walk.

"Well, well," Ramsey said in a contemplative voice. "Hungry Wolf himself."

"You don't think it's some kind of trick, do you, sir?" Callahan asked.

"I don't know," Ramsey answered. "Maybe so. No matter, Sergeant—if it is a crooked game, we will be holding the trump card, I assure you."

Inside, Ramsey was exultant. This was a gilded opportunity. Yes—if Hungry Wolf could be eliminated, the Kiowa leadership was bound to fall apart. And if Hungry Wolf could be killed or captured, Ramsey would be applauded far and wide. Everyone knew what sort of butcher the Kiowa chief was. Yes, Ramsey thought, this was the chance he had been waiting for.

Returning to his office, Ramsey again read the telegram from General Cox and drafted a reply.

"Received your instructions, and to that end have endeavored to arrange a meeting with the Kiowa leadership.
        Regards, Capt. B. Ramsey
        Commanding Ft. Cimarron."

That completed and given to Yount, the corporal of the day, to deliver to the telegrapher, Ramsey leaned back in his chair, hands folded on his lap, a peaceful look on his chiseled face. He tested his stiff right hand. Sore still, but healing. He leaned forward and took his map of the general area from another drawer and unrolled it on his desk, planning his tactics as carefully as if it were a military maneuver.

"What did he say, Eagle Heart?"

"At dawn. On the river, Nakai."

Nakai frowned. Always cautious, he considered his choice of location. Nakai reflected that it was good to have the river at his back to avoid encirclement in case of treachery. It would do. It must.

"What did you think of this soldier, Eagle Heart? Can he be trusted?"

"I do not know, Nakai," Eagle Heart said honestly. "He is one of those men whose eyes cannot be read."

Winter Owl commented, "I wish the old leader, Macklin, were still there. He, I trusted. This younger warrior I know nothing about. What do you think, Nakai?"

"It matters not what I think now, Cousin. We have made the arrangements. There is no choice but to go ahead with the meeting."

"How many warriors will we take with us?" Eagle Heart asked.

"None. The fewer of us who go, the better. Too many men might make them doubt our intentions." Also, Nakai was thinking, the fewer they were, the fewer who would be lost in case the white soldiers did have treachery in mind.

He said, "Winter Owl and I will go. That is all."

Winter Owl sighed inaudibly. Of course, it was his place to

go. He was the civil chief, after all. It was he who had made the treaty. Still, up until that moment, he had hoped to be left out of the arrangements.

"Cousin?" Nakai asked him.

"It will be as you say, Nakai. It is my place to be there."

"You must speak carefully, Winter Owl. They must be made to understand that we speak the truth and wish to uphold the treaty."

But did *they*? Did the whites really wish for that? The question plagued Nakai. He was hardly foolish enough to believe that these negotiations would be simple or that his adversary could be trusted in everything he said, but peace must be attempted. He did not want war. And the Kiowa were not *ready* for war. They had not even the core of their young warriors remaining in the camp. They would be beaten decisively in a pitched battled as matters now stood. There must be peace! Not as an ideal, but as a necessity if the People were to continue to exist on Cimarron.

Morning was clear with only a few low remnant clouds hanging on the southern horizon. The sunrise was golden and deep orange. The river where it was not a shadowed, murky purple, was bright with shifting gold as Nakai finished dressing with Rani-Ta's help, and applied fresh paint.

"I do not want you to go," Rani-Ta said for the tenth time as she finished braiding beads into his long hair. As each time before, Nakai ignored her. He must go; there was no choice.

Rani-Ta said, "I have dark feelings in my heart, Nakai."

"It is the time of the morning when people have dark thoughts, that is all there is to that," Nakai said, picking up his feathered war lance.

His pale war horse, also freshly painted, waited impatiently for him, and Nakai mounted the tall stallion. Nakai paused only briefly, then lifted a hand to Rani-Ta and turned the big horse toward Winter Owl's lodge. The two men met in silence and departed, Rani-Ta watching after them.

And from across the camp, alone in the dawn light, Ki-Ki-Tai also watched, her heart also filled with dark feelings and a yearning loneliness.

"It is a fine morning, Nakai," Winter Owl said as they approached the river ford. "Let us hope it augurs well for our journey."

Winter Owl did not wear his uneasiness well. His face beneath its yellow and red paint was strained. His mouth was a straight line tightened by care.

They found the ford and let their horses pick their way carefully across the rocks and sand beneath the face of the swift river.

Emerging from the river, they found themselves in the coolness of the oak grove. Still they heard nothing, saw no sign of the blue soldiers. Nakai reined in, raising his hand to indicate that Winter Owl should do the same.

"What is it?" Winter Owl asked uneasily.

Nakai shook his head. He sat his piebald horse in silence, listening, watching his pony to see if it smelled anything on the wind.

"I don't know. Nothing," Nakai said finally. "Let us continue."

Riding from the trees onto the long plains they saw the blue soldiers. There were only four of them. Two men held the horses while their two leaders stood watching the Kiowas approach. The soldiers were only tiny silhouettes before the bright ball of the rising sun. The man who seemed to be in charge stood with gloved hands on his hips. A saber, which Nakai knew to be a sign of rank, hung at his hip.

"Speak carefully," Nakai reminded Winter Owl in a low voice. "This is of immense importance to the People."

The two Kiowas rode slowly onward. The wind had risen with the sun, and it gusted across the plains, flattening the long grass, lifting the mane of Nakai's painted horse. The air was clean, but there seemed to be a desolate smell to it. Something ineffable; a secret it carried. Perhaps it seemed so only because they were now in the strangers' land. The fort was not visible from where they were. The land rose abruptly to a long, convoluted, treeless bluff.

They rode on.

"Do you think this'll work out, sir?" Sergeant Callahan asked as they watched the two Kiowa chiefs approach their position.

"I'm sure it will, Callahan," Captain Ramsey answered.

Callahan thought that was an odd answer, since the captain was always discussing the possibility of treachery, of having little faith in the Indians keeping their word. Callahan frowned, watching Ramsey's eyes now confident and overbright. It gave the sergeant pause to worry. His heart skipped one beat.

"Which one is Hungry Wolf?" Ramsey asked.

"I don't know, sir. I've never seen him."

"I think it's the one on the paint pony. Look at the way he sits his horse, the way he watches us. Yes, Callahan, I think that must be him."

Ramsey's eagerness was unmistakable now. Callahan felt his unease turn slowly into fear. Ramsey *was* going to talk peace with them, wasn't he? Then Callahan's eyes drifted northward and then westward again, toward the river, drawn by some tiny movement, and he saw a patch of blue uniform, the sun glinting on steel.

Oh, God! Callahan thought with dismay. He should have suspected something from the start. The morning patrol had consisted of twenty men when five troopers were the normal complement. "A precaution," the captain had told him at the

223

time. And the patrol had ridden out in the dark hours of the morning, long before their usual sunrise schedule. Callahan knew suddenly—Ramsey was going to do it. The fool was really going to do it.

"I'll have my horse, Huggins," Ramsey ordered.

"Sir?" the corporal said in confusion. Why would the captain want his horse now?

"I said I'll have my horse, Corporal!"

"Yes, sir," Huggins said with a shrug toward Callahan. The corporal brought Ramsey's gray horse forward and watched as the officer mounted.

Nakai saw this too as they neared to within fifty yards of the waiting whites, and he felt a tingle creep up his spine.

"Be cautious, Winter Owl. Something is not right."

Winter Owl nodded, but what was there to fear? Only one of the blue soldiers was mounted. He did not allow himself to think of the possibility of a trap. He had counseled peacefully with these men before.

"Nakai . . ."

"Halt here. Let the white soldier come forward to meet us," Nakai said. And after a moment, Ramsey did start forward, walking his leggy gray horse toward the two waiting Kiowas. He came on half the distance toward them. Then a little more.

Then Ramsey drew his saber and raised it in signal and a long line of mounted white soldiers appeared on the bluff behind him. Nakai roared a curse and shouted.

"Back to the river!"

He spun his horse around only to find ten or more mounted white soldiers approaching from concealment in the oak grove along the river. He cursed again. Winter Owl had halted his pony, frozen by fear into immobility.

"Cousin!" Nakai shouted at him, and then the rifles of the blue soldiers began to fire from both directions and Nakai saw

Winter Owl stiffen, his mouth wide, blood flowing from it. He slumped forward across his pony's withers as the horse raced away. Winter Owl fell to the earth only a few yards in front of Ramsey, who charged forward, his saber leveled.

Nakai heeled his pony into a dead run and rode directly toward the rank of soldiers approaching from the river. A bullet cut a burning groove across his right shoulder. He turned his piebald war pony sharply to the south and went to the side of the horse, his lance now lost. With his horse as a shield, he rode at breakneck speed toward the safety of the river as rifles popped all around him and gunsmoke rose in a dense haze. The pony took a bullet in its shoulder; Nakai could feel the impact as the horse staggered, lurched to the right, and then rolled, head over heels.

Nakai was thrown free to slam against the grass. He rose to his knees and glanced over his shoulder, seeing the charging soldiers close behind. Getting to his feet he ran toward the shelter of the trees, zigzagging in hopes of making them miss their mark. The oaks, cool and dense, were not that far ahead. No so far. Bullets whined past him as he raced on breathlessly, cursing all the while.

Suddenly he was in among the trees, weaving his way through the old oaks; the river, seen past their trunks, glinted in the morning sunlight. The soldiers were forced to slow their horses to weave their way through the dense trees, but Nakai ran on at full speed.

Reaching the river, he didn't pause. He ran three full strides into the cold water and then dove, swimming with all of his strength toward the far bank as the current swept him away southward. Along the bank behind him a dozen riflemen fired after him. Tiny spouts of silver water flared up all around him, some within inches of his head, but he swam on, his lungs burning, his arm numb from the bullet that had furrowed his shoulder.

The rifle shots dwindled to a widely spaced few and then stopped altogether as he was carried out of range by the swiftness of the river's current.

His arm, numbed before, now seemed deadened. It dangled uselessly. Nakai swam on his side now, struggling toward the far bank, which seemed infinitely distant. His progress was slow, the current continuing to roll and twist him as it pleased. White water spumed up here and there to fill mouth and lungs. He was slammed against unseen sawyers and rocks and carried on. He was a mile downstream before he felt his toes strike bottom mud and he tried to stand, gagging and panting, only to have his legs swept out from under him again by a violent eddy. His right arm felt like a log that was attached to his shoulder. He swam on.

The river made its way around a slow, sweeping bend, widened, and grew shallower. Nakai struggled nearer to the bank, reached up desperately, and grabbed the exposed root of a shaggy willow tree, clinging to it. Stunned and breathless, he remained there for long minutes, coughing up water as the river continued to tug at him, wanting him back.

With his breath recovered, but his head reeling, he struggled to climb the muddy bank, his right arm still dangling uselessly at his side. He clawed his way through the brush, over rocks and tangled roots. Eventually he achieved the flats above and flung himself down on the muddy, leaf-littered dark earth beneath the willows, lying flat on his back for a long while as the sun winked through the branches overhead and his arm returned from numbness to life with bludgeoning pain.

Nakai slowly sat up and ripped off his shirt to examine his shoulder. It was not good. There was much torn muscle and the hot blood still flowed, but he would survive this wound. There had been worse. He gathered some moss from the clump of cold granite boulders where he rested and pressed it into the wound to aid in the clotting. Then he cut a strip of elkskin from his shirt with his skinning knife to fashion a bandage. Then Nakai rose, staggering briefly from the loss of blood as his head spun and filled with colored dots.

Then with his heart as cold as the granite, he turned and started toward his camp—jogging, lurching, staggering homeward.

Ramsey wasted no time. Within fifteen minutes an entire company of cavalry was organized along the river. The captain summoned Callahan, who watched this all as if he were living in a dream. Dumbfounded, the sergeant reported to Ramsey.

"Get this to the telegrapher immediately, Callahan," Ramsey said, shoving a message into the sergeant's hand.

"Yes, sir."

Ramsey's attention returned to giving orders to his troop leaders. Callahan heard him say, "Every Indian in that camp is to be considered a hostile. A woman can kill as quickly as a man, remember that."

Callahan glanced at the note in his hand and then rode numbly back toward the fort, glad to have been given this assignment. Because Ramsey meant to cross the river; there was no longer any doubt of that. He was going to attack the Kiowa camp.

The message Callahan was delivering was addressed to General Cox at Fort Riley. It read:

"Kiowa attacked at peace conference this AM. Assuming field initiative pursuing Hungry Wolf's hostiles. Casualties.

Ramsey, Ft. Cimarron."

Casualties? What casualties besides one dead Indian? Callahan wondered. For that matter, what attack? Looking at the handwriting, Callahan could tell that the message had not been hastily scribbled in the field. It had been written in advance. Ramsey had been planning this for a long while.

"You're just a soldier, Callahan," the big sergeant told himself. Hand the damned message to the telegrapher and forget it!

It wouldn't be easy. Ramsey's last order to his men had chilled him. Callahan knew what it meant. Ramsey had virtually ordered a massacre.

The dawn light heightened the color of Ki-Ki-Tai's face, turning it to burnished copper. She carried a sack of seed corn in a leather pouch across her shoulder. Most of the women would be in the fields that day planting corn. Momo was hard at work scraping a buffalo hide—one of her nephews had killed a straggler from the large herd that had passed through the week before. Briefly Ki-Ki-Tai spoke to Momo and then continued toward the fields. It was hard for the two of them to speak of many things, partly because of their sons' involvement in the Ta-Hai-Kai. It was a fact well-known, but not easily discussed now that the Ghost Warriors had been banished and it was as if they had no sons.

Also Momo felt awkward still because of Rani-Ta's involvement with Nakai and the fact that Kianceta had run away with a white man and not kept her vow to marry Ketah. So their conversations were brief and constrained, nothing like the long laughing talks of what now seemed long ago. Ki-Ki-Tai passed out of the camp, seeing Winter Owl's first wife, Sho-Wata, parching corn. Sho-Wata worked diligently, but her eyes were on the distances, gazing beyond the river, watching for Winter Owl's safe return. Ki-Ki merely raised a hand to her and walked on, passing three small boys teasing a yellow pup. Woodsmoke flavored the morning air; frost still glazed the grass in the shadows.

Reaching the fields, Ki-Ki-Tai found herself alone, the morning's first arrival. She unslung her bag of seed and sat for a while on an old, barkless fallen oak. Across the field she saw two does with a wobbly-legged fawn grazing delicately on the new grass. A crow wheeled overhead, raucous with joy or with some petty annoyance.

Ki-Ki-Tai felt uneasy for no reason she could define. There was an odd current to the wind. Something touched her senses—an unseen creature in the woods, a sound of danger just beneath the level of conscious hearing. She could not define it. It seemed . . . underneath her the earth was vibrating, so slightly that it might have been imagined. She could see brown leaves quivering infinitesimally, but their movement was not caused by the wind. An earthquake? This seemed more like the trembling caused by a distant buffalo herd in passing.

The tremor became more distinct and Ki-Ki rose, frowning deeply. There was a distant murmur of indistinct sound with no visible source. It was growing closer. It seemed a violent sound although it was still quite small. The deer lifted their heads and looked toward the river and then bounded away into the trees.

Warriors!

Ki-Ki-Tai had lived through numerous raids. Apaches, Arapahos, Cheyenne. The sounds she now heard as well as felt were of raiding horsemen approaching the camp. Sudden confirmation reached her—a lone shot and then dozens. Hundreds. Ki-Ki-Tai leaped to her feet and started back toward the camp, jogging at first and then breaking into a dead run. She could see them now, weaving on horseback among the lodges. Blue-uniformed white soldiers. She halted, breast rising and falling rapidly. She felt cowardly for not continuing, but what could she do? A woman suddenly appeared before her, running to Ki-Ki-Tai. Blood flowed from her breast.

It was Rani-Ta. Ki-Ki hesitated and then rushed to the girl, catching her as she fainted. Ki-Ki-Tai took her under the arms and dragged her away into the shelter of the oak trees as the battle roared through the Kiowa camp.

Too late! It was already too late, he knew. Hungry Wolf had heard the first volley of shots and tried to hurry on, but his stumbling legs would not carry his wounded, exhausted body any faster.

It was already too late to warn the tribe, to evacuate the camp, too late to grab his Mexican rifle and fight off the attacking blue soldiers.

He staggered on, bursting into the camp, and then he halted, astonished to immobilization. It was no battle he was witnessing, but a slaughter.

He saw a white soldier thrust a pistol into Sho-Wata's face and shoot her. Horses trampled over their tipis and raced through campfires, spilling drying racks and pots. A child was killed as a soldier rode over its tiny naked body. Everything was a blur of color seen through the gray haze of gunsmoke: blue uniforms, the yellow war paint of Sakoom, the red blood of Ta-Ah-Omo, the youth who was not quite right in the head, as he stood waving frantic arms at the rampaging soldiers. The whites wheeled their horses, killing anything that moved. A white dog was shot, its leg blown off, and it dragged itself away, its howling inaudible above the roar of shouts, screams, and gunfire.

A hatless red-haired soldier spied Nakai and turned his horse toward him, charging down on Hungry Wolf. Firing from horseback, the soldier's rifle sprayed three shots wildly into the woods beyond. Nakai stood motionless, directly in front of the onrushing, frothing horse. Frantically the soldier reloaded. His face was young and frightened, nearly bewildered. His horse's shoulder brushed Nakai. Hungry Wolf leaped up and grabbed the barrel of the rifle as a shot exploded, barely missing Nakai. The young soldier's eyes went wide. Nakai twisted away and yanked hard on the rifle as the horse pounded past, and the white soldier fell from his saddle.

On his back, the soldier looked up through the dust to Nakai, his expression pleading. Nakai shot him in the head.

Grabbing the soldier's ammunition packet from his body, Nakai hurried on toward the camp, his shoulder flaming with pain, his lungs tight and constricted. He shouted to those who were still alive there, cowering behind flimsy shelters.

"Run! Into the trees. Run!" He yanked one woman to her feet and shoved her on her way toward the river oaks as a soldier on a standing horse raised his rifle to shoot. The bullet whipped past Nakai's ear. Nakai went to one knee and aimed his own shot more carefully. His bullet found the soldier's heart, and he fell to the side, his boot going through the stirrup iron. His frightened horse ran off, dragging the dead man through the camp.

Nakai knew there was no way to win the battle here, no way to even make a good fight of it.

Surprised by the sudden attack, most of the warriors did not even have weapons to hand. Nakai rushed to Rani-Ta's tipi through the smoke and roar of the battle. Throwing back the flap, he found her lodge to be empty. Emerging, he came face to face with a foot soldier and Nakai shot offhandedly. The shot, ill-aimed, sent a bullet tearing through the soldier's thigh and he went down. Nakai snatched up his rifle as well and ran crazily on.

All of the camp was on fire behind him now; the soldiers had thrown burning brands into their tipis. Black smoke curled skyward. The flames leaped from lodge to lodge, destroying everything. A following bullet sang past Nakai's head, but he didn't turn to answer the shot. He stumbled forward toward the dark shelter of the woods.

Reaching the woods he vaulted a fallen oak, placed one rifle beside him, and began firing with the other. He heard shouted commands and saw the soldiers slow their charge, begin to turn and regroup. He saw their leader, the one with the saber sitting his gray horse. Nakai steadied his rifle and fired at him, but the range was long, his hands unsteady, and he missed.

Now the leader of the blue soldiers raised his hand and he shouted something more, and the soldiers rode eastward toward the river ford, unwilling to confront the Kiowas in the depths of the forest. There was no reason for pursuit. The slaughter was vast. The camp was burning to the ground. The white chief would not take the risks of a continued engagement. Besides the two men that Nakai himself had killed, he saw not a soldier on the ground. The raid of the blue soldiers had cost the whites virtually nothing in the way of casualties.

Nakai rose, bracing himself against the trunk of the fallen oak tree. He found that his legs were still wobbly. His head hummed and his vision was blurry. He was losing blood again from his shoulder wound. Angrily, he snatched up the other rifle and went on, deeper into the woods.

In a tiny grassy clearing he came upon the two women.

He found Rani-Ta, the color drained from her face, blood across her shirt front with her head lying on Ki-Ki-Tai's lap. Ki-Ki was stroking Rani-Ta's head, speaking softly to the injured girl. Ki-Ki-Tai looked up sharply as Nakai approached, his face grim.

"Leave her alone!" Nakai shouted at Ki-Ki.

"I will care for her, Nakai," Ki-Ki-Tai said.

"No! Just leave her alone, Ki-Ki!"

Ki-Ki-Tai shook her head in refusal and turned her eyes

down, murmuring softly to the badly wounded Rani-Ta.

Spinning angrily, Nakai stumbled on. The acrid smell of burnt gunpowder still filled his nostrils, the smell of dust and burning hides, the scent of death.

"Nakai!" Eagle Heart emerged from the forest shadows, his face as grim as a skull. "Is this their peace?"

Nakai wordlessly handed Eagle Heart one of the captured rifles. Both men sagged to the grass and tried to catch their breath. There was a cool breeze off the river, but it could not carry the smoke of battle away. Nakai looked more closely now at Eagle Heart and saw that his scalp was bleeding horribly. Both men were smoke-smudged.

"Nakai? What went wrong? What will you do now!"

Nakai shook his head heavily and looked toward the smoking camp, toward the river and toward the white lands beyond. He answered Eagle Heart.

"I was wrong, my friend. Wrong to assume only I knew what was right and to honor the word of any man. I was wrong to find fault with the Ghost Warriors instead of guiding them. Wrong to let the whites think that Hungry Wolf had grown weak. Now, my friend," he said with his eyes on the distances . . .

"Now I shall come forth."

Rani-Ta had died.

Ki-Ki-Tai still sat with her inert body, Rani-Ta's head on her lap. The woods were eerily silent after the raid. Not a bird sang. Rani-Ta's eyes were open in death. They still held a pleading look. Ki-Ki-Tai realized that she had never really hated the girl. She could not blame her for wanting a part of Hungry Wolf for her own. She could not blame her for being what she was. So far as she knew, Rani-Ta had done her best to please Hungry Wolf in the brief time they were together. Approaching footsteps brought Ki-Ki-Tai's head up. Nakai stood looking down at them.

"So, she is dead," Nakai said, and it was almost an accusation, as if it were Ki-Ki-Tai's fault.

"Yes, Nakai."

"Find a place for her. There is no time for a proper ceremony."

"Nakai . . ."

"Do what I have told you. The other women and children are leaving now to travel to the winter camp."

"And you, Nakai? What will you do?"

"What do you think, woman?" he asked, scowling deeply. It was an expression she had never before seen on his face, dark and terrible. He bent over, placed a hand briefly on Rani-Ta's cool forehead, and turned sharply, striding away without a soft word for Ki-Ki-Tai.

Ki-Ki slipped from under Rani-Ta's weight and stood motionless for a time, watching after him. Her skirt was blood-soaked. Her hands and knees were dirty. Her heart was empty.

War again, forever; only this time Nakai would not be coming home. He would never come home to her again; they had no home; she could offer him none. Had he truly loved Rani-Ta so much, she wondered, or did he just hate Ki-Ki so? She did not know. She only knew that her husband was forever gone.

Momo called to her from across the clearing, waving. The other women were gathering together, carrying the younger children, preparing to travel southward. Ki-Ki-Tai said nothing. She turned away and walked toward the river.

Alone.

CHAPTER EIGHT

"I will not leave! This is my home."

Lieutenant Ramsey, sitting his gray horse in front of the O'Day's porch, studied her curiously. Tom, standing beside Elizabeth, said:

"Of course you'll go, Liz. Don't be foolish. It's not safe here."

"All of the local families are being taken to the fort for protection," Ben Ramsey said. "After what happened this morning—surely you heard the gunfire."

"I heard them, yes," she answered. "It doesn't make any difference. This is my home; I'm staying here."

"Liz," Tom said with exasperation, "it just isn't safe. Surely you can see that. It makes no sense to remain here."

"It does make sense—to me," she said. "Maybe not to you, Tom. After all, it hasn't been your home for the last four years. Maybe it just can't be home to you anymore."

"That's not the point!" Tom replied hotly. Now was she blaming him for fighting for the good cause during the war?

"It's only prudent, Mrs. O'Day," Ramsey put in.

"Is Isadora Kittinger going? Are Kent and Bettina going to the fort?"

Ramsey hesitated. "That's different, ma'am. They have virtually an army of their own on the Kittinger ranch what with the vaqueros and the men they brought up from Texas, a few they've hired since."

Elizabeth thought for a moment. Then she said, "No. I will

235

not leave the farm. Not unless someone ties me up and drags me away." Then she went back into the house, closing the door behind her.

Ramsey watched the plank door close and shifted slightly in the saddle. "What about you, Tom?" he asked.

"I'm coming along with you, Ramsey," Tom O'Day said, glancing over his shoulder at the closed door. "Elizabeth seems to think I should stay and work in the fields as if nothing has happened. Why wok on something that isn't going to be safe as long as Hungry Wolf is roaming the countryside? First things first, I say. I'll help you fight him.

"What did go on this morning, Ben?" Tom asked.

"The Kiowas tried a little trap that didn't work," Lieutenant Ramsey said. "A false peace conference. You know how the Indians are. We turned the tables on them. I had reserves watching in case something did go wrong. They tried to attack us and we countered. We pursued across the river. There was a little bit of stick and run tactics—well, you know they aren't going to mass and fight against our cavalry. We gave them back more than they counted on."

"You gave them back a little of their own?" Tom O'Day asked.

"That's right. Taught them just like we taught the Rebs."

"I'm glad you made it all right," Tom said.

"Well," Ramsey said with a rueful smile, "it was close. I can show you my other tunic with the bullet burn across the side. One of them damned near got me. But we were lucky considering we were outmanned. We only lost two troopers. We have another man who might not make it. The surgeon had to take his leg off."

"What is our next move, Ben?"

"We'll have to play it defensively for the time being. I've telegraphed Regiment and General Cox has wired back promising help. Reinforcements should arrive within three to four days. Then we'll disperse the Kiowas once and for all."

"And hang Hungry Wolf's scalp on your guidon."

"I hope so."

Tom nodded. "Can you give me a few minutes, Ben? I won't be long. I just have to grab an extra shirt and my rifle."

"Of course, Tom, you go ahead. I'll wait. It will be fine to have you at my side again."

Tom O'Day grinned crookedly. He wondered if, after all, he did not miss the war in some undefined way. He went into the house. It seemed so empty and cold. Anger flared up briefly. Why would any man want to stay around here? Elizabeth was about as warm as a snowball herself. Just why would a man want to stay around here! The boys were gone; she was hardly a wife anymore. Still gripped in irrational anger, he snatched his rifle from its hooks above the fireplace, found his extra ammunition in the corner cabinet, and went to the bedroom to collect a spare flannel shirt and some socks.

Elizabeth stood motionlessly at the window, looking out at the stubble fields. Crows hopped around it aimlessly as if they could find nothing there either. Tom spoke to her stiffened back.

"You're being plain silly about all of this, Liz," he said. When she didn't answer he repeated what he had said to Ramsey about the futility of planting crops until the Kiowas were defeated or driven from the land.

Elizabeth half-turned and smiled insincerely. "You're probably right, Tom," she said to avoid further argument. It was pointless to argue. They both knew equally well that Tom simply was no longer up to planting, physically or psychologically. Perhaps he had gotten too used to war in the end. Perhaps the whisky he drank, the opium, had drained all the reserves of his physical and mental strength. Perhaps he felt that this was no longer a home, as Elizabeth had believed for some time now, not with the boys gone. Somewhere, in some way she did not understand, the winds of war had blown away all of Tom O'Day's ambition where the farm was concerned.

"I wish you wouldn't go off to fight, Tom," Elizabeth said.

"Someone's got to," he told her as he had once before, all those years ago.

"There are soldiers for that, Tom. You're not a soldier any longer."

"I won't run from my duty. I didn't during the war; I won't now."

Elizabeth watched with dry-eyed, remote sadness as he stuffed his clothing into a cloth bag. How would he cope with this adventure of his! In Tom's mind he was still young and strong, alert and daring. But his mind danced and spun within the mists of his drugs. He was dragging an illusion into battle, and it could not do his fighting for him.

"I just wish you wouldn't go," she said softly.

"I'm going!" he said, growing irritated now.

"Just take care, then," Elizabeth said, going to him to look up into his haunted eyes.

"As if you care," he said cruelly, and now tears began to sting Elizabeth's eyes. "I can tell how much you care for me each night when I take you into our bed, Elizabeth."

"That's not necessary, Tom. Please don't hurt me anymore."

"Hurt you!" he laughed and shouldered his bag. "You have everything backwards, don't you? Everything. I don't believe you'd care if I never came back. Maybe you'd think it was for the best."

Then Tom turned and walked out, leaving the front door open as he joined Ramsey. Elizabeth felt a terrible, hollow loss. But she no longer wanted to cry. She no longer wanted to call out his name. The loss she felt was for the Tom O'Day who had brought her into this land years ago and been strong, rugged, and good. Tender and caring. She thought: maybe you're right, Tom. Maybe I wouldn't mourn if something happened and you didn't come back. You've been dead so long already; perhaps it is far too late to mourn.

The moon rose full, monstrously huge, and briefly red-gold before it gradually turned bone-white rising skyward beyond the camp of the Ta-Hai-Kai. Three fires burned low, sparks jutting against the dark sky, and around the fire men with their entire bodies painted with intertwined serpents, their faces painted into yellow masks, danced, blowing on eagle-bone whistles, thumping rhythmically on small drums.

Falcon, his leggings decorated with scalps, stood with his arms crossed, watching the younger men, the flames coloring his face with shifting shadows. His eyes had black paint around them and he seemed to be peering out of deep tunnels. The shaman, Washai, exultant and lost in some deep reverie, stood beside him. Falcon seemed emotionless, but the shaman was unable to restrain his excitement. His legs and arms twitched as if he were dancing in place. Washai's face was painted completely black, his teeth were tinted red. He had called for total war, but he had been met with resistance even from the Ghost Warrior's war leader, Opaga. Then word had reached their camp that the main Kiowa camp had been savaged by blue soldiers, solidifying his stature as a true prophet.

"They are bold enough," the shaman said to Falcon as he watched the young men dance.

"Bold enough, but still inexperienced, and we are too few, Washai."

"When shall we be strong enough, Falcon? When will the whites be fewer?"

Falcon only nodded. The shaman was right, of course. When would the numbers favor their side more than at this moment?

"Falcon!"

Yatha was running toward them, his face excited as he waved a hand in the air.

"What is it?" Falcon asked Koto's second son.

"They are coming, Falcon!" Yatha said, pointing behind him as he tried to catch his breath.

"Soldiers?"

"No, no! My father is coming and Eagle Heart—and Hungry Wolf. All of the older warriors."

"So," Falcon said meditatively.

"What do they want?" Washai asked sourly. The shaman knew that Nakai did not like him, and he did not want what might be his moment of triumph ruined by Hungry Wolf.

"We shall wait and see," Falcon told him. "Wait and see. I think I understand."

The two men moved away from the dancers. Catching Opaga's eye, Falcon gestured for him to come along with them. Opaga's eyes narrowed and he shrugged, rising from his blanket near the fire. He tapped Ketah on the shoulder and they started after Falcon and Washai. Hungry Wolf's other son, Tema, who sensed that something was in the air, followed after them.

"What is it?" Opaga asked in a dry whisper.

"Wait a minute and you shall see," Falcon answered mysteriously. They paused in the moon shadows away from the firelight to watch and listen.

They did not have long to wait. In a little while the long line of Kiowa warriors emerged from the trees and crossed the grassland toward the clearing. Hungry Wolf led them. His arm was bound up; his face was funereal. Koto, riding beside him, had an injured foot. Eagle Heart had escaped the attack unscathed, apparently, but his face was dark with determination. All of the older warriors wore fresh paint. Nakai halted his horse a few paces from Falcon. He looked from man to man, not knowing who the true leader of the Ta-Hai-Kai was, who should be spoken to.

Opaga made it clear when he invited them:

"Step down, Hungry Wolf, Father Koto. Eagle Heart. Welcome to our camp."

Sliding from their ponies' backs, the three older Kiowa chiefs were invited aside. "Let us counsel." The remainder of their band secured the horses and went to join the festivities. "You have ridden far," Opaga said. "Are you hungry?"

"No," Nakai replied. "Thank you, Opaga, but we need to talk as soon as possible."

Opaga nodded, his eyes curious still. He inclined his head and the group followed him to a smaller clearing away from the Ghost Dancers. The Ta-Hai-Kai carried no tipis with them, rapid movement being imperative in their guerrilla war, and so the warriors sat on blankets in the open.

The trees were black against the sky, firelight forming a shifting red background for them. The silver moon like some pocked war-survivor drifted high overhead against a clear, star-cluttered sky.

When they were all seated, Opaga asked without preliminaries, "What is it you wish to say, Nakai?" The young warriors' eyes were very fierce. Koto was astonished to note how his sons had changed in such a short period of time. Hungry Wolf's sons, Ketah and Tema, looked equally severe, although Nakai's younger boy still appeared nervous about meeting his father on equal footing.

"The time has come," Nakai said carefully. "I believe we must all wage war together if the People are to survive."

"I see," Opaga said evenly. He glanced at the shaman, who crouched beside him.

"*Now* you have come to ask for help," Washai half-shouted. "From those you cast out of the tribe."

"Be quiet, Washai," Opaga said with authority. "This is not your affair. It is time for the warriors to speak." Scowling, the shaman fell silent.

"Divided we are too few," Falcon said pragmatically. "Perhaps together we are still too few, but certainly we are much stronger."

Opaga was not listening. Falcon was stating the obvious. Opaga had other priorities. He had come too far to relinquish his personal power, his stature among the Ghost Warriors.

"Who, then, would be war-leader among us?" Opaga asked, his eyes meeting Nakai's, Koto's, and Eagle Heart's in turn.

Nakai sensed what was going on in the young brave's mind. He said, "We have come to join you, not to challenge you." If the taste of these words was bitter in his mouth, he gave no indication of it. "You are war-leader, Opaga."

Opaga looked steadily at Nakai for a long moment; then he nodded with satisfaction.

"I welcome you," was all he said.

"As you see, we are preparing to go forth tonight," Falcon said, gesturing toward the dancers beyond the trees. "Can you be ready so soon, Nakai?"

"I am ready at this moment."

"Good," said Falcon, the chief strategist of the Ta-Hai-Kai. "We will start at the southernmost white settlement and work our way north along the river, destroying everything in our path."

Nakai's head shook negatively. It was a very small movement, but Falcon noticed it. Perhaps he and Hungry Wolf were no longer friends, but Falcon was intelligent enough to respect Nakai's war sense.

"You find fault with the plan, Nakai?"

"Yes—since you ask me. The southernmost camp of the whites is the place where the woman lives alone with her husband. They have nothing. They cannot fight. It would be like squashing a bug—but," Nakai said, his eyes shifting to Opaga's face, "to burn that house would nevertheless alert the soldiers in the fort and all of the other whites that trouble was approaching. Nothing would be gained; the soldiers would be warned of our raids.

"I would say, no! The largest targets should be attacked first where the most damage can be inflicted, where the most is to be gained."

"You mean the men with the cattle?" Opaga asked thoughtfully.

"Yes."

"They have thirty warriors," Ketah said.

"We are making war, not game-playing, Ketah," his father told him. "Driving off the cattle would cripple the ranch, the soldiers, all of the whites nearby. They would no longer have meat in their bellies to fight on. To attack thirty warriors and defeat them is a beginning. To kill one woman is meaningless."

"It is the soldiers who must be defeated!" Washai said desperately. It seemed he felt he was losing his dominant position among the Ta-Hai-Kai with the arrival of Hungry Wolf.

Nakai smiled indulgently at this man who had never in his life engaged in personal combat, let alone planned a war.

"That will be done," Nakai said soothingly. "We begin tonight. No, not all of the soldiers will be defeated at once. Only a fool attempts to fell a tree with one blow; but it will be done, I promise you."

Opaga looked doubtful, but still he understood the logic of the more experienced warrior.

"Tonight, Nakai? You say we shall begin chopping down that tree tonight?"

"Yes. On this night many blue soldiers will die. This I promise you if you will listen to what I have to say."

★ ★ ★ ★ ★

Bettina Kittinger O'Day walked slowly past the south porch where her mother and Ben Ramsey sat outside, discussing something with muted laughter as punctuation. The jasmine in the back garden was just beginning to blossom and the sweet scent reached her through the closed French doors.

Bettina walked barefoot across the house, her hand resting on her swollen abdomen. Everyone said she should remain in bed until it was time for the baby to come, but lying in bed only made her back ache more.

Through the half-open kitchen door she could see Kent's crossed legs and gesturing hand as he talked to his father seated across the table. A sense of guilt stole over her. She did not like Tom O'Day, and there was nothing she could do to change that, although she had tried. There was something unhealthy about the bearded man, his heavy drinking aside.

Nor did she like Ben Ramsey or trust him.

There was a depressing aura that had settled about the ranch since her father had died and Ramsey had moved in, marrying Isadora only a week after Nesbitt Kittinger had been killed by the Indians.

Everyone told her that it was her pregnancy that caused her depression, but Bettina knew better. *That* was her only joy in life.

No, she thought, it was due more to the atmosphere of war. The men spoke of nothing but revenge, of killing. She would have thought that Ramsey and O'Day had seen enough of that during the War Between the States to last them a lifetime.

But they actually seemed to crave battle.

She could hear their words in the hallway, although they spoke in low tones.

"That's what Ben was saying." This was Kent.

"Within three days they should arrive? That will nearly double the strength at the fort."

"Yes." Kent's voice was light. "And we, of course, benefit all the way around. More soldiers to protect our homes. More soldiers who require our beef to feed them."

Bettina felt suddenly dizzy. There was a sort of tugging sensation in her abdomen. It was followed immediately by a contraction, quite hard. It couldn't be, she thought. It was too soon.

She was briefly frightened and then terribly excited. She fought down both emotions. Holding her belly with both hands, she entered the kitchen and asked Kent:

"Would you mind finding Missie and sending her to our room, Kent? I need to talk to her."

Tom O'Day looked at her with filmed eyes. Kent's face was briefly concerned, but she smiled at him, allaying his fears.

"Sure, Bett. She's probably in her room."

Bettina nodded and went back into the hallway. It *was* too early; she knew it was. But no one had told the baby that.

"I'll be back in a minute, Dad," Kent said, scooting his chair back, rising from the table.

"What is this all about?" Tom asked.

"Who knows, Dad? Women stuff, I guess."

When Kent had gone, Tom rose, bracing himself on the table top, and with a sigh he moved to the corner pantry where he kept his whisky jug. He drank so deeply from it that it rose into the membranes of his nose, burning terribly. Angrily he replaced the jug in the cupboard, staring at his bottled demons before he slammed the pantry door shut and walked out onto the front porch to stare at the moon hovering over the ranch.

A bullet from the darkness slammed into the doorsill behind him, tearing splinters from the oak wood of the frame. He was stunned and confused; nevertheless pure instinct sent Tom diving for the shelter of the house as a dozen more rifle shots followed. On the floor, Tom kicked the door shut, rose to drop the bar behind it, and yelled out.

"Ramsey!"

Ben Ramsey had heard the shots and he was already rushing toward the front of the house, his Spencer repeating carbine in hand.

"Here they come!" Tom shouted over his shoulder as Ramsey ducked into the room. Tom broke out a windowpane, knelt, and opened fire with his Henry rifle.

From out of the darkness a dozen Indians had appeared, their war whoops filling the air. Tom shot one horse behind the shoulder and saw it roll, crushing the painted rider. Ramsey nicked another Indian and the Kiowas veered aside, aiming a dozen more wild shots at the house.

"Kent!" Ramsey yelled without turning his head. "The back!"

A second wave of riders appeared then, charging in a widely spaced rank toward the house, and the two veteran soldiers glanced at each other. This was not going to be a brief raid then. The Kiowas had come in force to fight to the finish.

In the bunkhouse Miguel awakened with a start. Four of the other vaqueros had been playing cards, now they sat in tableau in the lantern light, none of them moving for long seconds.

"Kiowas," Miguel said, and he launched himself from his bunk, grabbed his rifle, and ran bootless to the door. He saw the blur of passing horses, moonlit and eerie, painted riders on their backs. He fired at one of them, missed, and drew three wild shots in return. Withdrawing to the bunkhouse, he slammed the door shut and stood with his back against it, loading his rifle fully. The Mexican hands crowded the windows, firing until their rifle barrels were hot and the room was filled with acrid gunsmoke.

In the other bunkhouse all of the Texans had been sleeping, with the exception of Pritchard, who had been reading his Bible by the light of a coal oil lantern, its wick turned very low. The first shots had brought the cowhands, who were used to trouble and always half-expected it, to life. They swarmed toward the gun racks like disturbed ants before they even knew who the enemy was.

"Kiowas, I think! Damn all!" Amos Starr yelled. He was wearing his trousers and flannel underwear, nothing else, not even his boots. Before Starr could get to the window, he smelled smoke. In seconds they saw the first bright curls of flame rising against the night.

"They're burning the shack down!" Pritchard bellowed. "We've got to get out boys. Open the damned door!"

"Go out low and shooting!" Starr shouted.

The first man out the door, a San Antonio cowboy named Frank Willis, didn't pay any attention to Starr's warning. He flung the door open recklessly in his panic, and as he did an arrow penetrated his neck. He staggered back and fell dead on the floor, his lips moving soundlessly.

Starr halted, cursing violently. Behind him the roof had collapsed in flaming wreckage. He decided he'd rather take his chances with the Kiowas than burn to death, and he leaped over Willis' body and flung himself onto the porch, firing three times before he had found a target.

Rolling to his feet, he darted into the shadows of a clump of sumac beside the bunkhouse with bullets flying past him.

Pritchard tried to follow him. Running in a crouch he suddenly straightened up and spun around, dropping his rifle. Picking it up again, he hobbled on weakly, shot in the lower back. He threw himself to the ground beside Amos Starr. The bunkhouse was being rapidly consumed by fire, the flames twisting high into the air, lighting the yard behind the main house brightly. Crimson washed the white walls of the mansion,

Starr rose up and shot one Indian from his pony's back. He fired at another warrior, missing him in the confusion of the darkness and flame. He cursed himself for not having grabbed extra ammunition when he had had the chance.

Pritchard was on his back. "They got me good," he moaned. "Look me over, Starr. See how bad it is, will you?"

Starr didn't even glance at his partner. His eyes were on the charging Kiowas. He fired once and then again. His rifle clicked on an empty chamber, and he grabbed Pritchard's rifle from his hand.

"They got the main house," Amos said to Pritchard, who was in too much pain to care.

The big house had indeed caught fire. Starr saw two of the Mexicans running toward it, perhaps intending to put the flames out. Maybe they were only seeking better shelter. It didn't matter. Both men were cut down by the Kiowa raiders before they could reach the house.

At the front of the big house Ramsey yelled to O'Day, who was kneeling at the other window.

"Tom! You've got to try to get to the fort. Get us some help down here. Now!"

Tom O'Day, following his wartime training, rose automatically to obey the order. His horse was still tied to the porch rail. It had tried to pull away when the shooting began, but Tom, who had lost other horses in the excitement of the moment, had the habit of tying his reins fast to the hitch rail. Frantically the animal had tried to rear and kicked about wildly, its eyes wide and panicked, but his knot had held.

"I'm on my way," Tom said without hesitation. He took a deep breath and lifted the bar from the door. Flipping his hat aside he dashed outside and ran in a crouch toward the horse, drawing two shots, one of which smashed through the window he had just quit. He got the reins loose with one practiced yank and swung onto the horse's back, starting it running before he was fully in the saddle. Low over the withers, he rode from the yard, war whoops from the night following him.

"Ben!" Isadora Kittinger crawled to where Ramsey knelt, reloading his rifle.

"Stay down! Get to the kitchen. It's safest there."

"What's going to happen!"

"We'll be all right. Tom will make it to the fort."

"What if he doesn't make it?" she asked. Tears streaked her cheeks. Her dress was torn, her lip trembling.

"He will. I know Tom. You get to the kitchen like I told you. Now!"

Hungry Wolf sat his horse beside Falcon, watching Tom O'Day ride for the fort in the night. The two men smiled at each other. Everything was going exactly as they had planned.

The shots continued to ring in the ranch yard. Miguel and Carlos had managed to work their way to the back of the big house, and at their own peril put out the fire smoldering there with buckets of water from the well. The smoke from the extinguished fire mingled with the gunsmoke. The yard, the house, everything was smothered in a dark cloud, veiling the moon. The two vaqueros heard the Texans fire one short, violent volley at the attacking Kiowas, and then their guns fell silent again.

"The Indians are pulling out," Carlos said from the shelter of the woodpile where they had taken refuge.

"Do you think so?" Miguel asked hopefully, peering out through the suddenly silent darkness. Then they heard more shots erupt in the distance and the following thunder of hoofs as the steers were brought to their feet by the invaders.

"Damnit! They got the herd."

Miguel could only shake his head sadly. There was nothing at all they could do about it. Not even a madman would ride out to confront the Kiowa warriors and a stampeding herd in the darkness. He sagged back against the woodpile, thinking of the months of labor it had taken to drive those longhorns north.

Inside the house Kent O'Day heard the rumble of thousands of running hoofs too, and he cursed savagely. Angered beyond frustration, he fired his rifle from the window until it was empty and hot, seeing no targets, hitting nothing at all.

Bettina moaned again. Missie stood at the foot of the bed, her dark face concerned and comforting.

"Push again, Miss Bettina," she encouraged. "Once more, I think."

Outside the guns continued to roar and were answered by shots from the house, Missie's face broke into a grin and as she manipulated it and pulled gently, the baby eased into its new life. *From darkness to darkness,* Bettina thought. The baby, wrapped in a blanket, was given to her as she lay there exhausted, proud and fearful. Missie dabbed at Bettina's perspiring forehead and began singing very softly, an odd and somehow fitting counterpoint to the raging battle.

"I'm so thirsty," Bettina said in a dry voice.

"I'll get water for you," Missie said. The servant wiped her hands on a towel and smiled down at mother and son; then throwing open the bedroom door, she went lightly down the hallway toward the kitchen pump. A random shot from outside caught her as she passed a window and Missie pitched forward onto her face to lie unnoticed and dying on the floor.

Tom O'Day had roused the fort with shots from his pistol and frantic yells to the sentries. Confusion reigned, but only briefly. Already on full alert, half of the troopers, under Sergeant Callahan, were ready to ride in minutes. The cavalry raced down the bluff and out onto the plains toward the sinking moon. Ahead of them, the fires at the ranch were winking red beacons.

Smoke lay in a dark halo over the land.

The soldiers had ridden on into the night for a little over a mile when Hungry Wolf led his warriors from the riverside trees, springing his trap. The raiders at the Kittinger ranch had been Ta-Hai-Kai, young, bold, and exuberant. The men Nakai led were experienced braves; Hungry Wolf's faithful few. Tough, battle-tested, highly skilled. They struck the unsuspecting soldiers with sudden, controlled violence.

A dozen mounted troopers were killed before a man among them had the time to aim his rifle at the night-warriors. The Kiowas rushed among them, overwhelming the Americans. Horses reared up and wheeled in panic. Men screamed and called out useless orders. Hungry Wolf, disdaining his rifle in these close quarters in the near darkness, used his war lance with deadly efficiency. He killed two men in the first few moments and drove his bloodied lance through the thigh of a third who survived to flee.

Panic swept through the ranks of the soldiers. Callahan's orders went unheard or unheeded. The troopers, in full retreat, tried to return to the safety of the fort. They were cut off by the Ta-Hai-Kai, who had disengaged from their raid at the Kittinger ranch.

The slaughter was terrible. The troopers had no real chance in the darkness. The Ghost Warriors acted with frenzied savagery.

Hungry Wolf, his emotions under control at all times in battle, broke away from the battle and surveyed the fort on the bluff. The soldiers who remained there, loosely organized and hastily mounted, now emerged from the gates. Nakai, realizing that they were soon to be outnumbered, began shouting orders to his warriors.

"The river! It is enough for now!"

His older braves, hearing the command, broke off the battle

immediately; some of the young Ta-Hai-Kai warriors, caught up in the frenzy of the moment, failed to heed his order and were caught between the two groups of soldiers. Nakai saw Yatha go down, shot in the face, and be trampled by dozens of horses.

"Now!" Hungry Wolf repeated at the top of his lungs. His horse turned in a tight circle. The battle still raged in a confused tableaux. War clubs rose and fell; pistols shot the young undisciplined Kiowa warriors from their ponies' backs. Clamping his jaw, Hungry Wolf started toward the river himself. When the fresh group of soldiers fanned out over the battlefield, they would be greatly outnumbered and the element of surprise had been lost.

Hungry Wolf kneed his horse, starting it running toward the river. He didn't see the white man standing beneath the shadowed trees until he had nearly ridden into him. Nakai gave a war cry and lifted his lance, but it was already too late.

Tom O'Day had his rifle shouldered, his sights aligned.

He shot Hungry Wolf dead.

Tom glanced back to where his own horse lay inert against the dark grass and then walked slowly out of the grove of oak trees. He started toward Hungry Wolf's pony, meaning to catch it if he could, but then changed his mind. Turning, he returned to Hungry Wolf's body, drew his bowie knife from its sheath, and scalped the Kiowa.

Rising with the bloody trophy in his hand, he spat on the body.

He never saw Ketah creeping up behind him through the moon shadows.

The sky was flushed pink in the east when Elizabeth rose and went out into the cool of morning. To the north heavy dark clouds hovered along the horizon, promising rain later in the day.

Circling the farmhouse, she looked out across her fallow fields, hands on her hips. She had seen them from her back window—perhaps two dozen steers stood singly or in groups in the fields, picking at the sparse grass and cornstalks. Having heard the flurry of shots the night before and seen the soft glow of distant fires against the night sky, she supposed she shouldn't have been surprised to see the scattered cattle. It was Kent's herd, she knew. It had been dispersed, or at least a part of it had, by the uproar, with these ending up on her property. Elizabeth walked toward them, shooing them with upraised arms, but they paid no attention to her. Perhaps they were too weary from the night before to bother running away.

Nearer the river she heard one of them bawling pitiably, and walking that way, she found that the steer was down on its side, a front leg broken. It rolled its huge brown eyes pitiably toward her.

"All right then," Elizabeth said to herself with a heavy sigh. Tom was not back; there was no telling when he would return. It was almost as if he had joined the army again. Perhaps he had!

Elizabeth went to the barn and harnessed one of their mules. Picking up a length of half-inch chain, she draped it over the mule's back and led it out into the pale glow of morning.

Going into the house, she emerged again with Tom's old Springfield rifle. Taking the mule's bridle, she walked it toward the riverbank.

She had never done a thing like this before; she did not want to do it now, but she knew how. Loading the rifle, she cocked it and placed the muzzle just behind the injured steer's ear. Turning her head, she pulled the trigger, the report of the rifle sharp and loud across the empty fields as the echo ran away.

The mule, startled, tried to bolt, but Elizabeth was quick enough to grab the harness again and soothe the trembling animal. Then she took the chain and looped it around the longhorn steer's head and horns.

"Come on then, Bo," she said to the mule, "let's take him home."

Even for the mule, it was not easy going across the rutted fields, but they managed, hauling the carcass to the rear of the barn where the broken cottonwood tree stood. Elizabeth looked up at the heavy bough, scarred with the marks of chains where the boys and Tom had hung hogs for butchering. She didn't know if she could manage to hoist the steer or not.

Leading the mule back to the barn, she pitched hay down from the loft to Bo and his harness partner, Dud. Then she looked around the barn's interior, and found the block and tackle and a coil of hemp rope.

She studied the bough and the block and tackle in puzzlement for some time. It was a job she had seen done many times, but like most jobs only observed, the finer points eluded her. There was nothing to do but try it. The options were to try burying the big animal or taking it somewhere to rot, an inexcusable waste.

Emerging from the barn, she heard the low distant grumbling of thunder. Looking northward she could see that the storm clouds were nearer, stacked higher against the sky, their apexes bright gold with the light of the rising sun, their bases flat and as black as sin.

The wind had freshened and it twisted her skirts around her legs as she tossed the block and tackle next to the dead steer and went to the house for the great butcher knife the men used for this chore.

When she came out again, Ben Ramsey was there in his buckskin shirt, sitting his gray horse.

"Hello, Mrs. O'Day," the army officer said. His tone was reticent. His eyes lacked their normal piercing quality. He didn't have to say anything else. Elizabeth already knew.

"Tom's dead."

"He . . . yes, Mrs. O'Day, Tom is dead. He died a hero."

Elizabeth closed her eyes tightly for a minute, not out of grief or shock; she was searching internally for *some* kind of emotion, but she found none. None at all.

"He got his horse shot out from under him," Ramsey was saying. He was trying hard to be comforting, but there wasn't a sincere bone in Ramsey's body and it was difficult for him. He settled for speaking softly; Elizabeth heard barely half of it.

"Tom got Hungry Wolf, Mrs. O'Day. Fought him and won. Some other Kiowa killed him when his back was turned."

"I see. Where is his body?"

"Kent took it," Ramsey answered. "He thought it would be easier for you. His body . . . the Kiowa desecrated it pretty much."

Elizabeth nodded. She should have been angry with Kent, not for taking charge of matters, but for failing even to ride over himself to inform her of his father's death. Oddly she could not even rouse that emotion. *What is the matter with me?* she wondered. *Have I died that much as well?*

"If there's anything I can do to help, Mrs. O'Day . . ."

"Yes, Ben Ramsey, there is!" Elizabeth said with strained heartiness. "You can help me hoist a steer's carcass."

Ramsey looked at her in puzzlement; then realizing the woman with the butcher knife in her hand was serious, he grinned crookedly and swung down, hitching his horse loosely to the rail.

Hoisted, the steer looked twice as large, dangling there on the bowed cottonwood limb. Ramsey said with a shadow of true sincerity, "I admire you, ma'am. Life must go on, right? Isadora, now, she's been crying all morning. She got some of the house paint scorched and lost her garden. Also, she doesn't know where she can find another maid way out here!" Ramsey smiled as if demonstrating his tolerance for his new wife's feminine quirks, but Elizabeth wondered how a man as strong as Ramsey really felt about what amounted to Isadora whining and complaining about trivialities.

"Do you want me to open the steer up for you, Mrs. O'Day? It's a messy job."

"No thank you, Captain. You would get your uniform bloody, wouldn't you?"

Ramsey looked at her darkly for a moment, reading something else in her words.

Elizabeth went on lightly. "I only have to go into the house to clean up when I'm through—besides it's about time I learned to do things for myself. Everything."

"Yes, Mrs. O'Day," Ramsey replied. "I suppose you're right."

"When you see Kent, tell him I'm boarding some of his cattle. He'd better send someone over to round them up."

"I will do that, ma'am." Ramsey touched the brim of his hat and with one last puzzled look, he turned and walked to his horse, riding away as the thunder in the north boomed again and the skies grew darker.

Elizabeth stood looking at the steer, hanging by its horns, dead eyes turned upward. She lifted the huge butcher knife and plunged the blade deeply into the belly of the carcass. Using two hands, she dragged the knife downward and steaming entrails flooded from the body cavity to lie in a serpentine heap against the ground. Elizabeth stepped back, feeling bile rising into her mouth. And she began vomiting. Then she began to cry until she could not stop and the first cold raindrops began to fall from the black and tumultuous sky.

The rain fell in a thunderous wash. The trees were swept by the wind, shuddering and bowing before the gale. The skies were as dark as dusk although it was not yet midday. The river roared past, strengthened by a thousand freshets, tumbling white water accenting the impetus of the curling brown flood.

She trudged on, soaked to the bone.

The little house lay ahead; she started that way, walking across the muddy fields. Thick red mud clung to Ki-Ki-Tai's feet, slowing her march. She paid no attention to that.

She was, after all, only a ghost—why should such trivialities concern a ghost?

Her heart had died the night before, crushed to death with the news that Hungry Wolf was dead, killed by the white man, O'Day. Nakai no longer walked the earth, bold and strong and confident, drawing the admiring glances of maidens, the respect of strong warriors.

When life was at an end, what did the roar and thrust of the north wind matter, the cold of the driving rain?

She walked on, lifting her eyes only occasionally to peer through the silver mesh of the falling rain, nearing the little house.

Reaching the rear of the house, Ki-Ki rounded a corner to witness an incredible scene.

There, beneath a dead, shattered cottonwood tree with the rain pitchforking down around her, stood Elizabeth O'Day with a butcher knife. Her hair was washed into her eyes. Her mouth was set in a tight grin that showed her teeth. Her hands and arms were bloody. As Ki-Ki-Tai watched, she lifted the knife again and again, hacking at the already mutilated carcass of a steer.

The knife rose and fell. The steer turned in slow circles with the force of her blows. At Elizabeth's feet was a cold pile of entrails. She stepped through these without knowing or caring. Ki-Ki-Tai watched for long fascinated minutes, forgetting her own intentions in her astonishment.

"Is that how it was done to Hungry Wolf?" Ki-Ki finally said, stepping forward until she was just behind Elizabeth's shoulder.

Startled, Elizabeth dropped the knife and spun around. Her eyes were glazed and unfocused. Slowly recognition dawned in them.

"You killed him!" Elizabeth shrieked and she leaped at Ki-Ki-Tai. The two women went down in a heap in the mud. Elizabeth clawed at Ki-Ki's eyes, but the Kiowa woman turned her head from side to side, avoiding her nails. Ki-Ki reached up and grabbed Elizabeth's hair, yanking her head back hard. Screaming soundlessly, Elizabeth struck back in a rage, slapping at Ki-Ki-Tai's face with all of her strength. The heel of her hand caught the Indian woman's nose and blood flowed from her nostrils. Ki-Ki's grip was broken and she rolled away, coming to her feet to face Elizabeth.

They stood facing each other, poised for one moment, and then they threw themselves forward, colliding as they clawed with nails and kicked wildly. Elizabeth was kicked on the side of her knee and it buckled slightly. Crazed with anger, she grabbed Ki-Ki's throat and yanked her toward her, biting the Kiowa woman's shoulder. Ki-Ki struck her in the ribs with a fisted hand, driving the breath from Elizabeth's lungs.

They circled each other slowly as the thunder rattled across the plains and lightning struck close by, the rain falling now in obscuring sheets.

Ki-Ki-Tai dove at Elizabeth's legs, driving her back into the mud. Elizabeth rolled to try to escape, but Ki-Ki was on her back, shoving the white woman's face into the mud.

Half-suffocated, Elizabeth writhed frantically, got hold of Ki-Ki's wrist, and twisted hard. Rolling over, Elizabeth banged her forehead into Ki-Ki-Tai's face.

Ki-Ki screamed in anger, rising to her feet again as Elizabeth dragged herself upright, her skirts and petticoats sodden and muddy. Elizabeth ripped off her hindering skirts and launched herself at Ki-Ki-Tai, clawing at her face, trying to bite, to kick her. Ki-Ki had lost one mocassin and her shirt was ripped down the front. They separated and stood panting, glaring at each other through the rain with hate-filled eyes.

Suddenly Elizabeth turned and just walked away. Ki-Ki watched as she crossed the muddy yard to her front porch. The Kiowa woman's hands were curled, dangling before her. Suddenly she yelled and raced across the yard through the rain, tackling Elizabeth as she reached the porch.

Elizabeth went down hard on her face. She was to her feet quickly and she and Ki-Ki fell into a battlefield embrace, clawing, slapping, kicking wildly.

Elizabeth was shoved backward. She made her way up the steps and was shoved again. The door behind her banged open. Ki-Ki-Tai pursued her. Staggering, Elizabeth reached out, picked up the globed lamp on the table, and hurled it at Ki-Ki-Tai. It caught the Kiowa woman a glancing blow on the temple and smashed against the wall beyond.

Ki-Ki charged forward, knocking over the round table where the lamp had been sitting. The table went over and the two women fell to the floor.

Elizabeth drove a knee into Ki-Ki-Tai's stomach and rose, her back to the sofa. Ki-Ki leaped forward and they went over the striped sofa and down again, the sofa falling over on top of them.

For a while they struggled futilely beneath the couch and then dragged themselves out from under it on hands and knees.

Gasping for breath, Elizabeth stood facing Ki-Ki-Tai. She hardly had the strength to raise her arms. Ki-Ki was holding her abdomen with both hands. She was muddy from head to feet. Elizabeth, in her petticoats, was soaked through. There was blood on her cheek. She could feel it trickling down her face.

The women's eyes met and held. Held for a long minute as their breasts rose and fell raggedly, as the rain drummed down on the roof and near thunder spoke again. Elizabeth stepped forward hesitantly and Ki-Ki-Tai stretched out her arms to her. Something that did not need to be put into words passed between them. Muddled thoughts about the futility of returning to violence, about the sadness of losing so many loved ones, of loneliness. Elizabeth stepped to Ki-Ki-Tai and embraced her. Ki-Ki's shoulders were trembling. She held Elizabeth tightly, kissing her cheek once as the tears streamed from both women's eyes, hot and healing. They stood together for long, long minutes. There was no need to speak. Their hearts knew.

After a while, Elizabeth stepped away. With her head down, she took Ki-Ki-Tai's hand and together they walked out onto the porch and seated themselves to watch the shifting black storm clouds, the occasional flare of lightning, the driving rain, and the roaring River Cimarron.

Chapter Nine

Inclement weather notwithstanding, Ramsey crossed the Cimarron with his re-enforced expeditionary force. Along with the supporting troops recently arrived from Fort Riley, he had half a hundred civilian volunteers from the local ranches and the young town.

The Kiowas were in disorganized retreat. They had struck the Rademacher farm, but it was no more than a glancing blow, deflected by the counterattack of a passing army patrol. There had been no more than ten warriors involved, it was estimated, and these seemed to have struck the farm only as a target of opportunity as they passed.

The Indians were definitely dispersing, and if they were not leaderless, they were acting as if that were the case. It was doubted that they would ever again dare to cross the Cimarron. Small pockets of Kiowas had been confronted here and there, often surprised as they made their night camps. Those who had not resisted the army had been removed to a stockade hastily thrown up north of the town. Those who resisted had been cut down. Ramsey's personal flag was flying high. A promotion to major had been approved by General Cox, Ramsey's own inflated reports being a significant factor in that advancement.

New settlers were arriving daily in the area as the word drifted east that the western bank of the Cimarron and the lands beyond that were certain to be opened to homesteaders soon.

The day of the Kiowa was already nearing an end.

They stood looking at the ignoble grave they had dug for Washai. The rain was light, the skies swiftly moving and gray.

"His magic was not strong enough," Opaga said. No one else in the heavyhearted group commented. The shaman had been killed by the suddenly appearing troopers at the Rademacher farm. The Kiowas had raided it in the hopes of finding fresh horses. They had lost so many animals these past days. There had been no time to stop and let them graze; others had been shot out from under them.

"We must leave," Eagle Heart said, lifting his eyes to Opaga. "We must travel to the winter camp. To remain here is madness. We are scattered, and to gather is to alert the blue soldiers to our location. The women and children have no men to hunt for them. They are camped before the wind with neither shelter nor warmth."

"How can we withdraw!" Opaga was virulent. The young war leader of the Ghost Soldiers challenged Eagle Heart with his eyes. "We have suffered a disgrace. The whites must be paid back."

"We have no chance, Opaga," Eagle Heart replied gently. "We are already beaten."

Opaga jabbed an angry finger at Eagle Heart and shouted, "You are the reason we are beaten! You and all the other old men. You would not fight with us when you were needed, and now again you want to quit the field, saying we are already beaten. You are the reason we are beaten, all of you!"

"One battle does not make a war, Opaga," Ketah put in. Nakai's son was crouched, drawing aimlessly in the damp earth with his forefinger. "There will be another day."

Eagle Heart said nothing more. Koto, beside him, was equally silent. The older warriors had already discussed this among themselves. Bravery won nothing. The strength of the Kiowa band had come forth because of their trust in Hungry Wolf, and their devotion to him. Without him and his experience in tactics, they felt they had no chance at all. The young warriors would destroy themselves in some wild, unbridled attack. It was obvious to the older warriors if not to Opaga, Ketah, and the other Ta-Hai-Kai.

"We will never stop fighting! Never!" Opaga swore. "Go if you must. Go to the women, like women yourselves."

Koto started toward his son, his fists tightly clenched, but Eagle Heart held him back. A little way away from them, the rest of the older warriors sat their ponies in the rain. They had already counseled on their own, already decided. If the People were to survive, they must go and protect their wives and children, give up the river to the white invaders. Their war was not a holy war, it was a matter of survival. Let the Ta-Hai-Kai do as they pleased.

"We are leaving," Eagle Heart said solemnly, lifting his eyes to gaze into the distances. He glanced at Koto, who nodded, and the two warriors rose to start toward their waiting horses.

"There they go. The men we so admired as youths," Opaga said bitterly. More loudly he said to those around him, "I will fight as long as there is a drop of blood in my veins. Who is with me! Ketah?"

"The white soldiers killed my father, Opaga," Ketah said. "I must fight on."

"Tema?"

Ketah's younger brother seemed to hesitate, but he nodded. "I fight with you, Opaga."

The truth was that Tema would rather have ridden back with Koto and Eagle Heart. What the older warriors had said made much sense. They could not win this fight. Not here, not now. His father was dead and that had taken the heart out of many of them. It had stunned Tema. In his mind his father had been immortal, unconquerable. Washai, the man who had promised them magic, lay buried on the plains. Opaga was too hot-headed to ever become a good war leader. The Ghost Warriors were forever doomed to have no home, to run and hide and scrounge for the meanest food. Still Tema nodded and repeated:

"I will fight on."

"What is it that you believe we should do now, Opaga?" Ketah asked.

"Retreat to the west for just a little while. We need to talk to the Comanche again."

"Osolo refused Hungry Wolf," Falcon reminded him.

"Yes, but perhaps they have had time to reconsider. The blue soldiers have crossed the river. How long can it be before the whites move onto Comanche land? If Osolo cannot see that, Wotasha must."

And so the Ta-Hai-Kai band started south and west toward the homeland of their Comanche cousins. All of them felt the same. Defeated they might be, but not beaten. Not just yet. If the Comanches could be talked into joining them, all the better. If not, the Ghost Warriors could still inflict terrible losses on the whites. All they needed was a little rest, fresh horses, and time. The Ta-Hai-Kai still did not really understand as the older warriors did that time was no longer their ally, but an implacable foe.

Eagle Heart and his fifty warriors rode slowly through the constant rain for all of the morning and into the afternoon. They were grim, their mood dark. Each man thought of his wife and children . . . sitting against the cold muddy earth with only blankets to shelter them, thrown over a nursing mother's head to make a wet tent for an infant, to leave an old man no warmer than if he had no blanket at all. With few horses—and those reserved for eating—when, if, they felt they could risk a fire built with damp wood. Sitting awake in the brutally cold night without a fire's light to cheer them, a hint of warmth to allow the blood to flow . . .

"The decision is the proper one," Koto said. He rode beside Eagle Heart, dour and stiff, hunched forward against the gusting wind.

"Is it?" Eagle Heart wondered. "What would Hungry Wolf have done?"

"The same as we are, Eagle Heart. The same. Nakai was crazed with anger when he led us to join the Ta-Hai-Kai. He knew that this war could not be won in their way, that the whites would cross the river at the first opportunity."

"Perhaps." Eagle Heart was not consoled. One of the riders in front of them suddenly yelled and pointed northward. He had seen the camp where the women, the children, the old, waited for the warriors' return.

Eagle Heart's spirits lifted. "Now if the rain would cease, Koto. Perhaps . . . it is important first of all that we put many miles between ourselves and the river."

Lifting their weary ponies to a swifter gait, they rode on through the rain toward the poor camp. They had been seen approaching and women stood pointing and shouting welcomes. Children ran out to greet their fathers—those who had returned from battle—for others there would be heartbreak and tears.

Momo was among those who came out to greet them, unharmed apparently. She waved frantically and Koto rode to his wife, sliding from his pony's back to embrace her stout, coldly damp body.

"Is it all right, my husband?" she asked him. "Will everything be all right?"

"Yes. Everything will be all right," he assured her.

"Opaga—is our son alive and well?"

"Opaga is well," Koto said. "We can talk about all of this later, Momo."

"And Yatha," she persisted as Koto began to turn away. "Is our other son well?"

Koto squeezed her shoulder, keeping his eyes turned away. "It will be all right, Momo," he said, and Momo knew that her younger son would not be returning to her.

"We must pack quickly," Koto said. "Take whatever you can snatch up and put onto my pony. We cannot stay here."

"There is little enough," Momo answered. "I can be ready in minutes."

"Good."

He watched her scurry off. Then he turned to look for Eagle Heart.

And his heart stopped.

The riders came out of the fog and mist of the dim day in a long blue line, moving at a walk toward the camp. The Kiowa camp was surrounded by white soldiers.

"Eagle Heart!" Koto yelled.

Eagle Heart turned from his horse where he had been tying provisions, and glanced eastward. He, too, saw the approaching soldiers then. There were other blue soldiers coming nearer. To the north and the south of the camp. They sat their horses in the silence of the shrouded day, dark specters of death.

"What can we do?" Koto asked frantically.

Several warriors had run to join them, their rifles in their hands. The children hid behind their mothers, the memory of the last white raid still strong and terrifying. Eagle Heart put his hand on Koto's arm.

"I will talk to them, Koto," he said.

"But we . . ."

"I will talk to their leader," Eagle Heart repeated. "Have the men put their weapons down. We cannot risk another slaughter.

I will not let these children, these women, die. It is over for us, Koto, it is all over now."

Eagle Heart mounted his spotted pony, deliberately raised his hands to show that they were empty, and started out through the gray mist to meet his conquerors.

"It is ended," Ki-Ki-Tai said with melancholy bitterness. Elizabeth looked across the table to where the Kiowa woman sat. Ki-Ki hadn't touched her tea. Since returning from her morning walk, Ki-Ki-Tai had fallen into an impenetrable silence. These were days seemingly dominated by pensive silences. Now she spoke.

"I met a young boy. His name is Kalaka. Thirteen years old," Ki-Ki said.

"Yes?"

"The soldiers have captured what is left of my band," Ki-Ki told her.

"They didn't . . . !"

"No, they did not kill them." Ki-Ki smiled tightly. She turned her teacup slowly around and around on its saucer. "They have been taken prisoner. The soldiers guard them day and night. Kalaka slipped away. He is trying to find the Ta-Hai-Kai so that he can join them and fight on."

"Perhaps no one will have to fight anymore," Elizabeth suggested hopefully. "If a new treaty can be signed, and . . ."

"They are taking everybody away, Elizabeth," Ki-Ki-Tai told her.

"I don't understand what you mean."

"They are taking everyone away. Putting them on a reservation—that is something like a prison, Kalaka said. They have taken all of the men's rifles and so they cannot hunt any longer. There is no food for anyone. The soldiers promise provisions soon, but . . ." Ki-Ki shrugged. "When is *soon* when babies are hungry?"

Elizabeth said nothing; there was nothing to be said. She supposed this had all been predictable once the army found an excuse to declare the Kiowas warlike, a threat to the white settlers, once enough new settlers arrived on Cimarron demanding land. Once Ben Ramsey decided it must happen . . .

"I cannot go with them, Elizabeth," Ki-Ki said. "My sons are not among them. Hungry Wolf is dead."

"What will you do?"

"Hide. Travel alone somewhere. They will never find me in the wilderness." She laughed dryly. "Besides, why would anyone come looking for one old woman? One useless . . ." She bowed her head, shaking with dry weeping. Elizabeth reached across the table and covered Ki-Ki-Tai's hand with her own.

"You must not think of leaving, Ki-Ki-Tai. You must stay with me."

"I cannot! What would I do here?"

"What will you do by yourself? You must stay here, Ki-Ki-Tai. For now at least. Do not go. Who else does either of us have now?"

The morning was clear, the river glitter-bright. Ramsey, astride his gray horse, his bright new gold oak leaves gleaming on the shoulders of his fringed buckskin shirt, rode toward the fort. Everything was now progressing according to his plans. Everything.

He rode on, considering what more he could do to further his advancement through the ranks. When the lone horseman emerged from beneath the canopy of river oak branches, Ramsey came instantly alert. Squinting into the sun, he could make out Amos Starr riding toward him. *Now what?* he wondered.

For a man who was supposedly a working cowhand, Starr did

virtually nothing on the Kittinger ranch. Kent had proposed firing him several times, but each time Ben Ramsey had intervened. It had puzzled Kent O'Day, but he had shrugged and let Ramsey have his way. After all it was Isadora's land and half of the cattle belonged to Nesbitt's widow.

"Morning, Major Ramsey," the dark-eyed Texan said as he drew up beside the officer.

"Hello, Starr. What are you doing out here? There's no work to be done on the ranch?"

"I suppose there is," Starr answered, tipping his hat back on his head. He looked at Ramsey with those strange muddy eyes of his. They were unnerving; Starr never seemed to look directly at anything. There was a shrewdness in them, however. Oh, yes, Starr was shrewd.

"To tell you the truth, Major, I'm kinda tired of cows. The ranch. The clothes I wear, the way I smell."

Bathing from time to time might help that, Ramsey thought but did not say. He had an inkling of what was up. That must be it—Starr wanted some money so that he could be moving on. Well, he considered, it would be worth a few dollars to get rid of Amos Starr.

"How much do you need?" Ramsey asked.

"Huh . . . ?" Then Starr grinned. He sat with both hands on the pommel of his saddle, relaxed and confident. "You got me wrong, Major. I don't want no money from you. I ain't going anywhere."

"You said . . ."

"I said I was tired of the ranch, of being a cowhand. Well, I am, and I figure you can help me out there."

Ramsey, siting rigidly in the saddle, waited, watching the Texan.

"Well?" he demanded. "What is it, then? What do you want, Starr?"

"You ain't been into the town for a while, have you?"

"No, I haven't."

"Well, those people have decided it's time to organize things, you see? They elected a mayor, a man named Dennis Shaughnessy. Coming up here soon, they got another election . . . for town marshal. I want that job, Major."

"Don't be absurd."

"Absurd?" Starr chewed on that word for a while. "That don't apply, Major. No, I want to be marshal, and you're going to see that it happens."

"Just how do you expect me to do that?" Ramsey asked.

"Oh, you can do it," Starr said confidently. "Right now you're riding high in this territory, Major. The man who killed Hungry Wolf and drove the Kiowa menace off. The man who opened the land west of the Cimarron."

"And you want . . ."

"I want you to stand for me, Major. Tell folks that you're behind me."

"Endorse you for marshal?"

"Just that, yeah. You and Kent O'Day."

"I can't speak for . . ."

"You and Kent O'Day, the biggest rancher in the area. I reckon you two are the most important men on Cimarron right now, wouldn't you say?"

Ramsey stared at Starr. This was the last thing he had expected. The new town—now named Bethlehem, the people having decided against "Cimarron"—deserved something better than Amos Starr as town marshal. He could see how the idea might appeal to Starr. A little power of his own. A little power of his own, undoubtedly to wield the opportunity to skim some money here and there, but it rankled.

"Why don't you do it my way, Starr?" Ramsey asked in a conciliatory tone. "I can offer you a good stake, and you could move on—wherever you wanted."

Anywhere away from here.

"I told you what I want, Ramsey. Now are you going to help me or not?"

As if there were a choice, Ramsey thought. How long would he be at this man's mercy? Maybe this would end; maybe his was all he would demand. They never mentioned what lay between them. The murder of Nesbitt Kittinger. But it was always in Ramsey's mind and in Starr's. Each day when Ramsey saw the indolent cowboy leaning against the corral, lazily coiling a rope or sitting in the shade, watching him. His little smirk as Ramsey strode past.

"If I do it—then what, Starr?"

"Nothing more, Major. You're off the hook for good and all."

"How do I know that?"

Starr tugged his hat back down. From the shadow of its brim, he replied, "Because, Major, I know what you are and I don't ever want to push you too far. I wouldn't want to end up in some alley or on the plains with a bullet in my back."

Then with a curt nod, Starr turned his horse aside. Leaving Ramsey tight-lipped and tense with anger, glaring after him

"You're right, too, you ugly bastard," Ramsey said through his teeth, "don't push me too far, or that is exactly what will happen."

Her name was Margaret O'Day, but her mother called her Ki-Ki and the child preferred that name, probably because when she was a very young girl it had been easier for her to say.

She was quick, agile, bright-eyed, and clever, interested in everything around her. There was no school where they lived in the La Junta Mountains. There were no neighbors except for the occasional wandering Ute hunter or solitary white trapper. Margaret could read and write very well indeed, though. She had learned as her father had from the Good Book and his John Bunyan. Too, Margaret had been fortunate in that she had been raised to speak two languages: English and Kiowa—which Kianceta said teasingly the girl spoke better than Oliver, despite their years together.

Now the girl stood watching her father. The old black dog sat beside her, its head cocked as it, too, watched this unusual work.

Oliver was tying his load of furs onto the black mule's pack saddle. Beaver, otter, and bear hides wrapped up in a bulky canvas tarp were strapped down snugly. Oliver O'Day stepped back, wiped his forehead, and looked with satisfaction at the load. It had been a good winter for trapping and for hunting. There were enough furs on the mule's back to see them through an entire new year.

"I still don't see why I may not go," Margaret said.

"You're still too young," Oliver answered.

"That's what you said last year, Father."

"Yes, I did. I'm surprised that you remember. But still you are too young. It's a long way and that town is not a good place for you."

He did not mention that a part of that was because she was half-Indian. It would never have occurred to Margaret, and Oliver didn't want her to know that people with such small minds existed until it was absolutely necessary.

She watched him with huge brown eyes, the lashes long around them. Her lips were parted, showing an even row of white teeth. She wore a buckskin dress with beading across the top.

"Oliver!"

"Yes, Kianceta."

She emerged from the cabin, as beautiful as the day they had met. No, more beautiful. Age had lent her a dignity, a bearing that few young women have.

"You will remember steel sewing needles and a hand mirror . . ." She glanced at Margaret. "Someone has broken mine."

"I will remember."

"It was an accident!" Margaret protested,

"I know it, dear." Kianceta stood beside her daughter, putting her arm around her shoulders. "I was teasing."

"I don't like being teased," Margaret said so soberly that both of her parents had to hide smiles.

"And what will you have from town, Margaret?" Oliver asked.

"Something sweet," she said immediately. "And . . . and a doll if you can find one."

"You have dolls."

"Only those Mother makes . . . Oh, I love them," she added hastily, "but, Father!"

"I'll look," Oliver promised. He stood for a minute in his buffalo coat and flop hat, hesitant to take his leave.

Beneath the buffalo coat Oliver was dressed in a beaded buckskin shirt and buckskin trousers. He wore a beard now, light brown and curling. His hair reached his shoulders and around his neck was a bearclaw necklace. He wore hard boots instead of moccasins and carried a Remington pistol and a bowie knife on his belt. They had no money to waste on clothes, not with buckskin so abundant and so much more durable than cloth, more practical for their wilderness life.

"Well, then!" Oliver said finally with mock enthusiasm. The journey would be long; he would miss them terribly. He walked to Kianceta and hugged her, rocking her slightly from side to side. Then he picked Margaret up and kissed her on the forehead, smiling as he looked into her adoring eyes.

"I'm off then, Kianceta. Margaret."

"Be careful, Oliver," Kianceta said. "Don't hurry so much that you will have an accident."

"I will be careful," he promised. "I will see you in three days then, all right?"

Regret had struggled to his feet, looking eagerly to Oliver.

"I'm sorry, old dog. It's too far for you these days."

Regret didn't accept that. He walked to Oliver, leaned his weight against his leg, and looked up with pleading eyes.

Kianceta laughed. "Oh, take him, Oliver! I don't want him staying up all night, leaping up at every sound, or howling for you! You know how he can howl!"

"All right." He crouched, taking Regret's huge head in his hands. "You can go. Do you know why? Only because you'd be a nuisance to the ladies if I left you behind."

Regret thumped his big tail happily, and when Oliver swung aboard his pony, lifted a hand in farewell, and led the black pack mule up the trail toward the distant town, Regret padded contentedly along behind him.

Margaret yawned prodigiously. She was tired but sleep was not coming easily. It was because she was used to her father tucking her in each night, to having Regret on the floor beside her to talk to. It was still very cold this early in spring at their altitude, and Margaret had her blankets pulled up almost covering her eyes as she half-slept, half-wandered, through imagination. She wished summer would come quickly this year. In the summer they frequently slept outside, in the forest along the beaver creek. Looking up through the lofty pines to the starlit skies was like looking all the way to heaven, she thought.

It had been a peaceful evening, sitting in front of the fire, reading until her eyelids grew heavy and Kianceta brought her to her tiny room.

It was the silence of the house, Margaret realized, that was keeping her awake, troubling her on some level. Always at this time of night she could hear Mother and Father speaking in low voices, Kianceta's occasional laughter.

When she was younger, Margaret had wondered what the grownups did out there while she slept. Creeping to the door, she had peered into the living room. There was nothing to see. Nothing. Just Kianceta and Father sitting close together, her head on his shoulder, his arm around her as he read or they both simply sat watching the play of the flames in the hearth, the twisting shadows they cast against walls and ceiling. She frequently wondered how they could simply sit there and be content, but they were, and now with her father gone, Margaret realized that she, too, found their quiet conversation, their uncomplicated evenings, comforting.

Nearly asleep now, she was startled to wakefulness. There had been a sound—or was it only a dream sound? She thought she had heard a horse outside the house. But her mother had not risen. The door had not been approached. Yawning, Margaret rolled onto her side and threw her arm over her eyes.

The door banged open and Kianceta yelled out. Margaret heard the table overturn, heard bootheels against the plank floor. She leaped from her bed and rushed to the bedroom door.

There were two men there, the front door open behind them. Huge men, they seemed, and Margaret's mother was on the floor. One man had her pinned to it as she thrashed wildly from side to side. The other man was tearing open the bureau, looking for something.

A scream froze in Margaret's mouth. She wanted to rush forward, to attack the men with her fists, but she had been taught to do otherwise. Told time and time again what she was to do if *anyone* broke into the house. Not to worry about Regret or her father, not even her mother. She was to climb out of the window and run to their secret hiding place deep in the pines. To not hesitate, to take nothing at all—there were blankets and a little food and water at the hiding place.

Still, now that something had actually happened, it was a long minute as her mother twisted and scratched and fought back against the laughing man who held her down, before Margaret could tear herself away from the scene, force herself to run to the window, step up on the headboard of the bed and crawl through, and run barefoot through the dark pines in the cold of night toward the hiding place.

It was fifty yards up the hill behind the house. There, screened by oak brush, were three huge boulders stacked together. It looked as if there was only a small opening leading nowhere between two of them, but Margaret knew that by squeezing through the narrow cleft she could reach a place where someone could remain totally hidden from view.

She could not bring herself to enter immediately. She stood outside in the chill of the mountain night, looking down toward the house, her breath coming in hot gasps, her heart flailing. She heard no sounds. Firelight still showed dimly. Smoke rose in gentle curls from the chimney until the gusting breeze whipped it away. She rested her hand against the granite boulder and stared through the blur of her tears toward the house, feeling somehow cowardly and treacherous. Still, she did what she had been taught to do, squeezing into the narrow cleft between the two upright boulders, entering the frightening darkness of the cold and terrifying night.

Margaret's teeth were chattering violently. By touch she found the blankets Oliver had cached there, shook them out, and sat, wrapping one of them around her shoulders to sit awake through the endless desolate hours of night.

The first thing Oliver noticed upon his return was the silence. There are different sorts of silence—the silence of a summer morning, the silence of a frozen winter night. There is the silence of the grave. The silence he felt now was nearer to the last. Uneasily he unsheathed his rifle and rode forward slowly into the small valley. He should have been seen already from the house, had anyone been looking, yet no welcoming cries rang out. They could not be sleeping—neither Kianceta nor Margaret were late sleepers. They believed in rising early to greet the joys of a new day. Could they be gathering? They could have gone to forage for blackberries or pinyon nuts. Fishing, perhaps? Margaret loved to fish although Kianceta didn't care for it except as a matter of necessity.

Regret, realizing that he was now home after their long journey, barked enthusiastically several times. Still no one appeared.

In his saddlebags Oliver had nearly fifty dollars from the sale of the furs, a few notions for Kianceta, and a doll for his daughter. Half an hour ago he had felt pleased with himself, the morning, and the world. Returning with enough money to support them for some time and some additional to put into the fund he saved to repay Donovan Hart should the day come they ever crossed paths again, his horse moving easily beneath him, even the mule content now that its load had been lifted, returning to familiar range, Regret trotting at his side, his wife and daughter waiting for him in their warm, dry cabin . . .

Now he felt that something was terribly wrong. Oliver tried to shake the notion. He supposed he always had had some vague dread that something would, one day, come along to spoil their serenity; this was different. Something did not *feel* right, and he could not ignore that feeling.

Approaching the house, he sat in the saddle for a long while. Regret ran to the porch, barking and wagging his tail, and Oliver called out:

"Kianceta! Margaret!"

There was no answer. The melancholy wind blew through the

long ranks of pine and blue spruce. Thin, high clouds drifted over the mountain valley.

Oliver O'Day swung down from his horse, walked heavily to the front door of the cabin, flung it open, and froze.

His motion stopped; his heart faltered. His mind, faced with the unacceptable, ceased to function for long seconds.

Kianceta, her skirt hoisted, her eyes wide, lay stiff and dead on the floor, her hands clenched, one leg twisted unnaturally to the side.

"Kianceta?"

In his disorientation, he went to her and grabbed her cold hand, shaking her. He yelled at her, knowing all the while that she was dead.

"Kianceta! Don't be so stupid!"

There was no movement. Regret nuzzled the dead body and Oliver slapped him away angrily. Then he went to his knees and stared down at Kianceta's still body. He thought he prayed, but could not be sure. If so, it was a blasphemous prayer. His lips moved, disconnected from his body. He still held her hand and now he let it drop. There was something he had to tell her . . . something about how she had made his life complete, given him love and strength and purpose . . . he couldn't frame these thoughts, they shot through his mind in a rapid, disorganized progression.

Then for a little while he cried. Or perhaps it was for a long, long time.

He took her still form in his arms and carried her out into the yard. He was surprised to find a shovel in his hand, but placing her gently against the cold grassy ground, he began digging, digging with a fury that heated his body, caused his muscles to ache and spasm and sweat to rain from him. He tore his shirt off and continued digging, almost frantically, wanting to end this, wanting to put Kianceta somewhere where he would not have to see her lifeless cocoon.

Margaret had heard the dog barking. Slowly, she crept from the forest. She watched shakily as her father dug furiously. She knew that her mother was dead. Slipping back into the house the morning after the big men had come, she had found Kianceta unmoving on the floor. In a blind panic, Margaret had returned to the hiding place, still following her often-repeated instructions. There was food there, but she did not eat, not for two days while she waited, crying, falling into tormented sleep, awakening to the darkness and the cold.

She watched as Oliver filled the grave. When he was finished he threw the shovel wildly into the trees and then sat beside the grave. He sat there for hours. Unmoving, his head buried in his hands. Still Margaret did not approach him. It seemed to her that her parents were communicating in some secret way as they did on those firelit winter evenings after she had gone to bed . . .

"Father?"

Oliver lifted haunted eyes. For a long minute he seemed not to recognize his own daughter.

Then he stretched out his arms and she rushed to him, clinging to him, crying as he stroked her back and murmured meaningless words of comfort.

"Come on," he said at length, rising to his feet. It wasn't good for a child to remain long in the presence of death. He took her hand and they walked back toward the house, Regret following at a distance, still unsure what sin he had committed to cause his master to strike him.

"I'm hungry, Father," Margaret said.

"All right. Can you cook something for both of us?"

"I don't know. Yes, I think I can."

"Fine. Listen, I have to tend to the horse and the mule. If you can cook something, then we'll eat."

"What do you want?" she asked.

"Anything at all. Do your best. I'm sure it will be all right."

In a confused waking dream, Oliver stripped the saddle and bridle from his horse, took the pack from the mule's back, and turned them free in the meadow to graze and drink from the stream. Storing the tack in the small shed, he returned to the cabin, his saddlebags over his shoulder. Margaret was sitting at the table, staring at the wall, her hands clenched between her thighs. Oliver attempted a smile.

"Look what I've brought you, Margaret," he said, taking a porcelain-headed doll from his saddlebags. It had a small, painted red mouth, apple cheeks, robin's-egg blue eyes, and a gingham bonnet and dress with a little white apron. He offered it to Margaret, but she didn't reach out to take it. He placed it beside her plate on the table. She looked up, half-smiled, and said "Thank you" perfunctorily, but she didn't touch the doll.

"You don't like it, Margaret?"

"It's beautiful, Father . . . I just don't think I shall ever play with dolls again. I'm sorry . . ."

Then she leaped up from the table and ran into her bedroom, and for a long time afterward, Oliver could hear her crying.

It wouldn't work.

Walking along the creek, occasionally bending down to pick up a stone to throw into the water, Oliver came to that decision. He could not raise the girl alone. Not out here. What could he do with her when he had to hunt or check his traps? Leave her alone in the cabin? After this! It was impossible. Also, she was growing up rapidly. He had no idea how to raise a girl-child to womanhood. It was just impossible.

His thoughts grew darker as clouds shifted overhead.

Who had done this? Who had destroyed his life, reduced it to ashes, snow, and stone! He didn't want to ask Margaret what she had witnessed. Not yet. Looking around the house carefully, he had found the tracks of two horses—both shod—and the boots of two men. He was able to track them for a little way to the east, but then the tracks had vanished over shale. Oliver wanted to hunt on, to find them and exact revenge, but there was the girl to consider . . .

The house had been ransacked, but nothing had been taken. What did they have that anyone would have wanted anyway? The little they had of value—the money set aside bit by bit over the years to repay Donovan Hart—had not been discovered beneath the floorboards.

They had only taken his entire world.

And Kianceta's necklace.

Oliver had noticed that as he carried her to the gravesite and bent his head to kiss her cold lips one last time. The silver and turquoise necklace, the wedding gift from Donovan Hart, was missing. He had looked around the house, thinking it might have been torn off during the struggle, but it was gone.

The next few days passed in brooding silence. Father and daughter barely communicated. Regret lay mournfully near the cold fireplace, head on his forepaws. No good. This was no good at all. The house was haunted; the long, beautiful valley was a sepulcher; the wind sang empty dirges as it moved through the tall pines.

"We have to leave, Margaret," Oliver said to his daughter on the final unbearable morning. The sun fanned brilliantly through the clouds and a doe and her fawn drank from the brilliant river. Still, it seemed the darkest of days. Margaret looked at him, saying nothing. She nodded; perhaps she, too, knew that they could no longer stay in this horribly shadowed valley.

"Where can we go, Father?"

"Away. Just away. I don't know."

But he did know. There was only one place, where Margaret could be taken care of by a caring woman who wouldn't care if she was a half-breed, who would welcome her with open arms, where Oliver could labor meaningfully. The only place where they could find shelter and warmth in this cold world. Home.

Back to his mother's house on Cimarron.

The day following they rode out of the little valley forever, neither of them sparing a backward glance for the place, the only home Margaret had ever known. Oliver led the black mule; Margaret rode Kianceta's paint pony. Regret hobbled along as best he could. The dog was getting so old; Oliver doubted it could make it back home. He hoped so for Margaret's sake. He never wanted her to see death again.

They crested the mountain trail and rode out onto the long plains. With spring arriving the new grass was bright green, bending with the wind. There was much game. They saw a herd of fifty pronghorns, dozens of mule deer, a cougar, and a fat grizzly bear with two roly-poly cubs waddling along behind her.

And on the third day they saw the approaching Indians.

There were two dozen of them, painted, angling toward their line of travel from the southeast. Oliver did not unsheath his rifle; there was no point in making himself appear warlike, but his hand did not stray far from his holstered pistol as the Indians drew nearer.

Ketah frowned. Still young, his face already showed the marks of a hard life. The lines that framed his mouth were like deep knife cuts. His black eyes were sullen and heavily lidded.

"What is this man?" Opaga asked. "Fearless, foolish, or mad?"

"It doesn't matter which he is," Ketah said. He was a white man, although he wore buckskins as did the girl with him. The man had light hair worn long and a light beard. A mountain man from the north, Ketah decided. *He should have stayed there.*

Ketah's mood was foul. The day before his band had been attacked by a force of Mexican soldiers, well across the border that the Kiowas had believed to be a line of sanctuary. They had lost eight Ta-Hai-Kai warriors in the ensuing battle. Tema had returned from the Comanche camp with bad news—Osolo and Wotasha remained intransigent. The Comanches refused to join them in their holy war. Dogged by white soldiers, unable to remain in one place for more than a day or two, the wandering Kiowas were weary, hungry, sick, and injured.

"There is something familiar about that man," Opaga said.

"I have never seen him."

"There is something, no matter. The girl, Ketah, she is Indian. I almost take her for Kiowa."

Ketah's eyes narrowed. As they drew nearer, he could see that there was something distantly familiar about the white man. And the girl almost did look to be Kiowa.

Opaga had lifted his rifle, but Ketah said, "Let's talk to them first." Opaga shrugged in response, lowering his weapon. It made no difference one way or the other when they killed the white man. Perhaps he knew something of value.

Oliver feared only for his daughter. His heart raced and his skin crawled with excitement; he was only human. But on another plane he did not care if he lived or died so long as Margaret could be placed in a good home before that happened. He glanced at the pretty young girl, her dark hair flying free in the breeze. She seemed unconcerned. It was her mother's blood rising in her, he decided with a surge of pride. He halted his horse and mule, Margaret at his side. There was no point in trying to elude the Indians. Their only chance was to try to talk the Indians out of killing them or taking them prisoner. If these were from a settled band, Margaret might be seen as a valuable captive to be raised to help with the women's work in their camp. If they were drifting renegades, which Oliver feared they were, they would have no use for either one of them.

Two of the Indian leaders rode slowly toward Oliver, who had already cocked his sidearm in its holster. Margaret had heard the ratcheting sound, but she had only glanced at her father, confident in his ability to protect them. He saw not fear, but defiance in her eyes. Both of the approaching riders looked belligerent and overconfident. And why would they not be?

As they waited, the Indians rode directly to them. Reining in, they both studied Oliver, and then, very closely, Margaret.

"The girl is Kiowa," Ketah said.

"Yes, she is," Oliver replied in their own tongue, surprising them both.

"How is this? What are you doing with a young Kiowa girl?" Keta asked.

"My wife was Kiowa."

"Your wife . . . ?" Ketah's eyes opened wide as he studied Margaret once more. He was looking into her eyes, at a face familiar since his childhood. The girl—it was Kianceta's daughter!

"What is your name!" Ketah demanded. "Tell me?"

"My name is Oliver O'Day."

Opaga leaned forward sharply, but Ketah put a restraining hand on his arm.

"And what is the child's name?" Ketah asked with difficulty.

"My name is Ki-Ki," Margaret said boldly in the Kiowa tongue. "Why are you braves bothering us!"

Ki-Ki! Ketah was stunned. Opaga laughed at the girl's audacity.

"Do you know who I am, Oliver O'Day?" Ketah asked.

"No, I don't."

"My mother's name was Ki-Ki-Tai. Is that why the child is called that?"

"Yes. Kianceta loved your mother very much."

284

Opaga interrupted. "Ketah! This is the man who took Kianceta!"

"Yes."

"The man whose father . . ."

"Yes. The man whose father killed my own, Hungry Wolf," Ketah said fiercely. "Did you know that, Oliver O'Day?"

"No, I did not. Kianceta and I left so that we would not have to live with a background of war. We had no way of knowing anything in the mountains where we lived, isolated as we were. I am surprised to learn this. I am sorry your father is dead."

"Sorry!" Opaga said scornfully. "*You* are sorry Hungry Wolf is dead!"

"Yes, I am," Oliver said sincerely. "Kianceta spoke often of him, too."

"Did she speak of me as well?" Ketah asked.

"No. I don't know who you are."

"I am Ketah! The one to whom she was promised in marriage! The one who killed the man who killed Hungry Wolf. The one who killed your father, Oliver O'Day." Stunned, still Oliver was not surprised. Saddened, he felt no anger against the Kiowa.

"Was it in battle?" Oliver asked.

"Yes."

"My father was a warrior. The time comes when every warrior meets his final battle. I am sorry for him. I am sorry for your father's death."

Opaga spoke to Ketah so rapidly that Oliver could catch only half of the words.

"What are you delaying for, Ketah? This is the man who stole Kianceta. Now she is dead. His father killed Nakai. It is his time to die now."

"And what of Kianceta's daughter?" Ketah asked. "What can be done with her, Opaga?"

"We could . . ." but he fell silent; they could do nothing for a young girl. They no longer had a camp, women to take care of her and instruct her.

"What shall we do then, Ketah?"

"I do not know." Emotions, mixed and confused, collided in Ketah's mind.

Ketah asked, "Kianceta? Was she happy? Did you make her happy, Oliver O'Day?"

Oliver searched for the right response, but it was Margaret who wasted no time in answering for him.

"My father and mother loved each other vastly. Kianceta laughed with every new day. Never were we hungry or cold. Never did my father strike my mother. He cared for us and kept us joyful in our hearts. No woman ever loved a man more than Kianceta loved him. She was happy beyond any words I have."

Ketah listened expressionlessly, wondering. If he had found them somehow years ago and taken Kianceta home to be his promised wife, what kind of life would it have been? War, fear, smoke and guns and blood. So much blood.

"And so Kianceta is . . . gone, now, Oliver O'Day?"

"Yes, she is gone now, Ketah. I have only the girl to remember her by."

"And so now you are going home?"

"Yes. To my mother's house on the river where the girl can have a woman's influence."

"Ketah!" Opaga's expression was still acrimonious. "This man is your enemy. Enough talking!"

"Bah!" Ketah said angrily. "What glory is there in killing one man who is not even a soldier? He is nothing. Let them pass. That is my decision."

Opaga's mouth opened and then clamped shut again. He sat his war pony glaring at Oliver. Eventually, however, he shrugged, shaking his head. Let Ketah have his way. "As you will have it then, brother," he said. He turned his pony and rode back to join the other warriors.

Ketah delayed for another minute, studying Margaret's face. "You ride to your mother's house, then?"

"Yes, Ketah."

"One day I may see you there, Oliver O'Day. I will have no weapon with me. One day . . . I may wish to see the girl again . . . one day."

Then he yanked his horse's head around and raced off to catch up with Opaga. Oliver waited as the Kiowas drifted on their way. When they were nothing more than indistinct figures nearing the horizon, Oliver turned to Margaret and said, "We'll ride on."

"I didn't understand all of that, Father," the girl said as they walked their horses eastward once more.

"Nor did I," Oliver admitted. "Nor did I."

That night they camped in the open while the cold prairie wind swept over them, but on the morning following they found the bright long-flowing Cimarron. Crossing it, they rode slowly, steadily southward, keeping near the riverbank until they came upon the small log house where two women sat watching their approach with deeply curious eyes until finally they leaped to their feet and began waving, calling to them. Oliver lifted his hat and waved it overhead.

"Who is that, Father? Where are we?"

"It looks, Margaret, as if we are home," Oliver answered, and they rode slowly on across the yard to where Elizabeth and Ki-Ki-Tai waited for them.

CHAPTER TEN

The seasons came and went on Cimarron. In the summer the corn flourished under the warm sun, ripening to golden yellow, the fields worked by Oliver and the women. The fall harvests had been good except for one dry year, and there was extra money for the small things that make life a little easier. Margaret was becoming a woman, groomed and tutored by the two older women, Ki-Ki-Tai and Elizabeth. The girl had never been sent to school through Oliver's reluctant decision. Not in Bethlehem, a town with a long, biased memory of the Kiowa wars.

Oliver himself seldom visited the town. He had always felt uncomfortable among so many strangers. Jostling, yelling, cursing, scurrying about to no apparent purpose.

Yet, on this fall morning with frost on the grass and the sun rising slowly into a clear sky, he saddled his horse and started toward Bethlehem. The army had honored a voucher for their corn and the money needed to be banked. With his money belt strapped beneath his shirt and a shopping list in his pocket, he rode toward the distant, low-lying town, the roan horse still exhaling steam through its nostrils as the morning slowly warmed.

Across the river he could see smoke from a dozen new houses. He shook his head; still a young man, he felt as if he had already outlived his time in these years of rapid change. The transcontinental railroad had been completed the year before; new towns like Abilene and Dodge City were booming. Kent O'Day had been shipping cattle east from his steadily multiplying herd—or so Oliver had heard. He never saw his brother. Kent still refused to visit his mother because of Kianceta and Ki-Ki-Tai. It was sad, but there was nothing to be done about it; Elizabeth had apparently given up hope of a reconciliation.

A solitary rider was approaching Oliver on the trail, and he squinted into the sunlight, recognizing Charles Kittinger. The boy looked nothing like Nesbitt Kittinger, but he supposed the coloring came from Isadora's side of the family. Meeting, the two men reined up to talk.

"Good morning, Mr. O'Day."

"How are you, Charles?"

"Fine as I can be."

"Isadora?"

"Mother's fine. Bettina as well."

"And her baby?"

"Baby! You'd better not let Louise hear you call her that. It's hard to believe, Mr. O'Day, but she's nearly eleven years old and almost as tall as her brother, Tad."

"It is hard to believe." Neither of them had mentioned Kent, Oliver realized, nor Ben Ramsey. "Are you headed anyplace special, Charles?"

"No . . . mostly I'm just out riding this morning, sir," the boy said, but he flushed faintly under his tan.

"All right. I'll be seeing you then, Charles. Oh," he said as Charles Kittinger started on his way, "I believe Margaret was doing laundry his morning—you'll probably find her out back, hanging clothes."

Charles' blush deepened a little. He mumbled a thank-you and rode on. Oliver smiled. It was hardly a secret that Isadora's son was smitten with Margaret. Or maybe it was a secret—to Ben Ramsey and Isadora. If they knew that their son and heir was seeing a half-breed girl . . . and what in the world would

Kent say! Oliver shook his head at that thought and started on his way again.

Bethlehem was still quiet in the morning coolness when Oliver reached the settlement. Long shadows crossed the rutted street. Only a few wagons were on the street, drawn up before the dry goods store, and there weren't more than a dozen hitched horses to be seen, and these in front of the saloons where the more determined of the drinkers had already begun to gather. Women, escorted or in pairs, walked down the new boardwalks. A few aproned storekeepers stood in their doorways, hands on hips, surveying the new morning or watching for customers, a few lazily sweeping off the porches of their establishments. Oliver knew not a single one of them.

There was some sort of commotion ahead of him—what, he couldn't tell until he drew nearer.

He heard several violent thumps, a muffled groan, a pleading voice. Then he saw what was happening. A mob of white men, six or seven of them, had an old Indian pinned against the alley wall of the blacksmith's shop. As Oliver watched another punch was landed. A narrow, red-faced man slammed his fist into the Indian's stomach, and he doubled up. At the fringe of the crowd was a man in a brown town suit and a bowler hat, leaping up and down in protest. A few yards farther along the alley one of Amos Starr's deputies, a big man with a thick black beard, the star on his shirt glinting in the morning sunlight, stood picking his teeth with a toothpick.

"Stop it!" the man in the suit was screaming.

"We don't allow no Indians in this town, Bonner! It's all your fault anyway."

"He's an old man—for God's sake, stop it!"

Oliver turned his horse into the head of the alley and walked it forward. He guided it directly into the crowd, his horse's shoulder knocking two men aside. Oliver kicked a third attacker in the chest with his boot.

"What the hell . . . !" the red-faced man spun around furiously. Oliver's rifle rested across his saddlebow, the muzzle nearly in the man's face.

"It's over," Oliver said evenly. "Get the hell away from him."

The narrow man stared up at the bearded, buckskin-clad intruder and sputtered a curse.

The deputy marshal started forward, Oliver watching his approach from the corner of his eye.

"Good morning, deputy," Oliver said.

"Good morning! Who the hell are you?" the deputy demanded. "What do you think you're doing here?"

"My name is Oliver O'Day. What I'm doing is stopping a bunch of spineless thugs from beating up an old man. Which I assume is against the law even in Bethlehem."

The deputy heard only a part of that. The name he had gotten.

"O'Day?" he asked blankly.

"That's right. Oliver O'Day."

"Your brother is . . . ?"

"Kent is my brother. That's right."

"Heard about you," the deputy muttered. The other men stood in a silent circle around them. Those who had been knocked to the ground had been helped up. One of them threatened Oliver: "You could be next, stranger."

"You don't feel like going home dead this morning, do you?" Oliver asked seriously. "I will shoot any man who makes a move toward me. I mean it. Now, step back and let the Indian go."

Slowly the men parted and the Indian, obviously a Kiowa, his face battered and bloody, looked at Oliver and then at the man in the town suit, his eyes bitter with trampled dignity. He walked away, holding himself erect. The white men dispersed with angry backward glances directed at Oliver. The deputy approached Oliver.

"If you weren't Kent O'Day's brother, I'd teach you a lesson, mister."

"I wouldn't let that stop you," Oliver said quietly. "I have to warn you, though—*I* fight back. But if you're determined that you want it that way . . .'"

The deputy hesitated, perhaps wondering what Amos Starr would say. He shook his shaggy head and laughed, "But I would make a habit of looking over my shoulder in this town, was I you."

"Mister, I formed that habit a long time ago," Oliver said.

The deputy and Oliver locked eyes for a long second, and then with a growl and a curse, the deputy turned and stalked away up the alley.

The man in the town suit and derby hat was still there.

Thanks," he said.

"It's nothing."

"It is," the man replied. "In this town it is something to stand up to Starr and his deputies. My name is Christian Bonner. It's more or less my fault that this happened."

"Oh?"

"Yes. I've just opened up a newspaper office here. We've only printed three numbers so far, but it seems I've already ruffled some important feathers . . . well," he said, looking around, "that's far too long a story to go into here and now. You probably would have no interest in it anyway."

"But I do," Oliver said. "Tell me where you office is, and after I've done a few errands, I'd like to come by and talk—if that's all right with you."

The newspaperman beamed. "It's more than all right. I'd be very pleased, Mr. O'Day. I take it that you've been around here for a long while."

"Most of my life. So far as I know my family was the first to settle on Cimarron."

"Then maybe you can give me a few pointers. I'm afraid I'm walking on very thin ice over a pond that I am unfamiliar with."

That was the impression that Oliver had already gotten. Christian Bonner was not a handsome man in any respect. He had shaggy eyebrows shading round brown eyes, one of which seemed smaller than the other, a large nose with a bump on the bridge, and a long jaw too large for the rest of his face. But there was a sincerity about him, a sort of subdued passion. For what? The truth? Facts? Social justice? Was he some sort of crusader living in his land of dreams? Oliver was still wondering about what sort of man Bonner was when, two hours later with his errands completed, he found the small newspaper office at the end of the street with a carefully written but unprofessional sign over it reading "Bethlehem Observer."

The interior of the office smelled of ink and machine oil. There was a platen press in one corner, for handbills and such, Oliver guessed, and a larger job press in the center of the room next to a font. A framed newspaper hung on the wall above a rolltop desk. Christian Bonner came out of the back room carrying a quart bottle of ink. He wore sleeve garters and a black rubber apron.

"Well, so you did decide to come over!" he said by way of greeting.

"I thought I might as well. You sort of piqued my curiosity."

"Did I?" Bonner asked, putting the ink bottle down, wiping his hands on a rag. "Well—that's something my newspaper doesn't seem to be accomplishing—except in the wrong cases, that is."

"Meaning?" Oliver asked.

"Oh, no one seems to care much about anything but the market reports and social functions, such as they are, except those who are quick to take offense. And they do take offense,

Mr. O'Day."

"Call me Oliver, please. By the offended, you mean . . . ?"

"Some of them? Marshal Amos Starr. Colonel Ben Ramsey
. . ."

"Ramsey?" Oliver said in surprise.

"You know him, I take it," Christian Bonner said. "Yes, I may
have cut my own throat there. Nothing like having a newcomer
swagger into town and attack a local legend like Colonel
Ramsey. Civil War hero. Brave Indian fighter. The man who
defeated the Kiowas and opened the land to settlers, making life
safe for the white families." Bonner sat down in his swivel chair
and leaned back, interlacing his fingers.

"I guess I have been missing something here," Oliver said.
"Do you want to tell me about it?"

"If you have the time," Bonner said with a sigh. He ran ink-
stained fingers through his thinning brown hair.

"Go ahead," Oliver invited. "I'm always interested when a
man has something to say."

"Well, I think I do," Bonner answered, "but getting the word
out to anyone is almost impossible. They've got me beat, Oliver."

"What do you mean? Are you thinking about closing up shop
already after just three numbers?"

Bonner smiled. "No. I still mean to print the paper, but I
can't get it out on the streets. I had two good boys working for
me here—the first issue went out on the streets and sold fairly
well," he said glancing at the framed newspaper on the wall
behind him. "A few days later both of the boys came back and
told me that their parents wouldn't let them work for me
anymore. I haven't been able to find any replacements."

"Ruffled feathers."

"That's it," Bonner said. "It was my mistake. I thought the
people here were ready for the truth; I was wrong. The power

on Cimarron is centered in three men—Ramsey, Marshal Starr, and—sorry, Kent O'Day. They represent," he counted on his fingers, "the Army, the Law, the economic giant."

Oliver said with a smile, "Funny. I'd never thought of my brother in that way."

"No? Well, he's amassed a lot of money over the years. His empire is based on cattle, of course, but it has extended itself. Land. Water rights. Now wheat. And of course the Ramseys have a ton of money as well. Isadora and Ben Ramsey control three large eastern banks through her father's legacy. The thing is that all three of them—Starr, Ramsey, and your brother—are interconnected, one might say interlocked, so that attacking any one of the three is like attacking the entire power base in this territory."

"Well," Oliver said frowning, "Ramsey's wife is my brother's mother-in-law, of course. But where does Starr come in to this?"

"I don't know," Bonner said, shaking his head. "I wish I did. But it's a fact that O'Day and Ramsey support him each election, and in a big way.

"And," Bonner went on, "it's a fact that Amos Starr and his thug deputies are the worst sort of law enforcement this town could possibly have. The saloons pay Starr off to leave them alone. It's pay up, or be closed down for any ridiculous infraction he can invent. Strangers are closely scrutinized. God help you if they don't like your looks. It's law enforcement with fists and clubs. And sometimes guns."

"I don't know my brother that well anymore," Oliver said, "but I thought I knew him well enough. I can't believe he would support Starr if things are as you say."

"I can't explain it. I just relate the facts. It's all Ramsey's doing, of course, somewhere along the line. You know he's planning to retire in three months?"

"No, I didn't."

"Yes, he is. That is why I want to have Colonel Ben Ramsey court-martialed soon."

It was a moment before Oliver could respond. "You *what?*" he finally asked.

"I intend to see the man court-martialed, Oliver."

"Blazes! You are a crusader. It's no wonder they're mad at you, Bonner. Court-martialed for *what* . . . ?" Oliver had an inkling of what the newspaperman might be getting at. Carefully he asked, "Does that Indian I saw this morning have something to do with all of this? You did say you were responsible for the beating he took in some way."

Bonner was nodding his head. "I wasn't careful enough, Oliver. I should have known better. The old Indian—his name is Eagle Heart, by the way—agreed to talk to me. I should have met him someplace else. Anywhere but Bethlehem."

"I believe I know what you're getting at," Oliver said.

"I thought you might."

"But you must know it's impossible, this scheme of yours. Ramsey can't be touched."

"Then you *do* know what I'm referring to. I had heard rumors about Ramsey's glorious victory over the Kiowas before, but Eagle Heart was there! He confirmed the stories. Ramsey instigated the entire incident. He used treachery and capped it with what was in no way a great victory, but a slaughter of unsuspecting people, women and children included!"

Oliver rose and stood looking out the window where a freight wagon rolled slowly past. With his back to Bonner, he said, "I knew it, Bonner. I've known it for a long time."

"You! But . . ."

"No, I wasn't there. I didn't witness it." He turned to face Bonner. "There's a woman who lives with us, she's Kiowa, a friend of my mother's. She saw it. She was in the camp when Ramsey attacked it."

Bonner grew excited. "But then . . . ! We've got him, don't you see?"

"No, I don't," Oliver said without expression. "For one thing Ki-Ki-Tai will not discuss it. Nor would she ever agree to do so publicly for any reason."

"But, still . . ."

"But still," Oliver said with a hint of anger, "you have nothing at all! Don't you know enough law to understand that an Indian cannot testify in a court of law against a white man? Especially not at a court-martial."

"I . . ." Bonner sagged back into his chair. "Yes, of course I knew that. I was just . . . wait a minute, Oliver! If the story *is* undeniably true, then there must be white soldiers who were there and . . ."

"And are willing to testify against Ben Ramsey after all this time!" Oliver scoffed.

"At least *some* of them."

"Yes," Oliver said sarcastically. "Those who wouldn't mind getting accidentally killed somehow the day before the court-martial. Bonner, that was a long time ago. Most of those men have finished their enlistments, died, drifted away or deserted years ago."

"Yes, yes, I know." Bonner rubbed at his eyes with two fingers. "Oliver," he said after a time, "there's still a chance, isn't there? There might be just one soldier who was there on that day who is willing to talk, to speak the truth."

"A man with nothing to lose, huh? Honestly, Bonner, what would one man's word mean against Colonel Ben Ramsey's anyway? I would like to see you pull this off, but the odds are so long against it. You'd only end up getting some people hurt—yourself probably included, that's all. Nothing would be accomplished except that you'd be run out of town."

Bonner began nodding his head again in a slow, constant,

determined rhythm.

"You're right, of course," he replied. Bonner sighed deeply, slapped his hands against his thighs, and rose. He smiled crookedly.

"The trouble is, Oliver, I'm just crazy enough to go ahead and try anyway. It's the right thing to do. Just the right thing. The man is a murderer."

"There's no way to change your mind?"

"I'm afraid not," Bonner said.

"Too bad. You leave me very little choice then," Oliver responded.

"What do you mean?" the newspaperman asked warily.

"I'm going to have to try to help you."

Bonner looked at Oliver with astonishment. Then he took his visitor's proffered hand in both of his own and shook it vigorously. His smile dimmed somewhat. "What can you really do? Have you an idea?"

"Maybe. Your earlier thought was the only real chance we have—find a soldier who was at the massacre who is willing to testify. Now," Oliver continued, perching on the desk to face Bonner, "I remember quite a few of the old-time soldiers from when we first moved out here. I can go out to the fort and try to look some of them up. If they've been discharged, I might try to find out where they've gone under the cover of friendship. Surely some of them remained around here. Others may have become career soldiers and stayed under Ramsey's command. I can come up with some sort of excuse for my digging around—as I say, I did know them as a boy.

"Even if I encounter Ramsey, I should be able to talk my way out of it. Something you would never be able to do," Oliver concluded.

"It might work, mightn't it?"

"Well, it might work as far as finding some of the old

soldiers—getting them to come forward is an entirely different matter. Discharged, retired or not, they will still cling to some sort of *esprit de corps,* if I know soldiers. Besides, Mr. Bonner, any man who was there at the time could be viewed as a criminal himself. They may be unwilling to admit it even in private, let alone in a courtroom."

"I understand. But it's worth a try, isn't it? Tell me this whole thing is worth it," Bonner pleaded.

Oliver smiled faintly and nodded. "Listen, Bonner—I've gotten on the wrong side of the law in this town already, it seems. Would Starr come after me?"

After a moment's thought Bonner said, "Because of this morning? No. Almost anyone else, yes, but being who you are . . ."

Oliver sucked thoughtfully at his upper lip. Kent had obviously become a bigger man than he had thought. He wasn't sure if that was for the good or for the worse.

"All right. Tell me, who was that big goon I ran into this morning? The deputy."

"Deputy Paine. His name is Brice Paine. Mostly they call him 'Stuggs'—don't ask me why," Bonner said holding a palm toward Oliver. "The other deputy—you'll see him around. Another big one, his belly hangs over his belt. Wears a handlebar mustache. That's Toomey. If he has a first name I don't know what it is. He's as mean as Paine, but not half as cautious. The man is apt to go off at any time. He's half-crazy if you ask me. Don't tangle with either one of them if you can help it, Oliver."

"I don't intend to." Oliver rose from the desk. "Well, I'll be going now. I'm going to swing by the fort and have a chat with some people before I ride home. If I learn anything, Bonner, I'll let you know."

"It's best if we don't meet here again," Bonner said.

"I agree. Why don't you give me a couple of days to look into this and then ride out to my mother's house?"

"All right. We'll do it that way," Bonner agreed. "Good luck, Oliver. Be careful, my friend. I hate to think what Ramsey might be capable of if he discovers we're out to hang him. His reputation is everything to him, and it is my firm intention to take that away from him."

The new fort was much the same as he remembered from his youth in physical appearance, but the atmosphere was different. The soldiers all seemed very young for one thing. There were no smudged faces or dirty uniforms. There were no Indians sheltering outside the post stockade. Not a man seemed tense or studied him with suspicious eyes.

He had no idea where to begin this quest. Certainly not the headquarters building; he was going to do everything possible to avoid Ben Ramsey. Pondering that, searching for an alternative, he spied a familiar face.

Smiling, Oliver guided his pony toward the building where three private soldiers sat drinking beer, playing cards. For there, talking to the soldiers was the sutler, Wiggins. His hair was thinning and gray, but Oliver remembered him well. The pouched eyes and hawk nose, constant narrow smile showing yellow teeth. Oliver swung down in front of the store, tying his pony to the rail as the off-duty soldiers watched him with casual interest. Wiggins turned his head toward Oliver, his eyes studying him with curiosity.

"Hello, Wiggins! Got any peppermint sticks?"

"Well . . ." Wiggins' smile broadened. "I will be damned. It can't be! Oliver? Oliver O'Day?" the storekeeper said, looking over the bearded, broad-shouldered man. "It is you! What are you doing back here?"

"What about you?" Oliver asked as the two shook hands. "I thought you pulled out long ago."

"I did," Wiggins said. "I wasn't having a lot of luck elsewhere so I came back a year or so ago. Come inside; let's talk, Oliver. How is your mother?"

"She's fine. Healthy and happy."

"Good, good." They entered the store, which smelled much the same as the one Oliver remembered from his boyhood. Leather and paraffin, carbolic, gun oil, pickles in the big wooden barrel.

"And you, Oliver? How have you been doing, son?" Wiggins asked, hoisting himself to sit on his counter. Two young soldiers were looking through the holsters and gun belts in the corner. A bluebottle fly circled and buzzed.

"It's a long story," Oliver answered with an expression that was half-smile, half-frown. "I went West, got married, had a daughter."

"My, my. Time does have wings, doesn't it?" the sutler said. "You have a daughter. And she'd be about . . . ?"

"Close to marrying age," Oliver admitted, barely believing it himself.

"My, my," Wiggins said again. "What brings you here, Oliver? I didn't ask you if you needed anything."

"I may look around later, try to find something for the women. But mostly I was wondering about the old bunch. They were a good group of men to help us out when we were new on the frontier. Helped us with the house, brought us little things we couldn't afford in those times."

Wiggins scratched his head. "You're taking me back a long way, Oliver. Swift, now, I know he was killed fighting the Kiowas over near Spring Creek. Yount . . . he's long gone. I believe he went back to Ohio to farm. Don't take that as gospel, but it seems I remember hearing that. Caffiter, now, I'm surprised you haven't run into him. He's running a stable down in Bethlehem these days."

That was something, Oliver thought. Assuming Caffiter had even been involved in the raid on the Kiowa camp that morning.

"And Sergeant Callahan?"

Wiggins shook his head. His eyes were like a mournful hound's as he lifted them to Oliver's. "He's around, too. I don't think you'd want to see him, Oliver."

"I don't understand you."

Wiggins sighed. He flicked a cloth at the circling fly. "He took his discharge and jumped right into the bottle. He's in town, but God knows where, probably in some alley dead-drunk or trying to figure out how to get that way."

"He's that bad, is he?"

"That bad. I expect to hear some day that they've found him drunk and frozen to death."

"I can't believe it. It's a shame."

"Yes, it is. Well, Oliver, some men can't handle that liquor. They think they can, but then when they've got no work to be done, nothing but free time and that pension check . . . well, Callahan is just one of those. You'd be lucky if he recognized you, let alone remembers the old days.

"The rest of those boys, I can't recall what happened to 'em. They tell me Huggins became some sort of traveling parson. Don't smile. Or," he said with a shrug, "maybe someone was just having a joke with me. Anyway, I don't know where he and the other boys have got to. I hope I helped you some," Wiggins said, sliding off the counter.

"You have, Wiggins. Thank you."

"Have your look around, find something for your mother— take it as a gift from me. She was quite a woman." There was momentary wistfulness in the sutler's eyes.

"She still is," Oliver said.

"Yes, I imagine." Then more briskly, he said, "Come back

any time and talk, Oliver. You might fill in some of the gaps in that short story of your life that you told me."

"I will do that, Wiggins. Thank you. I appreciate your time."

Not five minutes after Oliver had ridden away from the post, Colonel Ben Ramsey walked into the sutler's store. Wiggins, behind the counter, looked up from a new Chicago catalogue and nodded a welcome.

"Good morning, sir!"

"Morning, Wiggins." Ramsey was wearing regulation dress blues; his flamboyant fringed buckskin shirt hadn't been seen since his hero, Custer, had been defeated at Little Bighorn. He wore a closely trimmed gray mustache and his sideburns had gone a little gray as well. Otherwise he looked scarcely older than he had ten years earlier.

"You just missed someone, sir."

"Oh? Who?"

"Oliver O'Day! Can you believe that? I didn't even know he'd come back."

"He's been back for years," Ramsey said.

"Oh, yes, you'd know. Sorry. 'Course he'd of been visiting his brother and you'd of seen him."

"I haven't seen him," Ramsey answered, biting off his words. "Nor has Kent. Oliver took an Indian wife—a Kiowa squaw."

"Oh, I see," Wiggins said, unsure how to react. "I guess that explains why he sort of just sketched out his life to me. No real facts."

"He's been living up in the mountains in Colorado with his squaw."

Wiggins wasn't fond of the word "squaw" anyway—he himself had known some fine Indian women—but the way Ramsey said it, you'd think it meant something you kicked out of your way in the gutter.

"What did he want here anyway, Wiggins?"

303

"Nothin' much, sir. He just wondered what had happened to some of the men from the old days."

"He could have come to the office and checked the records."

"I don't know why he wouldn't," Wiggins said. "I suppose he just had a notion. It seemed he wanted to talk to me as well. It was just idle chatter, I guess. Probably didn't want to bother you."

"Probably." Ramsey was casually inspecting a new Colt revolver. "What did you tell him, Wiggins?"

"About the men, sir? There isn't much to tell, is there? Outside of Sergeant Callahan and Caffiter, there's none of them left around."

"No. Not any of them." Ramsey put the revolver down carefully on the counter and then spun on his heel and walked out, leaving Wiggins to watch his back and shrug. He returned to his catalogue orders.

"He was asking about the troopers who were there that day," Ramsey said. "Strange. Are you sure he was with Bonner this morning?"

"Positive," Amos Starr answered.

"What in hell are they up to?"

"Who knows," the marshal shrugged with unconcern,

"And what in hell was that Kiowa doing off the reservation anyway? Talking to Bonner?"

"I wouldn't know. Maybe he was just looking for hooch. That's your problem, Ramsey, not mine. Your soldiers are supposed to be guarding the reservation. Now and then, I suppose some of 'em are bound to break out."

"Yes, the young bucks. But what was this old dog doing off the reservation—and talking to a newspaperman!"

"I couldn't guess." Starr stretched his arms lazily overhead and yawned. In the rear of the jail someone in one of the three tiny cells moaned low. Starr glanced that way. "I know this Bonner sure as hell doesn't like me, Colonel."

"All right, but what could he possibly have against me? I've never so much as spoken to the man."

"Who says he does have anything against you?"

"How does it smell to you?" Ramsey demanded. "It's for damned sure he's up to something and Oliver O'Day is involved in it."

Ramsey did have an idea what the newspaperman was up to. Starr knew nothing about that. No one who was not in the Kiowa camp could guess. Probably the marshal thought that Bonner had somehow uncovered something concerning the death of Nesbitt Kittinger. Let him believe what he wanted. A suspicion that Kittinger had been murdered not by the Indians but by someone else still did not explain Bonner's interest in interviewing the old Kiowa warrior. No, it had to be the massacre.

"Do you want me to get rid of the newspaperman?" Starr asked in an unconcerned drawl.

"Bonner? No. That would really stir things up. We'll just leave him to wither on the vine as we planned. See how long a newspaper can last if we keep it off the streets as we have been."

"Whatever you say, Colonel."

"However," Ramsey said quietly, leaning across the desk toward Starr, "we may be forced to do something about some other people."

"Oh?" Starr asked, his eyes narrowing. "Like who?"

"Callahan for one."

"Callahan?" Starr laughed. He flagged a thumb over his shoulder in the direction of the cells. "That's him back there right now making that fuss. What can he do to anyone? It ain't worth getting him, Ramsey. He's trying as hard as he can to do himself in."

"I said maybe. Him and Caffiter."

"Mike Caffiter! Down to the stables?" Starr said in surprise. "What's he ever done to you?"

"Nothing. Nothing at all. We have to make sure to keep it that way, Starr."

"I'm going to tell my mother."

Margaret O'Day's eyes, always bright with amusement, clouded briefly. She put her hands on Charles Kittinger's shoulders.

"How can you, Charles? Isadora will be furious."

"I don't care. It's time. To do this secretly—well, it degrades our love. Something has to be said . . . unless you're unsure."

"Of you?" Margaret laughed, stretching up to kiss him. "No. Never. I know that I love you and more importantly, I know that you love me, Charles."

"Yes," the young man said seriously. He stroked her glossy black hair, warmed by the sun, as they stood close together along the river. "I do love you so very much. That's what I mean. Mother . . . well, I don't think Isadora will really object as much as you think. She doesn't really seem to know *what* she thinks unless Ramsey tells her. They tell me that once she was a strong-willed woman; I don't know about that. If so, my stepfather has managed to erode all of that strength over the years. And . . ."

"Ramsey hates me anyway," he said.

"Don't say that! How could he," Margaret said. "How could anyone hate you, Charles?"

"He just does. He wants me to become a soldier, I think. I've heard both of them talk about my father when he doesn't know I'm around. Both of them, in fact. 'Ned Kittinger was too weak for this country.' Things like that."

"Everyone is not a warrior, Charles," Margaret said, "I

wouldn't have you any other way."

"Maybe not; he sure wishes I were different. War is glory to him. He asks, 'Who does the world remember? School teachers, shopkeepers? No! They remember the great warriors! Alexander, Napoleon, Grant, and Lee. They will remember Custer.' "

"That is a terrible way to think," Margaret said. They had been standing in a long embrace for too long beneath one of the huge oaks along the river. Now the day was cooling, a slight wind rising, and she took his hand and started walking with him back toward Elizabeth's house.

"He is obsessed with war," Charles believed. "He is furious that the army never made him a brigadier. He was disappointed when the Kiowas moved on or surrendered. He wanted to join General Crook and fight the Comanches, the Apaches . . . anyone at all."

"What happened?"

"Crook refused his request without comment. You know," Charles said, pausing briefly, his frown deepening, "I don't understand something he said to me once, or *started* to say."

"What was that?" Margaret asked.

"He was half-drunk on brandy, I believe. He said, 'I cannot understand why you are so soft, why you do not wish to join the army. With the blood that flows in your veins . . .' "

" 'With the blood that flows in your veins'? But I thought he viewed your father as a weakling."

"I know." Charles shrugged. "Perhaps he meant my mother's blood, though no one could think of her as a warrior." Charles smiled tightly. He continued as they walked homeward:

"I will tell Isadora about our plans, Margaret. It must be done."

"There will be trouble, Charles."

"I know."

"I so want us to be happy," she said, leaning her head against his shoulder as they crossed the fallow field toward the log house.

"So do I. But listen, Margaret—there may be trouble, yes, but your own parents were driven from Cimarron, weren't they? How happy were they?"

"Very. Totally. I remember those times well. Oliver and Kianceta could have been no happier than they were."

"Well, then . . . ?"

She nodded. He was right. So long as the decision was right for him. She did not want to be blamed for any unhappiness that might arise in the years to come.

"Have you told your grandmother?" he asked.

"I haven't needed to. They know—Grandmother and Ki-Ki-Tai. They certainly don't believe you come over to visit *them* at every opportunity."

Charles laughed. "No, I suppose not. I love them both; they're dear ladies." He hesitated. "And your father? Does Oliver know?"

"I think he knows, but he's resisting it just a little. That is normal, I believe—he thinks of me still as his little girl. Why, I'm as old as Kianceta was when he took her away to be his wife!"

"Maybe I should talk to him," Charles said thoughtfully.

"It would be the right thing to do," she agreed.

"He would understand if anyone could."

"Yes."

"Oh, Margaret," Charles said with a sudden release of emotion, "I love you so much, so much." And he halted her, turned her gently, and hugged her for long, long minutes.

"The others can go to hell if they don't like it!" he said with passion. "I *will* have you for my wife!"

★　★　★　★　★

The evening sun was a pulsing orange ball on the western horizon, eerily distorted by the mist rising above the river as Oliver O'Day rode back to the town of Bethlehem. There was no point in putting things off. He would find Caffiter and Sergeant Callahan and talk to them if possible. He had no idea if he could convince them to testify against Colonel Ben Ramsey. It had been so long ago; did they really care anymore? Enough to disturb their own lives when it could be avoided?

He could only hope there was enough conscience in the old soldiers to urge them toward that decision.

Oliver decided to look for Sergeant Callahan first. It was still early in the evening. If Callahan followed the patterns of most drunks, he stayed up late, slept most of the day away, and rose with the setting of the sun to begin drinking again. Where did you look for such a man? Somewhere near a source of liquor.

Oliver walked his pony slowly up the darkening street. With the arrival of dusk, it was devoid of decent women. There were groups of vaqueros—Kent's men—and Texans standing in noisy knots on the corners, or congregated in front of saloons. On other corners soldiers from the fort stood laughing, drinking from whisky bottles. Oliver approached one of these groups. The young soldiers looked up with the suspicion they reserved for civilians. Their expressions ranged from amused curiosity to truculence.

"Good evening, men." Oliver leaned over the pommel of his saddle, tilting back his hat as he smiled down at the troopers. "I wondered if you could help me out. I'm looking for a man who used to be a soldier around here. Man named Callahan."

"Ain't no Callahan in our company," one of the more belligerent soldiers said.

"He used to be there, years ago."

"Then we wouldn't know him, would we?" the same soldier

said sarcastically.

"Wait a minute," another of the troopers said. He was fair-haired and smooth-cheeked. "He means old Callahan, the drunk."

"Is that who you mean?"

"Yes, it is," Oliver admitted. "Have any of you seen him?" Simultaneous with the question, he had taken a five-dollar gold piece from his shirt pocket. He polished the bright coin between thumb and forefinger.

"Go up to Third Street, behind the tack shop," one of the soldiers said immediately, "you'll find him."

Oliver nodded and tossed the soldier the gold piece, causing an immediate scramble and debate among them. Smiling, he turned his paint pony and started back up the street as a smoky gloom settled over the town. Now there was tinkling music along the avenue, shouted curses, the crash of breaking glass. *Bethlehem, indeed,* he thought. Bedlam would be more like it. He saw the two deputy marshals as they saw him. Paine he knew. And the other deputy had to be Toomey from Christian Bonner's description. He was a wide, paunchy man, wearing a waxed handlebar mustache. They were moving out into the night to crush some skulls and empty a few pockets. Bethlehem's night-vultures. Paine nudged his companion who was carrying a sawed-off shotgun, and the men exchanged a few words, but they kept on walking without saying anything to Oliver.

Oliver found Sergeant Callahan in the alley behind the tack shop, propped on a barrel, leaning dangerously back against the wall of the building. He held a small bottle in his hand, which he clenched without hoisting. His dead eyes lifted to Oliver as he approached the old cavalryman on horseback.

Oliver wouldn't have recognized the man if he hadn't known who he was. Slack-jawed, a whiskered wattle of slack flesh hanging under his chin, an unhealthily bloated belly. He was hatless, dressed in a pair of trousers too big for him, a brown coat with the cuffs two inches too short, a filthy shirt buttoned to the throat, stained and wrinkled.

"Hello, Sergeant Callahan," Oliver said. He swung down from his horse, the saddle creaking as he did so, watched by wary, unfocused watery eyes.

"Who the hell are you?" Callahan asked in a slurred voice.

"Well, damn all!" Oliver said, having decided on a cheery approach. "It's me—young Oliver O'Day."

"What d'ya want?"

"Well, I just heard you were still around. I thought I'd look you up and talk over old times."

"Don't feel like talkin' . . . who the hell'd you say you were?"

"Oliver. Oliver O'Day."

Comprehension slowly crept into Callahan's alcohol-fuddled brain.

"Well. Well, so it is! Damn me if it isn't." Callahan tried to rise, tipped the barrel forward precariously, and was more dumped than deposited on his unsteady feet. "With a beard and all . . ." Callahan said, rubbing at his throat as he studied Oliver. "My God! Has it been that long?"

"It has, Sergeant," Oliver said, shaking the grimy hand Callahan offered.

"Don't call me that," the old soldier objected. "Just Callahan, not 'Sarge.' "

"All right." Callahan continued to cling to his hand as one afraid of slipping away into some dark netherworld hanging onto reality. Oliver glanced at the half-pint bottle Callahan clutched in his other hand.

"Looks like you've got a dead soldier there," he said, indicating the whisky bottle.

"Well, he's badly wounded!" Callahan agreed with a raspy laugh that broke off into a rumbling coughing spell that lasted

311

nearly a minute. He turned his head and spat.

"Alcohol causes that, you know," he told Oliver. "Alcohol'll cut it if administered properly."

"Never let it be said that I'd let a man suffer when I had access to medicine," Oliver said.

He felt guilty about all of this. Acting cheerful in the face of such obvious and terminal dissolution, offering more liquor— the last thing in the world the man needed—just because it was the easiest and quickest way to make friends with a drunk. Using that proposed friendship to prod Callahan into doing something he wasn't prepared or equipped to do.

"Where can we get a bottle?" Oliver asked.

"Silver Dollar." Callahan was nearly in his face, his breath sour and smelling of broken teeth. "I can't go in there, Oliver. They don't like me much. But you could go in there and get us a bottle, couldn't you?"

"I can do that, Callahan! Sure. Just show me to the back door if they've got one. I'll take care of it."

Leaving Callahan in the alley, he entered the back door of the saloon, walking past crates of whisky and barrels of beer as a guard watched him narrowly. Inside the saloon proper, smoke from cigars rose in blue wreaths. The piano was loud, tinkly, untuned, inexpertly played. The women in their tired bright dresses and tired brightly painted faces swarmed over the cowboys and soldiers there, being squeezed, pinched, grabbed, and—Oliver imagined—ultimately abused and deserted. He longed briefly for the far, clean mountains. He found a place to stand at the end of the bar and waited until the bartender drifted that way. Ordering and receiving a bottle of whisky, he made his way out into the alley again, finding relief in the open air. Callahan waited like a dog for his bowl.

"Here you go," Oliver said, still using his mock-cheerful voice. Callahan used a pocket knife to draw the cork from the bottle and drank deeply, shuddering with delight. He handed the whisky to Oliver.

"Thanks."

"Here's to you," Oliver said. He feigned taking a drink from the bottle, wiped his mouth with the back of his hand, and returned the whisky to Callahan.

"Let's go somewhere warm and talk, Callahan," Oliver suggested.

"That suits me," Callahan said with alcoholic amiability. They ended up in a small toolshed behind the barn of the Bethlehem Feed & Grain Store. Callahan led the way. He was obviously familiar with the place. As the door creaked open, he put a finger to his lips, taking a lantern from a nail on the wall. He lit the wick and closed the door. The lantern light flickered on the plank walls of the shed, revealing rows of pitchforks, shovels, and baling hooks. There were piles of burlap sacking there as well, and the two men arranged these to make seats for themselves.

"Glad I ran into you, Oliver," Callahan said, lifting the bottle in a silent toast before he drank.

"Glad I ran into you, too, Callahan. It seems like a lifetime ago we last met. But I still remember all the help you were to us when we were trying to set up house. I recall you bringing horehound drops out to me and Kent."

"Did I do that?" Callahan grinned, rubbing at his whiskered chin. "Well, I guess I wasn't all bad. It's fine to know that sometimes good deeds are remembered. You know, Oliver . . . that *was* a lifetime ago. It was someone else's life you're talking about. Does it ever seem to you that maybe you've used up one life and God is making you live another one before you can die to pay for your sins?"

"I guess so," Oliver replied. "I think I know what you mean."

"Yeah." Callahan leaned forward on the sacking, the bottle

dangling between his legs. "It seems sometimes like I should have died a long time ago. It seems at times that I *did,* and no one noticed. Now I'm like a ghost chasing around on the earth going nowhere . . . do you think that's how ghosts feel, Oliver? I am just about invisible. No one sees me. My life . . . I ain't got one."

"Come on, Callahan! Cheer up. I'm seeing you tonight. You're alive, all right."

"Yeah." Morosely he drank from the whisky bottle again. Oliver decided that visiting Callahan *was* very much like talking to a ghost. He decided to press forward.

"I hear Ramsey is retiring."

A bitter expression came over Callahan's ravaged face. *"The bastard,"* he panted savagely.

Oliver tried to act surprised. "Why, I thought you two got along together well enough."

"Yeah, sure we did," Callahan said gloomily. "Glainvorious . . . vainglorious, I mean, don't I? Isn't that what they call men like that?"

"I guess it is." Oliver accepted the quart bottle from Callahan, again made a show of drinking the liquor, and handed it back. "I guess he does have some right to be proud, though. I mean, he was quite an Indian fighter in his day, wasn't he?"

"He was a lying bastard. A killer."

"In war there's always some killing."

"Sure. But a strutting peacock like him going around saying how bold he was—his reputation is based on slaughtering women and babies, Oliver O'Day."

Oliver put on a shocked expression. "That seems unfair, Callahan."

"You weren't there!"

"No," Oliver admitted, still playing the role of a dubious listener. "I wasn't."

314

"I could tell you . . ."

"Why don't you?" Oliver coaxed. "We've got the time," he added, nodding at the bottle, "and nothing better to do."

"I guess I won't," Callahan said, suddenly growing obstinate.

"All right. It doesn't matter. Let's talk about something else if you want to."

"I'd like to! I'd like to tell the world, but no one would listen to me. Look at me! People don't take me serious. Not now."

"Did they then?"

"Then I was a soldier. You don't go against your commander, Oliver. It ain't right. Besides," he added, lifting mournful eyes, "no one believes you."

Oliver waited. Callahan was sinking into a somberly reflective mood. He let the man pick his own words. They came hard to Callahan.

"I was there in those times, you know. Not at the fight across the river, but I heard. Everyone told me what happened."

"What did you see?"

"Me?" Callahan lifted rheumy eyes. "I saw everything afterward . . . when I saw the messages from General Cox."

It took Callahan a long time to tell his story, with many interruptions to drink, with verbal sidetracks, belching, and obvious memory gaps. What he had witnessed was critical evidence, Oliver soon realized.

Ramsey had reported a few skirmishes with the so-called "Ghost Warriors" to his commander at Fort Riley, General Cox, and had been instructed to seek a peaceful solution since the treaty with the Kiowas was still in effect. Ramsey had thereafter received word that the Kiowa leaders, Winter Owl, the civil chief, and Hungry Wolf, the Kiowa war leader, wished to talk to him about the treaty violations on both sides. Ramsey had set up a trap and ambushed the negotiating Kiowas, killing Winter Owl. Then, on the pretense that the army had been attacked after he had acted in good faith, Ramsey had crossed the river and destroyed the Kiowa camp.

"Gave the order . . . I heard him. In so many words . . . I heard him. 'Every Indian in that camp is to be considered a hostile. A woman can kill as quickly as a man, remember that.'" Callahan choked a little, a few tears trickled down his sallow cheeks. Was it caused by alcohol? The old sergeant again looked at Oliver and then toward some far distant point, some haunted memory.

"I suppose that meant that some little kid can kill you too if you don't do something about it."

"You weren't there—during the raid on the camp?"

"No, I was sent back to the fort as a courier to have the telegrapher send off a report of the . . . attack by the Kiowas to General Cox. Ramsey had already written it up, the night before. You could tell it had been written on a desk by how neatly it was done. It wasn't no battlefield communiqué. He took it neatly folded from his tunic and gave it to me."

"Was Mike Caffiter there—in the Kiowa camp when Ramsey attacked it?"

It would be helpful to have someone who was actually among the combatants to testify to the conduct of the raid.

"Mike? Yeah, he was there. Why?" Callahan asked suspiciously, drinking deeply from the bottle.

"I just wondered. I heard he was still around, that's all."

"He's around. He won't talk to me, but he's around." Something had alerted Callahan to the fact that something beyond casual conversation was behind Oliver's questions. He asked, "All right, Oliver O'Day, what are you up to?"

"I'll tell you the truth," Oliver answered, bending forward, his voice lowering. "We are going to try to nail Ramsey for what he did that day."

"What do you mean?"

316

"We are going to have him tried for his crimes."

"All these years on! You're crazy."

"Maybe, but if you despise the man that much . . . if you believe in truth and honor . . ."

"Hell, yes, I hate Ramsey! For the rest of it—you can keep your truth and honor for someone else. Is that why you bought me the whisky?"

"Yes."

"That figures. Why would I expect anything out of simple friendship?"

"Listen," Oliver persisted, "would you tell your story in a court?"

"No. It would be useless anyway, wouldn't it? Who would listen to me? The town drunk."

"We could sober you up. Taper off slowly, painlessly."

"Painlessly for who?" Callahan asked with a grimace. "For you, maybe. Besides, it wouldn't do any good, not a bit of good."

"We could try."

"It won't work!" Callahan waved a hand vigorously. "Do nothin' but stir up trouble that I don't need."

"So? What would you care, Callahan, really?"

"Huh?"

"It's pretty much like you said. You aren't much more than a ghost right now. Why not do one right thing before you drink yourself to death?"

Callahan didn't answer. He couldn't. He had bowed his head and was sobbing deeply, one hand pressed to his face while the other clenched the neck of the whisky bottle. So tightly that it seemed he was trying to snap it off. Oliver stood, placed a hand briefly on his shoulder and went out into the starry night. Feeling more than a little ashamed of himself. Was he right in doing any of this? Had he accomplished nothing at all except to further humiliate the broken man?

As he stood looking up at the cold silver stars, the door behind him opened and he turned to see Callahan's bulky silhouette framed in the doorway to the shack.

"Oliver . . . I'll do it. You're right. What do I care if they kill me?"

Then the door closed again and Oliver stood trembling in the night. He felt cruel and insensitive. He shook off the feeling, took a deep breath, and walked to his waiting pony. Swinging into the saddle, he told himself out loud:

"You have to remember what the purpose behind this is, Oliver. Ramsey must be made to pay for what he did."

"He'll pay all right!" the stableman said. "His Maker will see to that, O'Day. Oh, Ben Ramsey will pay for all Eternity without our help! What is the little punishment we could administer on this earth compared to God's justice?"

Oliver watched as Mike Caffiter finished currying the leggy roan horse and hung the curry comb on a hook in the stall of his livery stable's barn.

"It might do our own souls a little good to see that some punishment is exacted on this earth," Oliver said, adapting to Mike Caffiter's own formula of logic.

Caffiter had lost most of his hair. His pink scalp glowed beneath his silver-blond remnants. His cheeks were pink as well, puffy, almost like a baby's. He had a small mouth and wide blue eyes. As a young man, Corporal Caffiter, in Oliver's memory, had been flaxen-haired, wiry, good-humored. Perhaps he, too, was starting on his second life. It was hard to associate this roly-poly stableman with that lean young corporal.

A cowhand had entered, leading a weary-looking sorrel horse. Caffiter lifted a finger, indicating he'd take care of the man momentarily.

"Ike!" he yelled, and from somewhere in the rear of the stable, a gaunt assistant appeared, wiping his hands on his bib overalls. Caffiter nodded at the cowboy with the sorrel and then took Oliver's arm.

"Let's go to my office and talk."

Oliver followed along as Caffiter led the way to a small office hidden by the stairs leading to the hayloft, opened the door, and went in. The room was sparsely furnished. The puncheon desk held a small stack of papers—invoices and bills of sale. Overhead a kerosene lantern burned behind a green glass shade.

"Sit down, Oliver," Caffiter offered. Oliver took the straight-backed wooden chair indicated and waited as Caffiter settled behind his desk.

"Now, then. You would like me to go into court, a court-martial hearing. Tell my story of the Cimarron camp battle."

"Yes."

"Won't do it."

"Why? I take it you're a Christian . . ."

"Yes, I am. I was not without sin on that day, but I have made my peace with the Lord."

"Good. That only leaves Ramsey, doesn't it?"

Mike Caffiter sighed. He departed the realm of ethics and got to the practical aspects. "There's no way a single soldier is going to stand up before a court-martial and accuse his commander of something that happened fifteen . . ."

"Seventeen years."

"Seventeen years ago and be taken seriously. On the weight of what evidence? Why didn't I come forward sooner, they'll want to know.

"Oliver—I don't even know what started it all. We were being held in reserve on the bluff in case the Kiowas tried anything tricky. *Something* did happen. I couldn't see it, whatever it was. We were hidden, remember. But we were ordered to advance and we did."

"And you saw what on the plains when you reached them?"

"One dead Indian."

"So you believed it had been a Kiowa attack based on that?"

"I didn't believe anything. We were in full charge. Riding under orders. We were ordered to cross the river. Told there was a hostile force waiting there."

"And women and children?"

"Well . . . yes. But you see, Oliver, it's that way in a lot of Indian fighting, simply because you want to catch the enemy napping, and when he's napping there's likely to be women and children nearby."

"Maybe. The fact is, though, Ben Ramsey had the whole thing prearranged, plotted out."

"Who says?"

"Callahan. He saw the orders from General Cox and the wires back to Regimental Headquarters."

"Callahan! Sure. He also sees little pigs flying around some mornings. God, is that supposed to prove anything? He can't remember where he was yesterday."

"He remembers that day well enough." Oliver leaned forward, resting his forearms on the desk between them.

"And he's going to testify?" Caffiter asked.

"He is. And he'll be sober."

"I don't know." Mike Caffiter shook his head. "Maybe if it wasn't just me alone . . . Callahan, how do you know he'll be sober?"

"I'm making it my job to see that he is," Oliver told him. "If I have to lock him up somewhere, I'm going to see to that."

Caffiter's eyes were far away. "Who's behind this, O'Day? It's Christian Bonner, isn't it?" Oliver nodded. Caffiter laughed. "The man's insane. He takes on Amos Starr his first week in town. Now he wants Ramsey's neck? What's with him?"

"Maybe he's just a moral man, Caffiter. Moral enough to do

what's right without worrying about reprisals."

"Maybe . . . maybe," Caffiter said scratching his head. "Listen, O'Day, I'll think about it, all right? That's all I can promise you right now. If there's going to be another witness to back me up, well—just let me think on it, will you?"

Oliver left the stable and rode slowly through the town. Light glared from behind saloon windows accompanied by shouting, cursing, and the music of banjos and pianos. He considered stopping at Bonner's office to report on progress, but the place was closed and dark, so he continued on his way. Besides, they had both agreed that the newspaper office was a dangerous place to meet.

Standing in front of one of the saloons, the Red Rooster, Oliver saw the two deputy marshals, Toomey and Brice Paine. They stared at him darkly as he passed until a woman in a low-cut red dress leaned out of an upstairs window and yelled something down to Paine. He hollered something back and she laughed, closing the window. The deputies again turned their eyes to Oliver, who rode on silently.

The moon was a low, silver half-globe above the stealthily flowing river. The long, endless plains were black, silver themselves where moisture mirrored the moonlight. It was a beautiful night with the stars hanging bright against a clear sky.

All of it went unnoticed by Oliver O'Day. Suddenly none of it meant a thing.

Not the beauty of the balmy evening. Not Ramsey or Callahan. Not Bonner's quest. Nor Mike Caffiter.

He cared nothing for their troubles, nothing for the Kiowas' tribulations. It had happened when the woman in the red dress had leaned out of the window over the saloon.

She had been wearing Kianceta's necklace.

CHAPTER ELEVEN

The bear had four eyes in its head. A curious, ambling beast with blood on its claws, it rose out of the murky river in the night. Two identical silver moons passed rapidly overhead, growing bright before they sunk into ash in the far mountains. Growing nearer, the bear was attacked by soldiers, strange mounted men with black hollows for eyes. They fired at the bear with one long barrage of yellow-blue flame and the bear went to its hind legs, pawing at the air. Around its neck was Kianceta's necklace.

Oliver awoke in a sweat. The sunrise sky beyond the high narrow window of his room was pink and pale orchid, brushed with wispy clouds.

He lay still for a long while in the chilly gloom of the new morning, the dream fading in memory as he thought of what must be done that day.

Rising, he pulled on his trousers, buttoned up his shirt, and stamped his boots on. Going out into the living room, he found it empty. A fire had been lit already on this morning; the embers glowed softly still. Two empty teacups rested on the table. Oliver smiled. The older women were already up, already out at their chores. They were a remarkable pair, those two. Elizabeth and Ki-Ki-Tai. With their dreams shattered, blown away by the long winds, they had reentered a world without vistas with the same courage, the same optimism that each new day might bring some small gift of existence.

Oliver poured a cup of tea from the pot, which was still warm, stood drinking it for a few minutes at the fireplace, and then went to the closet, taking his coat from its hook. From the rear of the house he could hear Margaret stirring, making small noises as she dressed. He looked lovingly, sadly, at her closed door and went out to find his mother.

Elizabeth was feeding the chickens. She held the hem of her apron up, cradling their feed in it. Three dozen fluttering, clucking hens surrounded her. Feathers flew; small battles over a particular kernel of corn, important and understandable only to chickens flared up and were quickly forgotten.

"Good morning, Mother," Oliver said, kissing her on the cheek. She smiled gently at him. *Remarkable.* He often thought that word when seeking a description for his mother. For both of the older women. Both had gray in their hair, a bit of loose skin under their chins, a few sun-wrinkles at the corners of their eyes. But those eyes! Forever young yet shining with the kind wisdom of maturity.

"You were awfully late last night," Elizabeth said.

"Some things came up," Oliver told his mother. "Actually a lot of things."

"Oh?" Elizabeth scattered the rest of the chicken feed, brushed at her apron, and dusted her hands together. She asked, "Did you want to talk about any of it?"

"All of it, actually. If you have the time."

Elizabeth nodded. "If it's important, we can find all the time it takes, Oliver."

Returning to the house they passed Regret's grave. There was a fresh flower on it, a bright yellow daffodil cut that morning. To others it must seem silly, he supposed. But that was Elizabeth's way. There was a wooden marker at the head of the grave. They had carved "Loyal Friend, Regret" into it.

Going into the house, Elizabeth made fresh tea for them as Oliver told her everything that had happened on his eventful trip to town, beginning with meeting Bonner as the townspeople were beating the Indian.

"Did they say his name?" Ki-Ki-Tai asked as she appeared unexpectedly in the doorway. She crossed the room and sat with them at the table.

"It was Eagle Heart," Oliver said. "Did you know him?"

"Very well."

"He was not hurt badly, Ki-Ki."

"Thank you, Oliver."

He went on to tell them about Christian Bonner's crusade against the marshal and his deputies, and how his newspapers had been confiscated, the children frightened out of delivering them after the first edition had appeared. He told them about what Bonner had in mind next. Astonished, Elizabeth turned from steeping the tea.

"Ben Ramsey! Is he crazy? No one will hear a bad word about him around here."

"I don't know if Bonner is crazy or not, but that's what he's doing. And I am going to help him."

Elizabeth's eyes were briefly shadowed by concern. She asked him, "Do you have to get involved in this, Oliver?"

"No. I guess not. But I am going to be, Mother. It's the right thing to do."

She nodded and poured the tea, bringing their cups to the table. Oliver continued describing his adventure. "I went out to the fort and talked to Wiggins, did you know that he was back?

"By the way," Oliver said with a grin, "there's a carpetbag to hold your knitting in my room—I'll get it later—it's a gift from Wiggins. Apparently you've had a secret admirer all these years."

"So long as they send gifts," Elizabeth said.

"Anyway," Oliver continued, "I talked to Wiggins and he told me where two of the old soldiers from that day could be found." He described his meetings with Callahan and Mike Caffiter.

"I'm sorry to hear about Sergeant Callahan," Elizabeth said. "He was a nice man.

"Will anything good come out of this, Oliver," Elizabeth asked, "or will there just be more trouble?"

"I don't know," he admitted, "but it has to be done."

Margaret had come into the room, red ribbon in her glossy black hair, wearing a blue and white dress with tiny flowers in the pattern. She walked beside her father and kissed him on the cheek. She put her arms around him and the two briefly held hands.

"Maybe you should go out for a while, Margaret," Oliver said, looking up at his daughter.

"Why?" she asked in surprise. "I've heard most everything— voices do carry in this house, you know. Is there something else you did in town that I'm too young to hear about?" she asked mischievously.

"No," Oliver replied. There was unmistakable concern in his eyes. "All right—sit down then, Margaret. I must warn you that this will be shocking."

Having captured the attention of the three women with that remark, he proceeded.

"I was riding back from Caffiter's stable, wondering if I should stop and see Bonner," he began. He took the story ahead to seeing the deputies, exchanging glances with them, to the appearance of the lady in red upstairs over the saloon. He took a sip of tea, breathed in slowly, shook his head, and then told them:

"She was wearing Kianceta's necklace."

The silence around the table was complete. They could hear a killdeer singing in the fields. None of the women spoke.

Finally, Elizabeth, a little pale now, asked, "How can you be sure, Oliver? It's been so long since you saw it. There are many silver and turquoise necklaces, aren't there?"

"Many." He shook his head. "Not like this one. How do I know? I saw it every morning in the dawn light around the throat of the woman I loved. It was the necklace Donovan Hart bought in La Paloma for our wedding gift."

"How could this white woman have it?" Ki-Ki-Tai asked.

"Only one way I can think of," Oliver said grimly.

"One of the killers gave it to her," Margaret said, touching her throat with her fingertips.

"That's right," her father agreed.

"It could have passed through many hands by now," Elizabeth said, her tone urging caution.

"I know that. But I doubt it—if I were the man who stole it, I would do only one thing with it: give it to a woman. If I were the woman who received it as a gift, I would keep it, not give it away."

"It could have been anyone who gave it to her," Elizabeth said. "Anyone. A man long gone, dead perhaps, someone passing through who had too much whisky under his belt . . ."

"And it could have been someone who's in town right now," Oliver said. "I *will* find out. I mean to talk to that woman."

"That man she was flirting with. This Brice Paine," Margaret inquired. "Do you think . . . ?"

"I don't know. I am going to find out, though. I will do that," Oliver said firmly.

Margaret laughed out of nervousness and said to Ki-Ki, "Ki-Ki-Tai, isn't it funny how our days go by, years pass with nothing at all happening—and then to have a storm like this!"

"That's all of it, I'm happy to say," Oliver said.

Margaret looked to her grandmother and then to her namesake. She told Oliver, "No, it's not all, Father. There's more."

"I hope it's nothing so somber," Oliver said. "I feel like I've brought a cloud of gloom back with me."

"It's both good and bad, Father," she said, kneading her hands against each other. "I mean it's good . . . very good. But there are . . . corollaries which are not so good." She lifted those deep brown eyes, Kianceta's eyes, to his and he smiled.

"Am I supposed to guess what it is? Is that it, Margaret?"

She laughed, blushed, and then told him: "Charles Kittinger has asked me to marry him and I said 'yes.' "

"I see," Oliver said carefully. He watched the nervous young woman and waited for her to continue.

"He wanted to tell you himself last evening," she continued, with a rush of words, "but you were gone so long, by the time you would have gotten here . . . I mean, he did have to go home and explain . . ."

"And that is where the corollaries come in," Oliver said. He had rested a hand on her shoulder, then picked up her trembling hand and kissed it.

"Yes."

"Kent and Ramsey," Elizabeth said. "I don't envy the boy."

"They'll do everything possible to block it," Oliver agreed. "Margaret, don't take this wrong—is Charles man enough to stand up to it?"

"He is," she said with a bit of challenge in her voice.

"Were you, Oliver?" Ki-Ki-Tai asked. "Were you strong enough?"

"Maybe not," he said, rubbing his bearded chin. He smiled, "But Kianceta was."

"You two didn't have to stay here and live with the criticism," Elizabeth said.

"Nor will we have to!" Margaret said passionately. *Amazing,* Oliver thought. How like her mother she is. "I won't have Charles belittled or hurt. We are planning to go away as well. I'd like to stay here for the ceremony, of course . . ."

"You can stay here for as long as you like!" Elizabeth said.

"Yes, but his stepfather . . ."

"To hell with Ben Ramsey," Oliver put in roughly. Yet when Ramsey received news of the impending wedding of his son to an Indian woman, on top of the possibility of a court-martial . . . if he discovered what Christian Bonner and Oliver were up to . . . how vengeful could the colonel become toward a treacherous stepson?

"We have discussed this," Margaret said. "It is better if we leave."

"Where could you go?" Ki-Ki-Tai asked. "You are not Kianceta. You two could not live alone in the wilderness."

"We had no such plan," Margaret answered. Her eyes were cast down as she told them, "Charles and I want to teach school."

"School?" Elizabeth said in surprise.

"Yes." Margaret hesitated. "We want to start a school for the Indians. The Kiowas on the reservation. Charles has written to the Bureau of Indian Affairs. I speak the language. I *am* Kiowa," she said, looking at Ki-Ki-Tai. "Who will teach them if not us?"

"Sweet Christ," Oliver said. "Charles isn't going to tell Ramsey that, is he?"

"Yes, Father, he is."

"Lord have mercy on the boy." Oliver shook his head, visualizing that confrontational scene.

"You asked me if I thought Charles was strong enough," Margaret said. "Now what do you think?"

"I think if he can break that news to Ben Ramsey he's ready to take on the world."

"I'm proud of you, dear," Elizabeth said, taking her granddaughter's hand across the table.

"I am too," Oliver said.

"Can I take it that that is the same as giving us your blessing?" Margaret asked, still hesitant.

"Yes!" Oliver said with a short joyful laugh. "You may take it as that. Bring that young man over here and I'll tell him the same."

"Oliver . . . what about Kent?" Elizabeth asked.

"What about him? My brother has nothing to do with this."

"He won't look at it that way."

"He can look at it any way he damn well pleases," Oliver said, "just so long as he doesn't try to interfere with these two young people's happiness."

"Oliver," Ki-Ki-Tai said, interrupting, "I hear a horse coming."

Oliver rose and turned toward the door. There was tension in Ki-Ki-Tai's voice. He hadn't realized until that moment how tautly all their nerves were stretched.

He went to the window, Ki-Ki-Tai beside him.

"Do you know that horse?" Ki-Ki asked, peering out the window at the incoming rider.

"No," Oliver said, smiling faintly, "but I recognize that town suit. It's Christian Bonner. I'll go out and talk to him."

Bonner, sitting the saddle like a store's dummy, approached the house. He stepped down from the saddle with obvious relief, rubbing a haunch.

"I didn't realize how far out of town you people were," Bonner said. "It's a long ride."

"It can seem that way sometimes," Oliver replied, concealing his amusement. "Let's not hang around the house, Bonner. Walk down to the river with me. We can talk in private there."

They started toward the Cimarron, Bonner leading his horse. The river was gleaming in the yellow sunlight, like quicksilver flowing slowly southward. The two men walked into the shade of the crowded oaks and halted, Oliver leaning against the bole of a misshapen tree.

"Did you have any luck?" Bonner asked worriedly. Oliver

found himself wondering if the newspaperman had the nerve to follow through with this.

"I talked to two soldiers who were involved in the massacre," Oliver said, and he related the stories about Callahan and Mike Caffiter once more.

"I see. This Callahan, can you keep him sober?"

"I think so."

"Caffiter—I think I know who you mean, pudgy blond man—will he come through?" Bonner wanted to know.

"Again, I can only tell you what my feeling is. Yes, I think he will. His main concern is standing up alone in court, being the only witness with no one to corroborate his story."

"I can understand that. Is there a chance of finding other ex-soldiers?"

"It doesn't seem so, but I am going to look into that possibility a little deeper."

"All right," Bonner said with a sigh, glancing briefly at the smooth face of the river, "here's where we stand: as you know the decision to proceed with a court-martial hearing rests with Ramsey's commander—that is General Hayes at Fort Riley."

"Cox . . . ?"

"General Cox is dead. Quite a few years ago, unfortunately for us, because his own knowledge of the dispatches might have weighed in our favor. However, if I may continue? I have contacted General Hayes. The situation is unusual, to say the least. First, it has been so many years since the incident. Second, there aren't more than a handful of soldiers who have ever been prosecuted for their actions during an Indian war.

"However, Hayes strikes me as being a cut above many military men. Extremely hard-nosed, they tell me, jealous of the army's reputation. He's agreed to send an investigator down here to at least talk to us and see what we have uncovered. A man named Caldwell. Lieutenant Jefferson Caldwell. It's essential that we provide him with firm evidence."

"I see." Oliver was briefly thoughtful. "Well," he said, "that is some progress at least. Are you sure there is no way Ramsey can find out about this—until and if he's formally charged?"

"There's not supposed to be a way, Oliver, but you know how things go. Some brother officer might become privy to the information and feel compelled to notify Ramsey. Oh, there are a hundred ways he could be alerted, I am afraid."

"If there is a leak, we might find ourselves in real jeopardy."

"I realize that," Bonner said.

"But you're still determined to go through with this?"

"I am determined," the newspaperman said firmly.

"All right." Oliver puffed his cheeks and blew out his breath. "Then I'm with you. I'll start working on Sergeant Callahan, try to get him to taper off the alcohol. I'll try to keep an eye on him. I will also keep prodding Mike Caffiter—I think he can be convinced to go along with us if we approach him in the right way. With him it's important to keep things on a moral plane. Apparently he's become a very religious man."

"That happens to a lot of criminals and ex-soldiers, so I've heard."

"Yes, well, whatever the reason for it is, it's irrelevant to our objective. I think we can work with him on whatever level he chooses. Meanwhile I'll do my best to see if we can't come up with another witness or two. Those men have gone *somewhere*, we should be able to find some of them."

"Fine," Bonner said. "I was thinking of riding over to Fort Riley to talk to General Hayes personally."

"That might be a good idea."

"If I . . ." Bonner broke off suddenly, his eyes lifting in a startled gaze. "There's a rider approaching."

Oliver turned, looking toward the house beyond the trees.

"Damn!" he muttered.

"Do you know who it is?"

"I do. Bonner, you'd better leave right now. Keep to the trees. Follow the river for half a mile or so before you cut back toward town."

"Yes, yes, of course. But who is it?"

"It's my brother," Oliver told him. "Kent O'Day."

Oliver saw Bonner on his way. Then, when he could no longer see his horse, he walked out of the oak grove and stood in plain sight so that Kent, approaching the yard, had no trouble seeing him. Kent turned his gray horse toward his brother.

Kent reined in and leaned low in the saddle, studying Oliver. Kent wore a silver-blond mustache drooping half an inch below his upper lip. He wore a white shirt, black string tie, and black jeans. He had a noticeable paunch and was paler than was typical for men in this country.

"Oliver," Kent said with a nod. His eyes continued to search the face of his bearded brother—the brother he had not seen for so many years.

"I thought it would be better if we talked away from the house," Oliver said.

"It is." Kent swung from the saddle and dropped the reins to his horse, which stood there as if hitched. It was a well-trained, beautiful animal. But then, Kent could afford a horse like that these times.

"Let's not waste time or words, Oliver," Kent said. "Keep your daughter away from Charles."

"Don't be stupid, Kent."

"I won't. I mean to nip this thing in the bud."

"You're a little too late for that—how did you find out?"

"One of my vaqueros, Eduardo. Charles couldn't keep his mouth shut, he told Eduardo that he was going to marry your daughter."

"What does any of it have to do with you, Kent?"

"What! He's Isadora's son. Bettina's brother."

"And what does Bettina say about it?"

"Bettina thinks that everything in the world is just lovely, Oliver. Especially when it comes to romance."

"Meaning she would have no objection to the match?"

"Meaning she thinks like a woman. She hasn't a rational brain in her head."

"I see," Oliver said in a near-whisper.

"I hope so," his brother answered.

"I meant that I see who the irrational one is, Kent. Can't you see, it's none of your business."

"It is my business if a Kittinger wants to marry a half-breed squaw," Kent exploded.

"Careful, Kent," Oliver warned softly. "Any more talk like that about my daughter and I'll rip your head off."

"And you think you could do it, do you?" Kent asked his younger brother smugly.

"There's no doubt in my mind. Look at yourself, Kent. You're thin, paunchy. While you ride around playing overseer, eating rich foods, I'm up with the dawn, plowing, scything, splitting wood, pitching hay. And the tables have turned. At our time of life it's an advantage to be younger, not older in a fight. Yes, I can take you. Easily."

"Could you do it with guns?" Kent asked challengingly.

"I don't know about that. I don't think you'd carry it that far. If not out of love for me, with at least some respect for Mother."

"Maybe I wouldn't. Just heed carefully what I've told you, Oliver."

"It'd be better for everyone concerned if you'd heed what Charles is trying to tell you. He wants to marry Margaret. It might be impulsive; they might be too young. But it seems to me that most marriages start out like that, and these two are a lot brighter than many young people."

"He'll lose everything! Isadora will cut him out of her will."

"I expect he's considered that, Kent."

"He's a young fool. He has no idea what he's getting into. When Ramsey finds out . . ."

"What? What will Ramsey do, Kent?"

"There's no telling."

Oliver nodded. "You can tell Ben Ramsey what I told you. Tell him the same applies to him."

"You haven't changed, have you, Oliver? Not a damned bit. You haven't learned anything from your failed life. Look at you," he said, waving an arm. "right back where you started from!"

Oliver's voice softened. "Listen, Kent, so long as you're here . . . won't you bend enough to say hello to Mother?"

Kent thought for a moment. Obdurate as ever, he replied, "Not so long as she shelters Indians in that house."

"Ki-Ki-Tai? She's a great woman, Kent."

"Sure. And Hungry Wolf was a great man. All they did was massacre a hundred soldiers and civilians. Children too. Have you forgotten the Skoglund family? They killed Nesbitt Kittinger!"

"All right. I won't bother to argue that," Oliver said. "Going through it all again will solve nothing. I'm just talking about your mother, Kent. Your mother. Can't you at least say 'hello'?"

"It was hard enough to say hello to you," Kent answered in a wooden voice. Then, "You've been told how matters lie. You'd do best to heed what I've said." Then he collected the reins to his horse. Before mounting, he asked:

"Who was that I saw riding away, Oliver?"

"When? I don't get you."

"You get me well enough. It looked awfully like Christian Bonner to me, Oliver. If you have any sense at all left, you'll

stay well away from him. Amos Starr doesn't like people med-
dling in his business."

"The business of shaking down the town, beating men up,
skimming profits from the saloons who pay for his protection?"

"Prove that," Kent said.

"You know, Kent, you said I haven't changed. Maybe not,
but you sure have. You know that? When in God's name did you
put yourself in a position where you feel obligated to stand up
for scum like Marshal Amos Starr?"

Kent offered no answer. Sitting his saddle he looked at Oliver
for another long minute. He glanced once toward the log house
and then turned his gray horse, heeling it into a trot.

Oliver turned and started walking slowly back toward the
house where Elizabeth stood at the window peering out from
behind the curtains, staring after Kent who rode away with
seeming indifference. She let the curtain fall, wiped her once-
hopeful eyes, and began to build a fire to cook their evening
meal.

"I think it's wonderful! Exciting! I'm happy for you," Louise
O'Day told her uncle. Kent and Bettina's daughter was effusive.
Looking slightly sheepish, Charles basked in the glow of the
girl's pleasure.

"Thank you," was all he could bring himself to say. He was
only five years older than his niece and they had been more like
brother and sister than uncle and niece.

"Have you told my mother what you and Margaret are going
to do?"

"Yes. Bettina seemed pleased . . . a little nervous, maybe
about what we might be stirring up in the family."

"Well, that's understandable. She knows how my father will
react," Louise O'Day said. "That leaves . . ."

"My mother. And Ramsey."

"Ben will . . ." whatever Louise was going to say, she quickly abandoned the thought. "How do you believe Isadora will take the news?"

Charles shrugged. "I don't know," he said truthfully. "I think she'll be confused. My mother will accept my decision, I believe. At first. Then Ben Ramsey will go to work on her. The usual cycle."

"I don't know why she lets him have so much power over her!" Louise said in frustration. Living in the same house with them all of her life, she too had seen Isadora's will crushed to conform to Ben Ramsey's demands.

"It doesn't really matter," Charles said. "No matter what they say, I'm going ahead. There's nothing they can do to change my mind."

"You're so brave, Charles!" the young woman said. "I admire you. You must really be in love with Margaret."

"Totally."

"I envy you. Leaving the ranch. Starting a brand-new life! It will work out for you, Charles. I know it will."

"Thanks, Lou."

She went to tiptoes and kissed her uncle. She glanced toward Isadora's closed bedroom door and whispered, "Good luck," squeezed his hand, and skipped happily away, her pigtails bouncing.

Charles took a deep breath, stood motionless for a moment, gathering his courage, and then walked to Isadora's door, rapping on it. Her hoarse voice called:

"Come in."

Charles entered the room to find his mother propped up in bed, ruffled pillows behind her, white comforter drawn up to her waist. She wore a lavender peignoir and a thin volume of poetry—Wordsworth probably. Charles couldn't stand him, but he was mother's favorite. Her eyes were pouched. With age the

flesh had begun to sag over her once-sharp features dramati-
cally. She seemed to have no chin at all. Her jowls drooped un-
prettily. On the wall opposite, as if to defy time, was a huge
portrait of her as a young beautiful woman. At times Charles
thought uncharitably, "This is what Ben Ramsey has done to
my mother." True or not, it saddened and angered him.

"Sit down, dear," Isadora said, patting the bed beside her.
"Have you something to tell me?"

"You already know, don't you?"

"Yes." Her smile was half-sly. "Bettina could never keep a
secret. Not from me."

Charles kissed his mother's cheek, briefly hugged her, and sat
on the bed facing her.

"It's what I want, Mother. I love Margaret O'Day."

"I was angry at first. I could have slapped you," Isadora said.
"But haven't I always said that a person should take whatever
happiness he can find in life?"

"Yes, Mother."

"Or *try* to find it." Her eyes were briefly clouded. "Anyway,
Charles—no lectures, no advice from me. Will you have the
ceremony here?"

The voice thundered in from the doorway: "What ceremony!"

Charles turned to face Ben Ramsey. Rising, he felt his knees
quiver. *Dammit,* he thought. Despite preparing himself for this
moment, he still found himself trembling like a child before the
great Colonel Ramsey. Isadora seemed to shrink beneath her
bedcovers.

"I asked *what* ceremony?" Ramsey demanded again.

Charles blurted it out: "I am going to marry Margaret O'Day.
Mother asked if we were going to have the ceremony here."

"Here! With a bunch of painted Indians dancing around to
tom-toms?"

"Margaret isn't . . ."

337

"Shut up, Charles. The whole notion is not only ridiculous, it's repugnant. You'll not marry a half-breed."

"Yes, Ben," Charles answered quietly but firmly, "I will."

"Damned if you will!" Ramsey stepped forward sharply. His face was a mask. For some reason he was wearing his saber and his hand was on it, the knuckles white. "No son of mine . . ."

"I'm not your son!" Charles shouted back.

"You're . . ." Ramsey was momentarily speechless. His blue eyes flashed with emotion.

"My name," Charles said, "is Kittinger, remember, *Colonel*?"

"Yes, I remember," Ramsey said coldly. Isadora gave a small gasp, anticipating what was to come. She put her fingertips to her lips, shaking her head in a silent plea.

Ramsey was unstoppable. "Your name could be Jones or Green, Charles," the colonel said, approaching slowly until he was inches from Charles' face. "It could be Rodriguez or Zimmerman . . . but I know whose *seed you* are, and it is mine!"

"Ben!" Isadora screamed. "You promised . . ."

"Shut up, woman! It's time to tell him the truth."

"What . . . ?" Charles asked in confusion, "what are you saying, Ben?"

"I'm saying simply," Ramsey said, as he half-turned away, "that the plow that seeded your mother's fertile field was my tool."

"Bastard liar!" Charles said. He took one half-step toward Ramsey, his face twisted with fury before Ramsey turned and backhanded Charles with enough force to rattle his teeth. Blood began to flow from his mouth. Ramsey stood glaring at him. Emperor of the World, savior of the white race, bold warrior.

"I'll hear no more about you marrying a breed," Ramsey said, and then he strode out of the room, not sparing a backward glance.

Isadora was crying, face buried in her hands, her shoulders

trembling violently. Charles sat beside her again. He bent low and held her, his own body still shaking. He hugged her and then whispered to her.

"It doesn't matter, Mother. It doesn't matter at all."

Her hands fell slowly away from her face. Isadora reached out and touched his lip where blood still flowed. She pushed his hair behind his ear, smiling through the tears.

"Remember, Charles? Remember what I told you? You have the right to happiness. To *try.*"

"I won't see you again for a while," he said, rising.

"No. I know it." Her eyes closed.

"But I will never forget you. I love you, Mother. Goodbye." He bent and kissed her forehead. Isadora's eyes didn't open again until she heard him walk away, close the door, and start down the hallway. Then she dabbed at her eyes with a tiny handkerchief, sniffled, and returned to her Wordsworth.

Angrily Charles stalked down the hall. He went to his room, yanked shirts, trousers, underwear from his drawers at random, and shoved them into a canvas sack. He went out of his room again, leaving the drawers in disarray.

Passing the library, he saw Ramsey with a glass of whisky in his hand looking at him.

"Come in here, Charles!" Ramsey commanded. Charles kept walking.

"I said come here!" Ramsey repeated savagely. He stepped out into the hallway. Charles had halted, his back to the man. He didn't turn now. He responded in an even voice.

"Go to hell, Ramsey." Then he walked on, Ramsey shouting incoherently behind him. Charles went out and swung into the saddle of his big bay horse, hooking the drawstring of the canvas bag onto the saddle horn. Ramsey was at the door, whisky glass still in hand, as Charles started the horse forward, walking it from the Kittinger ranch, the shouts and curses behind him fading to silence as he traveled on, riding toward the river and a new world.

The woman's name was Bertha McCoy. She was plump, slovenly, jolly, and drunk. Oliver O'Day was responsible for at least part of that. He certainly had made sure that the woman had gotten drunk, and either he or the liquor in some combination had made her extremely jolly.

Bertha lounged on her bed in the room over the saloon wearing a red silk slip that could be seen through if you were so inclined. Oliver could hardly avoid looking at the breasts sagging heavily toward gravity's pull, the heft and sweep of her large hips. He kept his eyes from the silver and turquoise necklace she wore and whenever possible avoided her glazed brown cow eyes.

"Tired yet, honey?" Bertha asked suggestively. She poked at her dirty blond hair with painted fingernails.

"Not just yet," Oliver answered with a smile. They had been talking for nearly an hour about her pathetic and boring life, she growing increasingly drunk. Oliver had carefully picked his moment to approach the woman in the Red Rooster Saloon. A fight had erupted at the far end of the street between a group of soldiers and some Texas cowboys. Both of the deputy marshals, Brice Paine and Toomey, had headed that way on the double, anticipating the pleasure of breaking a few heads and the profit to be made by going through the men's pockets. Bertha McCoy had been left alone and Oliver had moved in on her.

A pint of whisky later they were in her room, where Bertha had slowly removed most of her clothing, complaining about the heat.

Oliver explained his reluctance to accept her obvious invitation. "I don't want your boyfriend to come back and find me here."

"Brice?" she laughed scratchily. "He doesn't care, so long as it makes money. And with you, cutie," she said, winking heavily, drunkenly, "I don't even care if it makes me any."

Well, Oliver thought, Brice just *might* care if he knew who Bertha was entertaining in her room.

"But if you just want to talk . . ." Bertha said, lifting herself clumsily to a sitting position, the bed sagging under her, "that's all right. I've had a few that's all they want to do. Gets lonely out on the plains, don't it?"

"Yes."

"If that's all you want to do, it's all the same to me." She picked up the whisky bottle, peered into its depths, and drank as if it were water.

"Have you know Brice Paine a long time?"

"Yeah . . . yeah, a long time. He and me knew each other back in St. Jo. There was a time we even thought of getting married." She laughed at that idea. "We was . . . well, we was kinda in business together back in Missouri."

Oliver could easily imagine what sort of business it had been.

"Then you just ran into him again way out here?"

"Naw. He knew where to find me—Topeka. He sent for me. Got lonely or something, I dunno. You never know what Brice is thinking. Why are you so interested in him?"

"I just like to know who the competition is," Oliver said.

"Sure." She didn't believe a bit of that.

"Is he the one who got you that necklace? I like it."

"Do you? Everyone does. I never take it off." She fondled the silver and turquoise necklace. "Yeah, Brice give it to me. Bought it down in Mexico, I guess."

Oliver's expression remained bland, but the blood was pounding in his temples. He could feel his muscles knotting with angry tension. Then it was true. Brice Paine was one of the men who had murdered Kianceta. And the other? It had to be his partner, Toomey, didn't it?

Attempting to break the tension he felt, Oliver got to his feet and looked out the window. Up the street the brawling men had mostly been dispersed. Two remained on the ground, one lying on his face in the dirt, the other propped up against a hitch rail post, holding his cracked skull with both hands.

"Hey!" Bertha said. Oliver turned toward her. She was holding up the pint whisky bottle, quite empty.

"I told you to get a quart, sweetie."

"Yes, you did. You were right," Oliver answered. He smiled down at her. She slipped her arms around his waist, her hands moving beneath his shirttail to the small of his back.

"I should have gotten a bigger bottle, but I didn't know what I wanted to do then," he said.

"Do you know now, Sweetie?" Bertha asked drowsily, putting her cheek against Oliver's stomach.

"Yes." Oliver stroked her stringy hair. "I know what I want to do now. I'll be back."

"Don't make me wait too long," Bertha said.

"No, I won't." Oliver took his hat from the bureau, strapped his gun on, and moved toward the door.

"You need a gun just to go for a bottle?"

"It's a tough town."

Oliver smiled meaninglessly and went out of her room into the carpeted corridor. Downstairs he avoided the smoky saloon and exited into the alley by way of the back door. He stood there in the darkness, taking in deep calming breaths for a few minutes. Inside the Rooster the night crowd grew more raucous. He had already made his decision.

He was going to kill Brice Paine and Toomey.

Oliver didn't like the idea, but what else was there to do? Have them arrested? By whom—Amos Starr? That was ridiculous. Have them tried? On what evidence. No, unfortunately, there was only one way to see that justice was done.

Remembering another chore, he briefly reentered the smoky saloon and got a pint of whisky, which he jammed into his hip pocket.

He found Sergeant Callahan in the alley at his usual spot, waiting like a dog for Oliver's return.

"I thought you'd got lost!" Callahan said. He stretched out a trembling hand for the bottle Oliver had brought him.

"How's it going, Callahan?" Oliver asked with real concern, crouching down.

"It'll be going better in a minute," the ex-soldier said, prying the cork from the bottle with his pocket knife, drinking deeply. Swallowing another swig, his shoulders shuddering as the liquor hit bottom, he said, "It's a little rough, Oliver. But I can make it."

"Just don't go wandering anyplace after that pint. No more drinks when that's gone, all right?"

"We made a deal," Callahan said. "I'll stick to it." He looked gloomily at the bottle, drank again, and held it up to the moonlight to see how much remained. "It's hard, though, Oliver. Real hard."

He asked, "Do you know what a drunk's first thought is when he opens a bottle of whisky?"

"No, I don't."

"It's 'Where's the next bottle coming from?' "

Callahan grew sly. "You can't leave me a buck so that I can get some coffee and breakfast in the morning, can you, Oliver?"

"No, I can't. I've fixed it up with the Texas Trails Restaurant so that you can get some coffee and something to eat in the mornings."

"All right." Callahan laughed. "Old habit, Oliver. I tried."

"Yes, you tried."

"It'll be all right. I'll pound this bottle down all at once and

343

go to sleep. Maybe save a little for morning—that's hard to remember to do, though. So if I don't shake myself to death, I'll make it."

"You can do it."

"I will," Callahan promised. "After this business is all over . . . I don't know," he said, shaking his head wearily. "I don't think I care enough to change for good and all, Oliver."

"You might find yourself thinking a little differently after we get you down off that stuff, Callahan."

"I might . . ." Callahan drifted away into his own hazy thoughts. Oliver patted his shoulder, turned, and walked slowly away. He should, he thought, find Mike Caffiter and talk to him . . . Oliver stopped dead in his tracks. At the head of the alley, directly in front of him, was Deputy Toomey, his sawed-off shotgun in his hands.

He looked as surprised as Oliver. Why was the deputy even here? There was that business up the street to be taken care of. No one but Callahan was to be found in the dank gloom of the alley.

"What are you doing here, O'Day?" Toomey asked.

"Why? Am I breaking a town ordinance or something?"

"You are if I make it a town ordinance," the man with the handlebar mustache said.

"Like any good lawman, huh?"

"That's right. Like any good lawman."

"How long have you been a lawman, Toomey?" Oliver stepped nearer. "You haven't always been one, have you?" Some secret fear seemed to flicker across the deputy's eyes.

He said, "Don't come any closer, O'Day. I'd take it as a threatening gesture."

"Would you?" Oliver took another step. "I was asking about before you became a deputy here in Bethlehem. What were you doing then, Toomey?"

344

"What do you care?"

"I care. Tell me—have you ever been near a place called La Junta over in Colorado?"

Toomey was frowning, perhaps mentally running over a list of past enemies. Had he met Oliver before and couldn't remember him? The bearded blond man looked half-crazy just then. Toomey didn't like this at all. Maybe . . .

"You and Paine," Oliver said quietly. "Did you ever come upon a lone Indian woman? All by herself in a little cabin?"

Toomey came instantly alert. His eyes widened. "You're the squaw man!" he shouted, and he swung the muzzle of his shotgun up. The hammers, however, had not been drawn back and he was very slow and clumsy in his reactions.

Oliver shot him through the heart with his Colt revolver, shot him again because he did not go down immediately, but stood swaying, perched on his toes as if performing a weird balancing act.

Shouts sounded up the street. Toomey's shotgun discharged into the earth at his feet and he folded up, falling on his face against the oily dirt of the alley. Oliver took to his heels, racing toward the foot of the alley. Before anyone had found Toomey, he had circled the block, and mounted his horse, walking the paint horse slowly out of town.

He supposed it was not a good idea to try to see Mike Caffiter again on that night after all. He pointed the horse toward home on Cimarron.

Brice Paine was in a foul mood. His mouth was dry and sour with whisky residue. The sun was piercingly bright through the window of his hotel room. Last night someone had killed Toomey. Who? Why? Well, there could have been a lot of reasons for *why*, knowing Toomey, but it was unsettling. Then Brice had gone up to see Bertha for a little relaxation before bed and found her drunker than usual, unresponsive.

He had gotten some information out of her, however. In a slurred voice from under her sheet, she had asked him if he'd seen Oliver O'Day. "Sumbitch said he'd come back with a bottle. Never came back."

O'Day? True, you were liable to find almost anyone up to and including Mayor Shaughnessy in Bertha's bed. But O'Day! He'd tried to question her about it, but her rambling drunken voice fell off into a rumbling snore. Shaking her vigorously did nothing but change the pitch of her snores.

To top it all, Marshal Starr had sent some Mexican kid over to pound away at Brice Paine's door at five-thirty in the morning, saying "The marshal had to see him right now, pretty quick. Very important, *señor*."

Grumbling to himself, Paine had dressed very slowly, pausing to take a drink of whisky between pants and shirt, shirt and boots, boots and gun belt. The liquor had little effect on his mood. He was still as grouchy when he stepped out into the cool of the morning. He looked up and down the dark, empty main street of Bethlehem and started toward Amos Starr's office.

Starr was standing by the window of his office, drinking coffee from a tin cup when Brice Paine arrived in the predawn gloom. In a surly mood still, Paine banged the door shut behind him and stood scowling at his boss.

Starr turned those murky, expressionless eyes on him. Unnerving, is what Starr's eyes were. With a normal man you could get an idea what he was thinking if you looked close. Not Starr.

"Sorry, Amos. It's damned early," Paine said finally, sagging into an office chair with a sigh. "What's up?"

"I wish I knew for sure."

"Does this have anything to do with Toomey getting killed?"

"I'm not even sure of that." Starr leaned against his desk,

folding his arms. "Do you know why Toomey was in that alley, Brice? I caught up with him last night after you'd got the last of the prisoners locked up from that fight between the soldiers and those Texas men. I told him it was a good night to do a job for me."

"Which was?"

"Getting Callahan. He has to be put out of the way."

"Callahan! Why worry about that old drunk?"

"Ramsey wants it done. I don't know why. I never asked. It just has to be done."

"So you think that maybe Callahan . . . ?"

"Shot Toomey?" Starr smirked. "He couldn't hold a gun steady enough to do that. Besides, I found him later passed out in a rubbish dump and he didn't have a gun on him. I didn't find a gun in the alley. No, it had to be someone else, but who?"

"Say, Starr! No . . ." Paine shook his head.

"Well, you know who it is that's been around talking to Callahan, buying him booze."

"You're right! Oliver O'Day."

"Now here's a coincidence," Paine said, and he went on to tell the marshal what Bertha McCoy had said about O'Day's visit to her room. "What do you make of that?"

"I can't see any connection, Brice." Starr looked directly into the deputy marshal's eyes now. "Unless there's something you haven't told me."

"No, nothing. Honest, Amos."

Of course Paine was lying. It had come over him suddenly, sitting there in Starr's office. The necklace! Why had O'Day been to Bertha's room? Well, didn't people say he once had had an Indian wife, that she was dead now? Jesus! It couldn't be, could it? That couldn't have been O'Day's wife back in La Junta all those years ago. It was just a weird coincidence, it had to be. But if it wasn't—Brice Paine knew he would be next on Oliver

O'Day's agenda.

Amos Starr was thinking other thoughts. O'Day was suddenly pals with Christian Bonner. Why was that? Bonner, who had already tried to smear Starr in his cheap little paper. There was something going on that he couldn't make quite come clear. Colonel Ramsey, now, he had another reason for wanting Bonner shut down. What was that about?

"We've got a lot of little problems, don't we, Brice?" Starr asked. He walked to the coffee pot sitting on the Franklin stove and refilled his cup.

"It seems so," Brice Paine answered solemnly. He was still wondering. *Could* that have been O'Day's wife? Damn all!

"We have to take care of things," Starr said. "A little at a time. One man at a time."

"I guess you're right."

"Yeah. For the colonel if nothing else. We wouldn't even have these jobs if it weren't for Ben Ramsey."

And why was that so? Brice Paine often wondered. Just why was the army officer such a staunch supporter of Amos Starr?

"The colonel wants Callahan out of the way, Brice," the marshal told him.

"I see," Paine said slowly. "And you want me to do it?"

"That's right."

"How?"

"Just after sundown, I want you to happen upon Callahan. You know where he hangs out. I think maybe you should be real nice to him," Starr went on. "Give him a quart of whisky, maybe."

"Yeah?" Brice Paine lifted an eyebrow.

"Yeah. Then maybe you and your pal can walk over behind the saddlery. You know that old well there?"

Light dawned in Paine's head. "Sure, I know it."

"It seems to me that if a man was pretty drunk and some

kids had maybe removed the cover from that dry well, a man could fall in and break his neck."

"I guess he could, Amos. It could happen easy."

"See that it does," Starr ordered.

Paine nodded. The deputy marshal cleaned his ear with his little finger, hesitated, and then asked:

"What about O'Day?"

"What did I tell you? One man at a time. I'd have to clear that sort of job with Ramsey. He's Kent O'Day's brother, isn't he? O'Day's married to his stepdaughter. We don't want Kent mad at us. I'll talk to Ramsey. Maybe we can come up with a plan. We can't have *everybody* falling down that well."

Then Amos Starr actually smiled. It was only the third or fourth time Paine had ever seen the ice-cold Texan with those strange cloudy eyes show that much emotion. Suddenly Paine wanted to be away from the office. Brice Paine got to his feet, adjusted his gun belt, and said, "I'll see to that little chore tonight, Amos."

"It should be easy, but still—don't take any chances. Make sure there's not a soul around."

"I'll be careful," the deputy promised.

Starr looked at him for a long moment with those dreadful eyes and then nodded, turning his back to drink his coffee, and Brice Paine left, glad to be away from Starr. Sometimes, as tough as Paine believed himself to be, Starr could give him the willies. Maybe after this was finished it was time to think about moving on. He had some friends who were doing a good trade in stolen cattle in Wyoming.

There was a hell of a lot of room in that dry well if Starr got mad at anyone. Paine did not intend for it to be himself down there.

Paine shook that gloomy thought out of his mind as he walked back toward the saloon with morning breaking. Passing the

Texas Trails Restaurant, he spotted Callahan, whiskered and grimy, eating breakfast, a pot of coffee at his elbow. Paine frowned. That was unusual. His mind shifted back to Oliver O'Day.

To hell with Colonel Ramsey and to hell with Starr. Given a chance, he was going to kill O'Day. Kill him and get the hell out of Bethlehem and on the trail to Wyoming. Paine knew O'Day had killed Toomey and he knew why. He did not wish to be next.

Yes—he decided—that was the way to go. Get it over with and head north. He had a little money tucked away. Maybe Bertha would go with him. Why not? Whistling softly, tunelessly, Paine continued down the dusty main street of Bethlehem in the orange glow of dawn, toward the Red Rooster, feeling better about things now that he had made a decision.

"Hello, Callahan," the voice from the darkness said. A friendly enough voice, Callahan decided, but not the voice he had been waiting to hear.

He opened his swollen eyes painfully. There was still a blur of deep crimson marking the western horizon. Stars had begun to wink on in the clear night sky. Callahan sat up, feeling rocky.

He had been dry all day. Drinking that pint of whisky Oliver had given him had seen him through the night. But with the morning the shakes had begun. His tongue, when he awoke, was cleaving to his palate, his mouth had been that dry. He had picked at a breakfast, forcing down a few bites of eggs and hot-cakes and drank three or four cups of coffee. Then he had returned to his alley nest to try to sleep the day away, but sleep came, overlayed with fragmented, jumbled dreams only in ten-minute segments. His clothing was soaked through with alcohol sweat. His eyelids felt as if they had been mucilaged together; the eyes behind them were swollen and sore. His liver hurt. But he had made it through the day! He had lasted until sunset. Oliver would arrive soon. He had promised to return with a pint of whisky. Callahan pried open his eyes to peer at the man in front of him.

"Paine!"

"That's right." The deputy crouched down. He was smiling a shark's smile.

"I ain't done a thing, Paine!"

"I didn't say you have, Callahan!" Paine answered in a robust voice. "You look like you're feeling a little rugged, Callahan."

"I'm hurtin'," Callahan admitted in a voice that was distantly hopeful.

"Come on," Brice Paine said, rising.

"Where? I don't want to go to jail, Paine!" *Not now!* Oliver would be there soon with his medicine.

"I'm not going to take you to jail. Come along with me and I'll buy you a bottle. I do have some heart, Callahan! I don't want to see a man shake himself to death."

Callahan studied the deputy marshal with mistrustful eyes. Why would Paine make such an offer . . . it didn't matter! It didn't matter a bit. What if Oliver didn't show up? Callahan felt panic momentarily cause his heart to race. Hell, he thought, a bird in the hand . . . and he dragged himself uncertainly to his feet and followed Brice Paine toward the back of the Red Rooster.

Oliver O'Day had a pint of whisky in his saddlebag for Callahan. He had waited until it was full dark before entering Bethlehem. He had heard no murmurs that anyone was looking for him in connection with the shooting of Toomey, but still he preferred to move about in the darkness.

Walking his pony up the alley, he frowned, not seeing Callahan at his usual post. He called out in a low voice several times and then swallowed a curse. Why had he taken a drunk's word for anything? The next day they seldom remembered promises made. He should have taken Callahan to his mother's farm and locked him in the barn. Maybe that's exactly what he would do. If he could find him.

He rode slowly out of the alley, checked out the shed behind the feed and grain store, knowing that Callahan went there sometimes, then rode through the cluster of cottonwood trees just north of the alley. Callahan was nowhere to be seen. It was unlikely that he would go far. Not in the shape he was in. Besides, he wouldn't want to be far from a source of liquor.

Leaving his horse in the trees, Oliver went to the rear of the Red Rooster and entered. The bored guard sat on a wooden chair among the crates of whisky, the beer barrels.

"You seen Callahan tonight?" Oliver asked.

"No, and if I do, I've got orders to escort him out."

"Anybody else? Anybody who just wanted a back-door bottle and left?"

"Nobody. Not unless you count Paine. He got his regular patrolling bottle," the guard told Oliver.

Paine? Oliver thanked the guard and went out again.

Paine? From what the guard had said it was a usual stop for the deputy as he made his rounds. But Oliver wondered . . . he returned to his paint horse and began a slow search of the alleys and back streets, growing more concerned as time went on. Returning to the cottonwood grove, his attention was caught by a muffled scraping sound as he wove his way through the trees.

What was that? He walked the horse more slowly forward. Emerging from the grove, he found himself behind the saddlery.

There in the starlight was Brice Paine, effortlessly dragging the heavy oaken cover from a dark chasm that Oliver recognized as a dry well.

"Heavy, isn't it?"

Paine lifted his eyes, his hands still on the wooden flat. Breath hissed from between his teeth. Oliver noticed the brown quart bottle of whisky, half-empty, on the earth beside the shaft. He swung down from his pony and approached Paine, who straightened slowly from his task.

"Damned kids pulled the cover off the well," he said. There was a smile on his lips. A con's smile inviting Oliver to believe his lie.

"Mind stepping away a little?" Oliver asked with his hand on his holstered revolver.

"What? What for?"

"I just want to have a look. There seems to be two sets of boot prints here."

"Other folks do walk down this alley," Paine said scornfully.

"Yeah." Oliver moved nearer, his eyes flicking from Paine's tense face to the open shaft at his feet. "It seems you dropped your whisky bottle," Oliver remarked, nudging the bottle with the toe of his boot.

"I tripped over the damned cover. Then . . ." Brice Paine swept back the skirt of his long coat as Oliver strode forward. The deputy knew there was no way he was going to talk his way out of this. In another minute, given the chance, Oliver would look into the dry well and see Callahan's broken form at the bottom of it.

Encumbered by the coat, fumbling in his panic, Brice never managed to draw his sidearm before Oliver launched himself against Paine's body, slamming a fist into the deputy's jaw. They went down together, rolled over, disengaged, and came to their feet in unison.

"Damn you," Paine growled, his head ringing from the blow he had taken, and he dove at Oliver, swinging his fists wildly. He tripped over Oliver's outstretched foot and tumbled backward into the open well.

353

He yelled with surprise and anger, but the cry was cut off. There was a small thump and then silence in the night. Brice Paine had come to the end he had feared.

Oliver wiped back his hair and looked into the well. There was just enough light reaching the bottom of the shaft to show him two bulky, unmoving figures entwined in death.

Cursing, muttering, he bent and dragged the heavy cover back over the well himself.

"So you killed both of them, did you?" the voice from out of the shadows asked. Oliver turned very slowly to find himself looking down the muzzle of Amos Starr's pistol.

Starr never trusted another man to do an important job. Not unsupervised. Long ago one of his many partners had taken off with all of the proceeds from a stagecoach holdup, leaving Starr waiting at their hideout where the law found him. Since then he had trusted no one.

He had sent Paine out to do the dirty work, to take the blame if caught, but Starr had shadowed him.

Well, it was done. Callahan was dead. Too bad about Paine, but thugs were a dime a dozen; he could be replaced. And chance had given Starr a scapegoat for the night's events.

"I suppose you killed Toomey, too," Starr said.

Oliver didn't answer.

"Too bad for you I happened along, isn't it, O'Day? I just can't figure out whether I want to waste the time trying you and hanging you or have it done with here," Starr said. "I've got every right to just shoot you, you know?"

When Oliver still didn't answer, Starr deliberately cocked his Colt. "What the hell," he said as he raised his pistol.

"Starr!"

Amos Starr spun toward the sound of the voice from the alley and fired wildly in that direction. Oliver rolled to one side, drawing his gun. It wasn't needed. An answering shot from the man in the alley boomed and Starr was spun around and hurled backward from the force of the bullet impacting into his body.

Starr hit the ground hard, his pistol flying free. Oliver jumped for the gun as Starr writhed and moaned, clutching at his wounded shoulder, cursing at the distant stars. Oliver rose from the ground slowly and saw the other man emerge from the alley. His eyes were narrow and bleak and familiar.

"Kent!"

His brother walked from the shadows of the alley to look dispassionately at Starr, who lay with his face contorted, still swearing at the night. Then he glanced at Oliver, holstered his pistol, and walked away.

"Kent!"

There was no answer. Kent vanished into the secret shadows of the night.

There were distant shouts sounding now. A back door opened from a shop onto the alleyway, sending a wedge of light out onto the ground. Oliver moved to where Starr lay.

"Let's go," he said, hoisting the marshal to his feet.

"My shoulder . . . hurts like hell. Broken to bits," Starr complained.

"I'll bet it does. We'll get it seen to," Oliver told him. "Let's just get the hell out of here first."

Starr managed to remain on his feet, where he stood swaying. He still held onto his shattered shoulder, grimacing, the blood flowing through his fingers. A .44 at close range can do a tremendous amount of damage. Starr was fighting the shock of the slug ripping into his body.

"Where are we going?" he asked, his hair hanging into his eyes.

"Where else?" Oliver said as pounding footsteps approached them. "To throw you in jail."

★　★　★　★　★

Shaughnessy was awake in the night. He had heard a few shots from uptown awhile ago, but that was the sheriff's business, not his. Still, as he rolled over, punched his pillow, and tried to fall asleep again, his mind was unsettled.

Someone was in his bedroom!

With the constant fear of a politician, he sat up and reached for his bedside pistol.

"You won't need that," a somewhat familiar voice said. Looking toward the sound of the voice, the mayor could make no identification of the shadowy figure.

"What do you want?" Shaughnessy asked with more strength than he felt.

"Just this—there was a shooting uptown just awhile ago."

"I heard it," the mayor said.

"I saw it, and I can tell you it was Starr's doing. They'll likely try to hang it on Oliver O'Day because he was there."

"Why tell me? Why not go over to the marshal's office and tell them or sign a statement to that effect?"

"I have no time or patience for that sort of business," the shadowy man said, "you do. I'm here to tell you to make sure that Starr stays in jail until trial. He's a dangerous man and if you recognize me, you know that I'm just as dangerous."

The door opened and then closed again as the night visitor stepped out. Shaughnessy had already decided to follow the man's advice. He didn't want to risk a second nightly visit from Kent O'Day. What did he care about Starr anyway?

Starr's moans had finally died away, the pain in his bandaged shoulder alleviated by whisky. Now and then he groaned in his sleep as Oliver and a grim-faced Christian Bonner spoke in the outer office of the jail.

"All of this does complicate things," Bonner commented.

"I know it, but it can't be helped." Bonner had made a suggestion and now Oliver followed up on his questions. "This Brigham Yates, are you sure he can be trusted?"

"He can. He's Mayor Shaughnessy's cousin. Our mayor isn't much, Oliver, but I for one believe he is honest."

"All right. We haven't much choice anyway. We need someone to act as interim marshal."

"You'll meet him soon. Brigham's a right enough man for the job. Shaughnessy will appoint him until the town can hold a new election."

"What did you tell Starr?" Christian Bonner inquired. The two men sat drinking bitter reheated coffee. The night passed by with somber slowness. They had been very busy—Bonner with Shaughnessy and his new headline story for the morning edition, Oliver with Starr and the doctor.

"I told him that he'll hang for Callahan's murder. I think he will believe me if we allow no contact with anyone outside this office, keep him in the dark. And don't let anyone in to see him. There are plenty of people in this town who'd love to be on the jury that convicts him, and he knows it."

"That's all well and good, Oliver, but what about the rest of it? What about the fact that we've lost Callahan as a witness in the court-martial of Ramsey? Where does that leave us? Perhaps we've been beaten after all." Bonner rose and began pacing the office, his face drawn, his eyes dismal.

"I don't know where it leaves us. We've got to try to keep a lid on the news of Callahan's death somehow."

"What good will that do us!" Bonner, still walking the floor, ran harried fingers through his thinning hair. He stopped his marching. "We have no other witnesses to what went on that day, to the wire sent down from General Cox, to Ramsey's refusal to obey that direct order, and the falsification of his own report of the massacre. You haven't been able to find another ex-soldier to testify against Ramsey?" he asked hopefully.

"We have Caffiter still, but no one else."

"Lieutenant Jefferson Caldwell arrived last evening from headquarters. I talked to him for an hour or so. I told him we had 'several' reliable witnesses."

"It can't be helped, Bonner. You know what has happened."

"I know, but . . ." Bonner was bewildered, frustrated by the turn of events. "What we know won't carry any weight at a hearing. Lieutenant Caldwell explained that part to me. Did I tell you? This is only a preliminary hearing to see if a court-martial is justified. If we don't have any witnesses . . ."

"We have Mike Caffiter, don't we?"

"One man. And, will he even testify once he finds out he's the only man willing to do so?"

Oliver put his coffee cup aside. He shook his head slowly. "Truthfully, I don't think he will, Bonner. Even if he does—well, as you have pointed out, one ex-soldier's word against that of a man of Ramsey's rank and reputation won't count for much at all. It counts to next for nothing."

"Then," Bonner said, staring at the floor, "we're beaten, aren't we, Oliver?"

"It looks like it, Christian."

"I should have known this was all folly," Christian Bonner said sadly. "It's just that I was fool enough to hope." He sighed. "There's still some hope, of course. Lieutenant Caldwell said that General Cox has been hearing rumors for months—from some ex-troopers and from some of the Kiowa allies as well. That's why he wants this all pried open again. But, unfortunately as far as supporting a legal case, it's all hearsay. We're sunk, Oliver. We're just plain sunk."

CHAPTER TWELVE

Colonel Benjamin Ramsey was completely at his ease in his dress uniform, his silvering hair and mustache newly trimmed. He sat behind the table in the county courthouse with his adjutant and advisors. Ramsey had chosen the courthouse for the informal hearing himself rather than drag the "circus," as he called it, onto his post.

Lieutenant Jefferson Caldwell, General Hayes' handpicked investigator, was far from being at ease. Tall, narrowly built, sallow, and nervously eager, he sat at a facing table shuffling through the thin stack of papers in front of him. All he had to work with was a hastily compiled, inconclusive smattering of evidence. From time to time Lieutenant Caldwell looked across the room to Ramsey with an almost apologetic expression.

In the front row of the courthouse chairs Mike Caffiter sat rigidly. His collar was too tight. He was perspiring freely, gripping the brim of the hat on his lap. He looked over his shoulder hopefully each time the door to the courthouse opened.

"Where's Callahan?" he hissed to Oliver, who sat beside him. Bonner, seated on his other side, said, "Don't worry."

That was no answer. Caffiter clamped his jaw shut and sat in bitter confusion. He felt like a small animal trapped for no reason it could understand.

Where was Callahan? Oliver thought. Why, he's dead as a mackerel at the bottom of a dry well. Probably where you'll end up as well, Caffiter.

Paul Joseph Lederer

Clearing his throat, Lieutenant Jefferson Caldwell rose to begin the proceedings.

"Gentlemen, this is not a court of civil law, nor a court-martial hearing. It is an investigation requested by certain citizens through the office of General Albert Hayes to investigate the conduct of Colonel Benjamin Ramsey during the last Kiowa war.

"I repeat, this is only an informal hearing, subject to no rules of order except those of simple respect for the court's officer.

"That having been said . . . it is incumbent upon those who have made the allegations concerning Colonel Ramsey's conduct to substantiate them. Therefore—Mr. Bonner, will you please rise and introduce said evidence?"

Christian Bonner got to his feet, glancing uneasily at Oliver, and took the floor. "Lieutenant Caldwell, we wish to present the evidence of eyewitnesses to . . ."

"Where's Callahan!" Mike Caffiter hissed. Oliver shook his head. Ramsey was staring coldly at Caffiter. Christian Bonner rambled on.

". . . The slaughter of innocent women and children while the treaty between our two nations was in effect, a savage, unconscionable attack . . ."

Lieutenant Jefferson Caldwell looked slightly embarrassed. Oliver could sense that the officer wanted Bonner to get to the witnesses. The *witness.*

"Where's Callahan?" Mike Caffiter demanded out loud, swiveling in his chair to search the courtroom. "You promised me I wouldn't be the only one!"

Ben Ramsey, erect in his chair, touched his silver mustache and continued to study Caffiter coldly. Bonner waded on through his peroration, stumbling over one line in his handwritten notes so that he repeated it twice.

"Where *is* he!" Mike Caffiter demanded again.

Oliver simply ignored him. He found that he was no longer listening to Christian Bonner either. The hearing had sagged in upon itself, becoming a farce. It probably wouldn't continue for another fifteen minutes. Bonner, his face glistening with perspiration, trudged on through his accusations. Unsubstantiated accusations.

The back door of the courthouse opened and closed. Caffiter spun around with eager hopefulness and then moaned. It was not Callahan, of course. Bootsteps approached Oliver and someone tapped him on the shoulder.

He looked up to see Bethlehem's interim marshal, Brigham Yates, a solemn, sardonic figure in a wide-brimmed hat.

Christian Bonner saw the marshal lean over and whisper into Oliver's ear. Oliver nodded and then beckoned to Bonner.

"One moment, sir?" Bonner asked Lieutenant Caldwell,

"Of course," Caldwell answered as if it made no difference at this point.

"I ain't testifying!" Mike Caffiter said loud enough to carry to the bench and to Ramsey, seated at the opposite table.

"Are you sure?" Bonner was asking Marshal Yates.

"I'm sure. Come over and talk to him yourself."

There was a buzzing in the court, uncomfortable murmurs. Lieutenant Caldwell was growing impatient.

"In the interest of expediency," the lieutenant said, "may we please proceed with your witnesses, Mr. Bonner?"

"One minute, sir, I beg you."

Mike Caffiter leaned forward and said in a quieter, firmer voice: "I ain't going up there. The hell with you all."

"Lieutenant Caldwell," Bonner said, turning toward the bench. "May we please have a brief recess?"

Jefferson Caldwell looked at the brass-cased clock on the wall. They had been assembled for exactly seven minutes.

"Unless it is absolutely necessary to the progress of this hearing . . ."

"I assure you that it is," Bonner insisted. Reluctantly Lieutenant Caldwell assented.

"Very well. Fifteen minutes?"

"Thank you."

"I'm not getting up there," Mike Caffiter repeated and Bonner startled him with a sharp response.

"Then get the hell out of here! Go feed your horses or something."

Then, with Bonner leading the way, the newspaperman, Oliver O'Day, and Brigham Yates tramped from the courtroom. Outside Bonner asked eagerly, "That's what he said?"

"That's exactly what he said," Yates affirmed. "Starr said, 'Get O'Day and Bonner. I ain't going to hang. I'm willing to make a deal that'll give them Colonel Ramsey's head on a platter if I don't fall for Callahan's murder.' "

"What in blazes could he have to trade?" Bonner wondered.

"He's been working for Ramsey for a long time."

"Yes, but . . ."

Bonner was too eager, Oliver thought. He understood it. The newspaperman wanted his reputation strengthened. Right now it was in danger of falling to dust. Oliver said, "Take it slow, Bonner. As a matter of fact, let me talk to him alone. I don't want to let him know how much we need his help."

Entering the jail then, Bonner stayed in the outer office fidgeting while Oliver went back to the rear cell and saw Starr, who appeared shrunken and desperate in the cold shadows. Blood stained his bandage, some private dread lurked in his milky eyes.

"Well?" Oliver asked, gripping the bars to the cell with both hands.

"Do we have a deal? If I talk?" Starr asked.

"I don't know. Talk first."

"You know I didn't kill Callahan! That was Brice Paine."

"You set it up," Oliver said evenly.

"No! No one can prove that."

"You tried to kill me."

Starr was gripping the iron chains of his bunk tightly. "Maybe someone could decide that," Starr said defensively. "But I never even shot at you, did I? What I did isn't a hanging offense, is it? For a lawman who thought he was doing his duty. Your brother came up on me in the dark. I didn't know who it was."

"I dunno," Oliver answered quietly. "With all of the enemies you've made in this town, some people might see it as a hanging offense, the way Callahan died."

"Don't let it happen, O'Day! I ain't ready to die yet."

"Then talk fast. I'll try to do what I can if you're straight with me, but we don't have much time."

Minutes later Oliver emerged from the cell block. Bonner looked at him expectantly. Oliver nodded, picking up his hat.

"Get the shackles out," he told Brigham Yates. "Amos Starr is going to take a little walk with us over to the courthouse."

Bonner was as excited as a puppy who had to pee and couldn't find a place. "Well? Well? What do you think, Oliver?"

"I think we can just chalk up the whole court-martial hearing to experience, Bonner," he said as Yates dragged a set of heavy shackles from the cabinet and walked toward the cells. "We never really had a chance anyway. We'll just have to let a civil court hang Ben Ramsey."

"He did it then?"

"Yes, he did it, but it's not what you are thinking of. No one will ever be able to prove what happened during the massacre in the Kiowa camp. What is provable is that he killed Nesbitt Kittinger for his money and his wife. Starr saw it. That's what the marshal's point of leverage has been—the threat of his revealing it has been hanging over Ramsey's head all these years."

"We've only got one minute to get back to the courthouse," Bonner said, looking nervously at his watch as Yates led Starr from his cell in irons.

"We've got all the time in the world, Christian. It's Ramsey whose time has run out."

Bonner and Oliver O'Day reached the courthouse first as Starr, impeded by leg irons, hobbled after them, escorted by Brigham Yates.

Inside the building the atmosphere was impatient. Spectators grumbled unhappily to each other. Lieutenant Caldwell looked up with weary forbearance. Mike Caffiter's chair was empty.

"Gentlemen, may we resume?" Caldwell asked.

"Sir," Bonner said, approaching the bench. "We have reconsidered, and with apologies for wasting your time, have concluded that we do not have the evidence in hand to justify the court-martial of Colonel Benjamin Ramsey."

The young army officer looked astonished. Had he ridden all the way from Fort Riley for *nothing*? Hadn't these civilians weighed their evidence? He started to complain to Bonner, but the back door of the courtroom again opened and everything changed course abruptly.

Oliver was watching Ramsey. The metamorphosis of his expression was incredible. Impatiently indulgent as they had entered, then a smirking confidence as Bonner made his brief speech, he turned his head and his eyes widened, his face paled, his mouth twisted into knots at the corners. The murmur in the courtroom grew to general confusion.

Amos Starr was led forward, the irons on his legs clanking heavily. Those opaque eyes of his were fixed on Colonel Ramsey. Ramsey asked a silent question with his own eyes.

Before anyone could react, Ramsey had leaped to his feet, the flap on his holster open, and he drew his service revolver.

"You son of a bitch!" Ramsey shouted and he shoved his way past his startled adjutant and shot Amos Starr between the eyes.

Behind Starr, Marshal Yates staggered back in astonishment. Yates managed to unholster his own gun as Ramsey ran wildly up the aisle.

"Stop!" Yates ordered, but Ramsey was not going to stop. It was flee or be hung.

Brigham Yates shot him twice and Ramsey fell dead to the floor as acrid gunsmoke drifted across the silent courtroom.

Oliver walked to Ramsey's body, touched the carotid artery, and found no whisper of a pulse. Yates stood trembling, his revolver dangling in his hand, looking down at the dead man. For a minute no one spoke, and then everyone was talking, shoving forward for a better look at the dead men, the clamor of the mob filling the room.

Oliver looked back at Christian Bonner, glanced at the clock on the wall, and went out. He had other business to take care of that morning.

Men were rushing toward the courthouse as Oliver went out. The shots had echoed down the street, drawing people magnetically toward the shooting. Oliver walked on, bumped shoulders with a man on the boardwalk, and then was halted.

Bertha McCoy was standing directly in front of him, wearing a green velvet dress and a little cocked hat. Oliver braced himself.

"Mr. O'Day?" she said. Bertha's eyes were puffy. Her makeup was smeared.

"Yes?"

"I heard . . . Brice is dead, isn't he?"

"Yes, he's dead."

"Did you kill him?"

"No. It was an accident."

She shrugged, a tiny movement of her heavy shoulders, which briefly threatened to become a quivering of her big body. In her hand was a small lace-fringed handkerchief.

"I guess this is yours, isn't it?" Bertha asked. She unwrapped the handkerchief. Kianceta's necklace lay in her palm.

"Yes, it is."

"I thought so. The questions you were asking the other night. Give it back to the woman it belongs to."

She pressed the necklace into Oliver's hand. Tears welled up in her faded eyes. Bertha turned sharply away toward the Red Rooster. "I guess I need a drink. I guess I need a lot of drinks."

Oliver continued on his way. The stagecoach had already arrived at the depot. There were fresh horses in the harnesses. He hurried on.

There they stood, just inside the doorway, looking expectantly up and down the street, holding hands and seeming very young and hopeful. *Is that the way Kianceta and I looked?* Oliver wondered.

Smiling, he walked to where Charles Kittinger and Margaret waited. His daughter came forward with a little cry of pleasure and threw her arms around his neck, kissing him.

"I was afraid you wouldn't make it," Margaret said.

"Of course, I would." He winked at Charles. He had decided to say nothing about the events in the courthouse to the young man. He would find out in time. There was no sense in marring this morning for the newlyweds.

"I have something for you," Oliver said, and he showed Margaret the necklace.

"Oh, *Daddy*," she exclaimed. It was the first time in years that she had called him that. "It *is* Mother's, isn't it? It is! Look Charles."

Oliver fastened it around her neck and kissed her on the

cheek. He whispered into her ear. "Give it to your own daughter, won't you, Ki-Ki?"

She smiled, wiped a tear away, and nodded. Charles was holding her hand again, more tightly.

The stagecoach driver had climbed up onto the box. They were ready to explore their new life.

"I almost forgot," Oliver said. "Here's something you might find handy, Charles." He withdrew the chamois sack from his pocket and handed it to the young man. It was obvious from its weight what the sack contained.

"I couldn't . . ."

"Yes, of course you can," Oliver said, folding Charles' hand around the gold. "I've been holding onto it for years. I don't need it. You just might."

"Thank you, sir," Charles said sincerely. "Thank you."

"It's nothing," Oliver said. "Anyway, by rights you should be thanking a man named Donovan Hart." Both of them looked at him curiously, expecting an explanation, but the stage driver turned his head and called out, "We're ready to go, folks!" There was only time for one last handshake, one last kiss, and then Charles helped Margaret into the waiting coach. The driver had gathered his reins and he snapped his whip, starting the team away from the station. Margaret looked back from the window, holding her hat, waving a tiny handkerchief.

Then they were gone. The dust settled slowly. People were returning from the commotion at the courthouse in twos and threes, discussing the events of the day. Oliver turned and walked across the street toward the stable, wanting nothing more to do with the town and its troubles.

He found his brother just inside the stable doors. Kent was looking up the empty street in the direction the stagecoach had taken.

"You were waiting here all that time?" Oliver asked.

"Yes." Kent shrugged. "Well, I didn't know what to say, really . . . I still don't Oliver."

"There's no need to say anything. Not to me," Oliver said. He walked to where his paint pony waited, tightened the cinches, and swung aboard. Kent glanced at his brother as he slowly walked his horse forward.

"Oliver?"

"Yes, Kent."

"Tell Mother . . . tell her I'll ride by one of these days."

Oliver nodded. Smiling, he started his horse down the main street of Bethlehem. The day was sunny; a few high clouds formed, changing shapes against the high sky.

Passing a saloon he saw an old man in a torn hat and a long, greasy buffalo coat peering hopefully into the window. At his side was a huge black, woolly pup. Annoyed by the puppy's whimpering, the man kept booting it away. Oliver reined up.

"That's a nice pup you've got there," Oliver said.

"What?" Weary red eyes lifted to Oliver.

"I just said, that's a nice looking pup."

"Damned lot of trouble is what he is."

"What'll you take for it?" Oliver asked.

"You want to buy that beast! I'll take just about anything for it, mister."

Oliver reached into his pocket and showed the man a shiny silver dollar. Eagerly the drunk scooped up the wriggling fat pup and gave it to Oliver.

Oliver gave the man the dollar and started on his way, holding the pup—black as coal, furry as a bear, huge paws indicative of size to come—across the paint pony's withers.

The town fell away and he found himself riding alone on the grassy plains. The sun glinted on the constant river and Oliver pointed the horse homeward to where the two old women waited on Cimarron.

ABOUT THE AUTHOR

Paul Lederer is a native of San Diego, California, and attended San Diego State University before serving four years in an Air Force Intelligence arm. He has traveled widely in the United States and in Europe, Asia, and the Middle East.

He is the author of *Tecumseh, Manitou's Daughter, Shawnee Dawn, Seminole Skies, Cheyenne Dreams, The Way of the Wind, The Far Dreamer,* and *North Star.* His most recent novel is the contemporary *The Moon Around Sarah,* published by Robert Hale, London (2013).

Now living in La Mesa, California, Lederer is an amateur musician and enjoys spending time with his two grown sons and his daughter.